The Centurion's Wife

Acts of Faith, Book 1

The Centurion's Wife

DAVIS BUNN
&
JANETTE OKE

BETHANY HOUSE PUBLISHERS
Minneapolis, Minnesota

The Centurion's Wife
Copyright © 2009
Davis Bunn and Janette Oke

Art Direction by Paul Higdon
Cover design by Jennifer Parker
Cover photography by Mike Habermann

Published by Bethany House Publishers
11400 Hampshire Avenue South
Bloomington, Minnesota 55438

Bethany House Publishers is a division of
Baker Publishing Group, Grand Rapids, Michigan.

Printed in the United States of America

Library of Congress Cataloging-in-Publication Data

Bunn, T. Davis.
The centurion's wife / Davis Bunn and Janette Oke.
p. cm. — (Acts of faith ; bk 1)
ISBN 978-0-7642-0654-2 (hardcover : alk. paper) — ISBN 978-0-7642-0514-9 (pbk.) — ISBN 978-0-7642-0655-9 (large-print pbk.) 1. Bible. N.T.—History of Biblical events—Fiction. I. Oke, Janette, 1935- II. Title.

PS3552.U4718C46 2009b
813'.54—dc22

2008041670

It may sound simplistic, but is meant wholeheartedly. We are so privileged to have the Scriptures written, preserved, and passed on to us. What an indescribable blessing it is for us to have easy and early access to the accounts of our spiritual roots. Writing a story involving the early Church has made this appreciation deepen.

It is also with a sincere sense of gratitude that we express our thanks to you, Gary and Carol Johnson, for your part in enabling us throughout our writing careers to share our faith base with many readers. Through your commitment, encouragement, sensitivity, insight, friendship, and good, hard work you have enriched our lives in so many ways. Our sincere thanks, and may God continue to bless you both. We know that you have left Bethany House Publishers in capable hands as you have moved on to enjoy all that God has in store for you in the more relaxed years ahead.

The Authors

NORTH SEA
BRITANNIA
ATLANTIC OCEAN
GERMAN
LUTETIA
GAUL
RAETIA
NORICUM
MASSILIA
PISAE
ITALY
TOLETUM
TARRACO
HISPANIA
ROME
NEAPOLIS
MEDITERRA
MAURETANIA
CARTHAGE
AFRICA
THE ROMAN EMPIRE 33 AD
0 100 200 300 miles

Judaea Province
Damascus
Phoenicia
Syria
Tyre
Mediterranean Sea
Galilee
Capernaum
Sea of Galiliee
Tiberias
Decapolis
Caesarea
Samaria
Jordan
Perea
Jerusalem
Bethany
Judaea
Dead Sea
0
30 miles
D A C I A
BLACK SEA
MACEDON
THRACE
Thessalonica
A S I A
Athens
GREECE
MESOPOTAMIA
Antioch
S Y R I A
E A N S E A
Jerusalem
CYRENAICA
Alexandria
Memphis
ARABIA
E G Y P T

CHAPTER ONE

AD 33, Caesarea, Judaea Province
Six Days Before Passover

USUALLY LEAH FOLLOWED the path briskly from the main kitchen to the baths. Today, with the Mediterranean breeze caressing her face and the sun not yet a scorching heat overhead, she could not help but slow her steps. She lifted her eyes at the cry of the seabirds. How peaceful it appeared. Only a few clouds hung in the sky, like a flock of spring lambs. Down below the walkway, sea waves lapped gently along the promontory's edge. Not even the first stirrings within the palace compound behind her could diminish her sense of delight.

For one further moment Leah drank it all in, her gaze sweeping across the panorama before her. Finally she turned away from the vast blue sea and studied the beauty of the city's setting.

Caesarea stretched like a royal necklace along the seafront, with the palace of Pontius Pilate its centermost jewel. From her position upon the rocky point, Leah studied the elaborate courtyard with its columns and statuary, the opulent ceramic-tiled baths, and the impressive marbled façade of the palace itself.

Broad, grand entrance steps rose up to gold double doors. In different circumstances, Leah would have found it all impossibly beautiful. Even though she had been raised as no stranger to fine things and elegant living, never had she dreamed of residing in the palace of the prelate of Judaea. Yet here she stood, strangely a part of it all.

In different circumstances . . .

It was the first occasion in a long time that Leah's thoughts had flown across years and countries to her grandmother. Whatever would she think of Leah now, standing here amid such splendor? Leah recalled how the old woman often stroked her face and said, "I see great things in store for you, my little one." Then she would pat her generous silk-gowned bosom with bejeweled fingers, as though sealing the promise in her heart. Her dear grandmother. What Leah would give for just a few hours with her beloved grandparent now. But she had been gone for eight long years. Leah would have that opportunity no more.

Leah sighed and turned away from the opulence of the palace and back to the contrasting beauty of the sea. *Its surface sparkles like Grandmother's jewels*. How easy it would be on such a dawn to overlook the reality that she was here because she had no recourse.

Far beyond the rolling waves lay her real home. True, there was no longer any place for her there, but it still held her heart. Would she ever see Verona again? And in Rome, her mother faced a new dawn as well. Alone. Bereft. Leah yearned to be with her, offering what love and comfort she was able. But she remained trapped within this imposing palace of a Roman prelate, surrounded by elegance she could appreciate only from a distance. Yes, she had been born to wealth and position, yet here she stood, little more than a slave. Bitterness filled her throat and caught her breath.

Another thought chased through her mind. If nothing more, she faced an easier circumstance than her two older sisters. She was free in spirit, if not in body. She was able to call her life her own, even if it was a life of servanthood. She would far rather be a servant in Pilate's household than slave to a man she neither loved nor respected, who ruled her every move. Hers was a bondage far more easily endured, she was sure.

Leah cast one more longing look over the blue expanse of sea, and with a determined lift of her shoulders walked on toward the bathhouse. Her first duties of the day would have her laying out fresh towels and robes and making sure that all the expensive unguents and soaps were readily available.

You must take what is good from the world for yourself, a quiet but firm voice echoed in her memory, *for the world will never come to you with outstretched hand.* Her father's words. Yet even as she recalled them, she was forced to admit that the philosophy had brought even him no lasting rewards.

The next morning, Leah's demanding day suddenly veered toward chaos. Like every other servant in Pilate's household, she always dreaded word that the prelate was moving to Jerusalem. For the servants and slaves it meant that their normal duties, already keeping them busy from early morning to late night, were multiplied many times over.

Leah struggled to meet the increasingly frantic pace. She had felt well enough the night before, when she had finally finished the day's work and retired to her pallet in the servants' quarters. Yet during the night she had tossed fitfully, and when she had lifted a hand to her brow, she knew she had a fever. Before dawn she had gone to the kitchen for water. She had slept some again and hoped her discomfort would pass. But now her strength drained away as her activities mounted along with the day's heat.

Leah knew her mistress, Pilate's wife, noted how sluggish Leah was that morning. She tried to add quickness to her step and lightness to her countenance. A servant's misfortunes, whatever their source, were not permitted to taint the lady's day.

But as the hours wore on, Leah found she was unable to sustain the brave front. Her body felt like it carried its own fire pit. Her stomach was unsettled, and she ached with a dreadful bone weariness from her head to her feet.

She touched her face with one hand, and her own fingers felt the unusual warmth. Though this was the first time she had ever suffered with the fever that swept the land at every winter's close, Leah knew its symptoms. She could feel the slow burn begin to scorch her limbs. *I don't have time to be ill,* she groaned inwardly. *Not today!*

A palace guard appeared from around the corner of the bathhouse and glanced her way. Despite the late afternoon light and the distance, Leah could see the scowl that touched his face. Had he noticed something? Were her steps dragging? Was she staggering? She forced herself to keep moving. Even though the sun was dropping into the western horizon, there was still much to be done. For on the morrow they all would leave for Jerusalem, where Pontius Pilate would take charge of maintaining the peace during the annual Passover festival.

She reluctantly turned away toward the servants' quarters. Maybe if she could rest for a few moments. . . . Midway there, however, she felt as though a wave from the sea were rising up and sweeping over her. She grabbed the wall as the light dimmed to grey, uncertain even where she was. She heard a voice call her name but did not have the strength to respond.

Leah did not fear the darkness that rose up to claim her. In fact, she welcomed it.

CHAPTER TWO

Nine Days Later

LEAH FELT MORE THAN HEARD the sound of her name. She sat up on her sleeping pallet in the early morning darkness to a whisper so tender it could almost be ignored. It vanished with her return to full wakefulness, but the memory remained, making her feel in some undeniable way that whatever the reason, the call came surrounded in love and gentle caring.

She did not realize until she was on her feet that the fever was gone.

For over a week she had lain in the servants' quarters, so weak she could not rise without help. She had counted the hours by the distance the sun traveled across the tiled floor. Now she washed her face in the basin against the wall and rolled up the pallet as though illness had never touched her. Her face was cool to the touch. She held out her arms and looked at her hands in wonder, for they no longer trembled. She shook her head, wishing she could recall the details of the dream. She was sure it had been a man's voice that had called her name with such kindness.

The dawn was a faint wash upon the eastern sky, still so muted the breaking waves below the palace grounds were just shadows of varying light and darkness. A pair of stars defied the rising sun. Two guards walked the palace perimeter, dousing the night torches as they went.

With almost everyone else in Jerusalem, the palace was utterly still. When Pontius Pilate was present, the house buzzed and the atmosphere was sharp and pungent with tension. Even when the night brought quiet, the place was filled with an air of expectancy, sometimes dread. There was hardly a private moment, especially for a young servant like Leah.

Leah entered the kitchen to find Dorit seated on her pallet. The old woman preferred to sleep close to the fire, though it meant rising with the arrival of the first kitchen slave. But even with the household help away, Dorit never slept past dawn.

The old woman's eyes widened. "Leah, what are you doing away from your sickbed?"

"I feel like I've just emerged from prison."

"You're better, then?"

"More than that, Dorit. I am well."

"Come, let me feel your face." Dorit stood and settled an age-mottled hand upon Leah's forehead. "I feared for you, child."

Leah's response was interrupted by a guard's shout from the direction of the palace gates. Leah straightened to the sound of approaching horses. She instantly recognized the voice that responded, coarsened by many years and battles. "It's Hugo," she remarked.

"That is not possible." Dorit slowly moved across the floor to sit at the table. "He left after you were felled by the fever. Surely he is still in Jerusalem with the prelate."

Leah did not waste time arguing. She bent to the kitchen fire, blew upon the embers until they glowed, and laid down kindling.

Footsteps stamped across the terrace, and Hugo's voice said behind her, "So you're awake. Good. I could kill for a bath."

Pilate's household guards came in all shapes and dispositions. Hugo was Leah's favorite, a grizzled veteran who had been with the prelate since his earliest campaigns northward in Gaul. Hugo had nothing to prove, unlike some of the others.

"There's no fire yet, neither for a bath nor tea." Leah turned and smiled a greeting. "But it's good to see you nonetheless."

The big man grumbled under his breath, then settled with a sigh onto a stool across the table from Dorit. The kitchen was a massive affair, a full forty feet in length and almost as wide. Two storage rooms opened off the eastern wall. The table ran down the kitchen's center, large enough to seat the servants and slaves at once. The guards were not permitted to enter the kitchen or the house proper, save for certain trusted soldiers such as Hugo. The others ate in the guardhouse, plaguing the unfortunate slaves sent to bring them their food.

Hugo groaned again as he stretched out his legs. "Been riding all night and all the day before. I was sent ahead from Jerusalem when Pilate departed."

Dorit exclaimed, "The lord is already on his way back here?" She struggled to rise from her place.

"Stay where you are," Leah said as she sawed at a portion of flatbread and set it on the table between the two of them, followed by olives and goat cheese and dried fruit. A soldier's breakfast. "Would our Hugo be sitting down if the arrival were imminent?"

Hugo grunted his gratitude and glanced at her face. "You're well again?"

"I am indeed." Leah filled a copper pot with water and hung it to boil. She hesitated and then said into the open flames, "This morning I dreamed of a voice. Someone called my name—a man,

I think. I woke up, and my fever was gone. More than that. It is as though I was never ill."

She felt more than saw Hugo's eyes lift again to study her, but he did not question or comment.

Leah turned and silently threw more wood on the flames. If he had asked for more, she would have had no more explanation to give.

They all dreaded the complicated and difficult transition from the one palace to the other. The governor loathed Jerusalem, and his foul mood tainted the entire household before every move. Leah never feigned illness as many did who hoped to be among the few left behind to tend the seaside palace, enjoying the breeze and languid days. No, her illness had been very real indeed. Frighteningly so. In her more lucid moments, she had heard other servants muttering predictions that she would not be alive upon their return from Jerusalem.

Hugo now said around a mouthful, "The mistress was worried about you. That is, until she fell ill herself." Leah turned her full attention to his words. "Dreams, nightmares she's been having. Since the night after we arrived in Jerusalem, she's suffered from nightmares strong as the plague. Her cries wakened the entire household."

Leah murmured, "I should go to her."

"She's coming to you, lass. They'll all be back before nightfall. I came ahead to alert you—"

"Pilate is traveling with his wife?" Dorit asked quickly.

"He's remained at her side the entire way."

"Surely her condition has improved for them to be traveling."

"Not when I last saw her." Hugo popped an olive into his mouth. "Is there meat?"

"I'm certain there is some salted pork left from our meal last evening," Dorit told him.

"And ale," Hugo added. "Like I said, I've ridden all night, and I've a terrible thirst."

Dorit untied the bundle of keys from her waist and handed them to Leah. Leah moved across to the locked chamber, found the proper key, and opened the door. She passed the shelves of gold and alabaster dishes meant for Pilate's table, as well as the amphorae of honey and fine wine. She stopped before the stacks of cheese and salted meat. Lifting a platter of pork from the shelf, she carried it out to the table, then returned to fill a mug from the stone vat.

When she had locked the door and brought the ale to Hugo, he lifted the mug and drained it in one long pull. He sighed with genuine satisfaction, set down the empty vessel, and declared, "There's been trouble over the prophet."

Neither woman asked of whom Hugo spoke. Dorit asked, "Was there revolt?"

"Would I be sitting here if there had been?" Hugo's gaze was on his plate as Leah arranged the slices of pork. "This land spawns trouble. And this prophet made more than most." He lifted a bite to his mouth, shaking his head.

Leah dropped pinches of dried leaves into three mugs, ladled in water from the steaming pot, and set one in front of Dorit. Hugo took his own, pushed his plate away, and said, "The Sanhedrin threatened Pilate with revolt. They said this rabbi, this Jesus, was a blasphemer against their Temple and their God. That he'd declared himself king of the Judaeans."

"He couldn't be any worse ally for the prelate than Herod is," Dorit said darkly.

"Pilate questioned the prophet. I was there for the trial, such as it was. Strange, like nothing I've ever seen. And I've seen more than my share."

Dorit pressed, "Tell us what happened."

"The man was innocent. His every breath said it. Pilate knew it, and so did I. The rabble garrisoned at the Antonia Fortress had their fun with him. He was scourged on Pilate's order, and still the council demanded his death."

"How—what did they do then?" Leah wasn't sure why she cared.

"They no doubt crucified him." Dorit grimaced. "I'm not sorry I missed that."

"You have never uttered more true words." Hugo's features were carved from decades of wind and sun and weather and war, yet something beyond the forces of nature seemed to have aged him in the days since he left Caesarea. He stared out beyond the kitchen at the rising sun and the lapping waters. His voice dropped and deepened. Both women leaned forward to hear him say, "A storm rose at the moment of his death, and the earth shook." He looked down at his hands clasped before him on the table. "I was afraid."

"You?"

"Terrified. I thought the gods were attacking. I still have not untangled it. It was as though the whole world lost all hope."

"But he's dead now, and the trouble is behind us." This from Dorit, the practical one.

"I hope you are right." The soldier's unfocused gaze and slack features left Leah shivering as though she had witnessed the moment herself. He shook his head and unclasped his hands, leaving them palms up in front of him. "But as I rode with only the moonlight to guide my way, I had the feeling that the trouble will be with us forever."

Leah entered Procula's bedchamber, opened the windows to the cool sea breeze, and laid out fresh bed linens in preparation for the woman's arrival. Using the key attached to her belt, she unlocked the wall chamber and counted out six silver *denarii.* She noted the amount on a rolled parchment she had placed in the chamber when the prelate's wife had turned over control of the household treasury to her. No servant before had ever accounted for the flow of money. She knew this because Dorit had held the responsibility before her, and Dorit could neither read nor write. And the one before Dorit had not done any such thing, because that servant had been a thief, taking what he called a tax collector's percentage with every purchase.

Leah had no idea if Procula ever opened the scroll, for nothing had been said. But Leah could not afford the risk of an accusation, even if it turned out to be false. Her father had been accused by dishonest partners of being a thief, then disgraced by bankruptcy. Leah wanted absolutely no such scandal attached to herself. She took a moment to count the jewels and the money, checked the tally against her latest entry, then shut and locked it away.

When she left the palace, the perimeter guards eyed her but did not speak. They could be rough with servant wenches, especially those not already claimed in some fashion by one of their own. But the household knew Leah as Pilate's niece, which was both true and not true. Her grandfather had been a close associate of Pilate's father. Leah's father had been adopted into the clan as an adult, a sign of affection that happened quite often at certain levels of Roman society. But then had come the financial calamity. The tales about Leah's disgraced father had been told and retold during her three years in Judaea Province. Daily Leah wished she could deny the bitter truth.

Large for a town of its size, the Caesarea market drew traders from as far afield as Arabia and Alexandria and even Gaul. Merchants displayed the finest goods in permanent stalls around the center plaza. Caesarea's entire administration was Roman, and most of its population was foreign to the region. Even the Judaean residents took pride in being Roman citizens and spoke Greek, rather than the Aramaic used in the rest of Judaea.

Leah flew through the market, impatiently ordering and bartering. She exacted the best prices she could, but today time was more important than saving a few denarii. She was in the habit of preparing an evening meal according to what she found fresh—forest mushrooms, smoked eel, newly caught redfish. There would be a soup of sorrel and sage to start, she decided, and to complete the repast the season's first fruit would be baked with wild honey and cinnamon. She left orders at each stop for the deliveries to arrive within the hour. Her final stop was the apothecary, where she bought a packet of a foul-smelling pollen that was absurdly expensive, looked like tar, and tasted worse. But it was the only medicine that relieved Procula when her headaches struck. Nightmares meant broken sleep, and whenever the mistress did not sleep well she was susceptible to even worse attacks.

Though Leah drove a hard bargain, she had become friends with several of the stallholders. These traders spoke with her this morning of the prophet's death and mused over the risk of revolt. Though she was not able to tarry long enough to hear more, from one she even heard a rumor that Herod Antipas also was coming to Caesarea from Jerusalem. For Herod to leave Jerusalem at the height of the spring festival season was unheard of. As the stallholder counted coins into Leah's hand, he wondered aloud if the sudden departure of both Herod and Pilate could be tied to the prophet's crucifixion.

Awareness of such rumors and speculations was how a servant survived in a household of power. Leah tucked away the information with the remaining coins and returned to the palace.

She was surprised to find Dorit and Hugo still seated at the kitchen worktable. She decided to use the opportunity to seek the soldier's help. She went to the vat and fished out a cucumber and a pepper from their brine of seawater, then sliced them thinly. She added some flatbread before setting the plate before him. "Will you take anything else?"

Hugo stared up at her and then dropped his eyes to the plate. "You've made a home here."

"And friends."

"Many expected you to try to lord it over the other servants."

"Including yourself?"

Hugo nodded slowly. "True enough. When I heard of your arrival, I said to myself, 'Here comes trouble.' "

"You're not often wrong." She smiled briefly. "Will you ask one of the guards to stoke the fires?"

"They loathe such slave duty."

"The baths won't be ready otherwise. You know Pilate will demand a bath as soon as he arrives. And I need to start preparations for the evening meal and ready the prelate's chambers."

Dorit said, "I can help with the rooms."

"No, you have enough to do here." Leah turned again to Hugo. "Don't *order* one of them to this duty—they'll only take it as punishment. Ask for a volunteer, and I'll feed him tonight from Pilate's provender."

"In that case, I'll do it myself."

This was what she had been after all along. As Leah thanked him and turned to the next task, Dorit said, "Sit with us a moment, child."

"I have a myriad of things to get done and too few hours." But something in Dorit's expression had her seating herself. "What is it?"

Hugo said, "I have heard Pilate speak of you." He would not meet her eyes. "The rumors are true."

Leah felt like she had turned to stone. Rumors had swirled

through the servants' quarters for weeks, about a centurion who commanded one of the province's outermost garrisons. This man, Alban was his name, had reportedly approached Pilate through a trusted emissary. The centurion had requested Leah's hand in marriage. How the centurion had even come to know of her was a mystery, for Leah went nowhere and sought the company of no man. Leah had done her best to ignore the talk, for she hoped with all her might that she would remain unwed all her life long.

Hugo continued, "Pilate has conferred with several of his officers. They all speak highly of this centurion."

"If Pilate wishes for you to wed the centurion, child, that is what you will do." Dorit reached for Leah's trembling hand. "Those who have met him say this Alban is most uncommonly handsome—"

"What do I care for his looks? They only serve to breed pride and arrogance," Leah retorted, her lips trembling. "Who speaks so of him? The maidservants whose hearts he has broken? Brothel owners? Tavern keepers?"

"Soldiers who have served with him in battle," Hugo put in quietly. "As well as men who serve under his command. They claim the commander is fair in his dealings."

Dorit spoke in a low tone to Hugo, "I told you she would be against this plan."

He shrugged. "A soldier obeys the commands of his officers."

"I am not a soldier!" Leah cried out.

She felt Dorit's grasp on her hand tighten. "Hugo speaks with you as a friend, child. If you will not hear what he has to say, how can you prepare?"

"There's no need to prepare for anything because it will not . . ." But the fire had gone out of her, and her shoulders slumped forward in defeat.

Hugo asked gently, "Why did your family send you to serve in

Pilate's household? Did you think you could remain hidden in the servant quarters for the rest of your life?"

Dorit reached for Leah's face to turn it toward her own. "You must listen, and listen well."

"I have served Pilate since he was still using a child's sword," Hugo went on. "I know him as few do. The man gives nothing away without an assured return. He will barter you for an advantage."

Leah's being was so filled with bitterness she could not speak. *Barter* whirled through her mind. Her last months at home had been overshadowed by her two older sisters begging and weeping and pleading not to be bartered into loveless marriages. But ultimately one had been sent to the bed of a man eleven years older than Leah's own father. The other sister had been wed to a man so stout he had not seen his own feet since childhood.

Hugo was saying, "I tried to find out what this centurion has to offer Pilate and came up with nothing save booty."

Dorit argued, "Pilate is already immensely rich."

"A man like Pilate never has enough of anything. I think the only reason this has not happened more swiftly is because Pilate needs time to decide what he wants to extract from this man." Hugo plodded forward with a soldier's relentless tread. "The day we left Jerusalem, Pilate sent his aide Linux off on the eastern road toward Galilee. My guess is Pilate is deciding what it is your man is going to provide to win your hand. And I suspect it will be something to do with the crucified prophet."

Leah dropped her face into her hands.

"Like it or not, your time is approaching." Hugo leaned forward until she raised her eyes to his. "We all know how your father was disgraced and died penniless."

"He was . . . he was cheated." The last word came out on a sob.

The soldier waved that aside. "He is dead and his debts remain unsettled. Where is your mother?"

When Leah did not respond, Dorit answered, "Rome. Residing in a widow's hut at the back of her sister's compound. Living like a pauper—"

"Stop." Leah covered her face.

Hugo continued nonetheless, sounding more friend than soldier. "So there is no voice from your own family to influence your fate. Pilate can do with you as he pleases. Mark my words, sooner or later you will be given to the centurion." He waited until Leah could bring herself to again lift her gaze. "You have a chance to make this marriage work to your own advantage."

The man leaned closer still and said, "You must decide what you want from this union. Then prepare yourself to fight for it."

Leah attempted to lose herself in the day's tasks. By habit more than conscious thought she set the joint to roasting and put the soup to boil. When a maid brought flowers picked from the palace grounds, Dorit arranged some at the table while Leah distributed them through the main rooms, one vase at a time. She forced her mind to other subjects, concentrating now on Dorit. The woman had been Procula's maid for years. Had come with her mistress from Rome. Service was the only life she knew, and she had continued the work long after most women her age would have settled for an easier routine.

Soon after Leah had arrived in the household, Dorit had broken her hip. The pain aged her as work never had. Leah had acted as Dorit's maidservant, doing what was needed before the woman was required to ask. It had been most difficult to see to Procula's demands while attempting to lighten Dorit's load. Leah had done so because something in the woman's eyes reminded Leah of her own mother. The silent sorrow in her gaze was the expression in her mother's the last days Leah had spent with her. What would be worse? To never have wealth, position, or honor, or to know it all and have it wrested from you? Whatever the answer, the eyes of both women had reflected the same pain and defeat.

But otherwise Leah and Dorit had little in common. Dorit had known nothing but the hard life of servanthood. Leah's grandmother, her mother's mother, had been a Judaean married to the chief official in Verona, Italy. Leah's mother, having been born into wealth and power, considered herself a Roman by birth and a Greek by culture and dismissed anything to do with her Judaean heritage.

So Leah had spent her first days in Judaea serving a slave in hopes that someone was offering her mother the same kindness. As a result, Leah had earned a friend who watched out for her in a house full of intrigue and hidden daggers.

How little all that matters now. Leah set the last vase in its niche. No one could protect her from her fate.

CHAPTER THREE

Nightfall

PONTIUS PILATE AND HIS ENTOURAGE approached the Caesarea palace just as the sun touched the edge of the western seas. Some three dozen officials—servants, slaves, and soldiers, coated with dust from the road—climbed the last incline to the gates. Despite the hour and their travel-weary state, they moved efficiently through the entrance and scattered to their familiar roles. Because of Leah's efforts, the servants found all was ready without the usual turmoil of the household's return. The cooks discovered a meal already filling the house with welcome fragrance. The governor's senior staff went straight to the baths, where they found the waters heated, fresh towels laid out, incense burners adding their own heady scent, and garden flowers adorning the changing rooms. The formal chambers were aired, the table set, and the sleeping accommodations were ready for the night. Leah received soft greetings from fellow servants able to breathe easy because she had organized and accomplished the work of a dozen.

Pilate remained by his wife's palanquin as Leah assisted Procula's descent from the conveyance in careful stages. Leah had seen the governor's wife in this state a few times before. Procula was not a complainer, even when she suffered the most dreadful of her headaches, and the worse the pain the quieter she became. Now she did not speak at all. She moved slowly with her eyes closed as Leah guided her through the formal chambers and into her bedroom. Pilate stood in the doorway as Procula was settled onto the bed. Leah noticed his normally severe features were softened with concern.

The prelate was by nature a stern man with a soldier's brusqueness, accustomed to being immediately obeyed. Most of the servants and guards were frightened of him and the power he held. Leah's interactions with him had been few and brief, but she had always found him a fair man. Yet she knew he could be deadly when crossed. *He has decided my future. . . .*

She shook her head and turned her full attention to her mistress. She bathed Procula's face with cool, scented water, then prepared a dose of the apothecary's draught. "Drink, my lady."

"I cannot." Procula barely breathed the words.

"You must, mistress."

Procula moaned. "If I drink it, I sleep. If I sleep, I dream."

"We both know the pain only passes in sleep." Leah kept her voice low and soothing.

Procula shook her head, then winced at the motion. "This pain shall never end."

Leah did not bother to ask what her mistress meant. There would be time enough for such discussions when the woman felt better. Leah lifted Procula's head and held the cup to her lips. "Drink."

Procula's breathing finally eased and she drifted into slumber as Leah gently stroked her forehead. Only then did Leah realize Pilate was no longer in the doorway. His presence lingered, however, like the biting odor in the air after a lightning strike. Or maybe it was just that Leah was thinking ahead to the confrontation that surely would occur at some point soon.

She shook her head again, gathered the used linens, and passed through to the servants' quarters. She was greeted in the kitchen by a few quiet words and a rare smile, her only rewards for her day's frenetic efforts.

With a sigh, Leah hurried out through the side door and deposited the armload of laundry near the large washing vats. She found Dorit seated on the ancient bench, staring out to sea and the sun floating on the western horizon.

The servants' quarters and the guardhouse formed a triangle with the kitchen's side wall, creating a narrow courtyard tiled in a dusty mosaic. Under cover of darkness, some guards and serving wenches used it as a trysting place. Leah preferred it now, when the walls radiated the day's heat and the setting sun turned the sea to bronze.

With no reference to their emotion-filled discussion earlier in the day, Dorit now said, "These moments have been the only times this spring when my bones have felt truly warm."

Leah leaned on the still-warm balustrade and listened to the waves lap against the stone foundations. Men's voices drifted from the sea-filled cold bath beyond the wooden screens. It should have been a peaceful and private moment, yet even here Pilate's power cast its pall and troubled her thoughts. "I would give anything not to wed," she murmured toward the sea.

Behind her, she heard Dorit pat the marble bench. "Come sit with me."

Dorit's lined face never held a frown. She did not raise her voice and rarely spoke an unkind word. She had been born to accept her lot and to smile at whatever her circumstances. But her gaze now was deep and knowing. The woman always seemed to understand Leah's feelings before words were spoken, which invited confidences. She knew Dorit hid a secret better than a sealed tomb.

The woman did not press her invitation. Leah said, still facing west, "I once knew a young man. He made me laugh. He bought me ices at sunset from the highlands, and we strolled along the river. I was fifteen and thought we were very much in love. After Father . . . after we lost everything, I never saw him again. He eventually sent word that his parents forbade our meeting. Nine months later, after my sisters became prisoners in two dreadful marriages, my father died. Soon after that, I was on a boat bound for Judaea."

Dorit said softly to Leah's back, "And you fear you shall never laugh again."

Leah turned to stare at the plain stone walls now flecked with sunset gold. She did not sigh, nor did her eyes glisten with tears. When she spoke her voice sounded low and flat. "Laughter is for children."

The sun slipped down beyond the sea's far horizon, though the colors remained in the evening sky. A lone gull cried out before returning to her nest. It seemed so peaceful in light of the chaos churning within her breast.

After a time Dorit said, "They say this centurion is from the north, from Gaul."

Leah walked over and seated herself on the bench. "Is that bad?"

Dorit pursed her lips. "It is hard to say with men. Still, he is a foreigner who has managed to rise to the rank of centurion. And he is the son of a chief, though not firstborn, of course. What chief would send his firstborn son to this forgotten corner of the empire? But these foreign chiefs have more offspring than a pomegranate has seeds. What is one more or less?"

They heard laughter drift up from the bathhouse. The sound seemed crude to Leah's ears. *Men!*

Dorit went on, "The centurion is said to be both a leader and a fighter. Which means he was likely considered to be a threat to the firstborn brother. It would have been easy to kill him in his sleep. It has happened many times, you know. But he is here. I believe he is only twenty-four years old."

"What does that matter?" Leah could barely hear her own voice.

"Remember, this is no son of a Roman general. This Alban is enough of a warrior to fight his way up through the ranks. His father must be proud, and his older brother should be terrified." Dorit cackled delightedly. "No doubt this Gaul plans to use you as a stepping-stone to Rome. He may find he has met his match."

Leah gripped her arms against her waist but could not entirely stifle the shiver of dread. "I know nothing of his intentions. I do not know him at all. . . ."

"Nor he you. What does that matter?

She whispered, "What of love?"

"Bah. Love is for poets and princes. For the likes of us, we must hope for a tomorrow without pain."

Dorit must have seen the sorrow shadow Leah's eyes, for her voice gentled. "My little one, listen carefully to what I say. You must set such futile dreams of love and happiness aside. And you must *plan*."

CHAPTER

FOUR

Northern Galilee
Ten Days After Passover

ALBAN WAS AWAKE when the guard changed two hours before dawn. He rose from his pallet, hefted his short sword, and walked out into the darkness. Like many able officers, he did not do well with waiting. Especially when the day ahead held such portent and danger.

He took his time checking the garrison's perimeter. He commanded a stodgy Roman fortress dominating the highest hill between the Sea of Galilee and the Golan, twelve miles northeast of Capernaum. The central parade ground, rimmed by simple structures of stone and wood, held corrals and barracks and baths and officers' quarters. As centurion, Alban possessed a rudimentary dwelling of his own. When he returned to his quarters, he found that young Jacob had laid out a soldier's breakfast on the porch table and vanished back inside. Alban's two main officers stood by the garrison's watch fire and pretended not to observe him. They all knew his habits. He insisted upon solitude before battle. They obeyed him, not just because he was their commander, but because he was that rarest of breeds—a Roman centurion who brought his men back alive.

The predawn wind up this high was cold for April. The moon was clear and strong, five days beyond full. Alban studied the horizon, the terrain nearby, and reviewed his plans for the day. A great deal rested upon his getting all the details right.

His thoughts moved over the battle tactics ahead of him, then flitted to the hoped-for reward. Her name was Leah, and she was Pilate's niece. Though he had never set eyes on her, Alban already knew a great deal about the woman. Leah served in Pilate's household because her family had been disgraced, their fortunes lost. He knew she was five years younger than his own twenty-four years, quite old for an unwed woman of Roman aristocracy. He had heard she was not considered particularly attractive by Roman standards. Both tall and strong, she was said to be extremely intelligent with a quiet and reserved manner. His informer had gone on to state that her nose was too straight, her lips too full, her gaze too piercing. Alban cared little for such trifles, or at least he cared for them less than the prospects of a union with the governor's family.

Alban was ambitious. He had asked Pilate for the woman's hand in marriage to further his goals. He might currently be assigned duty at a half-forgotten garrison in the borderlands between two unimportant Roman provinces, but he was determined to rise much further—maybe even to Rome itself. The woman would serve his purposes well. But only if he succeeded today.

The sentry by the main portal called a quiet challenge to someone Alban could not see. His two officers by the fire rose in unison with his own movements. The sentry drew back the door's crossbolt and opened it to admit a squad of dusty men. They saluted Alban's approach, huffing hard. In the torchlight, the road's dust had turned the soldiers' legs chalk white.

"Bring them water," Alban said to the sentry, then asked the squad's leader, "What news?"

"We waited for confirmation as you ordered," he answered through his panting breath. "The caravan will arrive at the dangerous region of the Damascus Road by midday."

Alban gestured to his sergeant. "Rouse the men."

The squad leader accepted the sentry's bucket and drank deeply. He handed it on to his men, wiped his mouth, and added, "Pilate has returned to Caesarea."

Alban frowned. This was unexpected. When the Judaeans celebrated their major religious festivals, Pilate used his presence to proclaim that Rome would allow no unrest. Judaeans traveled from Rome, Babylon, Damascus, Alexandria, even Alban's own native Gaul. Jerusalem was packed for the entire period, since many of the families who journeyed in for Passover remained there through *Shavuot*, the Feast of Weeks, fifty days later. The risk of revolt was never higher than during this time.

"The city is quiet, then?"

"There was some talk of revolution. The governor put the entire garrison on alert. The Judaean leaders blamed the problems on the prophet."

Alban closed the distance between them in two steps. "The one called Jesus?"

"The same. The Sanhedrin threatened a rebellion of their own unless Pilate ordered the man crucified."

This was a cruel blow. The rabbi had used Capernaum as his base and had even healed Alban's favored young servant, Jacob. "So he's gone?"

"A storm blew out of a clear sky when he breathed his last upon the cross." The squad leader quickly made the sign against the evil eye.

Alban hid his deep regret. In his opinion, there was never a man less likely to brew trouble and war than the prophet Jesus. But Alban was a Roman soldier, under Pilate's command. It would not do to let his men see his dismay. He could not risk his personal feelings getting back to his commander, this one who could decide his own fate. "You've done well. You and your men get some rest."

Alban walked out into the shadows that still clung to morning. So the prophet was dead. He shook his head sorrowfully as his whole being revolted against the news. Surely the Judaean elders knew they had no legitimate reason to crucify the man.

Young Jacob was alive only because of the prophet—of that Alban had no doubt. The lad had been terribly ill. Physicians had done all they could, to no avail, and declared the boy would be dead by nightfall. Alban had been desperate. Many whispered he had been too overwrought about the fate of a mere servant, especially only a Judaean lad taken in battle against bandits. Yes, legally Alban owned the lad. But deep within he knew that, in reality, his heart belonged to Jacob. Alban had no idea why he felt such affection for the orphan. His own family had taught him nothing about love. Yet he knew he would give his life for the boy.

He heard a soft whisper in the darkness, "Master?"

Alban turned toward the small form behind him in the shadows. "Yes, Jacob."

The lad stepped into the light. "I heard the soldiers speak about the prophet. Is he truly dead?"

Alban's voice sounded gruff to his own ears. "So they say."

"This is the Jesus who healed me?"

"He is."

"But why? Did he do something wrong?"

"I do not know the reasons. But of this I am sure: He did only good. Look at you. You are well and strong."

"Then why . . ." The voice trembled to a stop.

Alban reached out to touch the boy's shoulder. He felt a shudder go through Jacob's slender frame. Alban had no idea what to say to bring comfort. Alban released the lad, and became the commander once again. "You must prepare. We leave soon on our mission."

They moved out in fading moonlight, an hour before dawn. Alban led his troops from horseback. His second in command, Horax, was the only other mounted soldier. Horax led the rear guard. Jacob trotted at Alban's side, one hand resting upon Alban's right stirrup. The lad was only twelve and far too young to take part in the operation. Yet this day's success depended upon the lad's knowledge and connections.

They moved in silent haste and entered the mouth of the first Golan valley. The night air carried the vague scent of date palms and olive trees. To their right, a field of new barley trembled in the wind.

Alban looked around with a practiced eye. Eons of wind-driven dust had carved these narrow gorges into bizarre shapes. Most of the vales were virtual prisons that twisted and turned and led nowhere except back upon themselves. Only a few traced their way through to the province of Syria. South of them, within the straightest and broadest of these valleys, ran the Damascus Road. Parthian bandits had become increasingly bold of late, attacking along this barren stretch, then slipping into these secret vales and vanishing.

The squad turned south into a gulley that Alban knew ultimately led nowhere. Far on the horizon, dawn painted a tight sliver of sky. Down below, the wind moaned and fretted. As the rock walls closed in ever more tightly, Alban asked the lad, "You're certain he said to meet him here?"

"This is the chasm," Jacob confirmed with a quick nod.

Alban's horse shied with a startled neigh as a man suddenly

appeared on a ledge overhead. The shepherd grinned at the soldiers' surprise. Alban inspected the ledge and realized that what he had taken for just another morning shadow in fact held a cave. His soldier immediately behind muttered, "This place is made for ambush and death."

Jacob turned his face upward to Alban and said, "This is the man I told you about, master."

Alban saluted the shepherd. "Your name?"

"Samuel, son of Ishmael. And yours?"

"I am Alban."

"That is a Roman name?"

"No. From Gaul."

"I know not Gaul."

"Far to the north and west, beyond Rome."

"Yet you fight for Rome."

"We have been a Roman province for three generations."

The shepherd sniffed his disdain for all conquered folk. Alban hid a grin. The man might be dressed in dust and rough weave, but he carried himself like a prince. It was a trait he had seen among many Judaeans who lived at distances from cities. And it was one of the qualities the Romans most despised. How dare these uncouth peasants flaunt their independence before an empire that had conquered nearly all the known world!

The shepherd, leathery skinned and broad shouldered, showed a few strands of silver against his dark beard. "Parthian bandits are stealing my sheep."

"Then we have a common enemy."

Alban watched Samuel take his time inspecting the Roman band, his gaze lingering upon Jacob's hand and how it rested easily upon Alban's stirrup. Alban's men remained still because he did. The shepherd apparently found what he sought, because he said, "Leave your horses here."

Horax argued hoarsely from the rear, "But this gorge leads nowhere!"

The shepherd's dark eyes glinted with desert humor. "Just as the ledge held only shadows, yes?"

Alban raised his hand in signal and slipped from the saddle. He said to Jacob, "Stay close, lad."

The shepherd led them ever farther into the deep chasm. The gorge twisted and turned and finally split into three fissures. The wind did not penetrate there, and the sun was visible only for a few moments each day, so the stone walls remained cool. Even so, Alban sweated heavily. This was perfect territory for an ambush. Stones or arrows from above would leave none alive. Without hesitating, the shepherd took the right-hand fissure, so narrow the men had to pass single file.

A hundred paces farther, the fissure opened into a shallow bowl. The sand floor was colored a sunset red and still very cool beneath Alban's sandals. Nothing lived there. Nothing grew. Far overhead, the dawn wind moaned.

"This is as far as any outsider has ever come." The shepherd pointed to Jacob. "He says I should trust you. But he is your slave and can be forced into saying anything."

"You have asked about me in the markets?"

Reluctantly the shepherd replied, "My wife."

"What was she told?"

"That you were a friend to the Judaeans." The shepherd's tone suggested he found this very hard to believe.

"You were promised a reward if we found the Parthians, yes?" Alban kept his focus on the shepherd's face.

"Five denarii."

A small fortune. "Horax."

"Sir?"

"Pay the man."

Alban's adjutant moved through the soldiers grouped closely about the shepherd. He looked at Alban as if he would argue, but Alban motioned his intention. When the coins rested in the man's gnarled hand, Alban said, "Now we must trust one another."

Samuel slipped the money into a leather pouch, turned, and proceeded to walk up the seemingly featureless wall. Up close, Alban saw how narrow ledges extended from the wall, hidden by shadows and the stone's pastel shading. Another motion, and the troops were moving upward behind their commander.

The climb did not end upon the Golan plateau as Alban had expected. Instead they gathered upon a broad stone ledge, remaining well hidden from anyone moving through the valley. From below, their shelf melded into the surrounding ridges. This was an ideal encampment for men who wished to keep their location a secret.

Samuel traversed the broad stone block and started along yet another ledge carved into the cliff, only this path took them gently down. As they swept around a gradual curve, Alban heard the bleat of sheep. Another turn, a second set of steps, and they arrived inside an even more secluded world.

Samuel spoke for the first time since accepting Alban's coins. "This has been the haven of my clan for generations beyond count." He looked hard at the man whom he was trusting only on the word of a boy.

Alban met his stare full on. "Your secret will go on no report or map of mine."

And secret it was. Alban had heard rumors of such places yet had not believed they existed until now. They stood in a small valley, really no more than a depression between two hills, perhaps fifty paces wide and twice as long. Instead of cool sand its floor was covered in grass. A herd of black-faced sheep grazed the lush undergrowth. From the middle of the south-facing wall poured a small stream, enough water to stain the rock and form a pool as broad as a man was tall. A grove of stunted date palms clustered against the cliff face.

A young shepherd boy watched them with solemn eyes but made no attempt to approach. Alban's men took the opportunity to break out a breakfast of flatbread and goat cheese. After a time, Horax shifted over and squatted beside Alban. "I am amazed the shepherd trusts us with his secret."

"My guess is that the Parthians spotted his flock up on the plateau. They demanded sheep, tracked the shepherd, and now threaten to take everything. At least he has a chance with us." Alban spotted the man at the cliff's edge and rose to his feet. "Here he comes."

The shepherd signaled once and disappeared. Alban and his men again began a climb up the rocky path.

They were greeted up top by the best of an area spring. The wind was strong enough to cool the day's mounting heat and ruffled the knee-deep grass that still smelled fresh from recent rains. A second flock of sheep grazed contentedly. In a month's time, Alban knew, the grass would wither and the sheep would be reduced to eating thorns.

Alban turned to his young servant. "Wait for us here."

Jacob had not looked so distressed since his illness two years past. Or so vulnerable. He drew himself up as tall as possible. "I can help, master."

"You already have. I give you my word that the loss of your family will be avenged. The Parthians will pay for the death of your parents, your sister." Jacob did not respond. He simply looked a long moment at Alban and turned away.

The shepherd also watched as the despondent lad walked over to join his son with the flock. Jacob picked up a stick of his own along the way and gave the grass a frustrated whack. "He has personal reasons to loathe the bandits?"

"His family ran a caravan between Caesarea and Damascus," Alban said. "When he was only nine he saw them all slaughtered, and he and other youths were taken as slaves. We spotted the raiding party and gave chase. They only escaped by dumping the captured goods, including Jacob."

The shepherd studied the two boys with pursed lips. "The Parthians threaten us with the same."

Alban hitched his sword belt tighter still. "Not after today."

The highland pasture was bordered on all sides by sharp-edged cliffs. Alban ordered his soldiers to lower themselves prone, and soon his two squads of twenty-five men were just so many shifting mounds in the high grass. The shepherd used his staff to shove aside the animals and led Alban in a careful crouch to the southwest ledge.

The breathtaking view descended in a mad tumble of rocks and grass and scrub trees to the southern plains. Far below, the Damascus Road was a winding yellow river of dust.

The shepherd pointed with his staff. "There and there."

Alban nodded and muttered over his shoulder, "Horax? Do you see?"

"I see them."

Two bands of men, each some fifty strong, crowded on ledges below jutting from the rubble-strewn hillside over the highway. Far to the southeast, where the heat caused the air to writhe and tremble, came a long snaking line of men and beasts. The expected trade caravan was approaching.

Alban asked quietly, "Where are the paths?"

"Look to your left and your right. See how one shadow in each place forms a line from cliff's edge to valley floor."

Alban moved back a pace. A single bandit glancing upward would be enough to expose them and destroy the element of surprise. He lay on his back, surrounded by sweet-scented grass, and closed his eyes to the sun. "The question," Alban said, "is how to mask our descent."

Neither Samuel or Horax responded. Alban's adjutant rested on the grass beside him and remained silent. Watchful.

Alban turned over and carefully slid forward for another look. The bandits below were very much on the alert, watching for any outrider who might raise the alarm before the caravan drew close.

Fifty Roman soldiers descending from the plateau above them might as well arrive with trumpets and cymbals. To make matters worse, Alban's men would be attacking in single file against seasoned warriors massed on two ledges. Unless Alban could find a way to maintain absolute silence, he and his men would be decimated.

The shepherd moved back from the edge and swept his staff about him like a scythe. "The bandits saw us bringing sheep down to sell to a caravan they later destroyed. They tracked us back up and demanded a tax. Either in sheep . . . or in boys. Each time it is more. Last night they took half my newborn lambs."

A plan began forming in Alban's head. Once more he slithered forward on his belly and inched his head out over the precipice. This third inspection confirmed what he thought he had spotted. He reversed away from the ledge, then said to Horax, "Assemble the men."

As Horax glided away in a low crouch, Alban told the shepherd, "You need go no farther."

"This is my clan's pasture." He could tell Samuel had more than his share of Judaean pride.

"And I will keep it so. Now let my men do what we are trained for."

"I have fought brigands longer than you have been alive."

"Think of your sons," Alban said, his voice low.

More than half of Alban's soldiers were older than he. Four years earlier, they had greeted his arrival with sullen hostility. Now they watched him with the unblinking eyes of seasoned warriors. They trusted his ability to lead them into danger and bring them out again. They knew he had been trained for this role since childhood. He might be a chieftain's son, but he had never known a day when it had been within his power to choose a different life. Which, truth be told, was what bonded him most closely with his men and they with him. The power to choose one's fate was the prerogative of the wealthy and the firstborn.

Alban used his sword to diagram the cliff's border and the two paths in the rocky soil, then lifted his head to address the men now gathered before him. "We will split into thirds. I lead the group taking the eastern path. Horax, you lead the west."

The group scowled as one. They knew only one way of soldiering, the Roman way. Victory was achieved by the massed attack. The best-trained men and the greatest numbers were thrown forward in overwhelming force.

Alban pointed his sword at the most senior of the men and said, "You lead the third group from above."

"We're not to fight?"

"You will keep us alive." He stabbed his sword into the earth by the carved cliff edge. "You must crawl down among the rocks without being spotted. On my signal, you will dislodge the largest rocks you can."

"A landslide," Horax said thoughtfully.

"Aim for the two groups of men. Keep them so busy they can neither ready an attack nor escape."

Horax grinned. "It could work."

"If there are not enough rocks, use arrows. But you must keep the bandits occupied. Once we are in position, come down and join the outer wings." Alban slid his sword back into its scabbard and rose to his feet. He was desperate to move before one of the more experienced warriors spotted his plan's glaring weakness. "We move out."

Horax crouched alongside his centurion as the three groups crawled toward the cliff. "Split into threes we'll number far fewer than them. If the rock throwers are spotted before they're in position, we'll trot down those paths to sure death."

Which was why Alban had chosen the older ones for the rockslide. He hissed, "Quiet as snakes."

Crablike, Alban led his men to the cliff's far eastern corner, gliding forward until he could look over the edge. He watched Horax's face appear two hundred paces to the west. In between them, the third group slipped over the ledge in cautious stealth. Their goal was a pile of loose rubble perched upon a narrow outcropping above the bandits. Their progress was impossibly slow. Or so it seemed to Alban.

Like all good officers, Alban had learned to hide his fear. But his morning meal sat like a leaden lump in his gut. So much depended upon the success of this venture, yet so much was utterly unknown. It was difficult to concentrate fully on the task ahead. And Alban could afford no distractions—not for his men, not for the shepherd, not for himself.

The caravan's sounds carried through the desert heat, with jangling harnesses and shouting herders and the donkeys' sonorous protests. The noise was most welcome, because it focused the bandits' attention downward and masked the soldiers' hushed scramble.

At that point, the Parthians' evil strategy was revealed.

From the south rose shrill cries. Perhaps two dozen fighters on horseback and camels came screaming out of the valley's opposite side. Their exact numbers would be hidden from those walking the Damascus Road, for the dust and the heat would obliterate all but the leading bandits.

In a practiced motion, the caravan's outriders rode back to the procession's heart. They clustered together and drew swords, readying to meet the first attack. At the same time, the drovers and traders wrenched their beasts around and headed for the nearside cliffs, straight toward the bandits hidden below.

Then one of Alban's men slipped.

Roman sandals were not made for scrabbling silently on a stone face. A bit of rubble was unleashed to roll downward. Alban watched the tableau through an unmoving dread, as one Parthian after another looked up and the bearded faces opened to shout a warning.

Alban was already on his feet. "*NOW!*"

His men launched themselves downward, a howling Roman multiheaded beast. A hundred legs pounded the stone ledges. Swords and pikes rose like uneven teeth.

The soldiers on the cliff face let go of their boulders, which dropped in tandem. The two piles of rubble smashed into the second group of bandits while Alban's group frantically grabbed for handholds. Their combined weight had dislodged both piles, and they were threatened with following the cascading rocks to their own deaths.

The Parthians were caught in the instant of launching themselves downward. As the first raiders flung themselves down the ledge, those behind them screamed a shrill warning and turned to face rocks and Romans scrambling downward toward them.

"Hold hard!" Alban flung himself onto the cliff face, as more rocks tumbled and crashed from overhead. A stone struck his shield arm, almost dislodging him from the ledge. As soon as the tumult passed, he risked a glance upward, then shouted, "Attack!"

As he expected, the ledge used by the Parthians backed into a shallow cave. The ledge itself had been wiped clear of bandits. Either they had fled down the path, pursued hard by soldiers, or they had darted toward the cave's protection. Alban could hear the clanging of spear striking spear as the battle was struck below, but he knew Horax would be at the forefront and could be trusted to lead the men. His attention was on the cave mouth, which was now half filled with rubble and still-scrambling bandits. They were coughing and wheezing as they tried to grapple their way through the dust and debris.

"Bowmen!" The traditional massed Roman-style attack simply was not possible in such limited space. Now a quarter of his men fitted the shorter arrows into their bows and fired into the cave mouth. Shouts of rage changed swiftly to screams of alarm and pain.

Alban appointed a cadre of men to stand fast against any of the bandits who might try to return on the path. The rest stayed with the cave.

"Cease fire," he signaled his bowmen.

He shouted in Aramaic, the tongue used by all eastern border nations, "This is your only chance! Toss out your weapons, and you will be spared!"

Down on the plain, the situation had rapidly coalesced into victory for the caravan masters. Alerted by the rockslide, the traders had spotted the bandits before committing their beasts to the hillside. They drew their convoy into a tight defensive unit. Seeing that the allies on the hillside had been trapped, the bandits on horseback pulled up hard. The caravan outriders raced forward, their weapons glinting overhead. The mounted Parthians turned and fled.

But Alban had little time to peruse the fight below. His full attention was taken by the cave and its inhabitants. "Your cause is lost!" he informed them in a loud voice. "Drop your weapons or die!"

A dozen pikes and swords now clattered upon the rocks at his feet. He motioned his men forward. "Bowmen, stay on guard."

Alban turned to Horax, who had been gathering the men and taking stock. "How many of our men were lost?"

"One wounded, none killed, my lord."

Alban felt the tension in his body seep away like the sweat drying on his body.

As a raucous cheer rose from the valley, Horax lifted his sword and shouted, "Soldiers, salute your centurion!"

CHAPTER FIVE

Pilate's Palace, Caesarea

THAT MORNING AFTER HER MISTRESS'S RETURN from Jerusalem, Leah entered Procula's bedchamber and discovered the woman was sitting up. Leah quickly prepared the scented bathwater and laid out fresh garments. "You seem better, mistress."

"And what a relief it is." Procula rubbed her forehead. She still looked wan, her eyes sunken by past pain, but her voice sounded alert. "I would like to see my husband. Is he available?"

"Not right now, I'm afraid. He has a guest."

Procula's head lifted. "Who might he be entertaining at this early hour?"

"I believe it is a matter of state, my lady. Immediately following breakfast, he summoned Herod Antipas."

Procula sat up abruptly. "Herod? Here? But why?"

"I know not, mistress."

Both hands went to cover her eyes. Leah feared she was going to suffer another painful spell. "My lady?"

"This can bring no good." She lowered her hands and examined

Leah with a troubled expression. "You must observe them and bring me a report of this meeting."

"But I have no reason to intrude, mistress."

"My orders are your reason."

"How am I to gain entrance?"

Procula rubbed her forehead again. When she looked up, Leah realized she had a plan. Leah inwardly prayed to all gods, known and unknown, that it would be a plan with even a hope of success. If Pilate felt he was being spied upon, her life would be in extreme danger, whether or not she was his niece. That she was only carrying out his wife's orders afforded no protection.

"You shall serve them. Say that I have ordered them wine. For Herod, it is never too early in the day."

"But Pilate has his wine steward—"

"Greet Herod in my name and say I ordered it. If that sounds improper, my husband will attribute it to my illness. And linger," continued Procula. "Linger in the alcove behind the curtains until you know whereof they speak."

Leah bowed and turned, trembling. Her mistress was once again rubbing her forehead. "Trouble. Trouble. No end to trouble," Leah heard her murmuring.

Leah shifted the tray she was carrying and held her breath. She paused behind the crimson tapestry that covered the entrance to Pilate's audience chambers. All of the palace's formal chambers had windows facing the sea, and on this early morning the draft carried a noticeable chill. She put down the tray on the table next to the doorway. With only the slightest movement of her hand, she was able to shift the heavy drape just enough to observe the two men. Neither man glanced her direction. Pilate was pacing while Herod reclined on one of the velvet lounge chairs.

Herod lifted a plum from the golden tray and examined it idly. "What do you make of these rumors?"

Pilate continued his pacing. "I know not."

"I do wish you would sit. It is most difficult to speak to someone constantly moving about."

Pilate dropped into his chair. From her hidden position Leah thought his eyes appeared dark and haunted.

"Frankly," Herod said, "you look ghastly. Are you not well?"

Pilate rubbed a hand down his face. "I have not slept."

"It is troubling you, then?"

For a moment there was no answer. Then with the slightest nod Pilate admitted the truth. "That and Procula. Her health has been threatened, and by this same hazard."

"*You* are in charge. If things are out of control, you have the power and the might to fix them."

"True, but only when I can recognize the enemy." Pilate left his seat again and strode to the window. "Right now, I don't know where the danger lies, so how can I strike against it?"

"The danger arises from those fanatics who claim this carpenter's son is their Messiah. And to strengthen their claim, they are inventing all sorts of outlandish tales." As Herod leaned forward, grapes tumbled off his robe and rolled across the patterned tiles at his feet. "They are out to destroy us. If they can stir up a large enough rebellion, we will both suffer for it."

"How do you know this?" Pilate's tone was as sharp as the dagger at his waist.

"It's what they do. Always making trouble. No sense of—"

"So you have no proof? It is merely conjecture?" When Herod remained silent, Pilate turned back to the window. "My nights have been plagued with worry. We must determine what they are planning. But I have found no one willing to speak with me. Nor with you, I suspect, which is why we are having this conversation."

"We need to find some way into their inner circle."

"You mean, infiltrate their ranks."

"Get into the community. Yes. We need ourselves a spy." For one long moment Herod stared at his compatriot. "Surely, my lord, you can solve that problem. All it takes is gold. There are always plenty of peasants who will do anything for a price."

"We need truth, not more fables bought through bribery."

"Then what is *your* answer?"

Pilate began pacing once more. "There is a centurion, Alban by name, who is said to have made acquaintances in the Judaean community near Capernaum."

"You would trust a Roman soldier in the Galilee to bring you truth?"

Even from her hidden location, Leah could sense the tension in the room. Her hand fluttered to her breast, brushing against the curtain. The quiet stirring caught both pairs of eyes. Her breath caught in her throat as she quickly lifted the tray and stepped forward between the drapes. She hesitated long enough to dip a slight bow and then moved silently forward.

"Your wife sends her greetings to your guest, my lord. She has ordered that I offer you wine."

Pilate neither acknowledged her nor offered his thanks. She set the tray on a small marble table beside a plate of honey cakes. "Shall . . . shall I pour, my lord?"

"Here, girl. I'll have some." Herod's voice was as languid as his eyes. He watched her with unfeigned interest as she filled his goblet.

Then as quietly as she had come, she left the room. She could feel Herod's eyes on her back, watching her go.

Once again behind the safety of the curtain, Leah felt the shudder that vibrated through her entire body. How she wished to escape. Leave this whole terrible business behind her, along with all the fear and uncertainty and bitterness. She once more lowered the tray silently to the marble table. Though she dared not shift the curtains, she again listened carefully.

She heard Herod ask, "Who was that girl?"

"Her name is Leah."

"Of course. Your niece. How long has she been with you?"

"I'm not sure—three years, I think. She's my wife's maid until such time as she finds a suitable husband."

"Then you don't plan to keep her?"

"No. No, it doesn't seem fitting—her being family. I promised her mother . . ."

"Would you be willing to sell her?"

"She's *family*," Pilate said with annoyance. "She is with us until she marries. In any case, she is already spoken for."

"By whom?"

"The centurion I just mentioned."

Leah could hear Herod shifting his position. "This centurion you say may be of use to us?"

"Alban is young, but the men I have questioned speak highly of him. No doubt he sees my niece's hand as an upward step."

Leah heard the creak of the couch as Herod leaned forward. "This favored niece, how does she fit into your household?"

Leah felt her face flush with both embarrassment and anger. They were discussing her as though she were mere chattel.

"Her father lost everything. Names, titles, honor, life. When her family begged, I saw no way to refuse. My wife speaks well enough of her. Why do you ask?"

"You say this young centurion wishes her. Perhaps we could use her to, what shall we say, encourage him to find the answers. You haven't yet given this Alban your word?"

"We are still in negotiations."

"Alban is a strange name for a Roman."

"He's a Gaul."

"And the maid?"

"Mixed blood. Father was from a northern province. Mother was a Judaean, that is, her mother's mother."

Leah could hear Herod's intake of breath. "Perhaps we won't need as much gold as I had thought. The centurion Alban. Favorably disposed toward the Judaeans, you said. And this maid with Judaean blood. I do believe we have our answer."

Pilate's voice was heavy with impatience. "Then perhaps you would proceed to divulge it."

"Make the solving of the mystery the condition of the betrothal agreement."

"Betrothal?"

"A standard practice among Judaeans."

"A Judaean wedding? But the Gaul is not Judaean, even if the maid can claim Judaean blood."

It was all Leah could do not to cry out and disclose her hidden position. *A Judaean wedding*? She covered her trembling lips with a hand. She was no more of the Judaean religion than the Gaul himself. Much less did she desire a wedding of any kind.

"We will need to encourage one of the Judaean priests with a bit of gold. But you say this centurion has allies among the Galileans. Yes, this could be arranged."

"This Judaean wedding you are proposing. How does it work?"

"It's simple enough. First there is the betrothal. A traditional and rather legal ceremony once the conditions are agreed upon. The bride is presented, and following the ceremony she returns to her place of abode until such time as the bridegroom fulfills his conditions. Once that is done, he is free to collect his wife."

"So he is married, yet not married?"

"Precisely."

"I don't think the Gaul will go for it."

The couch squeaked again as Herod stirred. "Then you must convince him. We *need* a Judaean wedding. That is the only way we can ensure that the Gaul finds the required information. If he really wants the advancement that the woman would bring, he will do what needs to be done."

"Perhaps. Perhaps you are right."

"You must send for this centurion at once."

Pilate's feet scraped across the tiles. "I already have."

Leah could bear no more of this discussion. Surely she had enough information to satisfy her mistress. Silently she slipped away from the doorway and walked on numb feet down the servants' hallway. She did not enter the kitchen, however. She needed air and time to think. Time, as Dorit said, to plan.

CHAPTER

SIX

The Capernaum Garrison

THEIR DUSTY PROCESSION arrived back at the garrison under a cold moonlight. Alban let the wounded captives set the pace, though it left the small convoy open to attack. He stretched his men out as flanking guards while he and Horax moved about on their mounts, checking the perimeter. Alban did not realize how tired he was until he saw the fort in the distance. The hilltop glowed from the watch fires. He let Horax lead the cadre with the Parthians in chains through the fortified gates. Alban remained at the rear, watching for an ambush until the last man was safely inside.

He himself passed inside to the cheers of the entire garrison. His men had good reason to celebrate. The caravan masters had rewarded Alban's work with two sacks full of gold. The garrison had not been paid for almost six months, a common enough problem among the outlying posts. And Alban needed the money as desperately as any of his men. After an initial gift to Pilate, and another to the Jerusalem officer who had presented Alban's case to the prelate, he was nearly penniless.

Alban grinned at the cavorting men and answered their cheers with an upraised fist. He directed the night guard to use an empty stone enclosure for all the captured bandits. Then he spotted the strangers.

They approached Alban's horse and the lead officer saluted. "You are the centurion Alban?"

"I am."

The gentleman was impressive, with waxed hair and gold ornamentation on his uniform. He pointed at the enclosure. "Those are the Parthians, the ones most claim do not exist?"

"They are."

"How many men did you lose in the battle?"

"None." The soldier had addressed him in Latin, and Alban responded in kind. Even the few words on his tongue seemed strange. He had not spoken the language in months. He doubted that any of his men spoke more than a few words of Rome's mother tongue.

"You are to be congratulated, centurion. Your predecessor lost a quarter of his strength to the ghost battalions." The polished officer paused, then said, "Pilate commands that you attend him immediately."

Alban slipped from his horse and wearily rubbed the dust from his face. "Does he give a reason?"

"Only that the matter is urgent."

"Then we leave at first light."

"Centurion, we were ordered—"

"We will be taking with us the two Parthian leaders so Pilate can see them for himself." Alban pointed to the darkness beyond the garrison's main gates. "A mounted band of perhaps thirty more escaped on horseback. Do you wish to open yourself to attack at night from a mounted force? One that is incensed at their humiliating loss today?"

The soldier said doubtfully, "Pilate said nothing about bringing Parthians."

"Hardly a surprise, since no one knew of our raid." Alban dismissed the strangers with a weary hand. "We leave at dawn."

Tired as he was, Alban did not sleep well. He could not understand why Pilate had found it necessary to send an officer of his household guard to summon and accompany him to Caesarea. He tossed for hours, searching for some reason to hope that it all was good news, and came up with nothing that gave him calm.

Alban's greatest fear was not of death, not even of injury or shame. The dread that struck in the bleakest hours was over a loss of control. So little of his life had been as he had wanted. At the age of six, his own father had ordered him to begin preparing himself for battle. At twelve, his father had banished him to the compound of a retired centurion, where he was intensively schooled in the art of combat. He was permitted home only four times a year, for feast days and his mother's birthday. His father had visited from time to time, watching his progress as a swordsman, offering no sign of affection or affirmation other than his presence.

Alban lay and stared at ceiling beams that flickered and writhed in the oil lamp, and recalled the last time he had seen his father. The old chief had arrived on Alban's seventeenth birthday with gifts and orders both. They had ridden east toward the Roman legion garrisoned at Avignon. His father had spoken of great changes in the world, the chance Alban now had to elevate himself and the family name. He had handed him a small pouch of gold and a scroll appointing him adjutant to the garrison's commandant. Then he had saluted his son and ridden away. The tears Alban had refused to shed that day still burned behind his eyelids.

Alban had harbored no desire to become a soldier, much less a Roman legionnaire. But he had done as he was ordered. He lived a soldier's life. He strengthened his body and deepened his skills. He studied, and he served his commanders. He asked the wisest of them about lessons that came only through surviving in battle. He had returned home once a year. His last journey home had been for his father's burial. When he had knelt and promised the new chief, his elder brother, his fealty, Alban had seen the light of resentment and fear in the man's face. The next morning Alban had been ordered to Judaea Province. His brother could not kill him, so he had arranged for Alban to spend the rest of his days in the most desolate reaches of the Roman empire.

Alban pulled the covers over his eyes and did his best to shut out the bitter memories. He had never once broken a vow. But if he was ever granted leave to travel home, he would make his brother pay.

The officer from the prelate's household guard proved a good enough sort. His rank was *tesserarius*, a title that could mean any number of things and made him Alban's subordinate. But Alban knew Romans to be a prickly lot and vindictive if their pride was bent. So Alban treated Pilate's official messenger as though they were of equal rank. The soldier's name was Linux, and he hailed from a town in Umbria, a province to the north of Rome. According to Linux, Umbria was good only for growing strong pigs and weak wine. "I thought I'd already seen the nastiest place on earth—been there, seen it, and left immune to the worst. But this province turns out to be harder than iron."

Since Pilate was waiting for them, they all rode. Alban lashed the Parthian bandits firmly to their saddles and left the garrison accompanied by just one of his men. Jacob had begged to join them, but Alban said a firm no and turned away before his resolve could weaken.

His packhorse was piled with his share of booty from the raid. The Parthian leaders had carried shields of hammered gold, and their sword scabbards and hilts were jewel encrusted. Alban had never met a leader not cheered by a gift of booty.

Hours later, as they passed the small garrison marking the entry into Samaria, a guard called down from his tower, and the main portals opened so that the watch officer might salute Pilate's standard. Linux answered with a casual wave, then turned back to Alban. "For a Gaul, your Latin isn't altogether crude."

"Gifted by a centurion from Rome who had retired to a farm near my father's land. He was a rough sort, but a good fighter and a better teacher."

"Which explains the hint of gutter in your accent." Linux revealed an easy grin. "No offense, centurion. We Romans like a bit of the street. And your captives are testimony to your abilities as a fighter and leader both. As a matter of fact, Pilate himself mentioned that your ally in Jerusalem called you a hero in the making. What's his name?"

"The centurion Atticus. Based at the Antonia Fortress."

"Another good man, by all accounts." Linux sobered. "Your friend has known some trouble of his own."

"Atticus is ill?"

"In a way. You've heard about the prophet?"

"You mean the Nazarene, the one they call Jesus? Yes. Word came just yesterday."

"Your mate was put in charge of the crucifixion. It was hard on him. Extremely hard. And on Pilate. And worst of all on his wife, Procula."

Despite the desert heat, Alban felt the day chill slightly. "Pilate's wife?"

"Dreams, she's had. And is still having, according to some. Fever dreams, so bad she wakes the entire palace with her screams. Which is why we're traveling to Caesarea. Pilate and the province's entire administration left Jerusalem eight days ago to return to his seaside palace."

Caravan traffic converged around them, making further conversation difficult. They were joined at one point by a senior equestrian officer traveling from the Syrian province. Alban accepted the *tribuni*'s grudging congratulations for the successful raid, then backed away and watched Linux ply the crusty gentleman with aristocratic charm until the Syrians turned north toward Tyre.

They made good time and camped that night upon the fields of Armageddon. A large *caravanserai*, a trading outpost, stood at the juncture of the province's two main roads. To the north were Tiberias and the Galilee, from which they had begun their journey; to the west was the Roman capital of Caesarea. South lay Jerusalem, and farther north was Tyre, the region's largest port and home to the Roman navy. Where they halted, ruins of a fort from beyond remembrance jutted into the sunset. There local traders sold fresh fruit and bread and fodder for animals at outrageous prices, while their women danced in the firelight for gold.

The Romans camped well apart. As darkness fell the stars formed a gleaming wash overhead, while the surrounding hills glittered with firelight from Samaritan villages. Alban saw to his captives, personally pounding their stakes firmly into the earth, then told his sergeant he would take the second watch.

Their needs were tended by the soldiers who traveled with Linux. Though the pair wore the uniforms and cloaks of Roman legionnaires, Alban suspected they were trusted servants. As they made themselves comfortable by the fire, the officer revealed that his family ruled much of the Umbrian province. "My elder brother has the nerve to complain about it, as though being the most powerful man in Umbria is a burden he carries out of concern for my own weak shoulders."

"I've met such men."

"Sooner or later I'll be forced back into the fold. My dear elder brother is obliged to toss me a few crumbs. I'll be granted some drafty palace with a leaky roof, perched on some lonely cliff. All the servants will come to me suffering from diseases my brother wishes upon me." Linux motioned at his hovering servants. "Much like this lot, I fear."

The nearest one accepted the comment as soldier's humor and grinned as he announced, "Your meal is ready, sir."

"Well, serve it, man. Serve it." Linux shook his head and sighed an apology to Alban. "It will be all grit and road dust, I wager. So where is your home?"

"Here, as much as any place."

"Ah. Bad as that."

"Worse."

Linux accepted a plate from the servant and stared at its contents. "Where did you obtain this?"

"A Samaritan herder sold me a haunch of lamb roasted with rosemary and thyme."

Linux sniffed in appreciation. "Sorry, centurion. You were saying?"

"My father was a chief, my eldest brother a coward who fears my sword."

"And rightly so, no doubt. If I came upon you in battle I'd hoist my toga and flee like the wind." He pointed at Alban's plate. "Please, enjoy."

In between mouthfuls Alban felt the need to continue. "The life of a soldier was my father's desire. My eldest brother's first act after becoming chief was to have me shipped to Judaea. And you?"

"Military service is a long-standing family tradition. I might have a few generals scattered about my ancestry. One forgets. My brother ordered me to continue the tradition."

Alban snorted. "Brothers!"

Linux lifted his cup. "May they be plagued by pestilent sores."

Alban used his belt knife to slice the meat. "Why does a Roman aristocrat travel to an outpost on the Galilee border?"

"I volunteered for the duty. I was so relieved not to be left back in Jerusalem that I would have volunteered for almost anything." Linux shuddered. "Dreadful place, Jerusalem. Especially now. The city is one step from revolution, and Pilate leaves town because of his wife's bad dreams."

"You don't approve?"

"I don't approve of the whole province. Nest of vipers, if you ask me. But you, now. You've a reputation for making friends among the Judaeans."

"My region stretches from Tiberias to the Golan border, from Galilee almost to Tyre. I have but one hundred men. I could not rule effectively without making friends and cultivating local allies."

"I happen to agree with you, even if most of your fellow officers do not. They fear the Judaeans too much to ever form alliances. Especially now."

Alban read the man's concern in the firelight. Perhaps there was more depth to the man than he had first assumed. "You're speaking of the prophet?"

"Be glad you missed that little drama, centurion." The officer's careless manner turned serious. "Procula fears it will bring about Pilate's downfall, which worries the governor like nothing I've seen." He fed the remnants of his meal to the fire. "Dreams and women. Like oil on an open flame."

"Tell me what happened."

Linux was silent long enough that Alban assumed the man had politely refused. When he did speak, his voice was so low Alban had to strain to hear him above the sputtering embers. "How many crucifixions have you witnessed?"

"Enough." Though Alban had never ordered anyone crucified, his predecessor was notorious for littering the region with crosses. Road signs to proper behavior, the old centurion had called them on the day Alban had assumed command. Put up enough such road signs, and even the Judaeans will learn to read the Roman message.

Linux went on, "I've seen far too many of the dreadful killings. The emporer Tiberius is a great one for crucifying his enemies. But never in my life have I seen one like this, nor the trial which came before it. The Judaean council, the Sanhedrin, you know of it?"

"The name only."

"But you've heard how they fight among themselves, yes? The Sanhedrin is made up of two groups, the Pharisees and the Sadducees. They loathe each other." Linux shook his head. "Yet on that day they came together and stood in Pilate's court as one. They shouted the same words echoed in the streets by crowds they paid from their own pockets. The scene was one step away from riot. They all shouted, over and over, 'Crucify him.' Pilate had the prophet scourged, hoping that would satisfy their blood thirst. But they threatened the governor with open revolt. He washed his hands of it. The council won. The prophet carried his own cross to Golgotha."

Linux's expression had gone dark in the glow from the firelight. "I'd been sent to the south on an errand. I arrived back at the Lion's Gate just as it happened. A storm rose out of nowhere, the likes of which you can't imagine. The sky went dark as Procula's dreams. The wind blasted from all four corners of the globe. And then the earth shook. I've known earthquakes before. This one felt like the world was breathing its last."

Alban felt the same bitter dread he had known upon first hearing the news. "And Atticus was at the center of it all? No wonder he has fallen ill."

Abruptly Linux rose to his feet. "Sleep well, centurion. Tomorrow will be a momentous day."

"Wait." When Linux turned back, Alban asked, "What can you tell me of Pilate?"

"You have never met him?"

"For only a moment upon taking up my command. One of twenty new officers in an overcrowded room."

Linux inspected him carefully. "He gives nothing freely. Whatever you ask of him, he will exact the highest price you are willing to pay, then demand more besides." The Roman's eyes glittered in the firelight, full of warning. "Know well what it is you want, centurion, and be certain your desire is worth the price. Because pay you will. Pay with your booty or your blood. Maybe even your life."

CHAPTER SEVEN

Pilate's Palace, Caesarea

ALBAN HAD NEVER before visited Caesarea. His original troop ship had landed at the far larger port of Tyre. He could have visited the Roman center of power at any time, but he had avoided Caesarea for a very specific reason.

Outlying garrisons such as his were manned by mercenaries. He knew the elite of Caesarea considered them to be nothing more than gristle clinging to Rome's outer rim, scum who often disgraced their uniform. Alban had vowed he would only travel to Jerusalem or Caesarea when he had established himself, had become strong enough to prevail over such derision, when he would be singled out as a leader of men. Generals had become caesars. Why not a Gaul?

Never had Rome's might seemed clearer than on the approach to Caesarea. The city occupied nine seaside hills and a narrow stretch of rocky flatlands. The surrounding ridgeline was rimmed by Roman guard towers. Alban and Linux saluted the city's official watch master and entered Caesarea by the southern passage. The broad colonnaded avenue led them past the city's coliseum before turning north to flank the sea.

After months in the Galilee, the city's mix of odors—of camels and donkeys and spices and fires and men—was an assault to the senses. The farther they moved into the city, the more crowded it became. When the lane they traversed opened into a plaza, it was easy to see why visitors called Caesarea a miniature Rome. The hills might be golden sand instead of Roman rock and scrub, but the palaces were as fine as those of the empire's capital. The freemen he saw were dressed in elegant togas and took their ease at splendid inns or well-stocked market stalls. Their servants wore better clothes than any Alban owned.

To Alban's eyes, the governor's palace occupied the finest position in all Judaea Province. South of the port, a ledge of rock and shale extended far into the Mediterranean. The palace grounds occupied this entire peninsula. The guardhouse formed a low perimeter between the compound and the city. The main structure stood upon the highest ground, with an uninterrupted view of both city and sea. The descent to the Mediterranean was a series of polished steps, each as broad as the entire garrison Alban had just left.

As he dismounted, Alban knew a taste of nerves. So much depended upon the next few hours. . . .

Linux ordered the household guards to lock away the two bandits, then turned to Alban. "You and your man can wait inside, if you like. I'll go make my report."

"You're leaving me here?"

Linux saluted the approaching duty officer and lowered his voice. "You'll take counsel?"

"Always," Alban replied.

"No commanding officer likes to be caught off guard. The last thing Pilate expects is for a summoned officer to arrive bringing treasures and captives."

Alban knew a fleeting fear that Linux intended to poison Pilate's first impression, or steal credit. He pushed the concerns aside. "I am grateful for your wisdom."

The guard motioned Alban toward a room with a window overlooking the city's northern hills. But Alban chose to remain with his sergeant in the shade of the guardhouse roof. Between them and the port stretched the city's magnificent hippodrome, its oval track floored with fine white sand. The stadium had seats along three sides, with the fourth left open so that the fans could enjoy the azure waters.

His sergeant wiped a dusty face. "I do believe I smell roasting lamb."

Alban nodded. From the palace kitchen in the building just beyond the guardhouse he heard women's voices and wondered if one belonged to Leah.

"Mind you, they probably feed the ranks swill here, same as everywhere else," the sergeant complained.

"I'll make sure you eat what I am served. Then you're free until later." When the man did not respond, Alban asked, "Is there something that's bothering you?"

"Them Parthians. They're too calm."

"They are desert trained," Alban replied. "They have learned to mask their sentiments well."

"Not like this. Not the way they've been talking."

"You understand their tongue?"

"No need. I listened to them last night when they thought the camp slept. I was standing guard on the other perimeter. They were laughing like they were already freed."

Alban left his man and sauntered about the guardhouse. It was a substantial structure, holding barracks, cookhouse, baths, sleeping quarters, and one windowless cell. Prisoners were not held here long, of course. The chamber was intended only for those awaiting

Pilate's judgment. The sentries displayed the bored alertness of guards everywhere. "I'd like to see my prisoners," he told them.

"They are Pilate's now," the duty officer replied with a trace of a sneer, but he rose and reached for the keys. He kept his movements just slow enough to show what he thought of orders from a back-country centurion.

The two Parthians sprawled upon wooden benches against the inner walls. A single oil lamp granted the room's only illumination. The prisoners looked dusty and weary but far too composed. Only one of them bothered to glance over at him. The other remained as he was, stroking a beard with one manacled hand, staring at the ceiling and humming tunelessly.

When Alban returned outside, he found Linux waiting for him. The officer announced, "You're invited to enjoy Pilate's bath."

Alban leaned in close and muttered, "The prisoners are behaving as though they knew they have been granted a reprieve. Last night my sergeant heard them talking and laughing, like they were waiting for someone to slip them the keys."

Linux casually turned his back to the duty officer before replying, "From now on, you must assume everything you say and do will be observed and reported."

"Understood." Alban raised his voice and said, "My man needs a proper meal. And our horses need stabling."

Linux turned to the duty officer. "See to it." Linux left Alban, entered the guardhouse himself, and returned a few moments later wearing a thoughtful air. "Come with me." He led Alban around the kitchen and through a side door into the bath's changing room.

"What did you think of the Parthians?" asked Alban.

"Worth investigating." Linux motioned Alban to one of the changing cubicles, where they both removed their clothing.

The rooms were too well appointed for a simple soldier. Towels and robes were stacked upon trays of onyx and soapstone. Flowers sprouted from solid gold vases. The floor mosaics were adorned with semi-precious stones, and the utensils in the washroom were all hand-carved ivory. Alban was sure that the man who ruled Judaea from such a home as this had little use for a rough-cut Gaul.

A bath slave offered soaps and unguents in silver vials. There was an unending stream of fresh water, and new silver-backed razors for his face. They stepped into the first of three baths, the *caldarium*, the heated pool. Steam drifted in the languid air, causing the murals along the walls to spring to life and dance for him. They moved from there into the *frigidarium*, which was set in a chamber with only three walls, the far end open to the crystal blue sea. Two steps down led to a patio containing a third bath filled with heated seawater. A half-dozen figures lolled about the space. Alban felt eyes on him from every quarter.

He ate with Linux in one of the side alcoves. Across from them, a slave pummeled a large man on the massage table. Others ate plums and drank sweet wine, their talk of Rome and money and power.

When the chamber next to theirs emptied, Linux murmured, "If you want to survive in these waters, you enter every meeting well prepared. I left you at the guardhouse so I could speak with allies." Linux hefted the towel's edge and rubbed his face, mashing the quiet words so they were nearly indistinct. "Procula remains very ill from her dreams. After our return from Jerusalem, Herod paid a visit to Pilate, and now the prelate has sent a messenger to Herod's palace on the other hill above the hippodrome. They have been at odds for some time, but this prophet's death has brought them together in a way I cannot explain. I mistrust what I cannot understand."

In the distance, a voice called Alban's name. Linux responded, "Here!" To Alban he said softly, "Enter Pilate's presence as you would a battle."

Alban found a formal toga laid out for him in the dressing chamber. The cotton and linen weave was more refined than anything he had ever worn. On the side wall was the greatest astonishment he had seen yet in this house of wonders, a mirror with a polished surface that stretched from the floor to above his head. Despite the servant's impatience, he took time for a long look. This was the first time he had ever seen his own full image.

The man staring back at him was far more seasoned than the one who had entered Judaea's borderlands four years earlier. The cleft in his chin was matched by a scar that ran from his left temple to his hairline, compliments of an arrow that had almost robbed him of half his vision. His hair, originally a shade between brown and russet, was now more gold in color, and his skin was as dark as saddle leather. But what held him most were his eyes. He knew himself to have always been cautious, measuring, reserved. What caught him now was the hint of fear in his gaze.

CHAPTER EIGHT

Caesarea, That Same Day

FOR THE TWO NIGHTS since Herod's latest visit, Procula had wakened most of the household with her screams. Once awake she was again seized by the headache. Leah took to spending her nights at the foot of her mistress's bed. As soon as the whimpers began, Leah rose to give the governor's wife another measure of the medicine. Procula continued her weak protests, speaking in broken tones about the prophet now lost to the grave.

The other servants made no comment when Leah stumbled back to the women's sleeping quarters after serving Procula her breakfast and morning dose. The senior cook, a bitter woman who normally never had a kind word for anyone, gently awakened Leah personally in time to serve Procula her other meals. When Leah did sleep, it was in scattered snatches, starting awake from dreams in which she thought she heard the mistress calling to her.

This day, it seemed as though Leah had scarcely laid her head upon the pillow before the cook was touching her shoulder. "You must come now."

"The mistress calls for me?"

But the cook was already headed back through the door. "To the kitchen. Quickly!"

When Leah arrived, she found a newcomer seated at the center table. The soldier's beard was still wet from the baths. He plucked at the simple house robe and grumbled, "I prefer to wear my uniform."

Dorit was seated at the table's far end, peeling onions. "The prelate forbids uniforms and weapons inside his compound."

"And my lamb is not to be served in the guardhouse," the cook added firmly. She motioned Leah toward the fire. "Stir that soup, if you will."

Dorit said to the man, "You must be a trusted confidant to travel with the centurion."

Leah managed not to drop her ladle. She froze in place, then began stirring vigorously as the soldier replied, "We were in battle. This journey with him was my reward."

Leah kept her back to the room and its guest. The cook must have served him a plate because he rumbled what could be taken as his gratitude. From the corner of her eye, Leah saw the cook glance her direction, then said, "The prisoners you brought are bandits?"

"Parthians," he replied around a mouthful.

Dorit commented, "Some say the Parthians do not exist."

"Which is why Centurion Alban brought the two officers with us. To show the world how wrong those rumors are." The soldier continued to talk through his food. "Out in the borderlands we've known of them for years. But they've slipped past us until now."

Leah resisted the urge to turn and stare at Dorit. She knew the old woman had her own reasons to hate the Parthians. She heard Dorit ask, "You know this centurion of yours?"

"Well enough."

"Tell me of him."

"He's a good soldier. Brave. Looks after his men."

Leah heard the grudging tone. As Dorit must have, because she said, "But you dislike him?"

"I have no call to answer a question like that."

"I mean no disrespect, soldier." Dorit used her most persuasive tone. "It's just that the woman he seeks to wed is a friend."

The cook offered her own invitation. "Tell us about your officer, and I'll serve you another portion of lamb."

Leah heard the soldier drum his fingers on the table. "The centurion Alban is enamored by change and new ways. I'm for tradition. Old guard, old ways, old gods. They've served us well enough up to now."

The cook sliced more lamb and carried the platter to the table. "What can you say of the centurion's character?"

"The man is trustworthy."

"Even though you dislike his methods."

"He cares for his men. They do not die under him. He shares booty. He does not hold back when pay finally comes."

Leah could not resist any longer. She turned in time to watch the soldier drain his cup. He set it down on the table, wiped his mouth with an arm, and declared, "The centurion was born to rule."

To Leah's surprise, when she took the midday meal to Procula, she found the governor's wife waiting for her. Procula announced, "Your centurion is here."

Leah did not need to ask how Procula knew. Pilate's wife had eyes everywhere. Leah wanted to insist that the centurion referred to was not *hers*. Instead she said simply, "I saw his aide in the kitchen. How are you feeling, my lady?"

"Help me sit up." Procula allowed Leah to take much of her weight and held her breath tightly as her head moved upward.

Leah arranged another cushion behind her head and asked, "Shall I prepare another draught?"

"Later." Procula breathed out long and slowly as she settled back. The lines remained etched into the skin about her eyes and forehead. "Your centurion goes before Pilate now."

Leah felt her own breath catch in her throat. "I don't want to marry," she dared to say, her voice hardly above a whisper. "I would willingly serve you for the rest of my life, my lady."

Procula's head lifted away from the cushions. "Herod is there as well. I must know what is happening."

"Mistress, I have served you well. I have never asked you for anything. But I am asking you now. Please do not force me to wed this man."

Even wracked by pain, Procula possessed a queenly demeanor, dark and sharp and unreadable. "They say he is most handsome. And a fine soldier. Even Pilate refers to him as a hero."

"Mistress, I beg you. Do not force me to marry *anyone*."

"You are young and intelligent. You have fire. Others might not see it, for you mask your inner power well. You were not born for such a life as this. Do not bind yourself with fear over what may never come." She halted Leah's protest with an upraised hand. "You must learn to accept what the gods offer. I have learned the consequences of going against them. The Judaean God, in particular. Nothing is worth . . ." Her voice drifted away and she slowly turned her head to stare out the window. When she turned back, she finished quietly, "Believe me, it is not worth it. Now, go and observe and remember everything you see and hear. I will wait for your return."

Alban was aware that Pontius Pilate held several official titles, and the most commonly used was prelate. But the provincial governor preferred to be known as prefect. The title was held by a commander of the emperor's cavalry, someone known for grasp of military strategy. Pilate considered himself a warrior first, which was why he had been appointed to this troublesome province. In a calmer region, a prelate's first responsibility was taxation. But not in Judaea.

Pontius Pilate, prefect of Judaea, and his lone guest received Alban in a north-facing courtyard ringed by columns. The terrace had a fine view both of the sea and the hippodrome. White linen canopies stretched over the columns, offering shade where Pilate and his guest were seated. The palace doorways were hidden behind intricately carved wooden screens. A light wind off the sea caused the fabric to billow softly. On a table at the courtyard's other side was spread Alban's gift of bandit loot. Compared with the palace and its polished ambiance, the bejeweled sword hilts and shields seemed garish.

The courtyard's three divans, two chairs, two lampstands, and incense burner were all ornately carved and chased in gold. As were the cups and bowls and plates and utensils. Even the writing implements used to anchor the scrolls against the wind were gold. An empire's wealth was spread about the patio on casual display.

Only the two seats were occupied, low thrones set side-by-side upon an elevated dais.

Alban knew some of the prelate's history because he had made it his business to find out all he could. Pontius Pilate was born in Rome of Samnite heritage. The mountains south of Rome had bred a race of proud and stubborn people, whose men fought with brutal intelligence and ruled the same way. Pilate's father had been an *eques*, a member of the Roman knightly class. Pilate served in the emperor's personal bodyguard, then fought with the victorious legions in the Germanic wars. The newly appointed emperor Tiberius had decided Pontius Pilate was the ideal man to rule the troublesome province of Judaea.

Alban stepped forward and bowed low. As he did so, he noted a shadow behind the carved wooden screen. He forced himself to ignore the unseen watcher. "Greetings, my lord." He attempted to strike the proper note of subservience yet confidence. He would wait for Pilate's cue to acknowledge the other man.

Leah's first impression upon seeing Alban through the wooden screen was of the moment eight days earlier when she had risen from her bed, utterly free from the fever that had gripped her for nine long days.

Drawn from her bed by the sound of a man's voice calling her name.

Alban spoke for the first time. His voice was strong, clear, calm. She shivered, half relieved to know it was not his voice she had heard. Then she impatiently brushed the thought aside. She was not one for dreams and portents. Life was what it was.

And there was no place in her world for a man. She neither needed nor wanted one in her life—not now, not ever.

Leah knew soldiers. Her father had been a merchant to the local legate. Soldiers had been in and out of her house all her life. Many Roman officers used their brute force like a battering ram. She had learned to mark those who menaced others for pleasure.

She had also known a few who seemed like this man, the rare officer who was a true leader. Officers who could stand before men like Pontius Pilate and Herod Antipas and speak with the calmness of knowing precisely who they were. Not many, but a few.

His hair was neither brown nor red nor gold, but a color that combined all three shades. His eyes looked to be the copper color of a burnished shield. His shoulders were almost too broad for such a tall, slender man. She could not pretend to be blind to the fact that Alban was rather handsome—what she could see of him between the woven slats of the screen.

She held her breath and her trembling body as still as she could while she listened to others determine her fate.

"Greetings, Centurion Alban." Pontius Pilate made a vague gesture toward the nearest divan. Alban pretended not to notice. He had no intention of relaxing in these circumstances.

To his eye, Pilate was an aging commander who had possessed power for so long he wore it like a second skin. He was strongly built, particularly for a man in his forties. His gaze was level, measuring, and utterly ruthless.

The prelate motioned toward his guest. "You know of course the Judaean tetrarch, Herod Antipas."

Alban bowed a second time. "Sire."

Herod Antipas was a hyena in human form. His every gesture appeared to be a lie. His supposed ease, his smile, his quiet way of saying, "So this is your man."

"He brought us two Parthian captives. Is that not so, centurion?"

"Indeed, sire. With another eighteen kept at our garrison, awaiting your orders."

But it was Herod who responded. "Eighteen more, how fascinating." His narrow moustache slipped into a beard that was waxed to a shiny point. "And why, pray tell, are they not already dead?"

Alban directed his answer to the prelate. "No one but the caravan masters have believed the Parthians raid as far north as the Damascus Road. I thought you might wish to question them and determine whether they are gathering forces for a larger strike."

The silence was broken only by the waves far below and the flapping linen screen overhead.

At length Herod asked, "How can you be certain they are Parthians?"

"The leaders speak neither Aramaic nor Latin, or at least claim so. But several of their men have been more revealing. And their dress, their swords, their style of battle are as the war scrolls describe."

"The scrolls—ah, the scrolls." Herod wore a robe of midnight blue and embroidered gold threads. His every gesture glimmered and flashed. "Tell me, centurion. These are Parthian scrolls?"

Alban fastened his gaze at an invisible point between the two men and did not respond. Early on Alban had learned that there was safety in silence, especially with a monarch who sought trouble.

"But of course, they could not be Parthian scrolls. You don't speak Parthian, do you, centurion? Not a word, I warrant." His oily smile made Alban's hands go rigid at his sides. "So why could not simple Bedouin bandits merely dress up in Parthian style, after reading the same scrolls as you?"

The leather straps on Pilate's chair creaked as he shifted impatiently. "That would hardly make them simple, would it?"

"How astute of you to think thus." Herod moved his viper's leer to Pilate. "I would ask that these so-called Parthians be handed over to my custody. If they are truly bringing war to our borders, I must know about it."

"My men can ask such questions," Pilate replied.

"Indeed. But my own efforts are much more, shall we say, subtle." Herod leaned closer to Pilate. "And I must determine whether my brothers might have any hand in this."

Pilate finally nodded. "Any objections, centurion?"

Alban recalled the Parthians' languid ease in their cell. But he knew enough to reply, "They are your prisoners, sire, to do with as you please."

"Take them, Herod. Inform me of anything you learn." Pilate then shifted directions with a ruler's ease. "Centurion, I hear that you are considered an ally by the religious Judaeans of Galilee."

Alban felt a trickle of sweat maneuver down his spine. "My lord?"

"It is a simple enough question. Are you counted among those they call . . ." Pilate turned to Herod. "What is the term they use?"

Herod seemed to lick the words as they emerged. "They are known as God-fearers, prelate."

Alban said, "I try to maintain good relations with the local citizens, sire. But I remain loyal to Rome and steadfast in my duty."

Herod frowned. "That is no answer at all."

"On the contrary, it is a Roman answer," Pilate said.

"Ah yes, Rome." Herod spun the end of his beard between his fingers. "Which brings us to the crux of the matter, doesn't it? A soldier of Rome and a Judaean woman. Interesting."

Alban stood in absolute silence. Something was going on between the two men that he did not understand. It seemed that Pontius Pilate, the emperor's direct representative to Judaea, and Herod Antipas, tetrarch of Galilee and Perea, had been discussing him. And the woman mentioned? *Is it possible that Leah has Judaean blood?* None of this had come up in any of the information about the woman his colleague had gathered for him. The thought was so astounding he nearly missed the next words.

Herod looked rather smug as he turned to Pilate. "Well, are you going to tell him—or shall I?"

Pilate did not respond.

"Under Judaean law, the betrothal ceremony is a legally binding act," Herod began, as if speaking to a child. "To break off a betrothal requires a formal process of divorce. Yet the couple is not actually wed until the groom has fulfilled a vow. In between the ritual of betrothal and claiming his bride, the groom is required to fulfill a task, part of his dowry, as it were. Usually this means building a house or acquiring pastureland. In this case . . ."

Why was Herod spouting Judaean law? Alban's face must have revealed his confusion because Pilate said, "To be betrothed under Judaean law would open doors for the man desiring the hand of the maid."

Herod's face turned reptilian. "That is assuming the man is brave enough and determined enough to meet the conditions."

Alban was still at a loss to understand what was passing between the two men. But he knew now it somehow involved Leah and himself.

"May I ask—" Alban dared to begin, but Herod cut the words short.

"Oh, you may ask, centurion. And I'm sure that the honorable Pilate will be happy to explain. I have every confidence that you will be given every detail. Every detail. Isn't that so, Pilate?"

The prelate merely nodded.

"Then I shall take my leave. When shall my man collect your authorization for the other bandits, sire?"

"What is that?"

"Oh, did I misunderstand? I assumed your approval for custody was for both the officers and their men, particularly since your helpful centurion guesses some of them speak Aramaic. There can often be no better way to obtain answers than to question one while the others watch."

Alban could tell the prelate disliked the request. Alban was tempted to speak of what he suspected. But he had no evidence, nothing definite enough to risk the vengeful wrath that lurked within the Judaean ruler's expression.

"Have your aide present himself this afternoon," Pilate reluctantly replied. "I will have the release ready."

"I remain your loyal servant, sire." Even Herod's bow was a lie. "Good day, centurion. We shall meet again."

When they were alone, Pilate asked, "Do you wish to be seated?"

"Thank you, prelate, but I am fine as I am."

Prelate, prefect, legate, governor. Pilate's position may have carried many titles, but they all translated to the same thing: raw, brutal, Roman power.

Pilate said, "This alliance of yours with the Galilean Judaeans. I find it of particular interest."

Swiftly Alban recounted the problems he faced. One small garrison, the vast territory, the border crossings, the tax collectors, the bandits. Capernaum and Tiberias were the two main cities in his district, and both were dominated by the religious elders.

"Are you indeed what Herod spoke of, a God-fearer?"

The elders of Capernaum had asked him the same thing. Alban had had no answer then either. "I am a soldier of Rome," he repeated.

Pilate seemed satisfied. "I have yet to find anyone who speaks ill of you. Even among your men."

Alban was not surprised to hear there were spies in his garrison. "The prelate does me great honor."

"I suppose you've heard of the events in Jerusalem."

"The death of the prophet Jesus. Yes, sire. I have heard."

Pilate seemed to be alert enough to detect Alban's unspoken thoughts. "You disapprove of crucifixion?"

Alban shifted uncomfortably. "Sire, I thought I had been summoned to discuss my—my betrothal is it called?—to your niece."

Instead of answering, Pilate rose to his feet. Before he crossed halfway to the palace entrance, a servant appeared. Interestingly, the shadow behind the wooden screen had not moved. "Bring tea," the prelate barked. Then to Alban, "I seek to know your mettle, centurion. I have a pressing issue, and I must know if you are up to the task."

Still Alban hesitated.

"Speak! Your commander demands it."

"Sire, when I was but a lad, my father took me to a province northwest of our own, a slender stretch of highland valleys perched between the lowlands and the Alps. The year I was born the region had revolted against Roman law and Roman taxes. They turned each valley into a natural fortress and fought off the Romans for nine years. When the capital was finally taken, the Romans salted the earth and crucified every man and boy who survived the battles. The crosses stretched across the valley, up the far ridge, and off into the distance. My father wanted me to understand the danger of defying Rome. I dream of it still."

"The Sanhedrin accused this prophet of doing just that, defying Roman rule."

Pilate waited while the slave brought tea, ordered that Alban be served a cup as well, then continued. "I have been told that you had contact with this Jesus."

"Not face-to-face, sire." Alban gave his report in terse bits. He might have never met Pilate before, but he had years of experience in reporting to superior officers. Battlefield reports were all the same, the most information available packed into the smallest amount of space. All the while, his tea remained untouched on the table beside him.

Because Alban had aided in rebuilding the Capernaum synagogue, the local elders treated him as a God-fearer. The elders avoided direct questions that might have challenged their assumptions.

This Jesus had made Capernaum his base. The longer the rabbi taught, the larger grew the crowds. By day the city's roads became cloaked in clouds of yellow dust, by night the city walls were rimmed with countless campfires. The prophet took to walking with his disciples out into the desert to escape the hordes, but even then the crowds followed him into the dreaded Samarian wasteland, where, according to the stories, they were fed miraculously from his hand.

The Capernaum elders knew Alban had become attached to the lad, two outcasts making the best of the desert garrison. When Jacob was taken down by the wasting illness. The elders had spoken to Alban of the prophet's healing touch and offered to approach Jesue on his behalf. They explained that by doing so, they would act as a divine emissary—a term so powerful that to another religious Judaean, it might as well be the same person wearing a different skin. An ambassador with divine implications.

The first hint Alban had that the prophet Jesus had agreed to heal his servant lad was when the elders left Capernaum on the garrison road. From his fort's high position, Alban had seen the crowd start toward them. And he had known a distinct unease. Not because of the crowd's size, which was enormous, nor because of his own men's increasing discomfort at the sight of so many strangers headed toward the garrison. He had seen and heard enough to be certain that this man carried no threat with him.

Yet even at this distance, the prophet at the head of the crowd had made Alban unsettled in a way he could not describe, not then and not now while he stood before Pontius Pilate.

On that day, Alban had sent a second message with two friends, Galileans who ran local caravans and supplied the garrison with fresh provisions. He had asked them to tell the prophet that there was no need for him to enter the garrison belonging to soldiers, killers, mercenaries—men considered enemies of all loyal Judaeans. For even at that distance, Alban knew he watched a man of power. Alban had asked the merchants to say that Alban too was a commander of men, and if he told a subordinate to go, the man went.

Alban watched as they met the prophet on the road. And that instant, while Alban had stood on the guard tower and saw his friends converse with the prophet, young Jacob had risen from his sickbed as though he had never been ill, never suffered, never started down the lonely track toward almost certain death.

And when the caravan masters had returned, they had said a curious thing: They reported that the prophet Jesus had praised Alban's faith.

Which had only left him more uneasy still.

When Alban finished with his report, much more brief than the memories from which he supplied the facts to his superior, Pilate remained silent for a time, toying with his cup. Finally he said, "I ordered this Jesus brought before me. When I recall it now, my strongest impression was that the man was already gone. Though he still lived, he was utterly focused upon the beyond. This Jesus spoke of things I could not fathom. And all the while, the Sanhedrin bayed like hounds in the courtyard."

Alban ventured, "What did Jesus say to you, prefect?"

"I asked if he was truly the king of the Judaeans. He responded that his kingdom was not of this world."

"I feel the man was never a threat to Rome, sire."

"Exactly what I said to the Sanhedrin. But they accused him of blasphemy against their God and demanded his death." Pilate shook his head. "I have sent dozens of men to the cross. Hundreds, perhaps. But never, I fear, one as undeserving as this man."

Pilate set down his cup, stood, and began pacing. Alban waited. For what, he had no idea.

Finally Pilate said, "The man has vanished."

"Sire?"

"From the tomb. The prophet. He is gone."

"He did not die?"

"The Sanhedrin claim his disciples stole away his body. Does that make sense to you, centurion?"

Alban thought hard. "Weren't guards posted there?"

"Indeed they were."

"What do they say?"

"They reported to the high priest, who informed me they too claim the disciples stole the prophet's body."

Alban squinted at the floor by his feet. The statement made no sense. A soldier on guard duty who permitted such a thing was doomed to his own slow and painful death. Then a new thought came to Alban. "If the Judaeans planned revolt, if they wished to suggest—"

"That this man led them still." Pilate nodded his approval. "They could steal the body away and then make whatever preposterous claims they wished."

Alban's mind raced forward. "Or perhaps the Sanhedrin did it themselves and wish to disguise the fact by blaming the disciples while they foment their own revolt."

"Indeed." Pilate came to an abrupt halt. "You wish to marry my niece Leah."

Alban came to rigid attention. "Yes, sire."

"You seek advancement beyond the desert garrison."

"I do, sire."

"Here are my terms. You will be bound to my niece following the Judaean betrothal customs. Discover the truths behind the prophet's disappearance. Determine whether there is a threat against me or against Rome. If I am satisfied with your work, the wedding will take place."

As simple as that. Alban could not believe the words. "Thank you, sire."

But the prelate was not finished. "The position of *tribuni angusticlavus* on my staff is unfilled. Are you up to the challenge?"

Alban blinked away a sudden spinning of his world. Each senior legate could appoint as many as five tribuni, the personal knights who carried his seal and acted in his name. "I am honored you would think of it, sire."

"I have need of a man who can handle himself among the Judaeans. Serve me well, centurion, and I shall reward you better." He hesitated for a brief moment, then continued grudgingly. "Herod is of the opinion that Leah can be of use to you as your espoused wife. The fact that she is Judaean is to be widely circulated. This will allow her access into the Judaean community. Women talk. She might discover something that you would never learn on your own. You understand?"

Alban felt a faint trace of alarm. But Pilate's offer so seared his thinking he could scarcely see beyond that. "I accept your offer, sire," he heard himself saying, wondering if it was all a dream. Or the beginning of a nightmare . . .

CHAPTER NINE

One Hour Later

ALBAN AND LINUX left the palace, riding fresh horses from Pilate's private stable. The prelate had commanded them to make all haste, his imperious tone suggesting that usage of his baths followed by a good meal was all any Roman soldier needed in order to fully recover. And Linux was ordered to accompany Alban and see that the Jerusalem garrison granted whatever aid was required to accomplish his assignment.

Alban's mount was the finest horse he had ever set eyes on, a chestnut mare with a gentle nature, enormous strength, and a coat that shone. The horse's mane and tail were considerably lighter than her coat, and she tossed her head as if well aware of her beauty. Linux must have noticed Alban's admiring looks, for he said, "I am specifically ordered to return with both mounts."

"Horses can get lost," Alban quipped.

"Not that one. Not and either of us survive."

After Leah served Procula's early afternoon dose of medicine, she found Dorit in the kitchen in a chair pulled up close to the fire. The old servant watched as Leah cleaned the mixing bowl, pestle, and cup, then said, "It's true what they said, the centurion captured Parthian bandits?"

Leah's sigh came from the depths of her soul. "All I heard was how Pilate and Herod and the centurion have bartered me into a marriage not of my choosing."

Dorit remained silent.

Leah set the items back on the tray to dry and slowly made her way into a chair beside Dorit. "Yes, it's true."

"And he's as handsome as they say?"

Leah hesitated a moment. "What I could see of him was favorable enough."

"Even a soldier who resents the centurion's methods calls Alban a true leader of men," Dorit reminded her.

The weight of inevitability lay upon Leah like a stone mantle. "Does that make it right for them to chain me to him for the rest of my life?"

"Of course not." Dorit hesitated, then continued, "Still, after years of rumors and entire merchant clans disappearing into the sands, the centurion brings two Parthian leaders to Pilate. And saves a caravan. And loses no men in the process." Admiration colored her tone, and Leah could argue with none of it.

The two women sat quietly, staring into the flames.

Leah recalled how, soon after her arrival at the palace, Dorit had taken her into the town of Caesarea. Beyond the hippodrome, at the border of the portside market, stood a temple dedicated to Mercury, the winged Roman god of prosperity and messengers and merchants. The temple was a squat and orderly affair, built with all the practicality of a counting house. As they passed the side entrance, Dorit had adjusted her shawl as she checked in all directions, then leaned forward as though to place an offering in the temple bowl. Instead she had spat at the god's statue.

At that instant Dorit's calm mask had dropped away, and a bitterness turned her face as stern as death. Then she had carefully hidden her feelings away.

Only when they were on their way back to the palace did Leah ask about what she had observed. Dorit explained that she had once loved a caravan guard. After Procula had blessed their marriage, the guard went on a journey carrying wares of his own, which he had intended to sell and then buy Dorit's freedom. Neither the man nor the caravan were ever heard from again.

Dorit went on, "I would not resign you to the fate of growing old in the service of others, with nothing to look forward to besides lonely nights in front of a fire that refuses to warm away the hollow ache."

"Better that," Leah shot back, "than trapped in the house of a man who uses you to further his own ambitions. A man who views you as just another slave."

"You don't know that."

"I know men."

"Oh, is that so?" Dorit scoffed in a voice as soft as Leah's. "You know men, do you?"

"I know enough. I know they leave. I know they fail. I know they cannot be trusted." She held her face in her hands, hating the burning helplessness that filled her entire being. "There is no worse fate than to be chained through marriage to a man whom you do not know, whom you do not wish to know."

The afternoon found Procula much improved, enough so that she sought to speak with her husband. Leah's duties took her several times through the lady's private chambers, and she could overhear their voices from Pilate's apartment next door. They were not exactly arguing. But whatever topic occupied them must not have been a particularly pleasant one. Something told her they discussed her own future, and twice Leah was tempted to reach for the door.

Procula finally emerged just before midafternoon and announced, "We leave for Jerusalem."

Leah's expression conveyed her surprise.

"You and I shall travel in the first group." In the background, Pilate was bellowing for his secretary. "My husband will follow with the rest of the household when his work here is done."

"But, mistress, so soon? Your health—"

"The headaches have been as bad here as there. And my dreams are worse. Besides, I yearn to be on horseback and in the fresh air."

Procula made the household race by simply declaring she intended to leave within the hour, and whatever was not ready would be left behind. Pilate surveyed the ensuing panic with a severe expression but said nothing. He seemed to watch Leah as much as his wife, which only heightened Leah's dread.

Her anxiety was magnified when Procula declared, "Choose a gown for yourself."

"Thank you, but I have no need of such finery, my lady."

Procula showed a rare sharpness. "You have two choices: You can obey me, or you can arrive for your betrothal in a gown of my choosing."

The words hung in the air between them, as sharp as a blade. Leah knew instantly she had overstepped the invisible boundaries, and risked far more than her wedding garments. She spoke the first words that came to mind. "Please do not be angry with me, mistress. But if I am to be betrothed as a Judaean, perhaps I should be dressed as one. Not as a citizen of Rome or Greece."

Procula's frown deepened, but at length she said, "Very well. You may select something suitable from a merchant in the market when we get to Jerusalem. Now go! And tell the guards to bring my horse around front."

They left in haste, Leah and Procula accompanied by two other servants and nine guards led by Hugo. Leah found none of her customary comfort in the old soldier's presence. Nor did the sunlit vista or the open road fill her with any sense of adventure. For up ahead, beyond the road's next bend, lay only a hopeless future filled with foreboding.

Alban and Linux followed the road bordering Pilate's new aqueduct and headed south. The clouds piled up, threatening a late spring squall, and the wind threw fistfuls of grit in their faces. They came upon a trail leading to a ruined hillside village and took shelter, just as the storm started in earnest, in the only hovel that still possessed a roof. Other travelers must have done the same, for there was a square of smooth-faced stones blackened by fires, and beside it a scattering of kindling. Linux gathered more wood and started a blaze. "It always seems to rain harder in Judaea. Or perhaps it's only the contrast with the desert."

"No." Alban dumped the saddles and hung the blankets from a roof beam to dry. "All the seasons are fiercer here."

"I remember the rains of Umbria. Gentle as a maiden's kiss. When they passed, the world was washed so clean I could almost see Rome."

At a crack of thunder Alban's horse stamped nervously. He patted a flank and felt the muscles tremble. "It rained like this in Gaul. Every spring and autumn. Flash floods that sometimes carried away whole villages."

"Do you ever miss home?"

"I told you before, I have no home to miss." For once Alban did not mind the truth.

"Italia sings to me sometimes in my sleep," Linux mused. "Or I hear laughter, and I remember Rome. There always seems to be laughing in my memories of Rome. Or singing."

"I would like to have the chance to miss Rome." Alban crouched beside the fire, feeling in rare good spirits. Lightning struck in the distance and the rain fell harder still. He was warm, the hut where they sheltered dry enough, and he traveled with a likeable man for company on a mount he could kill to own. What was more, he carried Pilate's scroll in the pouch slung from his shoulder. Alban touched the document through the soft leather. It seemed to him the parchment was still warm where the prelate had melted wax and stamped it with his royal seal bearing the name and authority of not less than Tiberius, emperor of Rome. The cylinder was bound to a gilded staff crowned by the imperial eagle, and the text named Alban as Pilate's personal emissary, ordering all in Judaea to do his bidding.

Alban noted, his voice low, "I did not have a chance to see Leah. I've never even met the woman whom I am to wed."

"I've seen her about. She serves as Procula's personal maid."

"What is she like?"

Linux feigned blindness to Alban's heightened interest. "She's not overly fat, I suppose."

"Oh, and thank you for *that* most welcome news."

Linux fed more wood to the fire. "Other than a rather astonishing mole on her chin and the wandering eye, neither is she altogether plain."

"You are aware you're joking with a superior officer."

"I am indeed." Linux lay flatbread on the stones to warm. His tone changed. "She's unusually intelligent, your lady. The servants in any household are jealous of their own positions. A newcomer, particularly one both lovely and of superior heritage, could expect to be savaged."

Alban tried to keep his voice level. "She is lovely?"

"She is intelligent," he repeated. "Soon after she arrived, Procula's elderly maid became very ill. Without anyone assigning the duty, Leah began taking personal care of her. Imagine, Pilate's niece acting as servant to a slave. But this slave is a favorite to many of the servants and the guards alike. Leah's actions earned her friends throughout the household."

Alban mulled that over. "Have you spoken with her?"

"Nothing more than a greeting. She says little. I have heard she talks with no one save the old slave."

"An intelligent woman who is also private," Alban mused.

"She also is quite easy on the eyes," Linux finally added with a grin. "Too strong and direct and intelligent for my taste."

"But attractive."

"Indeed." Linux grinned again and shrugged. "Shame about that wandering eye."

Alban studied the other man. Linux had a good face. The firelight hardened the edges about his jaw and turned his gaze flinty sharp. Alban said, "Pilate suggested I contact one of the Sanhedrin. He said this Joseph of Arimathea would be a good starting point."

Linux slipped a cloth packet from the saddlebag. He laid out the rest of their meal on the flagstone between them—salt meat, dried fruit, cakes of honeycomb. "I've met several members of the Judaean council, but not that one. He's rich enough to barricade himself away from the likes of me. Not that I've any great desire to meet another Judaean. He's a Pharisee. You understand what that means?"

"I've known a few." Unlike the Sadducees, the dominant group on the Sanhedrin, some Pharisees traveled out to the provinces and visited religious communities like Capernaum, speaking in the synagogues, passing on Temple edicts to the priests and local elders. The Pharisees were well known for their distinct dress and the way they avoided even speaking to a Roman. A strict Pharisee would consider himself unclean after crossing so much as a Roman's shadow.

Linux asked the question that had hung between them since Alban had emerged from the palace. "How was your audience with Pilate?"

"So intense I am still sorting through the fray." He grinned crookedly at his companion. "Like after a battle, just as you said."

Linux stirred the fire. "You know what is an officer's best friend in battle?"

"Cunning."

It was a good answer, but Linux flicked his head in disagreement. "Cunning alone can trap you. Get a soldier into a pinch and allow him a way to escape, cunning gives him reasons to turn from warrior to coward. And too often he'll fall into the trap his enemies have set."

Alban picked up one of the flatbreads and tossed it from hand to hand until it cooled enough to eat. "What is it, then?"

"Cunning bonded to a secret rage. A good warrior lets the fury take hold only when the heat of war surrounds him. Then he lets loose, and cunning guides his aim." Linux inspected him gravely. "You have that rage, and you have that control, and you have that cunning. That is what I think Pilate found as well."

Alban rolled a slice of the meat and a bit of the dried fruit into his bread. He found himself silenced by Linux's observations. It was not often that a man read him as well as this one had.

The soldier continued to study him. "I for one wouldn't want to come up against you in a fight, centurion."

Leah and Procula were traveling light and made good time. They arrived at a simple inn on the road between Caesarea and Jerusalem with a few minutes of daylight to spare. Procula dined alone, served by Leah and the innkeeper's wife. Twice the woman started to speak with Leah, but whatever she saw in Leah's expression caused her to shrug, shake her head, and remain silent.

That night it was Leah who dreamed.

She stood in some flame-lit hall, dressed in finery not her own. In the murky distance a voice droned low and sonorous, the words reverberating with the beat of a gallows drums. She knew it was her betrothal ceremony, just as she knew without looking down that she was chained to the floor. Leah stood alone, but she felt eyes on her from every quarter. A mist clung to the floor and the walls, making it impossible to see anything clearly. The voice stopped, and the silence that replaced it seemed more oppressive still.

Then she heard another noise. Something breathed upon the back of her neck.

In her dream, Leah twisted about to face a huge beast leering down at her. He wore the centurion's skin, but the true creature lurking within the man was now revealed. The beast possessed a demon's face and fangs as long as knives. He growled his intent and lunged toward her.

Leah shot upright and rose from her pallet at the end of Procula's bed. Her heart pounded in her chest and her limbs were so shaky she was forced to support herself on the edge of the bed. Moonlight turned the room silver and revealed that her mistress was both awake and watching her. "Was it that man?"

Leah could only shake her head numbly.

Procula rose to a seated position and motioned Leah down to sit beside her. "Did the prophet speak to you from beyond the grave?"

Leah sighed over the confusion and defeat that had chased her from her slumber. "No, mistress, my dream was not about the prophet."

Procula slumped back against the pillows. It was doubtful she had even heard Leah. "I begged Pilate to have nothing to do with that man. But the whole Sanhedrin was on my husband like vipers, hissing and threatening to strike." Procula wrung her hands. "I fear for Pilate. I fear for us all."

Leah used the hem of her gown to wipe the sweat from her face. "I dreamed of . . . the centurion."

Procula's sat forward once more. Her gaze sharpened with her tone and her features. "I want you to listen to me. Your fate was sealed the moment you set foot in Pilate's household. What you want means nothing. Your betrothal to the centurion will take place according to my husband's timing."

Leah had heard Procula use such a tone only a few times before. It was the voice of a woman who held the power of life and death, as cold as the moonlight that etched shadows into everything Leah saw.

Procula said, "Look at me." When Leah lifted her chin, the woman continued, "I want you to do my bidding."

"It is all I have done for nearly three years, mistress."

"I am speaking about *now*. Our fate is tied up with the prophet's."

Leah blinked slowly, dragged from her dark well by the insistence in Procula's words. "But . . . this man Jesus is now *dead*."

"You heard what Pilate told your centurion. His body has vanished. The Jerusalem council claims it has been stolen by his disciples. Which makes sense, if they are planning to use his death as a rallying cry for revolution." Procula's head made a soft thump against the wall behind her pillow. "You do not know what it is like to face a provincial revolt," she continued. "You cannot imagine. The Roman legions reveal an unspeakable brutality. Regardless of how the uprising ends, Pilate would be ruined. He is charged to keep the peace, and in the Roman senate's eyes he would have failed. He would return to the emperor in disgrace. That is, if they permit him to return at all. More than likely, we would be banished."

"But what can I do?"

"My family's safety depends upon you and me. Pilate is at a loss as to how to find answers. I must know what is happening within this group. For the sake of us all, I *must know*. I want you to infiltrate the band of his disciples."

"Mistress, you cannot mean this."

"You are Judaean."

"My grandmother, yes, but my mother scorned the religious Judaeans of her ancestry. I know nothing about them. Nothing!"

"You are Judaean," Procula insisted. "You cannot be the only woman untrained in the old ways who seeks to know whatever it is they teach. Go to them. See what you can learn. And then you will report only to me. Do you hear? You will speak of what you learn only to me."

Procula leaned back against her pillow and closed her eyes tightly against the pain. She murmured, "And then I shall do whatever is required to protect us."

CHAPTER TEN

Jerusalem

ALBAN AND LINUX left the ruined village before dawn. At midday they began the long climb into the Judaean hills. When they crested the final rise, Jerusalem spread out before them, adorning the highest hill like a polished stone crown. The city wall was burnished by the afternoon sun so its reflection hurt the eyes. The scene struck Alban as belonging to some higher world, beyond the touch of mortals.

Linux reined in beside him, gave him a long look, and snorted. "Wait until you've been there a few days. Then you'll know this place for the snake pit it is."

Linux's cynicism could not quench Alban's wonder. They turned into the Kidron Valley, the city wall towering high to the left. They passed an assortment of structures so ancient they appeared to have grown naturally from the dust and the stone, as large as temples yet with neither door nor inner sanctum. "What are these?"

Linux did not bother to glance over. "Tombs. Kings and prophets and such. From the time when Judaea ruled itself."

An alert sentry saluted them through the Lion's Gate. The

ancient portal opened into a lane that was nearly empty of life. The only people who walked this cobblestoned lane were soldiers, a few merchants, and women who smiled invitingly as they passed. But up ahead they could see a cross street teeming with people and animals.

Linux halted at stables across from the main portal to Antonia Fortress. "The city is so crowded during the festival season we will make better time by foot."

"But this street is quiet."

"You'll see." Linux greeted the stable master by name and made certain the man understood these mounts belonged to Pilate himself. The man assured Linux he would care for them personally. Linux turned to Alban. "Baths or business?"

"I want to see this Joseph without delay."

"It may be wise. No doubt the Sanhedrin has spies in Pilate's household, and they could reach him first."

He and Linux left their saddlebags and set off. The closer they came to the first juncture of roads, the louder grew the din. To Alban's eye, it appeared they approached a solid wall of humanity. He turned to Linux to question him again about the contrast between the activity ahead and the quiet lane they were traversing.

Linux pointed to a set of polished double doors. "These lead to Pilate's new baths," he said, raising his voice to be heard, "dedicated to the emperor Tiberius. The Sanhedrin were outraged. Called them a desecration of their holy city. For once Pilate stood firm. Would not relent. No self-respecting Judaean will even set foot on this lane."

When they turned the corner the two were instantly trapped in a seething mass. Alban understood why Linux had left the horses at the fortress stables. Neither horse nor cart could have maneuvered through this throng. Their Roman uniforms granted them a tight ring of space, however, though the people they passed never looked their way. The Judaeans did their best to pretend the Romans did not even exist.

Linux led them up one hill and down another, turning to the right and left until Alban wondered if he was back in the Golan caverns. The city itself seemed astonishingly clean, and the normal stench he associated with packed humanity did not assault him here. Almost everyone he passed seemed remarkably unsoiled, their garments tidy, their faces clean. When Alban mentioned it to Linux, his companion remained unimpressed. "These Judaeans are as fanatical about washing as they are about everything else. Which makes their complaints about our own baths even more absurd."

"Ritual baths are part of the Judaeans' religion," Alban mentioned. "They disapprove of our habit of opening the baths to men and women alike." This information was based on his interactions with the Capernaum leaders up north. Alban endured Linux's odd look and changed the subject. "I've never known crowds like this."

"It's always like this during the festival season. Seven weeks in the spring and one in the fall." Linux kicked at a loose pebble. "I loathe this place most of all during the festivals. It's hard to draw a decent breath."

Alban did not respond, though in truth he felt overwhelmed by this city, as though its ancient might and splendor conspired against him. Against all things Roman.

He spent the remainder of their journey trying to formulate an approach to the Judaean and the meeting ahead of him. The previous night, as he lay in the hut and listened to the storm, it had all seemed rather simple. He'd assumed he would seek out the various parties, ask a few questions, and make his report. The issues were straightforward enough. Was the prophet dead, where was the body, and was there a threat of revolt? It was only now, as they left the market lanes behind and the city brooded down over him, that he wondered what threat might lie buried within his questions. And within the answers . . .

The house of Joseph of Arimathea was in the Upper City, which Linux said contained the finest residences. A stallholder directed them to an unmarked portal down an unnamed lane. The square doorway was tall enough to admit a royal chariot and framed by stone carved like a flowering vine. Yet there was none of the adornment that would announce the presence of a Roman villa behind its protective walls. Instead the Jerusalem dust so stained the ancient wooden door it appeared not to have been used in years.

Alban used his sword hilt to hammer on the portal. He waited, then hammered again.

A small door set into the larger portal opened to reveal a solidly built guard. He simply stared out at them.

"Is this the residence of Joseph of Arimathea?" Linux demanded.

"Who's asking?"

Alban stilled Linux's protest with a warning hand. "We come at the request of Pontius Pilate."

"Name?"

"The centurion Alban and his aide, Linux."

The guard slammed the door in Alban's face.

Linux glared at the portal in genuine outrage. Alban said, "Wait."

A few moments later, the portal opened again and the guard demanded, "You are the centurion of the Capernaum garrison?"

"I am."

"My master asks, are you a God-fearer as they say?"

Linux could hold his outrage no longer. "Are you aware who

it is you are addressing, guard? This man carries the personal seal of Pontius Pilate!"

The surly guard kept his focus square upon Alban's face. Alban replied, "The elders of Capernaum called me one. In truth, I do not know."

Oddly, the guard gave Alban's response a nod of grudging approval. The man bore no rank or insignia, yet clearly he had been given the power to decide whether Alban should be granted an audience. "You may enter, Roman. You and you alone."

Linux hissed at the insult. Alban murmured to his companion, "Return to the Antonia Fortress. Find the centurion Atticus."

"This man should be flayed!"

Alban stepped around to where his companion could not see him and the guard at the same time. "Find Atticus," Alban calmly repeated. "You said he was in charge of the crucifixion. If anyone can tell us whether the prophet actually died, it is he. Ask him to meet us. . . . I don't know the city. I need a location where he will speak freely."

Linux muttered, still indignant, "The public baths at the end of the lane fronting the fortress."

"Tell him to meet us there later tonight. Then find the guards assigned to the prophet's tomb. I want to see them before that, in a different location."

"There is a tavern on the main market avenue that welcomes us, just south of the lane leading to the fortress."

"I'll meet you there before sundown." He turned to the guard, who continued to bar the portal with his body. "Let us proceed."

Alban had been in such dwellings before. The wealthy Judaeans of Tiberias and Capernaum lived thus, in houses where all signs of affluence were hidden behind dusty masks. The major differences in this case were the residence's size and its guards, who were both numerous and extremely alert.

"Wait here," his guard told him.

Alban nodded and looked around. The central courtyard was a full thirty paces across. The large house itself was carefully understated and completely unadorned. Not a single mosaic framed the central fountain. Yet palace it was, with a colonnaded alcove framing three sides of the courtyard and opening into a multitude of chambers. The square's fourth side fronted an ancient city wall—not the massive fortress battlements which had been rebuilt by Herod the Great but something far older. This wall had been smoothed by eons to a dusky gold. Beyond the wall, Alban could see a massive structure standing upon a gigantic hilltop plaza, its angled roof reflecting the afternoon sun. Though he had never seen it before, he was certain he glimpsed the Temple to the Judaean God.

"This way." The guard had returned and now led Alban into the west-facing portico. The tall doors were fashioned of wood that had been polished until they gleamed. Inside, the chamber was also unadorned and vast. Simple, severe, serene.

A man was seated behind a table so long it could have accommodated thirty. Its surface was covered with scrolls and tablets. The man held a scroll as if he was beginning to unroll it. Light spilled through tall windows and gauzelike drapes. A male secretary stood behind the seated man, holding a sheaf of vellum pages.

Alban's Judaean host was dressed in the robes of a Pharisee, black and severe yet fashioned from some fabric as light as the drapes. "You have journeyed from Capernaum?" he asked, his tone well modulated, full of authority.

"From Caesarea."

"So our governor wished to interview you first. Very wise." He gestured with the scroll to the guard. "Our guest still wears the dust from the road. Have a servant bring water and a towel."

The instructions no doubt startled the guard as much as they did Alban. The Pharisees were extremely strict about religious protocol.

Everyone in this household would be religious. To order a servant to bathe a Roman's feet would be approaching blasphemy.

Yet when the guard did not move swiftly enough, the man lifted his eyes to stare directly at the man. His silence was command enough for the guard to spring into action.

When a young woman brought a ceramic basin, her trembling hands sloshed water on the polished marble floor. Alban saved her from further dishonor by taking the towel and the basin and washing his own feet. When he looked up, he found his host observing him with quiet approval.

Joseph of Arimathea was not a large man, but his presence was such that the chamber seemed filled with his aura. "What is it you want from me, centurion?"

"I believe you know the answer to that question, my lord."

His gaze was piercing. "When my manservant asked if you were a God-fearer, you gave a curious response."

"The elders of Capernaum say the Pharisees hold great store by the truth. I am giving as I hope to receive."

Joseph nodded slightly. "You may be interested to know that your response follows a passage from our teachings." He dismissed the guard and servant with a wave, turned to the secretary, and said, "Leave us."

When they were alone, the Pharisee repeated his query in different words. "Why are you here?"

"Pilate seeks three answers: First, is the prophet truly dead? Second, what happened to his body? And third, are his disciples threatening revolt against Rome?"

"The last question is the easiest to answer. Let Rome leave our borders and there will be no threat, not from any Judaean, not ever again."

Alban stood quietly and waited.

Joseph stroked his long beard. "As to the second question, the answer is, I have no idea where the rabbi is."

"Yet you approached Pilate and requested the body. You took it to your family tomb. You buried him, I have heard, with your own hands."

"All of this is as you say."

"And now his body is gone."

"I inspected the tomb myself. The day after the Sabbath, and every day since then. The body has indeed vanished."

Alban listened carefully but heard nothing to suggest the man had a hand in the theft. "Do you suspect someone?"

"The Almighty, perhaps?" His expression remained unreadable. His fingers again traced down a beard laced with silver, flattening out the curves. A gesture so often repeated he might not have been aware of what he was doing. "Certainly not I."

"You're suggesting the Judaean God came down from—"

"Heaven?" Joseph supplied, turning the word into a question.

"Your heaven."

"His heaven, centurion. Not mine."

"And stole away the prophet's body."

The Judaean began to sway slightly. Back and forth, as though intoning thoughts he now uttered very softly. "If our God did so, then the man now missing was not merely a prophet."

Alban noted dryly, "I will convey your opinions to Pilate."

Joseph of Arimathea then did a curious thing. He rose from his chair, walked around the table, and reached out his hand as though to touch Alban's arm. He did not quite make contact, for to do so would have rendered him unclean. "Come. We will be more comfortable out here."

He led Alban through the great doors and into the colonnaded plaza. The secretary, the guard, and the womanservant holding the basin all clustered nearby. Clearly they had been talking of their master and his guest, for when Alban appeared with Joseph, they gaped and stepped back. Joseph motioned them away with a gesture and pointed Alban to a pair of chairs set in the shade. "Please, you are my guest."

The wind passed through the fountain's spray, cooling their shaded corner. Alban realized the fountain's water was perfumed, the fragrance as sweet as a flowering meadow. "You live well."

Joseph dismissed the compliment with a thin smile. "My allies in Capernaum speak favorably of you, centurion. And the caravan you saved carried goods of mine."

Alban took this as an invitation. "What happened leading up to the disappearance of the prophet's body?"

"How much do you know?"

"Not much at all. Whatever I know has been hearsay at best. I came here first, straight from the road, as you see."

Joseph turned to stare out over the ancient wall at the Temple crowning the hill above. "The day before our Passover festival, the high priest Caiaphas called together a *beit din*, a council of judgment. Some cases go before the entire Sanhedrin, especially matters where all Israel might be affected. Other cases are tried by such smaller councils, especially civil cases or those related to religious protocol."

"A prophet whose followers extend the length and breadth of Judaea and beyond would not require the complete Sanhedrin?"

The Pharisee turned and called, "Guard!"

The man reluctantly appeared from the pillar's shadow.

Joseph said, "You should go to the kitchen for your evening meal."

"It can wait," the guard replied, his gaze never leaving Alban's face.

Joseph firmly waved the man away and waited until he was

out of sight. "Did I mention that members of the Sanhedrin are granted personal protection by the Temple guards?"

Alban understood instantly. "These guards are appointed by the high priest?"

"Caiaphas, yes. It is most helpful."

Alban stared at the point where the guard had disappeared. "A full gathering of the Sanhedrin would grant a voice to anyone who was both a council member and a follower of this Jesus."

Josephus merely stroked his beard.

"Were you there for the prophet's trial?"

"Caiaphas was kind enough to permit me to observe."

"But you were not appointed as one of the judges."

Joseph quietly repeated, "The high priest allowed me to observe."

"I see."

"Yes. The high priest's home has a private upper section for his family. The lower portion is given over to Temple affairs. There is a guardroom and a holding cell next to the courtyard used for such meetings."

"So the high priest chose to conduct this trial in his home."

"That is so."

"By this smaller group."

"A beit din. Yes."

"Filled with his cronies."

Joseph might have nodded. "Will you take tea?"

"No thank you. What were the charges?"

"Sedition, blasphemy, treason—quite a vast number of crimes. Witnesses came forward against the rabbi. Some had apparently been bribed, and their testimony was conflicting. The judges refused to rule against him."

"So he was taken to Pilate."

"To Pilate, then to Herod, then back to Pilate." Joseph's polished veneer cracked for the first time. He spoke with a bitterness that twisted his features. "Where he was scourged. Then, when that did not satisfy the crowd gathered by the high priest, Pilate washed his hands of the affair—literally and figuratively—and the crowd demanded that he be crucified."

"Did the prophet die upon the cross?"

Joseph resumed the gentle rocking that took hold of his entire body. "The man I carried to the tomb was cold and utterly lifeless."

"Then where is the body?"

"I have told you all I know."

"You must suspect someone."

"You might ask Caiaphas."

Alban leaned forward. "You suspect the high priest of kidnapping the body? Why? To foment further dissension among his people?"

Joseph rocked, his hand sliding down his beard over and over again.

Alban glanced back to where the guard had been. Could the high priest be intending to start a revolt himself? Alban prompted, "You approached Pilate and requested the right to bury Jesus."

"Which I did. I laid him to rest with my own hands. In a cave prepared for my own family."

"Alone?"

"I was helped by a friend, another member of the Sanhedrin named Nicodemus."

Something in the way the gentleman spoke, maybe the look of reverential awe that filled his features, left Alban both confused and unsettled. "May I ask what it is you are not telling me?"

The gaze that fastened upon Alban was luminous. "Tell me, centurion. What will you do if you find the rabbi's body—"

"*When* I find him."

The Pharisee's smile was otherworldly. "*If* you find him, what if the finding causes your entire world to be shaken to its very core? What if you indeed find the answers you seek, and everything you held as important, everything that shaped your world, all comes crashing down?"

"I don't understand your—"

"What if you do discover the truth, and the truth shatters your life?" Joseph leaned closer, until all Alban could see was the fire at the center of the Judaean's dark eyes. "And what if it forces you to leave behind all your ambitions and your desires? What then, centurion? What will you do then?"

CHAPTER ELEVEN

Late Friday Afternoon

THE JERUSALEM STALLHOLDERS no doubt found it extremely peculiar to have a lone centurion in dusty battle dress ask the way to the house of the high priest. But Alban was too conflicted by his conversation with Joseph to pay them any mind. His body ached from the road. He was hungry and yearned for the baths. Yet his instinct told him he needed to speak with Caiaphas before word of his meeting with Joseph arrived there ahead of him.

The house of Caiaphas occupied a promontory south of the Temple Mount. The house spilled down the cliff face and was fronted by four graceful patios. Caiaphas received Alban in a courtyard fringed by Lebanese cedars. Below them, a lane was jammed so tightly with penitents headed for the Temple that Alban could not see the cobblestones. Their voices, a constant drone, drifted upward on the hot afternoon wind.

The contrasts between Caiaphas and Joseph of Arimathea could not have been greater. The high priest wore robes of Greek design, his hair cut like an Aristotelian scholar. His every motion seemed planned for its effect, and his gaze held the same carefully disguised deadliness as that of Herod Antipas. He looked Alban up and down from his gilded chair. "My guard tells me you bear Pilate's insignia."

"Indeed, my lord." It was an inappropriate title for the man, and most Romans would have considered it insulting to address a Judaean in such a lofty manner. But Alban had found the Capernaum elders to be sticklers about matters of honor. He could only assume the Jerusalem leaders would be even more so. He handed over the scroll.

Caiaphas could not fully disguise his respect for the gilded eagle. "You may be seated, centurion," he said as he unrolled the scroll.

"My lord does me great honor. But I have been riding since before dawn. I would prefer to stand, if I may."

"You came straight here from Caesarea?"

"At Pilate's command, my lord, I went first to see Joseph of Arimathea. From there I immediately came here."

The man's face showed a flash of disapproval. "You are here regarding the pestilent prophet."

"Indeed, sir."

The high priest pretended to inspect the scroll. "What did Joseph tell you?"

"That the man was dead when they took him down from the cross."

"Well, of course he was. A Roman guard pierced his side with his spear."

Alban blinked his surprise. This was news.

"There were three crucifixions that day. The business had to be concluded before the Passover began. When they went to break the legs of the criminals, they discovered the imposter was already dead. One of the guards pierced his side to be certain." Caiaphas impatiently rolled the document shut and handed it back. "What else did Joseph tell you?"

"That I needed to speak with you, my lord."

"He did, did he?" Caiaphas did a poor job of masking his pleasure. "Most astute of him. I suppose he told you he was a follower of this rabble-rouser, Jesus."

"No, my lord. He did not indicate anything like that—"

"Of course it means nothing now. And Joseph never stated it outright. But surely you must have assumed as much, since he had the audacity to approach the prelate and request permission to bury the man."

Alban asked, "Can you tell me what happened to the body, my lord?"

"The man's disciples stole it away. The tomb was guarded by Roman soldiers. They reported it."

"Reported to whom?"

"To me, of course. The Sanhedrin was responsible for this affair." Caiaphas flicked his hand as though to rid himself of a pesky fly. "Really, centurion. Why Pilate should bother himself over such a trivial matter is beyond me."

"It is not for me to question my prelate's orders."

"No. Quite so." From the residence's main patio, a servant called down toward them. Caiaphas waved his acknowledgment. "Well, if that is all, I really must take my leave. Although I am not on duty at the Temple this day, I must make my Sabbath preparations."

Alban blinked. He had entirely forgotten today was Friday. "I am indeed grateful that you would take the time to speak with me, my lord. Could you tell me where I might find the tomb guards?"

Caiaphas froze in the process of rising. "Why, pray tell, would you wish to speak with them? I have told you what happened."

"Forgive me, my lord. But Roman soldiers on such guard duty would not give up the body lightly. How many disciples attacked them? Were the soldiers wounded? How were they defeated?"

"I'm sure I neither know nor care." Caiaphas motioned Alban toward the main doors. He obviously was accustomed to using his authority as a lever against any opposing force. "If you insist, we can speak another time. But now you really must depart."

Lengthening shadows painted the road as Leah and Procula's small group arrived at the outskirts of Jerusalem. Procula wisely insisted they wait out the Sabbath evening prayers at a hillside inn beyond the city walls.

The inn was run by Greeks who catered to non-Judaean guests. Situated on the same hill as the hippodrome, it was a pleasant enough stopping place. Leah was hot and tired and her body ached. She could ride well, but seldom was she required to travel such distances on horseback. Servants from several households were lounging at a long table by the inn's entrance, close enough to the main terrace to keep within sight of their patrons. Leah sat with her back against the inn's front wall, facing into the sunset and easing her throat with a drink of watered curds with honey. She had been to Jerusalem seven times in the years she had served in Pilate's household. The city unsettled her and magnified her sense of being an outsider in Judaea.

Between them and the city was another valley with a spring, where Pilate had permitted the Sanhedrin to set up a camp for the festival season. The Judaeans paid the Temple priests a rental fee, the priests gave a portion to the Roman tax collectors, and they in turn passed a tax on to Pilate. The prelate received his share of everything, including the Temple treasury.

The valley was overflowing with tents and makeshift hovels built of branches. A few cooking fires sent lonely pillars rising into the still air. A dog stalked the dusty lane leading down from their hillside. Otherwise the camp was deserted.

A servant Leah did not know muttered, "Where is everyone?"

Another of the household's personal guards replied, "Inside the city."

"Everyone? Doesn't that make Jerusalem very crowded?"

The servants all laughed at that, and the guard asked, "This is your first visit to Jerusalem?"

"We arrived from Rome only last week."

"Rome," another servant murmured. "What I wouldn't give to return there."

The guard explained, "Every week at this time, they go for their Temple ritual. It's all the worse during this festival season."

Leah, who listened silently, suddenly recalled the voice of her grandmother describing just such a scene. The yearly sacrifice, the trip to their Holy City, Jerusalem, the need for cleansing, for renewed commitment to a deep-seated faith that stayed with her grandmother even as a foreign culture pressed her to become another woman. *Why am I remembering this now?* Leah wondered. She had assumed those memories were buried so deep they would never surface again. Yet suddenly they were pushing to be released, relived. She wished she had listened more intently to her grandmother's recollections, her explanations of the Judaean ways, of their faith.

She forced her attention back to the conversation, putting aside her troubling memories.

"And in the autumn too," another voice was saying. "The same every year."

"But why?" The young woman clearly liked using her questions to remain the center of attention.

Leah did not know why she now answered. She seldom spoke in such gatherings. But today her thoughts made for uncomfortable companions. "The Judaeans' holy day begins on Friday night. Everyone is called to prayer. During the festival season they come from all over the empire. They like to gather as close to the Temple Mount as they can. Their prayers are supposed to mean more if they are inside the city walls."

All the servants were watching her now. The young woman asked, "Are you one of them?"

Leah stared into the golden valley. "My mother's mother."

The young woman pointed to the city walls fired a brilliant gold by the setting sun. "Why do they all come here?"

"The laws of their religion say Judaeans must come to Jerusalem three times each year and make sacrifices during certain festivals. One of these festivals, the Passover, just ended. Another is in five weeks. Most of those who travel long distances come for the spring festival and stay for the entire period."

"Why aren't you over there with them?"

"Because she's doing her duty, the same as us," the guard seated next to Leah put in, then pointed to the table by the balcony. "Your mistress is calling you."

Leah hurried over to Procula, sitting alone in a simple robe of grey felt. On the table before her rested a silver goblet holding the inn's best wine. Leah knew this because she had poured it for her mistress. Procula had not touched it.

Though Procula was approaching forty years of age, her hair remained dark and thick. Her face was smoothed in the lingering traces of sunlight. "Sit with me, please."

"Mistress, it is not proper—"

"I instruct you to take this chair."

Claudia Procula was true Roman royalty. Leah knew the family had been part of the emperor's court for three generations. Procula's mother, Augusta, had been married twice. First to Tiberius, who had divorced her for adultery. Augustus had then married a Roman knight, Procula's father, who controlled the island of Sardinia.

As Leah reluctantly seated herself across from her mistress, she reflected that the woman had never looked so regal. Or so lonely.

Procula said, "Once we arrive tomorrow, I want you to go directly to Herod's palace. You know Enos, do you not?"

"Indeed, mistress." Enos was Herod's chief servant in Jerusalem. "But don't you want me to help you settle—"

"We are not here for me to *settle*. We are here to *learn*."

Though the words had been softly spoken, Leah was certain the entire group saw and heard the tone and assumed she was being criticized for some great failing. "Yes, mistress."

"You are to be my eyes and ears. Starting immediately. We have no idea how much time we have."

Leah blanched at the sudden chill that struck her bones. "Before what?"

But Procula had leaned forward and missed the change in Leah's expression. "Help me with this clasp."

Leah realized what Procula intended and did not move. "Mistress?"

"Never mind, I have it." Procula lifted the gold chain holding the royal insignia from her neck, a replica of Pilate's official seal in miniature. She placed it in Leah's hand and said, "If anyone questions your right to inquire, show them this and say you speak on my behalf."

If Leah had any doubt about the importance Procula set upon this task, it was now gone. "I don't even know where to begin—"

"Someone in Herod's palace must know where the prophet's disciples are gathered," Procula said briskly. "For once, the festival is working in our favor."

Leah nodded. At any other time of year, the disciples most likely would have fled the city, dispersing throughout the province and beyond to escape any repercussions from their master's death. But these disciples were all clearly religious Judaeans. She understood they would remain within the city walls, bound by their ancient laws to a cycle of time they accepted as handed down by their God.

Procula now reached into the folds of her traveling robe and drew out a pouch. It clinked softly as she set it on the table between them. "This is the only language Herod's people understand."

Leah slipped the purse into a secret pocket sewn into the folds of her own robe. As she did so, the patio's chatter was silenced by a trumpet's piercing note, and Leah looked toward Jerusalem. The sound came from the blowing of the *shofar*, the Temple horn, and announced the arrival of another festival Sabbath eve. Leah shivered, struck by the sudden conviction that the trumpet had blown for her as well, announcing an unknown fate and future over which she had no control.

When Alban emerged from the high priest's house, he discovered that all the markets had closed and everyone in sight was headed in one direction. He finally reached a point where the way became impassable. The people around him seemed to accept this; in fact, they appeared enthralled with something he could not fathom. Alban inspected the surrounding faces and saw them gripped by a pleasure that bordered on ecstasy. Even young boys seemed caught up in something that remained invisible to Alban.

Invisible was precisely how he felt. None of the throng showed any interest in Alban. Even when he began pushing forward, the mass of people, mostly men, glanced at him, saw he was Roman, and turned away. As far as these people were concerned, this Roman simply did not exist, nothing more than a wayward thought. They focused completely upon something else, something so vital they could spare him no notice.

In the distance, beyond the towering Temple walls, a trumpet sounded. The crowd stopped pressing forward, and their fervor became even more intense.

Alban clambered up the sidewall of a shuttered tavern and stood upon the roof. Crowds completely filled every lane and avenue and alley. The ones on the stretch of road below him were all male. To his right, another lane was packed with women, as though they had segregated the very city in one silent maneuver. Every person he could see faced toward the Temple compound. The women covered their faces with the shawls draped over their heads. The men wore strange woven cloths with tasseled edges over their heads and shoulders. Though they held texts in their hands, few of them actually seemed to be reading. In fact, most everyone had eyes not merely shut but *clenched tight*. They dipped their heads in time to their droning voices. A great heaving mass of people, moving back and forth where they stood, murmuring in one gigantic voice.

The sun had descended below the western hills. The Temple itself seemed to hover above the city, drifting upon a cloud of golden dust and the chanting voices, more connected to the golden-blue sky than to the earth.

CHAPTER TWELVE

Antonia Fortress, Jerusalem

BY THE TIME ALBAN had made his way to the Antonia Fortress, the city was shrouded in the shadows of dusk. He'd become lost twice in the winding ways and had to search for someone to direct him. The empty streets only heightened his disquiet over the ethereal scenes of religious fervor he had just witnessed at sunset.

The tavern across from the fortress was the only establishment along the market lane still open. Linux, however, was nowhere to be found. The aromas of cooking food were enticing, and Alban ordered a flatbread filled with roast lamb and carried it with him up to the fortress baths. His body ached from the day and his mind from the burden of questions with no answers.

He paused in the passage between the entry and the changing rooms. As was customary for Roman baths, three alcoves held statues dedicated to minor deities—Abundantia, goddess of good fortune; Epona, goddess of good health; and Moneta, goddess of prosperity. The vessels before each idol held mostly *lepta*, the smallest coins, often tossed in with a laugh or jest. Alban had seldom even noticed such idols, they were such a common part of life among the Romans. Today, however, his mind still vibrated from the echoes of fervent prayer.

In the past he had visited the Capernaum synagogue and seen fleeting glimpses of the occasional man draped in his prayer shawl, rocking to and fro as he prayed. Alban had never witnessed an actual Sabbath service, of course. Or a festival like this one. He frowned at the figures in their small shrines. Who was to determine which was the god men should turn to?

The new baths were a true Roman affair, with room for half Alban's garrison in the caldarium alone. He discovered Linux in the steam room. The air was thick with vapor and the smell of healing unguents. Linux sat with his elbows planted on his knees and a towel draped over his head. He gave no sign he noticed Alban settling in beside him until he muttered, "Every time I leave this city I swear I won't return. But here I am. Ordered by the prelate to remain here for how long I don't know. And it's your fault."

"Sorry," Alban said, though in truth he was glad for an ally within the city walls.

"I'm commanded to expedite your every request. Me, a prince of the realm."

Alban felt the welcome heat of the baths begin to work its way through his weary muscles. "It's your brother who's the prince."

"A trifling detail. His black heart can't keep beating forever."

Alban shrugged. It was a soldier's right to complain. Often it was his only defense against orders not to his liking. Alban wiped his sweating face and said, "I became trapped by the crowds."

An unknown voice carried through the chamber's fragrant mist. "You didn't know enough to get back before sundown?"

"The centurion has never been to Jerusalem before, and I forgot to warn him about the Sabbaths during festivals." Linux wiped his own face. "We arrived from Caesarea just after midday today."

"The crowds were unlike anything I have ever seen in my life." Alban felt another surge of sweat with the memory. "I climbed on a roof. You know what I thought when I surveyed the mob?"

Linux looked at him for the first time. "An army?"

"The fact is, they seem to move as one." He shut his eyes and again saw the crowd and heard their murmurs wash over him like waves of a human sea. The chants themselves were not alarming, but the sound *as of one voice* held implications of a power he could neither understand nor truly describe.

Alban finally realized why Pilate was so concerned about revolution. The man ruled this province with one irregular legion, mostly mercenaries, few fully trained. Against him stood a people who were united only by prayer. But united with a mysterious bond totally foreign to any Roman Alban knew.

Roman gods were fickle allies to be bribed into cooperation, at least temporarily. Many of his own Gauls worshiped certain trees and hilltops, or spoke of faeries and wood sprites by name. But nowhere had Alban seen anything like the way these people worshiped. The intensity they shared, the passion. They truly *believed*. All they needed was one voice, one man to claim the right to lead them. And every Roman in Judaea and the whole province would be swept into the sea.

Alban spoke almost to himself, "If they can be so joined by a simple act like prayer, think what would transpire if they decided to revolt."

The voice from the sauna's other side held a veteran's gruffness. "Where are you stationed, centurion?"

"Capernaum."

Alban saw through the mist a man rise and head for the exit. "Every arriving soldier should be brought to Jerusalem for a week," he growled over his shoulder. "It's the only way to understand the threat we face here."

When the door shut behind the departing soldier, Linux stood and walked through the steam, making a circuit of the entire chamber. He returned to sit beside Alban and whispered, "I was not able to find your Atticus or the guards."

"If the sauna is empty, why do you whisper?"

"You really are a provincial, centurion. Pilate was right to have me watch your back. Without me, you would perish within the hour."

"I made it back from the high priest's house, no thanks to you." But Alban made sure his tone held no malice.

"I fear I deserve that." Linux leaned against the wall and stretched out his legs. "The fortress commandant spent a good half hour dressing me down, if that's any consolation."

"What did you do?"

"Other than breathe the air of this pestilent city, I have no idea. I asked around in the guardroom where I might find the two who had been stationed at the tomb. I might have been talking to the floor beneath our feet."

"They refused to help you?"

"They claimed to know nothing. I then asked the duty officer where I would find the centurion Atticus. The officer didn't know, he said. The next thing I knew, the commandant had sent his aide with two armed legionnaires to fetch me. The commandant demanded to know why I was pestering his men." Linux rose to his feet. "Come, my provincial friend. It's time we cooled off."

Alban followed Linux into the cooled waters of the smaller bath, its water piped directly from an underground spring. After rinsing off, they chose an alcove at the far end from the entrance. Alban asked, keeping his voice low, "What can you tell me of the commandant?"

"He's a veteran campaigner. He earned the rank of tribune in battle. This tribune also asked me who rode one of Pilate's own horses. He knows his steeds, that man, and he has eyes and ears everywhere."

"But why did it seem as though he might arrest you?"

Linux dragged the towel over his handsome features. "Before commanding the Jerusalem fortress, he served the governor in Damascus."

"Ah." Alban nodded his understanding. Originally Judaea had been under the direct command of the regional governor in Damascus. Nine years earlier, Emperor Tiberius had changed all that when news of a possible Judaean revolt alarmed him greatly. Not because of Judaea's strategic importance, which was paltry, but rather because of all the Judaeans living throughout the entire Roman Empire. Tiberius feared the prospect of such a revolt spreading through the realm and toppling his own rule. So the emperor elevated Judaea to full provincial status, personally choosing his ally Pontius Pilate to become its new governor. He refused to submit Pilate's name for senate approval and ordered the prelate to answer directly to him, which enraged the senate.

It also enraged Herod's brother, who lost his governorship. A man loyal to Damascus was a natural enemy to Pontius Pilate. And vice versa.

Linux went on, "The tribune demanded to know why we had been sent here during the busiest period of the year. He could not grasp how Pilate would place such importance on one more bothersome Judaean, particularly one who was already dead. I'm probably only here because I found opportunity to tell him about your authorizations from Pilate himself." Linux leaned his head against the tiled wall. "One more thing I can tell you for certain: The tribune hates Gauls."

The next day, Leah left Pilate's Jerusalem residence and walked around the outer wall to the corner and to the main portal of Herod's adjoining palace. It included a fortress that guarded the Jaffa Gate into the city, and the grounds contained vast ornamental gardens. The whole complex was so large Herod Antipas had offered Pilate one wing as his own Jerusalem residence, an attempt to strengthen their alliance.

Unlike Pilate, Herod permanently staffed each palace. He loved to rub the noses of his Judaean subjects in his lavish way of living. Pilate was conservative with his money and left only a few trusted older servants in his absences.

Leah exchanged greetings with the guards. Notorious for troubling the young and pretty, Herod's guards left Leah alone. The two men only nodded and saluted as they opened the wide outer door to her. She gave her name to the first servant who passed, and settled onto the bench used by supplicants seeking Herod's aid.

Enos, Herod's chief of staff, appeared shortly, looking shocked to find her waiting on the supplicants' bench. "What, pray tell, are you doing out here, Leah my dear?"

"Resting."

"This won't do at all. Come with me." Enos snapped his fingers at a passing slave. "Bring water for washing and wine and food."

"Not wine, please," Leah said. "I'm afraid I would sleep and not wake up again."

"Tea, then," he called to the slave. "And hurry or I'll give you the lashing you've been asking for." Enos sniffed as the maid scurried away. "As if they ever learn the meaning of the word hurry."

In a household known for every possible excess, where pleasure was the only idol to be worshiped, Enos was a curiosity. He had the look of an ascetic and wore only white. He was as lean as a whippet, and his nose thrust out from his cavernous face like a great hawk's beak. He wore his thinning hair in a long silver tail that trailed over his right shoulder. Yet his simple robes were of the finest material, and his skin gleamed from daily baths and rich ointments. Herod's slaves were terrified of him, yet to Leah he had always appeared friendly enough. Even so, Leah was certain that given opportunity for personal gain, Enos would sell her to Parthian slavers for a handful of silver.

There was only one thing that Enos loved more than money. And that was gossip.

Enos ignored Leah's protests and ordered the maid to wash her feet, as for a visiting noble. When the maid was gone and a table by the central fountain had been spread with food and tea, he said, "Weren't you too ill to travel here with the governor?"

"That was the previous time. I'm well now."

"Indeed. You do look healthy—if you were one of my maids I'd suspect you had been faking to avoid Jerusalem during the festival season." But his tone was jovial.

"That is not my way."

"No, you never were one to shirk your duties. Unlike my own servants. Procula is fortunate to have you." He folded his hands and leaned toward her in a familiar manner. "How is your lovely mistress? Recovered, I hope."

"Her headaches come and go. Actually, she is here."

He showed genuine shock. "What, back in Jerusalem?"

"It is not an official visit."

"You're certain? You can't be wrong about this!"

Enos's visible unease was justified. Throughout the Roman Empire, governors were the center of social, political, and financial life. Pilate's official presence would require the city's governing structure to shift drastically.

Leah replied, "The prelate will not arrive for another week or more."

The head of Herod's household blew out a sigh and relaxed. "Why is *she* here?"

"My mistress seeks information about the crucified prophet. She is hoping you might be able to help her."

Leah had half expected the man to dismiss her out of hand. Instead Herod's servant gave his nose a thoughtful rub. "She was having dreams."

Leah did not bother asking how the man knew. "Nightmares."

"About that man Jesus."

"Yes."

Enos continued to rub his giant beak. "The prophet may be dead, but he continues to trouble others as well. How much do you know of Caiaphas?"

"The high priest? Very little, in fact."

"Caiaphas was actually appointed to the position by Gratus, the governor who preceded Pilate. I have never known anyone to love gold as much as that man."

Leah blinked. To have Enos make such a statement was astonishing indeed. "So Caiaphas bribed Gratus for the job?"

Enos smiled indulgently at her. "What a delightful young woman you are. *Everyone* bribed Gratus. He actually sold the position of high priest to five different people. Only Caiaphas was devious and powerful enough to actually hold on to the job. I have heard the amount he paid to Pilate to keep the job was his own weight in Temple gold. But that is not the only reason he still holds the position today. Caiaphas is the son-in-law of Annas, who was a high priest before him. Annas remains the most powerful man on the Sanhedrin."

"And what does this have to do with the prophet?"

"All I know for certain is this: Caiaphas—and probably Annas also—is still extremely worried about a man who was most definitely crucified and buried. The body of this Jesus has vanished, but I suppose you already know that."

Leah nodded slowly. "My mistress wishes for me to speak with the prophet's disciples. But I have no idea where to begin."

Enos gave a slow smile, the one he showed all supplicants seeking an audience with his master. "I am ever ready to stand in the service of Pilate's lovely wife."

"Procula suggested I offer a . . . a reward for your help." Leah retrieved the pouch from her pocket. "I have no idea how to go about this, or even what to say."

"Your honesty is almost too charming." With the delicacy of a bird drinking from a fountain, Enos dipped his fingers into the pouch and quickly retrieved two gold coins that just as quickly were secreted into his robe. "I will see what I can learn, my dear."

CHAPTER THIRTEEN

Antonia Fortress

THE JERUSALEM GARRISON'S commandant, Tribune Bruno Aetius, was a crusty veteran of a hundred battles. The fingers of his right hand remained half curled even when empty, as though the soldier were unable to relinquish his sword's haft. Close-cropped grey hair and beard set off a broken nose that angled slightly to the left. The scar running from a corner of his mouth to his ear made him appear to leer, certainly when angry. Which he indeed was now.

After keeping Alban waiting in his antechamber for almost three hours, the tribune greeted him with a roar. "Front and center, soldier!"

"Sir!" Alban came to rigid attention as his feet smacked the floor and saluted. "Centurion Alban reporting to the garrison commander, sir!"

"I caught your mate skulking around here yesterday. You are of the impression that tossing Pilate's name about is going to impress me?"

"Indeed not, sir!"

"Alban—that's no Roman name."

"I hail from the north, sir. From Gaul, sir."

Bruno Aetius offered a few choice remarks about Gauls pretending to be Roman soldiers, then noted, "Aren't you the one assigned to that pestilent outpost crammed with other mercenaries?"

"Along with other foul beasts. Yes, sir, that would be the one standing here at your command."

The tribune must have caught a glint of humor in Alban's response. He barked, "Something strike you as amusing?"

The man's gruff demeanor took Alban straight back to his childhood. His first teacher and dearest friend, the retired centurion, had sounded so similar to Bruno Aetius they might as well have been brothers. Alban replied, "Only that it's good to be in the company of a real soldier again, sir."

The tribune's eyes narrowed. His next volley lacked some of his former ire. "If you expect my men to bow and scrape, you're soon to be disappointed."

"Indeed not, sir. I was merely hoping to ask the commandant's advice."

"I'm not in the habit of advising mercenaries." But the tribune's growl was now a mere rumble. "You have some ill-considered reason for being so far off post, some odious purpose for fouling my quarters?"

"I was hoping to report to you about Parthians and the Damascus Road." Swiftly Alban recounted the raid, the capture, the summons from Pilate, the strange response the Parthians gave to their captivity.

The commandant pondered for a time, then conceded, "Splitting your men like that and using a landslide was rather clever. Where did you come up with that one?"

"My homeland lies not far from the Alpine slopes. A neighboring province rebelled against Rome around the time I was born. Landslides were a favorite tactic. They once took out almost six hundred legionnaires. The Parthians outnumbered us and were holed up in a pair of caves overlooking the caravan. I needed to keep them from attacking while we moved into position."

Bruno Aetius gave a single nod of approval. "I fought the Gauls. Farther north than your homeland. Across the sea, west of a town called Londinium. Fierce, they were. Terrible fierce." He turned and shouted for an aide. Then he said, "Seat yourself, centurion."

"Thank you, sir."

The aide appeared and looked startled at the sight of Alban seated across from the commanding officer. His eyes widened further still when Bruno Aetius asked Alban, "Some tea?"

"I wouldn't say no, sir."

When the aide departed, the commandant went on, "The Parthians call their land Persia. We don't know how far it spreads or how many they number. All we know for certain is they care nothing for the lives of their men. We kill ten thousand, and they send ten thousand more. You're wondering why the Parthians were so casual about their captivity."

"Just so, sir."

"That's easy enough. Because this province has more problems than there are fleas pestering a donkey's hide!" He brought his fist crashing down on the maps and scrolls littering his table. "There's not a decent Roman legion in the entire province! Then Herod Antipas is permitted to have his own forces, as is the high priest Caiaphas, not to mention a dozen or so merchants who claim they need private armies for their caravans. They're all little more than villains in fancy robes!"

It was a complaint Alban had heard many times before. He let the officer across from him fume a moment, then changed the subject. "I became trapped outside the fortress by the Friday prayers."

"My men have strict orders to be either on base or on the city walls an hour before sundown. Which you would have known if you'd reported in as you should." At a knock on his door, he barked, "Come!"

Alban accepted his tea. He had not come to discuss the Parthians, and he suspected the commandant knew it. He'd merely brought the incident up as a means of establishing his credentials with the tribune. Alban spoke now as a fellow warrior. "I was ordered by Pilate to go straight to the home of Joseph of Arimathea. We'd been traveling so hard and fast I overlooked that it was Friday."

The eyes tightened, but the anger did not return. "So what is this errand the prelate has sent you on?"

Alban recounted the story of the prophet's missing body, or at least he started to, because the commandant cut him off. "This province breeds rabble-rousers like Rome does rats. What difference does it matter if the disciples steal his body away for whatever reasons they might have? The man was dead, I tell you! Dead!"

"I was hoping to speak with the ones ordered to guard the tomb where Joseph of Arimathea placed the body."

The commandant snorted his disdain. "That arrogant high priest is responsible for the guards."

"Caiaphas?"

"He keeps a few of my men on hand during the festival seasons. Some like the assignment because the duty is light. Others detest it because they serve with the Judaeans under the whim of the high priest, who is an old goat in fancy robes." He noticed the aide still hovering by the door. "What is it, man?"

"Forgive me, sire. But Herod's man is outside. He wishes to have a word."

"Well, he'll have to wait." He waved his aide away. "Where was I?"

"Caiaphas uses your men as extra guards during the festival season."

The commandant grunted. "This festival has been the worst of all. It won't end too soon for me or my men, I can tell you that."

"The prophet Jesus caused you trouble?"

"His name was everywhere. And the ruling council, the Sanhedrin, they were frantic. That man had them worried like nothing I have ever seen."

Alban ventured, "Did the prophet or his disciples preach revolt against Rome?"

Alban had expected the commandant to brush the question aside with a veteran officer's claim that any threat against Rome would be crushed. Instead the commandant stood and walked to the window. "This is your first visit to Jerusalem, you say?"

"Indeed, sir."

"This city is unlike any place on earth, and I've served Rome in some strange and dangerous regions, I don't mind telling you." The commandant squinted into the daylight and mused, "I don't know what to tell you about the prophet they call Jesus of Nazareth, except that he was crucified and buried, and now his body is gone."

Alban stood. "Thank you for your time, sir. And for the tea."

But as he started for the door, the commandant halted him. "Who else was with you at your meeting with Pilate?"

Alban turned back. "Herod Antipas, sir."

The commandant growled, "That man is a snake."

Alban did not respond.

"A snake! And now his man is outside, waiting to speak with me. No doubt interested in our little exchange. As though a Roman tribune need tell a Herodian snake anything." The tribune turned from the window to face Alban full on. "Herod wouldn't be worried about our conversation without a good reason. Do you have any idea what that reason might be?"

"Perhaps Herod is in league with the Parthians," Alban said, finally giving voice to his suspicions. "He feeds them information about caravans run by his own subjects. And I have—"

"Herod will not like you stirring his pot, centurion." The commandant returned to his desk. "If I were you, I'd watch my back."

Nothing moved swiftly enough in Jerusalem. Over the next week, Alban remained confined by the crowds and bound by currents he could neither name nor identify. He and Linux returned to the high priest's residence and were met by a secretary who knew nothing and offered less. Not even Linux's threats could dislodge a useful word.

In desperation, Alban finally went back to the commandant's office. But the tribune was away and his aide proved equally unhelpful. "Wait till the spring festival season ends," the man said laconically. "They'll turn up."

"You seem surprisingly relaxed about men under this command," Alban commented. When the junior officer eyed him crossly, he added in a placating tone, "This is my first time in Jerusalem. I seek wisdom as much as the missing men."

The officer laid his stylus aside. "I am telling you, they are not missing at all."

"Explain for me. Please."

"The garrison has but one duty in the festival season. This duty takes precedence above all else."

"To maintain order," Alban guessed.

"Precisely," the tribune's aide confirmed. "The high priest is as frantically busy and overstretched as we are. Perhaps he was troubled by bandits stealing lambs being brought for the slaughter. Perhaps there was a rumor of trouble in one of the camps. He might have ordered his men to go, only then discovered there were no free guards. So he sent ours. But this is not officially permitted. The Roman garrison is restricted to patrolling Jerusalem. Are we going to object? Are we going to raise a fuss?"

"Not if there is no trouble," Alban said, nodding now. "Not if you don't know."

"So the men have vanished. Perhaps they slipped away and are spending the festival season in a tavern's back room. It has happened before. They will show up."

Alban asked, "What about the missing centurion, the one named Atticus?"

"His mates claim he was taken ill. His sergeant says he has not seen him."

"This does not worry you either?"

The officer hesitated, then nodded. "The commandant knows and likes Atticus. He is asking around. But quietly."

Alban set the scroll bearing the golden eagle on the officer's desk, then pulled out the purse holding Pilate's gold. "I wish to offer a reward in the prelate's name."

The officer could not keep his gaze from the royal scroll. "The tribune wishes to save the centurion Atticus from official censure."

"Atticus is a friend of mine. I am in his debt. I seek to protect him as well. I am after information, nothing more." Alban set a pair of gold denarii on the table beside the scroll. "For your troubles. And another two for the soldier who leads me to Atticus."

The officer could no longer disguise his amazement. A legionnaire earned a third of that amount each year—if he was paid at all. "They will be at each other's throats to hand you the man."

"And another two for the man who brings me the missing guards." Alban turned to the door. "Tell them speed is everything."

Centurion Atticus was precisely where his sergeant had said Alban would find him. The man had chosen a tavern well removed from any of his Roman colleagues. Which was a good thing, for the centurion was far beyond bedraggled. The tavern was located in what once had been the main Greek quarter and was now the caravans' central gathering point at the Damascus Gate.

Atticus slouched within shadows at the back of the tavern's main chamber. The flooring was sand and its walls Bedouin cloth. The front was open, with a view of the noisome corrals for donkeys and camels. The other patrons feasted on roast lamb with the single-minded intensity of those facing a long trek and a longer time until the next decent meal. Atticus watched Alban's approach with eyes that seemed almost dead. In fact, his entire person seemed to have collapsed in on itself.

Alban seated himself across from him and asked, "What's happened to you, my friend?"

Atticus drained the pewter mug and hollered for the innkeeper to bring more ale. "Who's the man you left stationed by the front?" he muttered.

"Linux. He's on Pilate's staff."

"Thought I recognized him. He scouts the road like it's enemy terrain."

"We seem to have made a foe of Herod Antipas."

"Then I'm talking to a dead man."

"I might say the same thing."

Atticus gave no sign he had heard Alban's words. He nodded as the innkeeper refilled the mug. "My first year in Jerusalem, Herod Antipas held a banquet. The daughter of his new wife danced for his guests. The girl is quite the beauty, or so I've heard. Like her mother, who let herself be stolen away by Antipas from his own brother. After the girl danced, Herod was in such a state he offered her anything she wanted, up to half his kingdom."

"I wanted to know—"

"The girl asked for the head of this Judaean by the name of John. Apparently she'd been put up to it by her own mother. This prophet was known as the Baptizer by those who followed him. John had condemned Herod and the girl's mother for marrying after she'd divorced Herod's brother. Anyway, Herod makes the girl his offer, and the girl asks him for the head of this John—on a platter. Herod serves him up as the banquet's last course."

Alban remained silent and waited. He marveled that the man could speak so coherently after the amount of ale he'd obviously consumed.

"His father was worse still. Do you know Herod the Great heard about the birth of this Jesus from Magi who claimed to have read the signs in the stars? Herod the Great's own advisers found writings in old Judaean scrolls that spoke of a king rising from a lowly birth. That Herod had every male infant in the boy's village slaughtered." The centurion drank deeply, swiped his mouth and beard with a filthy sleeve, then added, "The things you hear in this city are enough to curdle a man's gut."

Alban asked, more softly this time, "What happened, old friend?"

"I was there."

"Where?"

"Golgotha." He drank again. "If I could have the day to do over, I would abandon my post and flee the city."

"I was told you saw the prophet crucified."

He drained the mug and shouted for another. The innkeeper was ready this time, for scarcely had the centurion raised his voice when another foaming goblet was set upon the stained table. But when the soldier reached for it, Alban clamped his hand on the soldier's arm.

The centurion's face darkened. But just as suddenly, the fight went out of him. He slumped forward, seeming to curve inward around a hollow core. "You know what they're saying now?"

"Who?"

Atticus swept his free arm in a broad circle, taking in the entire city. "Some of the Judaeans. Three days after it happened, I was down in the Lower City. I heard them talking about how the body had disappeared from a sealed tomb. Some claimed the prophet had simply swooned. That he wasn't actually dead when we took him down."

Alban admitted, "I've heard that too."

This time, when Atticus tugged, Alban released the arm. Atticus lifted the mug, then lowered it back to the table. "I've seen death. We were sent to do a job. There were three of them crucified that day, two thieves and the prophet. I was in charge. Do you think I'd walk away without being certain?"

"Absolutely not."

"I watched him die." The man slumped further still. "The Judaeans were frantic about getting the three of them down before their Sabbath. My men broke the legs of the other two. But when they came to the prophet, he was gone. When we took him down, he was cold, rigid. No blood flowed. I swear to that."

"I need to know what you haven't told the others." Alban leaned closer. "Pilate has ordered me to learn if there is a threat against Rome. He worries that the prophet's disciples stole the body to start such rumors and cause the people to revolt."

The older centurion gave no sign that he had even heard.

"You're my oldest friend in Judaea," Alban tried again. "I need to know—"

"It haunts me." The words were a groan wrenched from the

man's core. "Every time I shut my eyes I'm back on my horse on that cursed hill. Before we hung him on that cross."

Alban sat and waited.

"The streets were packed with the festival crowds. I was on horseback. They saw me and got out of the way. They'd heard of the scourging and the Sanhedrin's threats and Pilate's decisions. News travels fast as the wind in Jerusalem. They knew, and they stood aside, and they wept. They reached out to touch the prophet as he passed. They were weeping and wailing and tearing their garments. The sound chills my bones."

Alban did not move or breathe. Did not even blink.

Finally Atticus dragged in an uneven breath. "We made him carry his cross for a time, but he was torn apart by the scourging. So I had one of my men pull in someone from the crowd. We brought Jesus to Golgotha, and it seemed like the entire city was there. We nailed him to the cross. The people screamed like we were hammering the nails into their souls. He hung there for a few hours. Not long. Then it happened."

This time, when Atticus did not continue, Alban pressed with quiet urgency, "Tell me."

"He called out to his father. Since that moment, night after night I hear the man's cry echoing in my soul. He speaks like no man I have ever heard before. He invites one of the thieves to join him that very night in the heavens. He asks his father to forgive us. He asks his father why he is forsaken. And then he says three final words: *It is finished.* And he leaves."

Alban felt a tight wind, as strong and silent and cold as death itself, drift through his chest. "You mean, he dies."

Atticus looked directly at him for the first time, an emptiness in his eyes. "I mean, he leaves. He is gone. Like it was his own will—his decision." He dropped his gaze back to the table between them. "The sky darkens, like the breath of life is sucked from the entire world. The earth shakes."

"I heard there was a storm."

"Not *was*." Atticus's fist struck the scarred wood. "The storm is with me still."

Alban rose from the table. "Come. I will take you back to the fortress."

"There is nothing for me there." But the older centurion did not struggle when Alban gripped his arm and pulled him to his feet.

Alban did not speak further because he knew Atticus would not hear him. Even if Pilate's seal was not enough to gain him clear answers, at least he could repay a friend's favor by bringing him back from the abyss.

CHAPTER FOURTEEN

Pilate's Palace, Jerusalem

JUST OVER A WEEK after their arrival at the governor's palace in Jerusalem, Leah was summoned from the kitchen with news she had a visitor. Leah had never been called on by anyone save the occasional merchant and one Temple guard who had spied her on the street and wished to pay court. Leah had made it abundantly clear she had no interest in his attention. Today, as soon as she entered the courtyard foyer, she knew the one awaiting her came from Herod's household. The lovely young woman possessed a knowing gaze far beyond her years. She was dressed in the Greek style, including a lined outer garment and a necklace of semiprecious stones. "You are the one they call Leah?"

"Yes, I am."

She dismissed Leah's simple cotton garb with a condescending glance. "My master wishes to speak with you."

"King Herod has arrived?"

"Of course not *him*. Enos bids you attend him immediately."

"One moment." Leah hurried back to her alcove in the servants' quarters and drew out a plain grey hooded robe. The summons from Enos could mean one thing only—he had discovered where the dead prophet's disciples were hiding and would give her directions. Leah wanted to begin her explorations in a modest and inconspicuous fashion.

Herod's servant gave a sniff at Leah's choice of outer garment. "Come."

The morning had started dark and blustery, and it still threatened rain. The maid did not speak to Leah again. They hurried back down the hillside avenue. The palace guard saw them coming and held open the main outer portal. As soon as they passed through the inner doors, the maid called, "She is here."

The plaintive tone that responded was all too familiar, though Leah could not see Enos. "Could you possibly have taken any longer?"

The maid adopted a tone as pained as the head servant's. "She insisted on dressing herself for the visit."

"Come on then. No, not you. Over here, Leah." The maid sniffed a final time and disappeared. Enos complained, "As if I had nothing else to do with my day but wait on your convenience."

Leah remained where she was. The double portals led into one of the palace's receiving rooms. Like everything else about Herod's residence, it was so ornate as to appear garish. Enos stood by an inner window, and in the dim light a figure knelt upon the carpet before him. Leah had seen the position well enough for her own stomach to clench with dread. The figure was clearly female, with long black hair spilling about her. The robe she wore was as plain as Leah's, which was odd, for everyone else in Herod's household tended to dress as flamboyantly as their master. Yet the woman was clearly a servant, for she remained in the position adopted for punishment. Enos held a supple cane and tapped it lightly against his other hand. Leah had seen it applied all too often. In her recent fevered state, she had dreamed about it, and though she had never felt the cane herself, she had heard herself scream.

Leah's voice was low but clear. "I have no desire to witness this."

"Oh, do behave sensibly and come in. I have far better ways to spend my hours than delaying a simple lashing." He smiled thinly as the woman at his feet shuddered. "This troublesome slave ran away. Didn't you—what's your name?"

"Yes, master. I'm . . . I am Nedra." The voice that spoke was not young. Nor, another oddity, did it hold the typical mixture of whining and terror.

"I knew she was gone, but I had not yet alerted the authorities," Enos said. "Yesterday she went away on an errand. She did not return. But some of our maids can slip away from time to time. So long as Herod is not here, I grant them a bit of freedom. I am far too indulgent, I know." He tapped the cane once more against his open palm. "I do hate the sight of blood. It upsets the other household help."

The woman at his feet trembled but did not speak. Normally by this point the slave to be punished would be reaching for the master's feet, begging and pleading for a mercy that seldom came.

"Then what happens," he continued, "but the slave returns this morning. Alone. And she tells me the most curious thing. Didn't you, Nedra?" When the slave remained silent, he prodded her with the cane. "Tell our guest what you told me."

"They . . . they ordered me to return, master." Her voice shook but the words were clear.

"And who, pray tell, told you to do that?"

"The prophet's disciples. They said . . ."

"Yes, go on. We are fascinated by what you are telling us. What could these riffraff possibly have told you that would have forced you to return, knowing the punishment that awaited you?"

"They said, sir, that I must remain in my earthly position until the Messiah brings our final freedom."

Enos studied the kneeling woman, then turned to Leah and asked, "Do you have any idea what she is talking about?"

Leah shook her head slowly, her eyes never leaving the kneeling figure.

"And yet I have the strange feeling that the slave speaks the truth. At least, as much truth as she is capable of." He tapped her back but not hard. "Nedra, listen carefully to what I have to say. This young woman's name is Leah. She wishes to go to the prophet's disciples. You will take her, do you hear me? This is not a request. You will take her, and you will do whatever she asks of you."

The woman did not move. She appeared not to be breathing.

"Do this, and I will be gentle with you. I will show you mercy you do not deserve." When the woman did not respond, he tapped her again with the cane. "Tell me you understand."

"I hear you, master."

"Now tell me you will obey."

"I will do as you say."

Enos's lips drew down as he glanced at Leah and shrugged, clearly having expected more of a struggle. Either that or the woman's unearthly calm unsettled him as it certainly did Leah. He started to say something further, then shook his head and told her, "You may rise."

Nedra unsteadily got to her feet, then stood with head downcast. Enos flicked the supple cane, causing the air to whistle around the woman. The slave flinched but did not move. He warned, "Your fate depends upon your doing exactly as I ordered."

"It will be as you said, master."

"Wait for Leah by the outer gate." When the door shut behind her, he said, "I'd heard the man had secret followers everywhere.

But never, not in my wildest dreams, did I expect to find one here in Herod's house."

"They sent her back?" Leah still could not fathom it.

This was troubling Enos as well, Leah knew. "You will tell me if you find something that explains what we just heard, yes?"

"Of course." Leah took that as a dismissal and bowed. "Thank you for your help. My mistress will be most grateful."

"Wait, I'm not finished." He pointed to a scroll unrolled across the nearby table. "Word came this morning from my master. Herod bids me to make preparations for your betrothal."

Had it not been for what she had just witnessed, Leah would have wailed aloud at the news. Instead she saw herself in the slave's position upon the floor, kneeling and helpless, awaiting the lash. She shivered and did not speak.

Enos went on, "Herod travels here with Pilate. They arrive in three days. The betrothal is to take place the following week."

Leah feared if she tried to speak she would retch. She turned silently for the door.

"One further moment." When Leah paused and looked back at him, Enos showed his thin, humorless smile. "It is customary at such moments to reward those who do your bidding."

Leah fumbled at her waist and drew out more coins. They disappeared as quickly as they glinted in her palm.

Nedra stood in submissive patience by the gate. The daylight had strengthened somewhat, though the sky remained shrouded in gloom. The slave's eyes were a remarkable combination of sorrow and calm.

Leah sought something to say that might partly erase what she had just witnessed. "You were very brave to return."

The slave merely turned to the open portal, ignored the guard, and started down the hill. Leah hurried to walk abreast of her. "I want you to know, I do not mean you or your fellow disciples any harm." The woman gave no sign she had heard.

At the juncture of the palace avenue and another of Jerusalem's many crowded lanes, the slave stopped and turned to Leah. "Enos loves to inflict pain almost as much as he enjoys ruling with fear."

"I have no doubt of that."

"I have seen women beaten until their ribs were exposed. I have seen . . ." Nedra shuddered and blinked, dislodging a tear. "And yet he let me go unpunished."

"I told you, I intend no harm either—"

"Listen to what I am saying, I beg you. I did not agree to bring you because of my master's threats." Even though her dark eyes remained filled with tears, they burned into Leah's. "My brethren told me that the Lord our God would protect me this day."

Leah's mind floundered over what she was hearing. "Your . . . brethren?"

"They said I must return to Herod, and I could trust in the Lord God to be my shield and protector." Another blink, another tear, then, "They said this was the season of miracles, and I was to trust in the risen Messiah, the one you know as Jesus of Nazareth."

Leah felt swept away in a tide as strong as the tumultuous crowd pushing down the lane behind Nedra. "Risen?" She could hardly form the word.

The woman turned away. "Come and see."

The Tyropoeon Valley divided the lower half of Jerusalem into the Upper City to the southwest and the Lower City to the southeast. The Upper City was located on the slope of the city's western hill and contained Herod's palace and the residences of most members of the Sanhedrin. The Lower City was where most commoners lived. Leah had visited this area a few times, for most of Jerusalem's craftsmen and woodworkers had their shops along the Lower City's market avenue.

Nedra led Leah along the overcrowded Lower City market street, the crowds thick as dust. Somewhere up ahead, toward the Pool of Siloam, Leah heard the crash of cymbals and shrill cry of flutes, no doubt a wedding procession. The thought clenched her insides tight. But before the pageant came into view, Nedra had turned onto a side lane and began climbing a steep cobblestone lane. At its crest was a narrow stone-lined plaza.

As every other open space within the teeming city, the square was packed. Yet it also held a strange sense of calm. Nedra asked, "Who should I tell them you are?"

Leah could think of only one reply. "Tell them the truth."

Nedra looked at her. "It is true what you said, that you mean them no harm?"

"I have been sent for information only."

"And what about those who sent you?"

"I do not know. I am a servant. I do what I am told."

Nedra appeared satisfied by the answer. "Wait here."

Leah walked over and seated herself on the bench rimming the courtyard's public fountain. Common enough in desert cities, this was a simple pool set in an octagonal stonework frame, intended to be used for drinking and washing and supplying the neighboring houses. The people who filled the plaza were as unadorned as the fountain. Leah wore the attire given to all Pilate's servants, a Roman dress made from one strip of unadorned fabric called a *stola*, covered by her grey cloak, called a *palla*. Yet she was far better clothed than many she saw there. Most wore the sort of homespun garments used by shepherds and the poorest villagers.

Nedra emerged from a doorway on the plaza's opposite side with another woman, and all eyes turned toward them. Leah rose to her feet at their approach. The woman with Nedra was an enigma. She too wore the simple clothes of Judaea's poorest, a dress gathered about her waist with a simple cotton tie. Her head was covered in the modest fashion of a religious Judaean, a long shawl lined in pastel blue. There was nothing Leah could point to as the reason this woman seemed to catch everyone's attention. Leah herself felt unsettled.

"You are Leah?"

"I am."

"Sit, please. You are of Pilate's household?"

"Yes."

"The prelate sent you here?"

"His wife."

The woman spoke in a voice as calm as flowing water. Her gaze held a vivid tranquility. Leah also was filled with a conviction that the woman saw to the heart of her. "I'm sorry, but you are . . ."

"My name is Mary Magdalene."

The name meant nothing. Mary was perhaps the most common of Judaean names, and Magdalene could signify either a family connection or the region of her birth. Leah said, "My mistress, Procula, sent me to inquire of the prophet's disciples."

"I am a follower of Jesus. Please inform your mistress that she is welcome here at any time."

Leah blinked. The idea that the wife of the most powerful man in all Judaea would venture into such a gathering on this side of town was unthinkable. Leah doubted Procula had ever entered the Lower City at all. Yet this woman made the offer as though it were the most natural thing in the world.

Mary Magdalene added, "She suffered from nightmares before her husband crucified our Lord."

To hear of palace intrigues recounted by this woman was shocking. "How, may I ask, do you know of this?"

"I was with our Lord that day. I saw her speak with her husband."

The sorrow welling up in the woman's features was so unmistakable Leah felt it as a weight in her own heart. "I'm sorry."

"I saw Pilate's wife come out onto the veranda where he was seated. We heard later how she reported that she had been told in a dream that they should have nothing to do with the rabboni."

"I'm sorry, who?"

"Rabboni. In Hebrew, the word is rabbi. It means teacher, great one."

"My mistress continues to have these dreadful dreams—not every night, but when they come it is very bad." Leah thought back to the early hours of that morning. "Last night they were bad indeed."

"I shall pray for her."

Leah inhaled quickly, again at a loss. The offer was made so easily she could have dismissed it as meaningless. Yet she was certain nothing about this woman was either false or unthinking. "Forgive me, but who are you?"

No face Leah had ever seen held as much joy, or so much sorrow, or such calm, as this woman's. "As I said, I am a follower of our Lord Jesus. That is my whole life. Before he rescued me from my fate, I was a village madwoman. Many also called me possessed with demons. They were probably right. All I can say for certain is that the Lord healed me, delivered my life from destruction."

There was nothing in those words that should have caused Leah to weep. But suddenly her carefully prepared questions, all her own worries, seemed as meaningless as the dust beneath her sandals.

"What does your mistress wish to know of us?"

Leah forced her mind to concentrate. "Who is this Jesus, and what happened to his body?"

"He is risen."

That word again. "He was taken away?"

"He took himself away."

"You mean, he didn't die?"

"He died. He was buried. And he rose again after being in the tomb three days."

Leah would have scoffed were it not for the illumination that filled this unusual woman's face. Leah finally asked, struggling to form the words, "How do you know this?"

Mary Magdalene almost sang her answer. "Because I have seen him and spoken with him. And felt the touch of God."

CHAPTER FIFTEEN

Jerusalem
Six Days Later

LINUX WORKED HIS CONNECTIONS within the Antonia Fortress and elsewhere in the city, but despite the offer of gold, no word about the missing guards surfaced. Alban spent fruitless days searching the crowded city, in the meantime gradually learning his way around. He and Linux had taken lodging above the fortress stables, close enough for the commandant to feel he was in charge of them. Yet here they remained independent of garrison life. The pair of cramped rooms included a narrow balcony overlooking the corral behind the stables. Alban liked waking to the odor of horses and leather. It was a familiar note in this alien city.

On the sixth morning after finding Atticus and restoring him to the legion, Alban awoke to the scent of fresh bread. His servant lad must have finally arrived from Capernaum. "Jacob?"

"Coming, master!" The boy appeared in the doorway, a grin firmly in place. "I have heated your shaving water."

"Tea?"

"That is also ready, master."

"Is that lazy dog in the other room awake?"

"I have found no dog, master. But there's an officer with a look of the royals about him, and he still snores."

Alban laughed. "Have you grown since I saw you last?"

"No, master. I'm still the runt you left behind."

"I have never called you that. Scamp, most certainly. Scoundrel, almost daily. But never runt."

"That's the word the sword master used when he refused to teach me his craft."

"That will come in time." Alban sat up and accepted the hot mug. After a sip he asked, "How was the journey from Capernaum?"

"Magnificent, sire!" The lad's face was now split by an enormous smile. "I tended two camels!"

"I'm sure you were a great help to everyone." Alban nodded to the figure that appeared yawning in the doorway. "This is Linux, my boy. He is indeed a lesser royal. They decided they could live without him in Rome and sent him here to pester me."

Jacob gave him a slightly awkward salute. "It is an honor, sire."

They breakfasted on bread that Jacob had found in a shop nearby and goat cheese and fresh pomegranates. Jacob waited until Alban had shaved and dressed for the day to announce, "I slept in the tent of the Capernaum elder whose caravan brought me to Jerusalem, master. I passed on the message you sent back to the garrison with your officer. The elder said to tell you he awaits your visit."

"Excellent news," Alban exclaimed. "Well done, lad."

Jacob beamed. "Thank you, master."

Linux must have noticed Alban's relief. "You have a plan?"

"A hope, nothing more," Alban replied, then asked Jacob, "Where is the Capernaum contingent camped?"

"At the amphitheater, master, by the city's easternmost border."

The lad had the look of a young lamb, all knobby angles and huge eyes. Overlarge hands and feet suggested he had a good deal of growing left to do. "Jacob, I could use your help with something."

The lad's eyes grew round as Alban described what he had in mind. "It will be as you command, sire!"

"Take no risk," Alban warned. "I want you to go and return unnoticed. If that cannot happen, you must leave the task for Linux and me."

"I will do as you say!" Excitement captured the boy's whole being, and he looked as if he was ready to spring out the doorway at a mere nod from his beloved master.

"Do you still have money?"

The boy slipped the pouch from his belt pocket. "More than half of what you left with me, sire."

"Go, then."

When the lad darted from the room, Linux observed, "He worships you."

"His father was a minor merchant dealing in sandalwood and oil. The family's caravan was wiped out by the Parthians. He and a few others were saved alive. We gave chase, and rescued them, and I found Jacob."

"He is fortunate to have you." Linux nodded his own admiration, adding, "You make allies everywhere you go."

"Let us see if these allies can actually do us some good."

When the two came downstairs, they found a young officer in the gleaming uniform of Pilate's household guard awaiting them.

"Linux Aetius, the prelate sends his greetings and requests your presence."

Linux's languid air vanished. He straightened and demanded crisply, "The prelate has summoned me, and you've been waiting about down here?"

"Pilate said you were free to report at your convenience, sire."

"When did the governor arrive in Jerusalem?"

"Last night. Herod came with the prelate's company."

"Is the centurion to come with me?"

In response, the soldier saluted Alban and said, "Pilate sends his compliments, sire. He asks if you are ready to make your report."

"Not yet, but soon," Alban said, fervently hoping it was indeed true.

"Then the prelate says you are to proceed with your duties. He also says that your betrothal is set for next week."

Linux grinned at Alban's evident shock. "Don't tell me you'd forgotten."

"No, of course not. But . . . well, will you attend as witness since I have no family here?"

Now both officers grinned at Alban. Linux replied, "That's one skirmish I wasn't trained for. But yes, if you wish, I'll guard your back. Little good it will do you."

The only way Alban could mask his feelings was to turn away. "I will speak with the Capernaum elders and meet you back here tonight." He forced his leaden legs to carry him away.

"The greatest problem with this camp is water." The chief officer overseeing the amphitheater settlement was a young sub-lieutenant likely on his first command. He carried himself with an air of self-importance. "We have just three wells for over a thousand families. And these are not families in the Roman sense, centurion. The Judaean clans are far more extended. We have no way of determining how many people actually are dwelling here."

"I am not here to survey your command," Alban assured him. He had not wanted to meet the lieutenant at all. But a guard had challenged him as he had turned off the main road. Few of the Judaeans had horses, and the guard had met Alban with spear held horizontally to block his path. Now they stood by the main guardhouse, in plain view of anyone entering or leaving the camp. Alban said, "I have confidential business with one of the Galileans here."

But the lieutenant stood his ground. "Forgive me, sire. Romans are forbidden entry."

"Under whose orders, may I ask?" This was not what Alban had expected.

"The tribune of the fortress, Bruno Aetius. In past years, some of the younger soldiers came out here looking for trouble. At least that was the Galileans' protest. The Romans claimed they merely came to observe the city's visitors."

"There have been altercations?"

The lieutenant bristled. "Not a whiff of trouble. Not under my command."

Alban reached into his satchel and retrieved the scroll. The lieutenant's expression altered immediately at the sight of the Imperial Eagle. Alban said quietly, "I am here under orders from the governor."

The lieutenant saluted, as much to the unseen prelate as Alban. "In that case, I will accompany you."

"That will not be necessary."

"Centurion, I am personally responsible—"

"I seek the assistance of the Capernaum elders on a very delicate matter." He took his time returning the scroll to its place. "I do not wish to meet them accompanied by the might of Rome. I must perform this duty alone."

The Roman eagle flashed in the sunlight as he stowed away the document. He could feel the lieutenant's gaze on him as he walked into the camp, but the man made no attempt to follow.

The tents formed a colorful tide that washed up against the amphitheater's boundary wall. Linux had told Alban that the massive arena had been completed by Pilate's predecessor, but only after several riots, because that governor had siphoned Temple funds to finance the structure. As usual, Rome had won, and the extra money was used to erect the largest amphitheater east of Rome.

Alban endured hostile glances following him along the meandering lane between each clan's collection of temporary dwellings. The pathway was deeply rutted and fouled by the donkeys the Judaeans used as pack animals. Otherwise the camp was amazingly clean and orderly for such an overcrowded settlement.

As Jacob had instructed, Alban headed east into the morning sun until he arrived at the camp's perimeter. From there he picked his way along an outermost row of tents. The amphitheater occupied a hill only slightly lower than the city, which crowned the region's highest ridgeline.

A young lad about the same age as Jacob climbed over a rocky ridge ahead of him. "Are you the centurion Alban?"

"I am."

The lad answered in words loud enough for the men scowling in Alban's direction to hear. "My grandfather salutes you and invites you to join him in his tent."

Simon bar Enoch, the Capernaum elder, was also one of the city's senior merchants, and his clan controlled some of the region's richest grazing lands. The tent reflected his standing, and a series of interconnected chambers formed a small inner courtyard. The walls were draped with colorful tapestries, matched by brightly striped carpets piled upon the ground that made the tent's floor. Within this protected central area, children played, chasing a newborn lamb that leaped about on trembling legs.

The grey-bearded elder received Alban into the largest chamber. One outer wall was rolled up so that they looked out toward the Temple compound, its marble walls capturing the eastern light. Alban had known the man since his first week at the Capernaum garrison, but never before had Alban been invited into a private chamber with him. They had always met at the synagogue Alban had assisted in rebuilding.

"I and my family are honored by your presence." The elder gave a formal Judaean gesture, lifting his hand from heart to mouth to forehead, then swept into as deep a bow as his years would permit. "The Centurion Alban is welcome in any abode I care to call home."

Alban greeted a number of other Capernaum elders, most of whom he already knew, who were gathered in the chamber. He was granted a place of honor, reclining upon the cushioned support with a splendid view of the city towers. The elders were lying or sitting as was their preference, while the central carpet was filled with fragrant dishes brought in by women of the clan. A young woman offered a wet cloth to bathe his face and hands and feet and served him a tea made from wild mint and elderflower. Like all the women in this household, she wore a long shawl as a head covering. One end was draped about the lower portion of her face, used as a veil in the presence of a stranger. Alban took care not to look directly into her eyes. In the Hebrew tradition, he broke off segments of unleavened bread with his right hand and dipped it in the communal dishes. And he waited.

When the elder finally motioned the young women away, he said to Alban, "I understand you wished to ask my assistance with a matter of some importance."

In truth, Alban had requested this meeting without knowing precisely what he would ask. But the Capernaum elders were allies, and he assumed by the time this meeting could be arranged, something would have arisen. Which most certainly had happened.

A trio of women remained by the rear wall. The central figure said, "First, my husband, ask him about the lad."

Alban had no experience with Judaean customs in their private chambers. But a Roman woman, no matter how senior, would not dream of interrupting a discussion among elders. Yet the old gentleman merely stroked his beard and said, "My wife is concerned about young Jacob."

Alban resisted the urge to turn and speak directly to the woman. "He is a splendid lad and serves me well."

"Simon bar Enoch, if you do not ask him, I will." Her voice held both deference and strength.

The elder merely sighed and stroked his beard.

Realizing the elder might be wishing to avoid making a direct request of a Roman, Alban ventured, "Jacob has expressed a desire to you?"

The woman now spoke directly to Alban, her eyes snapping with indignation. "The boy does not know enough to ask. It is a disgrace to the memory of his family."

A few of the other elders glanced askance at one another. Clearly there was concern over a woman addressing a Roman officer in that manner.

Alban realized the elder had agreed to this meeting because of this personal matter. He risked a glance at the woman. Her eyes were rather bold, inviting no argument. "Did you know his family?"

"He is a Judaean. That is enough," she replied.

Her husband said, "A Judaean male is expected to go through a rite of passage to manhood. My wife has become very attached to the lad. She wants him to have a proper *bar mitzvah*."

"He should study the holy texts. He should know what it means to be Judaean," she added, then turned and said to her husband, "Tell him the rest."

One of the other elders said quietly, "This is unseemly—"

"No, no," Alban countered. "We are in agreement. Jacob is as fine a lad as ever I have met. We have become very attached to one another. I want to do right by him."

The tension in the tent visibly eased. The woman said, "Among Judaeans we are taught to forgive all debts on the seventh year."

"The centurion is Roman," one of the gathered elders told her. "He is not bound by our laws."

"He is bound to the lad," Simon bar Enoch noted. "He has proven himself a friend to all in our province."

Alban nodded. "You wish me to grant the lad his freedom."

Another elder spoke directly to Alban for the first time. "There are many among us who no longer follow all the edicts of the Law. Particularly about debts and slaves—"

"We should pay him," another put in. "The Law demands that early release of a servant requires the owner to be recompensed for the years of service remaining."

"First we must determine if he is willing to release the lad."

Alban always relished his interactions with the Galileans. Without the usual Roman discipline and orderliness to their discussions, they all said what they were thinking, voices overlapping one another with varying degrees of passion. They could be fierce in their opinions, yet even angry disagreement did not mean disrespect. But ultimately they followed their elders' lead. It was a remarkable balance between the individual and the group, something quite alien to Roman culture.

Alban understood the uneasiness behind many of these comments. Most of these elders possessed slaves of their own. Added to this was the fact that he was a Roman. A Roman soldier. Of the occupying force. And he had a Judaean slave, as did many Romans in the region.

But Alban was different. Perhaps. And this was the key. This was why they were inviting him into their home, why they spoke to him in such a frank manner. They considered *him* to be different.

To show he understood, Alban said quietly, "The Judaean God makes certain requirements of you."

The elder corrected, "Our God is the God of all."

"Of heaven and of earth and of all who dwell here," another intoned.

Alban persisted, "But this God makes special demands of you. He seeks to have Judaeans be slaves to no man, no other temple, no other deity. You are to worship him and follow him. And my ownership of Jacob disturbs this. You care for the boy, as do I. You trust me enough to make this request."

The entire chamber settled back and sighed as one. The woman used a corner of her outer garment to dab at her eyes. Simon bar Enoch turned to his fellows and said, "Was I not right to call this centurion a God-fearer?"

Alban announced, "I will not sell Jacob." The group held its breath. He went on, "But I am about to become betrothed. It is a practice among my people to celebrate a high moment in life with the fulfillment of an obligation."

Simon protested, "I have lived under Roman rule my entire life and never have I heard of such a thing."

"This particular tradition comes from Gaul," Alban said.

"You are not Roman?"

"To the core. But I was born a Gaul. In many respects, a Gaul I will always remain." He paused a moment, then declared, "I will free the lad. He will study for your rite of passage. He may then choose whether he wishes to remain in my service."

"We are in your debt," the elder replied solemnly.

"Wait, please. There are two conditions to my offer. First, if anything happens to me, you will personally take responsibility for the lad."

"He will enter our household," his wife declared.

"As a freeman," Alban clarified.

She nodded agreement. "I will treat him as I do my own sons."

"And second," Alban went on, "Jacob has expressed a desire to become a legionnaire. If this remains his aim, you will grant him your blessing."

The wife was aghast. "Become a Roman soldier?"

"I agree," her husband asserted.

"You cannot!"

"The lad will choose his own destiny," the elder persisted. "Even if it means losing him to the army that occupies our homeland."

"But—"

"My decision is final." The elder waited to ensure that his wife would not protest further. Then he turned to Alban and said, "You had a matter you wished to discuss."

"I have come in need of your help," Alban said, inclining his head to the group.

"On this day," the elder replied, "I and my clan could refuse you nothing."

CHAPTER SIXTEEN

Pilate's Palace, Jerusalem

"THIS WOMAN SAID SHE WOULD OFFER a sacrifice for me?" Procula still looked astounded.

Leah stood in the center of Procula's bedchamber, basket at her feet, her grey cloak draped over her left arm. Procula's summons had come just as Leah was leaving for the city's market. "The word she used, mistress, was *pray*. She said she would pray for you."

This conversation had been repeated several times now. The afternoon after Leah had returned from the plaza and discovered Procula sitting up in bed, her pain vanished. The second time was the next morning before Procula had sent her off again. And now, a week after Leah had originally visited the square.

The entire palace staff was talking about the change in their mistress. She had never suffered from such headaches as those over recent weeks, and never so often. Yet when Leah had returned from that first meeting with the rabbi's disciples, Procula's headaches seemed to have been banished. Leah glanced out the window. The morning was cool in the desert manner. The sun had not yet shown itself over the eastern hills, and the sky through the palace windows was a lovely mix of gold and palest blue.

"The woman said she would pray to her Judaean God," Procula reiterated, speaking each word very carefully, as though weighing them individually. "For my well-being."

"Yes, mistress."

"And this woman is not a temple priestess?"

"No, mistress." Leah shut her eyes, and instantly the face of Mary Magdalene reappeared. The calm and penetrating gaze, the light that suffused her features, the ethereal beauty that defied time and the woman's obvious bittersweet emotions—sorrows from the past and, more recently, healing related to the prophet. Once again Leah felt herself shaken to the core by something she could not name.

"Leah."

She jolted back to full awareness. "Forgive me, mistress. I was . . ."

Procula was watching her curiously. "You were what?"

"Remembering the woman."

"This village madwoman."

"Please excuse me, mistress. But the description does not fit her now, if it ever did. Though I doubt she would speak an untruth." Leah struggled to find the words. "Whatever she once might have been, there is no sign of such now."

Procula leaned back in her seat. Swallows stitched the sunrise to the horizon and filled the room with their piercing song. Procula settled the coverlet closer about and said thoughtfully, "So this woman invited me to come and join them."

"I do not think she meant any offense by it, mistress. In fact, I am sure of it. And then yesterday . . ."

"It is not like you to hesitate so, Leah. I have ordered you to speak freely."

"Mistress, I do not know how to put this into words."

Procula waved an impatient hand. "I command you to make the attempt!"

Yet not even her mistress's irritation cut through Leah's confusion. She began slowly, "There is nothing I can point to and say, *Here, this is what is so mystifying*. I returned yesterday and saw neither Nedra nor Mary Magdalene. I sat in the plaza for much of the day. No one approached me or spoke to me as they observed the Sabbath. But there was no sense of being excluded. They knew who I was, I am sure of it."

"They?"

"The people who filled this plaza."

"These are the prophet's disciples?" When Leah did not respond swiftly enough, Procula's voice rose a notch. "Well?"

"Mistress, I have no certainty about who they are. There is a doorway at the back of the square. People go in and out. Several times I have seen the entire plaza turn and watch someone, as they did when Mary Magdalene came to speak with me. But they hold themselves apart. I think . . . I have the impression there are people—a large group—who follow Jesus, and a smaller circle who are his very close disciples."

"You speak of the now."

"Pardon me, my lady?"

"You said, 'follow Jesus,' as if they follow him still. Even though he is dead."

Leah found her hands trembling and clasped them together in front of her. "Mistress, I have told you. Mary Magdalene believes this Jesus is alive."

"He died, and yet he lives."

Leah did not know how to answer. She finally said, "Yes, mistress. That is what she—"

"She did not say this to trick you?"

It was not the first time Procula had asked the question. Leah replied as she had before, "Mary Magdalene spoke of having seen him herself."

"The dead prophet. Who lives again."

"That is what she said. He died, he was buried, and yet he lives."

"You are an intelligent woman who has always spoken the truth to me." Procula seemed to be reminding herself as much as Leah. She turned away toward the strengthening daylight. "What do you think this all means?"

"Mistress, I really have no idea. But one thing I am certain of. The two women I have spoken with, Nedra and Mary Magdalene, they do not seem capable of lying."

The table beside Procula's bed was her favorite, set upon bronze legs. The onyx top was inlaid with mother-of-pearl. Without turning from the window, Procula reached over to trace a finger along the edge of the intricate design. "Not capable."

"When they speak of this prophet, they . . . alter somehow. They seem to have a . . . a confidence. . . ."

Procula nodded slowly. "Here is what you will do. As soon as you finish with your errands in the market this morning, you will return to the square. And you will seek to enter that doorway. You will speak with someone from the disciples' inner circle."

"Mistress, what if they do not permit me to enter?"

"Take the slave from Herod's household. What is her name?"

"Nedra."

"Give Enos my compliments and tell him you have need of Nedra's assistance. You still have gold?"

"Yes, mistress."

"Pay Enos what he asks. Go back with Nedra. See what more you can learn."

As Leah approached the door, Procula added, "Something

further. I spoke with my husband this morning. Your betrothal will take place tomorrow."

"Mistress—"

Procula stilled the protest with an upraised hand. Hard and majestic and implacable, she said, "You lost the right to choose your life's course the day you entered my husband's household. You have but one freedom left to you. One freedom, one chance to recover your family's reputation. I urge you to make the most of what is now being offered you."

The rising sun burnished the city's eastern rim, while the sky was now the deepest of blues. Swallows continued to sweep overhead, cutting swift lines through the desert morning. The dust that stirred about Leah's feet was cool as it settled on her sandals. She carried her dread of the morrow with her as she walked along a quiet lane, her mind mulling over everything Procula had said. She tried to push aside concerns over how to seek out the prophet's disciples, only to be confronted anew by the irrevocable ceremony looming over her.

Leah found solace in the everyday duty that took her to market. She much preferred the fresh air to standing over the kitchen's sweltering fires, preparing a meal for which she would receive no thanks. And even the taciturn head cook agreed that Leah obtained the best produce at the best prices.

Part of her secret was being one of the market's first customers. Normally she preferred to complete her work there before sunrise, when the produce was freshest and she had her pick as the stallholders were still setting up. Today, however, the conversation with Procula had delayed her. She hastily selected first the fruit and then the vegetables for delivery. The meat stalls would be her last visit, hopefully comprising lamb freshly butchered and poultry recently plucked.

She mentally reviewed the items as she moved quickly through the aisle of spices, sniffing her way from one stall to another, nodding here and there to vendors she had dealt with in the past, doling out coins where purchases were made and giving instructions for deliveries.

She was reaching for a cluster of leeks when a noise from the market entrance captured her attention. It turned out to be an angry stall owner chasing two small street ruffians who had attempted to steal grapes from his cart. She heard a nearby vendor utter some curses, saw another hide his smile while an elderly woman shook her head in apparent sympathy. Without turning her head from the scene at the end of the street, she reached again for the leeks.

But instead of the vegetables, her fingers closed about another's fingers. Startled, Leah found herself looking into a pair of beautiful dark eyes framed with long eyelashes. The young woman stepped back a pace, her expression flashing from surprise to puzzlement and then a trace of fear.

The girl lowered her gaze and spoke softly, "Excuse me, please. I was not watching."

"It was my fault as well. Please do not concern yourself." Leah assumed from the woman's simple garb that she was a servant in some Jerusalem home. As with many of the young Judaean women, when out in public she wore a long shawl swept up and around the lower half of her face. Even so, Leah had the impression that before her stood a lovely young woman.

"I should not have been so careless."

"We were both watching the street scene." Leah motioned at the vegetables on display. "Please select what you are after. Then I will choose."

Something about this young woman stirred deep longings.

Dark eyes contained humor even when she was trying so hard to be respectful. Leah found herself thinking of her sister Portia. As she watched the young woman, a tremor passed through Leah. How she missed her older sisters, especially Portia. They had been very close. Portia with her teasing ways and light heart. She had the ability to turn any mundane event into an exciting adventure, any day into a celebration. At least, until she became chained in marriage to a man she loathed. For a moment Leah feared that she might dissolve in tears. But she had much experience at hiding such emotions.

Even so, the young woman must have noticed her distress, for she withdrew her hand and asked, "Is something amiss?"

"No . . . It's nothing." Leah even managed an awkward smile. "Let us select together. Come. Reach into the basket at the same time I do."

The young woman chuckled softly and stepped up beside Leah. As one they reached toward the leeks, each lifting a different bundle. Leah felt like a child again. *Oh, if only* . . . But Leah would not allow her thoughts to travel further along that sorrowful memory. This was not Portia, and she was no longer a little girl. She was a servant with vital duties that awaited her. Already she had lost precious time.

Leah took one more look into the deep, appealing eyes of the young woman before her, nodded, then turned away.

Simon bar Enoch entered Jerusalem on a donkey led by his grandson, a nearly grown youth. Alban walked alongside, leading his own horse by the reins. It was easier to match the donkey's slow gait on foot. Plus he did not wish to be in a position of having to look downward toward the old man. The elder told him,

"Our Lord God has granted my clan prosperity. I can afford to take rooms inside the city for the festival. But I know what the people of Jerusalem think of us Galileans." He thumped his bony chest. "I follow the Law. I teach the Books of Moses in the ancient tongue. I keep the flame of faith alive."

"I don't understand," Alban said. "Aren't you also Judaean?"

"When we were freed from slavery in Egypt and brought to the Promised Land, each tribe of Abraham was apportioned a province. But the sons of David, our great king, fought one another, and after the reign of Solomon we were divided into two kingdoms. It was the beginning of our downfall, both because our strength was split and because we defied the edicts of the Most High God." Simon bar Enoch seemed to address Alban as he might a youngster eager to learn, enlarging on whatever Alban asked. "The region containing Jerusalem belonged to the tribe of Judah, and the southern kingdom took that name. The north, including the Galilee, became the kingdom of Israel. Nowadays the people of Jerusalem take great pride in calling themselves the only true Judaeans and look askance at the rest of us."

They left their animals at stables just outside the gate named after Herod the Great. The stable master and his three assistants were amazed at being handed a steed with a saddle blanket bearing Pilate's own stamp, then watched in further awe as the Roman officer offered the Galilean elder his hand to aid the old man in descending from the donkey.

Alban now asked, "What do you think of the Sanhedrin?"

"Most are beyond absolution. They—"

"Papa," the strong young man supporting his father admonished. "Shah, Papa."

"We are among friends," the elder replied with a wave of his hand. He went on, "Too many of the Sanhedrin are disgraceful in their habits and decisions, but still there are *haredi* among them."

"What is that term?" Alban wondered.

"*Haredi* is Hebrew for fearful. It means a devout man who stands in awe before the Most High God. A few of the council hold to the true path. Including Joseph of Arimathea, the one whom you wish to speak with today."

Alban had requested the elder's help in setting up this second meeting with the man. Alban wanted to talk with him alone, without guards. Even within his own house, Joseph had been careful not to order the Temple guards very far away. Clearly the man was beset by pressures Alban could not fathom. How the council member might now respond to Alban's request was very worrying. The man was both wealthy and powerful, and he was extremely well connected. This was not a man to have as an enemy.

But it had to be done. Alban desperately needed to confer with the missing legionnaires. He accepted the word of Atticus that the prophet had died upon the cross. Now he needed a Roman soldier's word that the right body had indeed been buried in that tomb. The longer it took to locate the guards, the more certain he became that they held the key to his own understanding.

Still, he hated asking Joseph's aid with nothing to offer in return. Yet what could a centurion manning an isolated garrison in the back of beyond offer to one of Judaea's richest and most powerful men?

Alban dragged his attention back to the sunlit avenue. "What is your opinion of the high priest Caiaphas?"

The grandson shot Alban a warning glance and said in a low voice, "His spies are everywhere. And you are Roman. This conversation is not safe, even here."

It was all the response Alban needed.

The crowds closed in, pressing Alban against the elder and his grandson. Simon bar Enoch did not seem to mind the jostling, even if it was with a Roman soldier. The elder continued, "Some of the haredi, the true religious, have forsaken Jerusalem entirely. They are called *essenes*, the separate ones, the inviolate. They have formed communities from the Dead Sea north to the Golan. They say they will not return to Jerusalem until Jerusalem has been returned to God."

His grandson murmured, "Perhaps that time has come."

Alban glanced from one face to the other. When neither spoke, he pressed, "Are you speaking of the dead prophet?"

"If he is indeed dead," Simon bar Enoch said in a low voice.

They passed the Pool of Bethesda and entered the warren of streets known as Bezetha, the city's northernmost quarter. Alban asked, "Do you think the prophet is still—well, does he remain someplace out there?"

"What I think," the younger man said, "is that your prelate scourged the prophet and then crucified him. What I think—" his tone grew more firm—"is that in speaking like this with you at all we take a great risk for little gain."

Alban nodded his understanding. "I do not wish to bring any harm on your house."

The grandson studied him a moment, then acknowledged, "Since you took command of the Capernaum garrison, there has been less trouble than under any other centurion."

"Indeed so." The elder smiled. "And it is a great thing you have done for young Jacob. To have rescued him from death, taken him into your service . . ."

"I care deeply for the lad," Alban confessed.

"Never before have I found a Roman willing to see the world through a Judaean's eyes." Simon bar Enoch pointed to a shadowy doorway along the market avenue. "Now let us see if we can convince a member of the Sanhedrin that you are worthy of aid."

A child loitered in the doorway, playing with a wooden top.

When he spotted Alban's approach, however, he stiffened, poised to raise the alarm.

Simon bar Enoch moved forward and reached out a hand to place on the boy's head. "The Roman is a God-fearer," the elder said quietly. "And all is well."

Even so, the lad watched Alban pass with grave eyes.

The three entered a dusty forecourt ringed by a dozen entrances. Alban had seen countless such places before, and he knew each door led to a humble dwelling where many family members shared cramped quarters. The trapped heat was so fierce Alban found himself recalling the stone-walled valley far north in the Golan hills. He remembered the battle that had followed and wished for his sword.

The elder led him through one of the innocuous entrances and up a set of stairs. At the top Simon bar Enoch knocked on a nail-studded door. A small gate opened at eye level, and a voice growled in a language Alban thought might have been Hebrew. Simon bar Enoch responded in the same tongue. The guard gave Alban a hard stare, and Simon spoke again, more forcefully this time. The guard unbolted the door and stood aside, glaring as Alban passed.

Inside was an astonishment of high-ceilinged alcoves circling a broad hallway. Many of the entrances were blocked by ornate drapes. Those Alban could look into were framed in carved wood and contained low tables and reclining benches. Young lads in white robes scurried about, bearing copper trays of tea and sweets and roasted meats. The boys cast astonished glances Alban's way as they passed.

An older man rushed over, nervously wiping his hands upon a towel. Simon bar Enoch greeted him formally. The man gestured toward Alban and replied with a few sharp words. Two of the nearest drapes flicked back and forth as whoever was inside cast glances his way. Finally the overseer bowed them fearfully on, avoiding eye contact with Alban. One of the servant lads led them down a hall painted with murals of idyllic desert scenes: an oasis slumbered beneath a quarter-moon, a windswept dune looked down upon a peaceful village, a caravan walked through a high-sided valley. The lad stopped before the last alcove and spoke softly. Someone behind the drapes murmured a reply. The lad drew back the drapes and bowed them inside.

Joseph of Arimathea said in greeting, "Ah, centurion. I had hoped you were the reason for this surreptitious meeting in borrowed quarters. I am pleased we have another opportunity to talk."

CHAPTER SEVENTEEN

Jerusalem

"THIS MORNING I HAD a most remarkable experience." Joseph of Arimathea stood by the window, leaning on one hand in the narrow opening while the other stroked the silver-streaked beard. "We Judaeans are called to pray at certain times each day. We pray at sunrise and again at sunset, and before each meal. We offer prayers before we drink. We will sometimes pray before ritual acts such as washing. But you as a God-fearer must know these things."

Alban did not respond. Nor was he certain he was expected to. Thus far the meeting had followed the standard Judaean practice. Their conversation had remained at a polite level while tea and sweetmeats were served by the servants of Nicodemus, in whose home they were meeting. Only when Joseph was certain Alban and Simon and the grandson were refreshed with all they desired did he rise and move to the window.

Joseph went on, "This morning, in the midst of my prayers, I had a sudden image. I watched the city come to life as sweetly as a baby shaking off slumber. It burst into activity with a song that I could actually hear. The vendors rushed toward the gates and laid out their wares. The shopkeepers bustled down the lane beneath my balcony, massive keys jangling from their belts. Potters and merchants and money changers, all there to serve the crowds who have descended upon our beloved city. But in my vision something was missing." He turned and looked at Alban. "There were no Romans."

The Jerusalem elder stood so he was sliced by the afternoon light. It caught a shimmering thread in his robe as he continued, "I wondered if perhaps it was a message from the one God that our time had perhaps come. Then my vision faded, and outside my window I heard the soldiers riding through the Upper City on their splendid stallions. I could hear their cloaks with the Roman insignia flapping in the wind. Without glancing over the balcony wall I knew what I would see. The soldiers glared from side to side, their chins thrust proudly, hungry for some small crime so they could show off their might and their authority."

Beyond the alcove's closed drapes, the establishment bustled and clattered and talked. Inside their alcove, however, the three visitors remained silent, their attention rapt. Joseph of Arimathea mused, "For most of my life, I have hated you Romans. It was one of two forces that bound us Judaeans together. The Sanhedrin, the Pharisees, the Samaritans, the Galileans, the caravan masters and the shopkeepers and the religious and the zealots—all of us quarreling and raging at one another, yet held together by our enormous loathing for all things Roman. And second, by our Temple. For religious Judaeans, the Temple means life. It is the only remaining thing that totally belongs to us. It too holds us together as one."

He waited then, as though granting Alban a chance to object. When the alcove remained silent, Joseph went on. "I despised your empire with every fiber of my being. You have no right to be here. This is the land of Judaea, of Israel. Promised and given to us by Jehovah himself. You outsiders are brutish tyrants. Because of you, we are nothing more than slaves in our own homeland. We can't even walk our own streets without stepping aside for your arrogant soldiers. A scourge. A plague."

But Alban did not hear a man filled with hatred. Instead here was a man confessing. The extraordinary admission was mirrored on the faces of Simon bar Enoch and his grandson, as though they not only shared Joseph's thoughts but already knew what the Jerusalem elder intended.

After a moment, Alban ventured, "Then you met the prophet Jesus."

"If he was merely a prophet," Joseph replied, looking out to the sunlight and the view beyond the window, "you would not be here."

Alban nodded, though not in understanding, for he did not truly comprehend Joseph's words. But they now had arrived at the reason for their meeting.

Alban said, "Please, would you tell me about him?"

Joseph continued to stroke his beard, seemingly an unconscious gesture as natural to him as breathing. But the silence was comfortable now, shared by men drawn together by a common desire for the truth. Finally Joseph said, "When he looked at me, I saw my own soul. His gaze broke through all my assumptions, all my barriers. I was stripped to the very essence of my being. He saw all my lies and my failures and all my sinful ways. And yet he loved me still."

Beside Alban, Simon bar Enoch drew a tremulous breath. His grandson sat as still as stone.

Joseph continued, "When he spoke, he illuminated a truth I had always yearned for and yet always run from. I am known as an authority on the holy texts, and yet when he spoke, I realized I knew nothing. And what I did know, I had cloaked in my own selfish interpretations. In so doing, I had turned the truth into lies."

Alban now found himself able to voice the question that had awakened him during recent nights, a question that rocked him with the fear that to know its answer would shatter his world. He asked, "Is Jesus alive?"

Joseph turned and looked at him, his features bright with far more than the sunlight streaming through the narrow window. He said, "The first time I met Jesus, I was part of a crowd coming to condemn him. We sought a reason to denounce him as just another false prophet. We have known so many, you see. Our land has suffered beneath the heel of one conqueror after another. Our people are in need of a leader who will free them from these harsh times. We await a Messiah, the Anointed One of God, who will lead us to freedom. We seek him and fear him in equal measure. Because when Rome falls, so too will the Sanhedrin. So many people have come to see us as an extension of Roman rule, surely we will be cast aside as well. I did not see this then. But I see it now, with the clarity of one whose own lies have been exposed."

Simon bar Enoch coughed and sipped noisily from his cup. Alban wished he could trust his own hand to lift his own cup, for his throat was locked tight.

Joseph continued, "Jesus told us that anyone can love a friend. Even the unbelievers do so, even the Romans. But we as believers are called to love our enemies." He paused and stared down at the floor. "I left that meeting a broken man."

Alban did not recognize his own voice. "And does he live?"

"If so," Joseph replied, looking directly at Alban, "he would be far more than a prophet. You yourself know that to be true. I see in your face that you accept the fact that Jesus died. You heard me say it, and you believe me. It is true, yes? You acknowledge that the body I laid in the tomb was cold and without breath. So if he lives, it would mean that he has done the impossible. He has conquered death. The Messiah walks among us. The Anointed One of God is here. Do you understand what I am saying, Roman?" He paused again to stare into Alban's eyes. "It means we are called to worship him as the living God. It would mean that four thousand years of prayers have been answered."

Joseph turned once more to gaze out the window. "But how did we respond to this gift? We crucified him. We all stand convicted, guilty of a crime so horrendous the very heavens shook. I was there that day, Roman. I witnessed an astonishing event. The curtain between the Temple's inner chambers and the Holy of Holies, where our Lord God is said to dwell, was split from the top to the bottom. Do you hear what I am saying? *From top to bottom*. This is impossible, for no man can reach that high. Yet it happened, without anyone touching it. Why is this important? Because it means the division between God and man has been abolished. Vanished. How? Because the great Jehovah, the One whose name may only be whispered once each year by the anointed high priest, had sent—yes, *sent*—his Son to be crucified. Why? How could the eternal Lord of all do such a thing?"

Beside him, Simon bar Enoch covered his eyes. Joseph moved across the room to settle his hand upon the old man's arm. Simon cleared his throat and drew an unsteady breath. He answered the question. "Because we could not save ourselves."

Joseph of Arimathea nodded his agreement. "So, Roman. Here we sit. Sinners bound together by the impossible command to love our enemies."

Alban felt the light pour from the Jerusalem elder's gaze. Impossible that he should feel so moved by the man's words. He was a Gaul, trained from birth for war. He was a Roman soldier upon the brink of realizing his lifelong goals. He was a man of reason, not to be influenced by outlandish stories.

Yet his entire being felt the ashes of lies and misdeeds, of selfishness and cruelty.

Joseph smiled once more, as if Alban's confused silence was

the finest answer he might ever give. "So, Roman. Tell me. What is it I can do for you?"

Nedra did not seem the least surprised, either by Leah's appearance in Herod's palace or her request. The slave did not speak until they reentered the familiar plaza, and then it was only to say, "Wait here."

When she disappeared inside the doorway, Leah settled herself down at the same spot, upon the southern wall, where the shade was strongest. The plaza was hemmed in on all sides by buildings scarcely more than hovels. The shutters and doors fronting the plaza were all weather-beaten and in various stages of disrepair. A woman passed leading an overburdened donkey laden with firewood. Sparrows pecked at the stones and drank from the central fountain. Glances were cast Leah's way but did not linger. The conversations that surrounded her were as constant and soft as the fountain's trickling water. A rooster crowed from some unseen garden. She smelled peppers being cooked in oil. But what she noticed most of all was the sense of calm. She leaned her back against the wall and drifted into memories.

Leah rarely indulged in recollections. They were so painful and led to nothing save bitterness and regret. Especially now, when she was facing yet another upheaval, yet another bitter event, on the morrow. Yet here she sat, images rushing through her mind for the second time in days. First the market and now here, both times leaving her helpless to stem the flow.

Her father had shown the world a gentle face. He affected a slight stoop, though he could walk for miles in the hills above Verona and not tire. When meeting people for the first time he often turned his head and cupped his ear, though in truth his hearing was very keen, as sharp as his mind. He had liked to smile and sing, and he filled their home with good friends. The quality of their table had been known throughout the province. He had often noted they made stronger allies over dinner than most nations did through decades of negotiation.

Yet none of this had helped them, not when his two partners had fed him to the wolves. In one season they had lost everything. Their house, her mother's inheritance, the family titles, her father's wonderful smile, all gone. Her sisters had been shunted off into marriages that had turned out to be nothing more than slavery. Leah had sensed her father's desperation, made sharper by the knowledge that any attempt to restore their former life was utterly futile. He had turned a deaf ear again, ignoring her sisters' tears and entreaties, leaving them to fester and grow bitter within the peculiar loneliness that only the unloved and ill-used wife will ever know.

Leah realized someone was speaking her name.

She opened her eyes to find Nedra standing in front of her, and beside Nedra was Mary Magdalene. Leah hardly realized she spoke the words welling up inside her. "I am so afraid, and I don't know what to do."

Leah followed the women toward the doors at the plaza's other side. The torment her words unleashed now swept about her in a whirlwind of heat and dismay.

The double doors were the height and width of a loaded cart. Inside was a traditional craftsman's residence, or that of a small merchant. They went through into a narrow alcove, fronted by a second set of doors that could be barred at night. They stepped into a narrow courtyard, perhaps twenty paces long and ten wide. The small patio was surrounded by stone pillars supporting the second floor. The shadowy lower floor was divided by chest-high walls into chambers the size of animal stalls, perhaps their original use. Or possibly the craftsman's apprentices had worked their trade here, or the merchant had stored his wares. Whatever their previous purpose, it was lost now to the tide of people gathered in them.

There was little difference between the people here and those outside. Leah saw the same clusters speaking in low tones. Perhaps there were more women in here, some seated and talking, others busy with chores. She was startled to recognize the young woman from the market, the one who had reminded Leah of her sister, tending a cooking fire. But swiftly she turned away, and Leah decided their chance meeting would go unmentioned.

A bearded man in a shepherd's robe rose from his group and walked over. "Who is this you have brought inside?"

"Her name is Leah."

"She is the one you spoke about?" The man was not so much unfriendly as concerned. "The servant in Pilate's household?"

"Yes, she is—"

"You allow a possible spy into our midst?"

"What do we have to hide?"

The man blinked quickly. "I do not think—"

"Say the word," Mary replied calmly, "and I will ask her to leave. But my heart tells me she should be granted entry."

The man, tall and broad shouldered, was burned dark by years of labor in the Judaean sun. He chewed upon the end of his beard for a moment, then turned away, saying simply, "I do not like it."

Mary waited until the man had climbed the stairs, then said to Leah, "Your mistress is welcome here, as are you."

Nedra asked, "How are her headaches?"

"Since my first day here—since you offered to pray, they have not returned."

Mary Magdalene repeated, "Your mistress should come with you and see for herself."

"That is not possible. Pilate would not permit it."

Neither woman disagreed. Instead Mary said, "I am supposed to be preparing the noonday meal. We can talk as I work."

"Please, I would like to help."

Mary smiled. "Come, then."

They passed through the narrow shaft of sunlight at the courtyard's center, the only space where the second floor's overhanging roof did not shade, and entered the kitchens at the rear of the compound. Mary Magdalene lifted her voice above the commotion to announce, "I have brought another set of hands."

A tall large-boned woman glanced over at the newcomer. "If she is as unskilled at cooking as the men who keep pestering me, I'd be better off alone."

"Her name is Leah, and she is a servant in Pilate's household."

All work ceased in the kitchen area. Finally the big-boned woman demanded, "Can you cook?"

"I can," she answered. "What needs to be done?"

The woman tended a great simmering cauldron. She pointed to vegetables piled at one end of the table. "You may begin by preparing these for the pot."

"This is Martha and her sister, Mary," Mary Magdalene told her. "There are a number of Marys among us, including the Lord's mother. This is why I am known by my other name as well."

"The mother of Jesus is here?"

"She is."

Leah saw the group, including Nedra, go through a subtle change. A curtain had been drawn, not in hostility, but in a sense of unified protection. Leah allowed the silence to linger long enough for the question to disappear.

The chamber was open to the courtyard and had another three

small windows along the opposite wall, no doubt overlooking a rear alley. Even so, the heat was stifling. Leah had endured such conditions before, however. She quickly selected a knife from utensils piled by a stone washbasin. Like everything else in the cooking area, it was immaculately clean. She washed the vegetables, stripped off the outer leaves, and chopped them into segments. The women watched her for a time, then seemed to accept that she knew what she was doing.

Leah asked, "Are the prophet's disciples here?"

"We are all his followers. But our Lord selected twelve to be his closest disciples."

"And they are here?"

They seemed to accept Leah's questions as simple curiosity, and one answered, "The eleven who remain are in the upper room, where they had their last supper together."

Mary Magdalene said, "She is Judaean. She knows what Passover is."

Leah corrected, "My mother's mother was Judaean. My father was Roman."

"If your mother was Judaean, by our law you are as well."

Leah responded to the unasked question. "My grandmother followed some of the rituals, like the lighting of the Sabbath candles. My mother, though, took pride in being Roman."

No one criticized or questioned her. Instead their silent acceptance was so natural it invited further confidences. Leah felt herself pulled in two, her mind following parallel tracks like the deep ruts of an overused road. One side sought information to satisfy Procula's questions. The other searched frantically for a way out of the impossible dilemma facing her the next day. Only the practiced movements of her hands held her emotions in check.

Mary Magdalene spread flour over the table's opposite end and began kneading dough. "Do you wish to tell us about your difficulty? You said you didn't know what to do."

"I am to be betrothed tomorrow." The words brought glances from the other women. "To a man chosen for me by Pilate. A soldier. I need to escape, and I was hoping—well, maybe I could find shelter someplace here for a time. . . ." Leah stared at the knife in her hand. She blinked fiercely, then picked up another vegetable, holding it so tightly it was crushed nearly to pulp. *I will not cry*, she told herself over and over.

When her vision cleared, she realized the women were watching her. Mary Magdalene said simply, "That is not our way."

Nedra added, "I also came begging for sanctuary. You were there when I returned to Enos as I had been instructed."

Mary Magdalene said, "Our task is to carry the Lord's peace into every situation, into every duty."

Leah used a cloth to wipe the ruined vegetable from her hands. She continued to rub the cloth over her palms, as if to scour away her sorrow. "I have some coins," she offered hopefully.

No one laughed. Instead Martha left the cauldron and walked over. "You must find this all very confusing. But know this: Understanding comes from within, from knowing and trusting in the Lord."

She touched Leah's shoulder before returning to the simmering vat. "The men will soon be asking where their meal is."

One of the other women offered, "Know you will be prayed for."

Leah looked from one of them to another. "You would pray for me?"

"I do so already," Mary Magdalene replied. "I have since our first meeting."

Leah did not sleep. Voices chased her through endless dark hours. Her father's endless tirades against the gods, the echoes of her sisters' pleas, her mother's silent and helpless regret. She heard them all.

Only now there were other voices.

She saw herself once again standing in an overheated kitchen at the back of a narrow courtyard in the poorest section of Jerusalem. Women spoke to her, strangers who shared their duties and their words with the ease of lifelong friends. Leah tried to dismiss them and what they had told her. Despite their poverty, their tragic pasts, their own sorrows, they stood before her in strength and spoke with a wisdom that defied their circumstances.

As dawn brightened the eastern sky, their words echoed in a refrain countered by near panic. Leah rose heavily from her pallet and washed her face. The Jerusalem palace was already bustling with those working in the kitchen and stoking the fires that fed the bath's warming pipes.

This day her duties had been assigned to another. The previous evening Procula had sought her out and questioned her, then made her repeat everything she had already reported about her visit to the followers. Leah had done as she was instructed, this time leaving nothing out. Not even the way the women had responded to her own plea for sanctuary. Procula had looked hard at her when Leah had confessed her desire to escape but said nothing further to the implied plea, once again, for her mistress to spare her this day, this hour, this future.

CHAPTER EIGHTEEN

Antonia Fortress

ALBAN TOSSED IN RESTLESS WORRY. In mere hours his future was to become intertwined with that of a woman he had never actually met. The fact that she was Judaean was as great a mystery as this betrothal ceremony. To a soldier's rational mind, it sounded like all of the responsibilities of marriage with none of the benefits. Time and again he fought against the fear that he was making an enormous mistake. His simple request for a wife, one who would contribute to his successful future, had turned into something else entirely. It was now being used as leverage in someone else's hands—out of his control, and certainly out of hers.

Added to this were growing concerns over young Jacob. Alban had heard nothing since sending the lad off on his errand. He tried to tell himself that the boy was resourceful and smart, that he likely would return soon. Finally around dawn, Alban slipped into a fitful slumber.

When he awoke, he discovered two crumpled forms snoring in the other room.

Linux looked like he had spent weeks in the saddle. His lanky body was dusty and sweat streaked. A filthy Jacob sprawled upon the floor by the window, wrapped in Linux's blanket and snoring louder than the officer.

"A fine sight!" Alban stood with hands on hips. "I've been very worried! Where have you been?"

Linux groaned. From Jacob there was no sound at all.

Alban walked over and nudged the lad with his toe. "You young hooligan! What have you got to say for yourself?"

Jacob rolled over and covered his head with the blanket.

Linux muttered, "Where did he come from?"

"You're asking me?" Alban nudged Jacob again and was rewarded with a sleepy sound. "Where have you been?"

Linux staggered to his feet. "Did I make it back in time?"

"For what?"

Despite his evident fatigue, Linux summoned a grin. "You can't possibly be that relaxed about your own betrothal."

Alban nudged the boy once more. "I command you to explain yourself!"

The lad at his feet groaned. "Water. Please . . ."

Alban walked to the corner table and poured a cup from the pitcher. He knelt beside the lad. "Here. Drink."

Jacob rolled over, sat up, drained the cup, opened one gritty eye, and croaked, "I found them, master."

Alban roughed the lad's hair, or tried to. It was like rubbing his hand through oily sandpaper. "How did you get so filthy?"

The lad held up the cup and pleaded, "More." Then added, "Master."

Alban shook his head, rose to his feet, and returned with both water and ripe plums, along with the previous day's flatbread. The lad ate quickly. Alban filled the mug a third time, then ordered, "Speak."

Jacob coughed to clear his throat. "No one would say where

I might find the prophet's disciples. I could tell people knew. But they did not know me. And they would not reveal it. Not even to an unarmed lad."

Alban pulled over a chair. "The Judaeans are protecting plans for revolt?"

"No, master. At least I do not believe so. I saw no weapons. I heard no talk of battle."

Linux padded across the floor and washed his face. Toweling off the water, he demanded, "How did you locate them?"

Despite red-rimmed eyes and hoarse voice, Jacob's face shone with pride. "I joined the orphans."

Alban and Linux exchanged glances. The packs of young children who survived by picking pockets, stealing from the stallholders, and scouring the garbage heaps were evident wherever one went in the city. Despite his anxious hours worrying about the lad, Alban was impressed. "And then how did you get them to show you where the prophet's disciples were located?"

"I told them of my healing. I said I wanted to pay my respects. Which is true. They took me."

"Clever." Linux sniffed one of the remaining plums and bit deep. "Very clever indeed."

Jacob went on, "They occupy a merchant's house at the highest point of the Lower City. How the group found it is a tale told far and wide. The day before Passover, the prophet sent his disciples into the city. He said they would see a certain man and should tell him their master had need of his house. They did, and the owner gave it to them."

"You're not making up this story?"

"Oh no, master. I heard the same thing from more than one person. The disciples come and go, but they always return to the upper room where they shared the Passover meal. I heard that story too. How the Rabboni broke the bread and shared the wine and declared that this was of him, his flesh and his blood."

"Do you understand this?" Linux asked.

Jacob shrugged and shook his head.

"Nor do I," Alban said. But he recalled the conversation with Joseph of Arimathea, and his heart was stirred. "What else?"

"The plaza that fronts the house is filled with people, men and women alike. They leave, but they always return."

Linux asked, "They guard the disciples?"

"Not with arms, sire. They watch, but they do nothing except talk."

Alban asked, "What do they say?"

Jacob's young face creased with concentration. "Things I did not understand, master. They argue yet without anger. They speak words I have never heard before. They talk about Jesus being the Messiah. Some say he is, and others aren't so sure. They ask if he is to restore Israel."

"Do they ask if he is alive?"

"No, master. They sound like they are sure of this."

"What?" Linux looked offended. "The man was not crucified?"

Jacob's features showed an even deeper bewilderment. "Sire, they are as certain he died as they are that he now lives."

Linux protested, "These Judaeans are insane!"

Alban patted the boy's shoulder. "You did well."

The lad's grin split his coating of grime. "Thank you, master."

"And I should still flog you for causing me such worry."

"You'll have to leave the lad's punishment for later," Linux declared. "You are to be betrothed the hour before noon, and Pilate commands us both to report before then."

Alban took a deep breath and nodded his agreement, but he kept his gaze upon the lad. He crouched down so he could look directly into Jacob's face. There was one thing that could not wait. "Jacob, I am giving you your freedom."

The lad's face crumpled. "You're sending me away?"

"Of course not." Alban gripped the boy's arm and shook him gently. "Listen to me. Your freedom is my betrothal gift to you." He explained what he had agreed upon with the Capernaum elders, then repeated it all to ensure the lad truly heard him.

Jacob rubbed at his eyes with grimy hands. "I can stay?"

"As long as you wish. But as my free servant, not a slave." Alban ruffled the filthy head again and found his throat closed up so tight he could scarcely shape the words, "You young scamp. Go get yourself into the baths."

Leah could not remain secluded for long. An hour after she sought to lose herself in the palace gardens, she was discovered by Dorit, who had arrived in Jerusalem with the prelate and his entourage. "Our mistress, Procula, wishes to see you. And I would not keep her waiting. She is in quite a state this morning."

Leah had no choice but to follow Dorit back into the palace. "What does she want with me?"

"Something about betrothal garments. I know not what the tumult is about, but Procula is quite frantic."

Leah sighed. Was there to be no end to all the fuss over this distressing ceremony? What difference did it make what she wore?

Dorit noticed Leah's expression and admonished, "There are far worse fates than yours."

Leah checked her response. There was nothing to be gained by quarreling. Her world, her life, was totally out of her control.

"There you are!" Procula exclaimed when Leah appeared. "This is hardly the time to be slipping away! I have sent for the maid from

Herod's household. She knows what is needed and will accompany you to the vendors to choose the proper attire. Now go. You have little time. Nedra is waiting."

"Yes, mistress." Leah did not recognize her own voice.

"Here are the denarii you will need." She thrust a handful of coins at Leah. Leah knew in an instant she would not need the amount of money her mistress was holding out to her, but there was no time to argue. She nodded, took the currency, and as she walked, tied it into a corner of her shawl.

Nedra sat on a bench in the hallway connecting the servants' quarters to the royal chambers. She looked nervous and agitated but brightened when she saw Leah. "They have a chariot waiting to take us to the market street."

"A chariot?" Leah stopped in midstep. Never in all her trips into town had she ever traveled in such a conveyance.

"They say we must hurry." As they rushed toward the palace entrance, Nedra went on, "Lady Procula asked me all sorts of questions while they sought you. She is most interested in this coming ceremony. There have been messages sent back and forth between the prelate's court and Herod's. Enos has become more pompous than ever." Immediately, Nedra's hand flew to her mouth. One did not criticize one's overseer without severe punishment.

"You and I will keep that our secret," Leah said. She was rewarded with a look of pure gratitude

True to Nedra's word, their transport waited at the gate with an impatient driver and a pawing bay horse. Leah clung to the side as wheels rumbled and hooves clattered over stone-paved streets. The driver skillfully wended his way through pedestrians and flocks alike. Nedra looked terror stricken, her eyes wide with fear and white-knuckled hands clinging to whatever was within reach.

Leah wished they could just drive on and on. Through the city, out the other side, and away through the countryside—perhaps all the way to Egypt. *Or northward to Italia and Mother. . . .* But it was not long until they had reached the street of shops.

Face drained of color, Nedra descended gratefully. When she could finally speak, she turned to Leah. "This is Lemuel's shop. He carries everything you will need."

Nedra almost pushed Leah through the doorway. Before Leah stretched an array of colorful garments and shawls. She didn't know where to begin.

"Perhaps it will be easiest if you choose your head covering first," Nedra suggested.

"I have worn one when I am out, but I really don't understand—"

"You need one for the betrothal."

"It is not part of my culture. We are accepted as . . ." But she wasn't sure how to describe Roman women's place in society. Many of them, like her sisters, were viewed as chattel, to be bartered off wherever a father could get the best reward—the best bride price. That was freedom?

"We are accepted as well," Nedra was saying. "Accepted—and treasured."

"Treasured?"

"Our men—our fathers, our brothers, and our husbands protect and care for us."

"And that is shown by hiding you under this shawl?"

"It's not hiding us, Leah. The shawl, this head covering, is a declaration before man and God. His divine Law proclaims women to be of great worth and orders that they be protected. First through their father, then their husband. If the husband dies, then women are protected through next of kin. And if there are no next of kin, the community. If this is not fulfilled, Leah, it is not the fault of God's Law, it is the fault of those to whom his Law was given."

Leah had never heard the explanation before. She certainly could use protection. Would welcome it. Then a new thought seized her imagination. *Could I use this covering to provide a means of escape?* To find opportunity to become lost in a crowd, slip away with travelers, find a transport ship, flee to another land? Even flee back home?

Leah nodded to Nedra. "Which shawl would you advise?"

It did not take Leah long to make her selections. The robe she chose was much simpler than Nedra would have liked. The long shawl was matching in color, a robin's egg blue with a lining the shade of fresh cream. Nedra showed her how to take one end of the shawl and drape it across the opposite shoulder, hiding all but her eyes. New sandals completed the outfit. As Leah laid out the required coins, hardly diminishing the fistful she tied back into her shawl, the shopkeeper frowned his disappointment. In a matter of a few minutes she and Nedra were once again in the small chariot and on their way through the cobbled streets back to the palace.

Leah turned from Nedra's obvious discomfort at their speed and squared her shoulders for the day ahead. Much as she hated to acknowledge it, the occasion she had dreaded was truly going to take place. Every turn of the wheels reminded her that her future was now numbered in hours. She would soon be joined to a man she did not even know.

Leah returned to the palace to discover the baths had been temporarily closed to the men. When she entered the courtyard, she was met by two servants whom Procula had ordered to prepare Leah for the ceremony. Her feeble protests went unheeded. Leah's skin was scrubbed with soap mixed with sand as fine as flour, then gently scraped with an ivory baton intended to remove its outer layer. She was settled upon the marble massage table. Unguents spiced with the immensely expensive myrrh were worked into her skin. Her hair was washed and straightened and dried and combed into an ornate style adorned with fresh flowers. Leah dared not object further for fear Procula would revise the orders concerning the gown and insist she wear something more fashionable for the ceremony. After all, her hair would be hidden under her head covering and her oiled skin well covered by her robe.

She recalled childhood dreams in which her beloved would appear and sweep her away into a palace that would be hers, filled with love and light and song and children. Now she shuddered. Just like her sisters, she would be trapped within the locked cage of marriage for the rest of her wretched life. If only the gods—if there were any gods—had dealt more kindly with her. For the first time in her life Leah was thankful her grandmother was not here to see her now.

Alban arrived at the guard station before Herod's palace compound with Linux and Jacob in tow. Outfitted in a new linen toga, hair washed and combed and coiled, Alban looked ruddy from a thorough cleansing. The breakfast Linux had forced on him sat in his belly like a stone. He could not decide which he feared most, the meeting with Pilate or the ceremony that was to follow.

He saluted the guard and asked, "Is there someplace my young companion can wait?"

The man waved toward the courtyard wall. "There is the bench used by merchants."

Alban settled Jacob into the shade and promised, "Linux will come for you as soon as we finish our meeting with Pilate."

A young officer of Pilate's contingent was waiting for them and led them through Herod's grounds toward the adjoining palace. They made their way by large gardens filled with every imaginable flower. Birds Alban had never seen before flitted from branch to branch while fountains splashed and waterfalls emerged from palace walls.

They passed through a newer wall that separated Pilate's Jerusalem abode from that of the Judaean tetrarch. The prelate's authority and power were immediately evident. The surroundings were more austere, the military presence far more evident. A trio of officers bearing the standard of the Damascus legion waited on benches shaded by date palms. Linux and Alban saluted them as they proceeded through open double doors. They halted and bowed to the figure seated before them on the low dais.

Pilate finished dictating to his secretary, then rumbled, "Well?"

Alban's heart squeezed in cold fear before he realized the prelate addressed Linux. The officer replied crisply, "As you ordered, sire, I traveled to the Capernaum garrison. The officer in charge, a man by the name of Horax, insisted that he gave up the captured Parthians only upon receiving your signed command."

"Herod's soldiers claim that the Parthians were gone when they arrived."

Linux responded with military silence.

"Horax. What kind of name is that?"

Alban spoke up for the first time since entering the prefect's presence. "He is a freeman from Damascus, sire. And a very good officer."

"You trust him?"

"With my life."

Alban knew a moment's dread that Pilate would demand just that. Instead he addressed Linux. "You believe the man?"

"I do."

Pilate grunted. "What of the Parthian officers?"

During their morning bath, Linux had explained to Alban what had happened after Herod had taken custody of the two bandits. Herod's men reportedly had been attacked while transporting the Parthian officers from Jerusalem to the infamous prison within Herodion, the walls of the fortress city built by Herod's father. The tetrarch's men had been killed, so the report went, and the Parthians had escaped.

Linux now answered the prelate, "I traveled to where the Damascus Road meets the turnoff to Herodion. I found no evidence of a recent battle. I went into the surrounding hills and spoke to the Samaritan elders at both villages overlooking the road. None of them knew of any recent disturbances."

"None that they saw," Pilate corrected sternly.

Linux said, "The villagers have been attacked twice in the past year, sire. They keep careful watch over the lowlands. If there had been something to see—"

"Well, centurion? What do you have to say for yourself?" Pilate demanded.

Alban snapped to rigid attention and related his investigations over the past two weeks. Pilate maintained an intent silence after Alban was finished. After a time he asked, "How did you get the centurion at Golgotha to speak with you?"

"I promised him protection in your name, sire."

Pilate's frown deepened. "You gave amnesty to an officer who vanished at the height of the festival season?"

"Atticus is a good man, sire."

"He has an unusual way of showing it!"

Alban felt sweat trickle down his spine. "He is a favorite of the tribune Bruno Aetius, sire. I felt it was more important to obtain the truth than to punish."

Pilate conceded gruffly, "If he has won the approval of that old warhorse, there must be something to be said for him."

"I intend to offer the same amnesty to the tomb guards, sire. That is, if I can find them. And of course if the prelate does not object."

Pilate rubbed his chin, his fingers rasping over the day's beard. "That was very clever, using the village elder to set up a secret meeting with Joseph of Arimathea."

"Thank you, sire."

"But Caiaphas will already have heard of it, you mark my words. Nothing that happens in this city escapes the high priest's notice. Be prepared. He will call for you to give an account."

"I am grateful for the prefect's counsel."

"Now, centurion." The hand formed a fist and dropped to the gold-covered chair arm. "Tell me what you have concluded from your search thus far."

Alban was ready for this. "There are three issues you commanded me to resolve, sire. First, did the prophet die? Second, where is his body? And finally, is the disappearance tied to a revolt?" Alban resisted the urge to wipe perspiration from his face. "I have two firsthand reports that the prophet Jesus of Nazareth was indeed crucified and breathed his last upon the cross. His side was pierced by a Roman spear. He was brought down by trusted Roman soldiers who are certain the man was dead. Then Joseph of Arimathea and a friend took the body and wrapped it in burial garments, and he set it in his own tomb. Joseph has confirmed that the body was lifeless and cold."

When Alban hesitated, Pilate barked, "Proceed!"

"Sire, some of his followers are certain the man now lives."

Pilate said, "You mean the man's disciples believe he did not die?"

"No, sire. They acknowledge that Jesus of Nazareth did indeed die upon the cross. They say he has now risen from the dead." Alban swallowed hard and stared at a point just above the prelate's head. "They accept this as fact."

"This makes no sense."

"No, sire. Even so, not just his close disciples believe this. It is a story I am finding throughout the city and beyond. The Capernaum elders discuss it with utter certainty."

Linux broke his rigid stance to turn and stare at Alban.

Alban went on, "They do not quarrel over whether the prophet has risen from the dead. They argue over what it *means*." Alban related Jacob's report, adding, "I have heard similar discussions around Jerusalem's plazas. They have begun using terms that I have never heard before. The most common one is *Messiah*."

"This is a military term?"

"It is from the ancient Hebrew tongue, sire. It has been explained to me as meaning the Anointed One of the Judaean God."

Pilate's closed fist now beat softly upon the armrest. "What of your final task, that of discovering whether they plan revolt?"

Alban took a breath. "Sire, the followers of Jesus are waiting for him to tell them."

Both men gaped at him. "They seek guidance from a dead man?"

"Yes, sire."

"Not from his—what is the term they use for those chosen?"

"His disciples. I have not yet met any of their leaders, sire. But from what I have heard, it appears they too are waiting. For what, I have no idea."

CHAPTER NINETEEN

The Betrothal

THE ONLY POINT when Leah nearly wept was upon her departure from Pilate's house. She would be returning later that day and remain until the bridegroom fulfilled his obligations to Pilate and Herod. Yet as Leah passed through the gate for the second time that morning, her entire being was filled with an appalling sense of finality. She had known a similar sensation twice before—on the day her family learned her father had lost everything, and the day she left Italy for Judaea.

One of Pilate's maids held her elbow as Leah walked the cobblestone lane toward Herod's palace. Some turned her way and smiled. *How do they know?* she wondered. She was very glad indeed for the shawl's protection.

Herod's palace had never seemed more outlandish, more overdone. The overwhelming combination of coverings and drapes and mosaics and fragrances had never seemed stronger. The incense burners were filled and smoldering. Every surface she passed held vases filled with flowers. Leah knew the decorations were not for her benefit. Herod Antipas was in residence, and he demanded the immediate satisfaction of his every desire. Leah had known this about him since her first year in Judaea. Just as she had known that no matter how his eyes might track her movements through a room, she was safe. Herod would not dare make unseemly overtures to Pilate's niece.

She was led into a small antechamber and seated on an ornately carved ivory bench. Enos appeared a moment later, followed by a young maidservant. He snapped his fingers and pointed at the table by Leah's bench. "Set the tray there."

The maid's hands trembled as she attempted to put it down without spilling its contents. "Now, straighten up, child," he ordered. "You're not a limp vine. No one wants to see you all bent over like that."

Although the words were intended for the maid, Leah straightened as well. She tried to ignore the tears welling up in the young woman's eyes.

Enos said, "All right, slave, you may return to your duties. And what will you do if Herod chooses to notice you?"

"I-I will bow, master."

"And what else?"

The young girl's swallow was as choked as her voice. "I will smile."

"Go. Go." When they were alone, Enos sighed. "How I deplore the task of training new slaves."

Leah moved over in compliance with his motioning hand. Enos settled down beside her on the bench. "So this is your betrothal day. Might this unworthy servant be permitted to have a glimpse behind your veil?"

Without speaking she raised the shawl so that it framed her face. Enos inspected her gravely. "You are as beautiful as you are sad. And you are very sad indeed."

Silently Leah settled the covering back in place.

He gazed into her eyes, then reached over, filled a goblet from the carafe, and placed it in her hand. "Drink. It will help you to concentrate on what is ahead."

But that was precisely what she did not want to do. Even so, Enos watched her with an expression that allowed no argument, so Leah took a small swallow.

"You'll be wasted on the centurion, no matter how fine the fellow may look."

It was not like Enos to offer an opinion on such matters. Surprise caused her to ask, "What makes you say that?"

"Because he's a Gaul." Enos spat out the word as he might a rotten seed. "None of them can be trusted. Herod has hired enough as guards for me to know. And now your young Gaul is making us wait." Enos crossed his arms and snorted. "The best of them are scum."

"His men call him a true leader." Leah could not understand why she was defending him. "One of his sergeants told me the centurion was born to rule. Procula called him a hero."

Enos blinked slowly. "What else did she say?"

Leah paused to remember what she had heard. "His father was a chief, and his grandfather swore fealty to Rome. His eldest brother rules the province now. The centurion has risen up the ranks through merit." It was little enough to know about a man with whom she was to live the rest of her life. She sighed. "He keeps the peace in Capernaum."

Enos did not seem impressed. "The Galilee is a long ride from civilization. You'll be stuck in the back of beyond, grubbing out your garrison existence, a lovely flower among brutes and mercenaries."

"He is said to be ambitious. Perhaps we will not stay there long."

"Do you actually think this Gaul has any hope of advancement?"

"He's been promised a promotion to tribune."

Enos could not hide his astonishment. "Pilate has offered to take this Gaul into his personal staff?"

"I . . . I heard him speak the words myself." Leah was sure she should not be saying all this to Enos. She clamped her lips together, determined to offer no more.

Enos stared at her for a moment, then allowed, "The young man will find you to be a great asset."

A silver bell chimed in the distance. Enos leapt to his feet. "Herod calls. For all our sakes, I hope it's to say your centurion has arrived."

The air condensed until Leah could scarcely catch her next breath. Then a remarkable thing happened. One moment, she could think of nothing more appealing than turning away from life itself. The next she had the distinct impression that she was no longer alone.

Leah was sure she could feel the prayers, even the presence, of the women who called themselves followers of the prophet. Her mouth opened, as though she could call to them and they would hear. They were that close. Her breath slowly released from its iron grip of terror. She shut her eyes and tried to sense their voices as they spoke her name. Women who were a universe removed from her world of intrigue and tragedy. They spoke not to her, but rather to a God she did not know. In her very soul she felt sure that, just as they had promised, they prayed to him about her in this most difficult moment, and she knew the same peace she had felt in their kitchen facing the inner courtyard.

Leah had no idea how long she remained like that, resting in a sea of impossible calm. Then a sound drew her back. She heard sandals scrape across a marble floor. She opened her eyes. A wooden screen divided the chamber where she sat. On the screen's other side loomed a shadow with a warrior's form.

Leah felt herself back in the grim reality of the moment.

Enos stepped back into the chamber and announced formally, "We are ready to begin."

The rabbi was a slender man with pointed features and a wispy beard. He made grand gestures and droned so loudly the walls echoed with his strange speech. The Judaean tetrarch sat on a padded chair with gilded arms and a high back topped by a golden eagle, a miniature version of the emperor's traveling throne. Herod was attended by two maidens, one of them the young woman with ancient eyes who had summoned Leah eons ago, the other the new maid who had nearly dropped the tray earlier.

Pilate's chair was empty. Procula had offered formal apologies, saying her husband had been called away by the Sanhedrin. Leah's mistress sat on a throne only slightly smaller than Herod's. Behind the trio of gilded chairs stood an officer and a young lad with a wide grin. Leah had seen the officer often enough, as he served in Pilate's household guard, but she could not remember his name. He was handsome in the manner of one born to wealth and position. The officer observed the proceedings with a languid smile.

Farther back stood Enos, surrounded by other members of the two households.

Leah did not look at the man standing at her side, but she could feel his eyes upon her. For a moment, the chamber was so silent she could hear his even breathing. He stood a full head taller than Leah, which was uncommon, for she was taller than all of the women and some of the men in Pilate's household. The centurion radiated a sense of raw power, like some young lion whose strength and speed and claws threatened even when the beast was still.

Alban was still looking at her when the rabbi addressed him. "I asked, centurion, if you are a God-fearer."

"The elders of Capernaum have called me thus." His voice was far deeper than when she had overheard him speaking with Pilate. The sound pushed through Leah's benumbed distance, drawing up her gaze to his against her will. Alban stared at her with eyes that held an unsettling intensity. Quickly Leah looked away.

She saw that the rabbi was frowning over the centurion's response. But Herod waved a hand and declared, "I say the word of the Galilean elders is all we need."

Leah watched Herod's rabbi start to protest, then shrug his acceptance. He asked Leah, "And you are Judaean?"

She touched her tongue to her lips and whispered, "My mother's mother. Yes."

"Then by the laws set down by Moses, I am able to perform the betrothal ceremony." With a ritual flourish he produced the parchment bearing the royal seals of both Pilate and Herod Antipas. He read the document, halting at several points to explain the details. Leah knew she should be paying careful attention. But the words spilled about her like rain.

She knew some of the maidservants were jealous. They noted the centurion's good looks and saw her marriage as an enviable chance to escape servitude. Leah clenched her teeth and dug her nails into her palms.

The rabbi leaned over until his face filled her vision. "I said, do you understand the terms of the betrothal?"

She breathed a sigh. "Yes."

"The bridegroom may recite his pledge."

Leah had not been prepared to hear vows made by Alban. *Please*, she inwardly pleaded, *please don't make me say anything.*

But the rabbi's eyes were on Alban. Something deep within Leah made her feel it was only fair that she look at him while he recited the promises, though another part of her wished to stare straight ahead.

Instead she lifted her shoulders and turned to meet his gaze. She would not shrink before this man.

"I, Alban, take you, Leah, as my bride. I will depart. But upon the fulfillment of the pledges I have made, I will come for you and receive you to myself and into my household. That where I am, you may dwell also."

It was most unsettling. His eyes seemed to suggest that the day, however quickly it transpired, would not come soon enough. Leah felt a shiver pass through her body and was once again glad for the shawl veiling her face. She let her eyes drop and turned ever so slightly to hide the chaos of her bewildered thoughts.

The rabbi invoked a flowery blessing on them in what Leah assumed was Hebrew, a language of which she knew not a word. He produced a stylus, inked the tip, then passed it to Leah. "When you sign this document, in the eyes of the Law you are wed to this man," the rabbi announced in sonorous tones. "If Alban were to die before your marriage is consummated, by the Law you would be treated as his widow."

The words penetrated her numbness. Her fingers were so stiff she almost dropped the pen. "Pardon me? I don't—"

"A widow," the rabbi confirmed with a nod. "Your betrothed must fulfill the terms set in the betrothal document. But the Law now considers you married to him."

She took a deeper breath. "How long?"

The rabbi was obviously nonplussed, clearly expecting

nothing but a subservient silence from the bride. "You are asking, how long before what?"

Alban, misreading her question, answered in a husky voice, "My task should be completed in a few weeks."

"Sign the document," Herod instructed brusquely.

Leah signed.

She waited as Alban added his signature next to her own. The rabbi invoked another prayer. He held out bread on a silver plate to Alban. He took it and turned to Leah. She moved her shawl just enough to allow him to slip a small portion between her lips. It rested in her mouth, a lump as tasteless as mortar. She fed him a bite of the bread, making sure her fingers did not touch his mouth. The goblet was offered, and Leah took one small sip before settling her covering back into place. The rabbi prayed once more, then, "*Mazel tov.*"

It was done.

CHAPTER TWENTY

The Celebration

AFTER THE CEREMONY, the guests and bridal couple were ushered into an adjoining chamber. Servants hurried around the ornate room with trays of sweetmeats and honeyed wine. Leah and Alban were seated on a small dais with two chairs. The crowd talked and laughed and swirled around the two, glancing occasionally in their direction.

Leah ate and drank without tasting anything. She simply sought some action that kept her attention off the stranger seated next to her. The tiny seed of hope planted during the signing ceremony remained a mystery. Even so, the feeling was too strong to be dismissed. She felt calmer than she had all day. Could it simply be from hearing that one word, *widow*?

Alban shifted in his seat and cleared his throat. "You have lovely eyes, my lady."

Leah gave a brief shake of her head. But it was a response for herself, not him. She knew she would never be able to arrange another person's death, no matter how desperate she might feel.

"Forgive me if I do not speak correctly," he began again. "This all is very new to me. I have never taken part in, or even observed such a ceremony. . . ."

His voice drifted off. He lifted a platter toward her, the delicacies glistening with syrup. "Will you take another sweetmeat, my lady?"

"I would ask that you not call me by that title." Her voice sounded metallic to her own ears.

He put down the tray. "I meant no disrespect."

"I am but a servant in Pilate's household."

"You are also Pilate's niece. That makes you—"

"It makes me nothing but another servant. I survive by assuming no station or airs that are not mine to claim."

She was astonished that she had spoken thus. She, who went for days without speaking a word beyond the minimum responses required by her duties. Offering up such confessions was unthinkable.

Alban waved a hand, and she saw the creases of war made by the leather straps used to protect his wrists and arm from sword and spear. "You may serve in another's home this day. But you have the beauty and bearing of a lady of Rome."

She opened her mouth, intending to silence him with the same haughty retorts she used with household guards who dared cast impertinent comments in her direction. But a servant came just then with another tray, departing with the first one.

Alban picked up where he had left off. "Your gown is most becoming—"

"Nedra, a servant, helped me with the purchase." She shook her head again, willing him to stop. She did not want to hear these sincere-sounding words. "I have nothing. Not even a second name."

"I'm not sure what you mean."

"My father died disgraced and destitute. My mother dwells in a widow's hut behind the servants' quarters of an unwelcoming relative." She did not want to tell him these things, yet the words continued to emerge, drawn from the simmering cauldron that was her heart. "I sleep in the same chamber as the household slaves. I own nothing. I am dressed at the whim of my mistress and ordered to obey commands I often find loathsome. How could I use the prelate's name?" Leah stared at him for the first time since entering the salon. "So you see, my ambitious centurion, I have nothing of any use to you. Not position, not title, not even a name to help you scale your way into Rome. And legally I am a Judaean."

He met her gaze above the veil with unblinking intensity. This close, she saw his eyes held a remarkable contrast. They were not brown, as she had first thought. Their copper depths were flecked with a remarkable mix of gold. The same was true of his hair, which was woven so it fell over one shoulder, the locks bound by a simple gold ring. He wore the formal Roman toga, white save for the lone blue stripe that signified military service.

Alban said quietly, "We hold more in common than you realize."

Leah caught her breath. She had expected a lashing of anger, bitterness, spite, and disappointment. Instead his voice had returned to that same husky tone she had heard during the ceremony.

Alban rose to his feet, crossed the room, and called, "Linux."

The officer put down his goblet and moved quickly toward the centurion.

Leah knew a disquieting regret that Alban was leaving on such a note. Yet that made no sense at all. She wanted nothing to do with him. How could she possibly care how or when he came or went?

But then two men moved back toward Leah. She heard Linux say to Alban that they needed to leave.

"Soon. Hand me the satchel," Alban told him.

Linux slid the leather sack from his shoulder. "I remind you we are in Herod's palace," he said, his voice low enough that Leah could barely hear the words. "And you are not exactly a royal favorite right now. . . ."

But Alban merely motioned him away and returned to seat himself again across from her. She dropped her gaze, only to find herself staring at his hands as he unfastened the satchel's straps. He said, "In my homeland, the clan's name is a title used only by the eldest son. For all other sons, such as myself, we may use just the one name."

He looked at her a moment, as if to ascertain whether she understood the parallel with her own story. He pulled a rough woven cloth from the satchel, the sort of bundle a shepherd might use for carrying his meal. Alban went on, "Not long ago we captured a band of Parthians who had been attacking the caravan route between Judaea and Syria. Most of my allotment went to Pilate as payment for your hand. All the wealth I had managed to collect before then had gone as a first offering to the prelate, and to reward the man who spoke on my behalf."

Leah did not want to hear anything further, but she found herself unable to speak.

He unknotted the bundle and opened the cloth to reveal a wreath of woven gold. The circlet had been damaged and was misshapen. Even so, it was clearly a prize of great value.

Included with the circlet were five jewels. Leah recognized three of them as emeralds. The other two were rubies, she knew, from her dealings with her mistress's jewelry.

"I was planning to have these made into a necklace, my betrothal gift to you." Alban fastened up the bundle again as he spoke. "But I want you to have them now, if they will help you look beyond—"

"Please, no." Her throat felt constricted, as though hands were throttling her neck. "I cannot accept this."

"I will hold them in trust for you." Alban quickly retied the bundle and rose to his feet.

She sat numbly. His gaze seemed to pin her to the chair.

"My lady," he said, his voice a husky burr that drew a shiver from her. "Please forgive me, but I cannot call you by any other title at this time. I have never regretted my lack of fine words until this moment. I know that I stumble over my own tongue. But I wish you to know this: I shall do all in my power to restore to you the place and position you rightfully deserve."

Leah's breath again caught in her throat. She could only stare as he turned to follow Linux out of the room.

CHAPTER TWENTY-ONE

After the Ceremony

ALBAN HAD NOT EXPECTED Leah to be so regal in bearing, or to have such an honest and intelligent manner. She held none of the haughtiness of other Roman ladies he had known. Alban had crossed paths with enough of them to know they wore too much scent. They drew their mouths into pouts as though the expression could hide the avarice in their eyes. They wore elegant robes belted by ropes of gold, their clothes simply another opportunity to flaunt their wealth and position.

This Leah was clearly someone else entirely. She was surprisingly tall and held herself so erect as to appear queenly. Yet she moved as though wishing to go utterly unnoticed, disturbing not even the air.

Alban recalled the way she had looked at him, with emerald eyes darkened by loss and splintered by pain.

He looked to his side and noticed Jacob was speaking. "What did you say?"

"I have seen her before, master."

"Who?"

"The lady. The one beside you at your betrothal."

Linux scowled. "Did you not hear anything the lad has been saying?"

"Apparently not."

"She was at the plaza, sire."

"Leah?" Alban stopped to look directly at Jacob. "With the disciples? Why?"

"I do not know, sire. But she was there. And she spoke with someone who came from inside the compound."

"She met one of the disciples?"

"No, sire. She spoke with a woman."

Linux must have read the concern on Alban's face. "Perhaps the lad mistook her for another."

"It was the same lady as came from the governor's chambers just now," Jacob insisted. "And she talked with one of the women from inside the disciples' quarters. They talked for a long time. I know—I was watching them."

Never had Leah's bed seemed such an enemy as that night. Never had the dark held so many conflicting voices. Every time she began to drift off, she was startled back to wakefulness by the memory of two unblinking eyes the color of copper at sunrise. Alban had seemed immensely still, a man so secure in his abilities that he needed no adornment or even motion to establish who he was. He did not merely sit in a room, he took charge of the space around him.

Leah hugged her pillow to her chest and tried to tell herself that such a man as this would thrive on domination—brutally, if need be. That it was only a matter of time before her own laments joined the grief of her two sisters.

Then she remembered the centurion's final words to her and shivered anew.

When dawn finally stole through her window, Leah rose almost in relief that she no longer had to struggle to sleep. She began her duties. Procula's tray was ready long before her mistress awoke. Procula took the same breakfast every morning. Her instructions were very precise and came from the emperor's own doctor. A handful of special leaves were to be twisted and clenched but not broken. The water was to be poured over them only after it had reached a hard boil. This was prescribed against the night humors, which the doctor was convinced were behind Procula's headaches. Bread from the previous night was warmed along the edge of the morning fire until it became as hard as small bricks. Procula ate these spread with clotted cream and a sweet confection made from rose petals. One small orange when it was in season. A second mug of the tea.

In preparation for Leah's departure, Procula had a new maid, Katurah, a silent wraith from Samaritan heritage. Katurah found mornings difficult, which meant Leah could maintain at least this small portion of her familiar duties. She balanced the tray on one hip, knocked on the door, and at the sound of Procula's voice, entered the bedchamber. "Good morning, mistress. I hope you slept well."

"There was neither headache nor pain." And indeed, the woman did look refreshed. She inspected her servant closely as Leah set the tray on the dressing table. "But I see you have not slept at all."

Leah adopted the formal pose, hands folded before her, head bent. "What clothes shall I lay out for you, mistress?"

"One of the formal gowns. Pilate expects me to attend an audience of visitors from Damascus today."

Leah began brushing Procula's remarkably thick hair while the woman held a small polished mirror before her. The dark tresses were accented with henna, as with most Roman matrons. But the hair was all hers. She wove in no plaits of others' locks, a common practice among wealthy women.

Procula asked, "When do you leave for the disciples' gathering place?"

"You wish me to return?"

"Of course I wish it. What kind of question is that? Did you expect your betrothal would change my wishes? Or a few nights without my dreams?"

"Mistress, forgive me, no. It is just, I fear I am learning nothing of real value to you."

"Nonsense." Procula's tone held an implacable force. "In this short space of time you have moved from being just another outsider to someone they trust within their inner keep."

"In the kitchen," Leah corrected.

"Where better to learn what threat they pose to my husband's rule?"

"Mistress, I confess that I have found no sign of threat whatsoever."

Procula watched Leah's reflection in the mirror, her eyes dark and unfathomable. "Then why," she demanded, "was I so plagued by dreams of this prophet?"

To that Leah had no reply.

Leah was donning her cloak and preparing to carry out her mistress's continuing assignment when Herod's maid arrived to announce, "My master wishes to speak with you."

"Herod orders me to appear?"

The eyes gleamed with the pleasure of knowing more than Leah. "The tetrarch has already departed for Herodion. My master Enos says you must come now."

Leah followed the maid back through the gardens and into the smallest of the formal chambers, where Enos greeted her. "Ah. Do come in, my dear. How good of you to join me." Enos sat in the thronelike chair used the previous day by Procula. Herod's chair was placed against the side wall, awaiting the ruler's return. Even Enos would not have risked one of the servants informing Herod that he had usurped his master's seat. "Will you take tea?"

"Thank you, no."

He motioned her to a backless chair with arms curved like an open vase. "How is your dear mistress this morning?"

"She has rested well, I am glad to say."

"Please do remember me to her, and tell her how grateful Herod Antipas was that she could stand in for the governor yesterday."

Leah folded her hands into her lap, her senses on full alert. "I shall do as you command."

" 'Request,' my dear. It is hardly my place to order you to do anything." Enos toyed with an oversized ring. "Especially now that you are wed to a centurion in Pilate's favor."

Leah held herself stiffly erect. "Betrothed," she murmured.

"Quite right." His eyes were narrowed in what might have been humor. "I was merely looking ahead to that splendid day when your marriage is fully consummated."

Leah gripped the chair arms to hold herself steady and moved to rise. "Forgive me, but my mistress has ordered me to other duties, which—"

"Of course, a servant holding Procula's confidence could hardly have time for pleasantries with the likes of this poor servant." He sighed theatrically. "How fortunate you are to find yourself in a position to grant favors to those who care for you and your mistress."

Leah now understood. She slipped the pouch carrying the remainder of Procula's gold from her cloak. She balanced it on the arm of the chair closest to Enos. "My mistress has ordered me to be generous with all who assist her."

Enos rose to his feet, flipping his robe's trailing end about his arm, and as he did so he made the pouch vanish. "Come, my dear. The courtyard is particularly attractive this time of day."

He said nothing more until they were well inside the central gardens. Herod's interior plaza covered a space as large as the portside market in Caesarea. A dozen servants did nothing but tend the tropical growth. Enos led her to the back wall, where a bench rested against flowering vines and faced the smallest of the courtyard's six fountains. Enos indicated she should be seated, then leaned over to murmur, "I have news. But to reveal it places my life in your hands."

She inspected his face but found no reason in his expression to disbelieve him. "I am known to be a safe haven for all secrets."

"Which is the only reason I speak with you at all." He leaned close enough for her to smell the balm coating his skin. "Herod is in league with the Parthians."

A pair of hummingbirds flitted about the perfumed air. "Forgive me. I don't know—"

"Your centurion captured bandits attacking a caravan. A caravan, I might add, financed by Herod's brother in Damascus. Do you understand what I am saying?"

"I . . . I believe so. Herod is using an alliance with the Parthians to attack his brother, who in turn, seeks to depose him."

Enos nodded and lowered his voice further. "Herod has secretly released the Parthian leaders captured by your centurion. He asked only one thing in return."

Leah said nothing, but she thought she knew what was coming.

Enos continued, "Alban's victory means both the Parthians and Herod have reason to hate him. They are conspiring to kill your centurion."

When Leah did not respond, Enos said, "The Parthians have vowed he will not return to Capernaum. They will seek a moment when he is removed from the city and its crowds and the Roman guards. One murderous moment is all they will need." His expression held something slightly sinister. "Such news is worth far more than half a pouch of your mistress's gold."

Somehow she managed to keep her voice as steady as her gaze. "I am in your debt."

"I knew I could count on you."

"I must go and warn my betrothed."

The glimmer of mirth returned to his face. "Of course, my dear," he murmured. "Of course."

CHAPTER TWENTY-TWO

The Disciples' Courtyard

LEAH WALKED QUICKLY through Jerusalem's streets toward the now-familiar plaza. A meager breeze found its way through crowds turned irritable by the heat and dust. When she arrived at the plaza, those there seemed unaffected by the heat. Their swift inspections of Leah were accompanied by momentary silences, then they returned to their discussions and activities. Leah retreated to the sidewall that offered a narrow slice of late morning shade. She sat and stared at the razor line of light and dark that split the cobblestones at her feet. And then the thought came, *All I need to do is . . . nothing*.

Over and over the stark words whirled through her mind. She could be free. Free to join her mother. Free from being consigned to a loveless marriage. Free to return to Italy. She would be a Judaean widow, but she would be *free*.

She needed only to remain silent. Do nothing with the warning Enos had passed along. *And why not?*

It was not as though she held the dagger. She had not enraged the Judaean tetrarch. She was not the assassin. She was not arranging anything.

If she simply sat and waited, it would be done for her.

All that would be required of her was to allow a good man to die.

"Leah? Why haven't you come inside?" A woman's form enlarged the shadow at her feet. "We've been so concerned. How was the ceremony?"

Leah grew aware that she was rocking slowly, back and forth, like the religious Judaeans who filled the streets about the Temple on the Sabbath and the High Holy Days. She stilled herself by gripping her arms against her waist. "I am ordered by the prelate's wife to come here day after day. I am commanded to report back what I find. But no one will explain what everyone is talking about, or what is *happening*."

"The answer to what they discuss and why you are kept at a distance are closely linked." Mary Magdalene seated herself beside Leah and laid a hand on her arm. "Four weeks ago, everyone you see here was in mourning because our beloved Rabboni had been crucified. His death was ordered by the man whose wife has sent you here.

"But even so they do not weep and wail and accuse the Romans—or even Pilate—of robbing them of the most important person in their lives, the man whom they expected to become their king. The Anointed One, sent to restore Israel and purify the Temple. They have not turned away from you in anger or with accusations, dear girl. And actually, they have questions that are not all that different from the ones you bring."

She caught Leah's hand. "Now, Leah, tell me about the ceremony."

Leah shook her head, tears pushing behind her eyelids. The

truth was, she could not. Not without confessing to the dreadful temptation that tore into her soul.

She had not wept the day the ship pulled away from the Venetian harbor, wrenching her away from her beloved home and mother. She had not wept at the news she was ordered to wed a man she had never even met. Yet here she sat, in a narrow strip of shade at the edge of a sunbaked plaza, surrounded by people who would prefer she stay away, listening to a woman ask about her betrothal in most loving tones.

Leah wiped her face and took a deep breath. "I don't understand why, day after day, I am forced to return here." She turned to stare at the woman beside her. "I have told Procula that your prophet is *dead*."

Mary's gaze was now fastened on a doorway at the plaza's other end. "At the start of the week after Passover, after the terrible crucifixion, the Master's disciples were gathered in a room above the courtyard. We had prepared a meal, and they were eating. Or rather, they would have been if they had not been so troubled. And confused. Because, you see, I had told them that I had met the Master."

Leah blinked fiercely to clear her eyes. "You met the rabbi. Jesus."

"Yes."

"After he died."

"On the third day after his crucifixion."

"You mean, you believe you saw his wraith."

"It was no being from beyond the grave that I saw."

"How can you say such a thing?"

"I reached out to embrace him, and he told me I should not do so. That he had not yet been brought before his Father. So I knelt with the others and touched his feet."

"Others?"

"There were other women with me. We saw wounds where the nails had been driven through his feet into the wood of the cross." Mary stopped, still staring at the distant doorway. Then she said, "I went back and told the disciples. Several ran to the tomb and saw his burial garments. Among them was his prayer shawl, the folded cloth that had been settled around his head in the burial. Peter saw this and believed. So did John. Others did not." Her gaze had moved to the shuttered windows above the ancient doors. "That night the disciples gathered in the chamber and locked the door because they feared the ones who have sent you. Which was understandable, for these same people had crucified our Lord."

Until that moment, Leah had not realized many of these followers of the prophet were afraid of her. She was viewed as one with the Roman power that had killed their leader.

And despite this they had not sent her away, had not excluded her from the group.

Mary Magdalene, now watching Leah closely, went on, "And then it happened."

Leah searched the face looking into her own. What made Mary Magdalene so unique—and so believable—was her *innocence* in spite of her past. Her face was filled with a purity as intense as the sunlight. "What happened?"

"While they debated our report, arguing over what we had seen and whether we had seen it, and the significance of the empty burial tomb, Jesus came. Though the door was locked, he appeared. He stretched out his arms and he said, 'Peace be upon you.' He asked for a bit of fish. He showed them the places where the nails had pierced his hands and feet."

"This man who was crucified."

"Yes."

"And died. And was buried." Leah shook her head. "I do not understand how you can believe this."

"Most of all, Leah dear, it is your unbelief that isolates you from the rest of us."

Leah was stung. "I do not understand how so many people can sit here, day after day, arguing over whether the man they once knew has done the impossible."

"You misunderstand." Mary Magdalene swept one hand about, encompassing the crowded plaza. "These people no longer argue whether the Master has risen. The time for doubt is over. The Lord has appeared four times now. Twice to the men inside the locked upper room, once to his followers upon the road to Emmaus, and also, as I told you, to several of us outside the grave that could not hold him."

Leah shook her head so her entire body swayed. "No. *No.*"

Mary Magdalene persisted, "What occupies us now is *why*. But before you can begin to delve into the why with us, you must first conquer your own unbelief."

Leah found frustration welling up to where she almost shouted the words, "I do not understand why my mistress insists I return and ask about such things. The man is *dead*. It is *finished*."

About the plaza, people shifted around to stare at her. But their expressions were not guarded or suspicious. They seemed to look at her with calm acceptance.

Her companion rose to her feet. "Would you take a walk with me?"

Mary Magdalene went back inside the inner keep and returned bearing a cloth satchel, the sort of shoulder bag that many local women carried when purchasing bread, vegetables, or other wares. Mary Magdalene cradled it within both of her arms, clutching it tightly to her chest as they passed through the crowded market lanes.

They walked down the central craftsmen's avenue, which ran in a straight line from the Upper City boundary to the Dung Gate.

The farther they traveled away from the Upper City, the more basic and primitive became the market stalls. Beyond the Pool of Siloam, the alleys branching off to either side were occupied by leather workers and tanners and butchers. Leah had never left the city by this gate. She had no reason to, since this led to the juncture of the Kidron and Hinnom Valleys and the city's burial grounds.

Mary Magdalene must have noticed Leah's rising unease, for she said, "Have no fear."

Beyond the gate they took a path that led them along the valley floor. They entered a grove of desert pines, stunted trees clustered together like a crowd of old men. But the shade was welcome and the trees scented the air with their resin. Mary Magdalene said, "The last time I walked this path was just before dawn on the Sabbath after Passover. The soldiers had cut my Master's body down from the cross. . . ."

She faltered, and tears dimmed her eyes. She tripped over a tree root and would have fallen if Leah had not been there to catch her arm.

"This is more difficult than I thought," Mary whispered.

"Here, sit yourself on this rock. Shall I fetch water?"

"No, no, join me, please."

"There is not room."

"We can make ourselves small." Mary sidled over and patted the surface beside her. "Please."

Uncertainly, Leah settled onto the cool stone. In truth it felt good to give her feet a rest. The day was hot enough for the cobblestones to have baked through her sandals.

Mary Magdalene stared at the sunlit expanse beyond the trees. "A wealthy man by the name of Joseph of Arimathea was a secret follower of our Lord."

"I know that name." Leah recalled overhearing the discussion between Pilate and Alban. Her mind leapt from there to the choice

Enos had unwittingly placed before her. The scalding indecision bit deeper still. She cleared her throat. "This Joseph asked Pilate for the prophet's body."

"Joseph of Arimathea's burial chamber is carved from the hillside just over there," Mary said, pointing. "Several of us followed him and another man, Nicodemus is his name, as they brought our Lord here. They were hurrying, for the Passover Sabbath was approaching. I was in no condition to recall the exact hour though. The sky was bleak and dark as my heart. You see, if Jesus was dead, then he was not who we had thought him to be, for Jehovah cannot die. He was not the Messiah as we had expected. He was an imposter. We were all overcome with despair. We held one another and wept—not just for him—but for ourselves as well."

Mary lifted an edge of her shawl and wiped her eyes. "We returned before dawn on the first day of the week. We had agreed to meet here at sunrise, and I was the first to arrive. I was in this grove, almost in this very spot. The earth shook and I saw a flash of light beyond the trees. I was frightened at the earthquake and waited for a while. When I thought it was safe to approach the tomb, the stone was gone, and the soldiers were no longer here. The tomb was empty. Angels told my friends, who had by now arrived, that the Lord was gone from this place. I did not understand and could only stand outside and weep.

"And the Lord appeared to me."

Mary looked a long time into Leah's eyes, then reached into the satchel and pulled out a beautiful alabaster urn. "Each of us had come with spiced ointments to embalm our Master's body. There had not been time to do so before the Passover began. But they were not used."

"I . . . I don't understand."

"My Lord was alive. Alive! There he stood before me. The

knowledge of my forgiveness washed over me again. I was free. Free from my sin. From my wretched past. I could see it in his eyes—and then he spoke my name. Just my name. But it told me everything I wanted to hear."

Leah realized she was trembling. Tears were running down her own cheeks, though she could not have said why. She wiped them quickly on a sleeve and tried to shake off the intensity of her emotions.

Mary went on, "He didn't stay with us for long. I was anxious to return and tell the others that he was alive. I assumed he would be with us again as before. But it is different now. As I said, he has visited us several times, but I feel . . ." She shook herself as though to bring her thoughts back in line. "We are fickle people at best. The enemy of our souls takes full advantage of that fact. Shamefully, I admit that in the days following, I had times of doubt. Had I been dreaming? Was it a cruel vision? Had it been wishful thinking that had brought me to simply fanciful thinking?

"That morning I returned home with the jar of spices." She held the jar out in front of her. "Each morning when I would arise, I would look at the jar and I would say to myself, 'We went to the tomb to anoint him for his burial. He was not there. He had risen, as he promised.' As I said the words, relief washed over me in the knowledge that it was true. It is as real as life itself."

For a moment the jar was poised between her hands, then she held it out to Leah. "I want you to have this."

She knew how much the jar of spices meant to Mary, how expensive it was, both the alabaster itself and its contents. "I can't accept it."

"The jar is now yours. I don't need it any longer, Leah. I am fully assured that he is alive. Even on the days I do not see him." Love shone from Mary's face. "Because I accept this, I am beginning to understand now why he had to die. He was the sacrifice for our sin. Not just mine. For all of us. The perfect Lamb that God promised to send. But this work is finished now—just as he said. Through him, we no longer stand condemned. It is almost beyond comprehension. We are free, Leah. Forgiven and free."

Leah's numb fingers closed over the base of the jar. Her entire being struggled against the words. But how she wished it were true. *Free . . .*

Mary rose from the stone. Silently she rested a hand on Leah's shoulder, then slipped through the trees and away. Leah stared at the point where the woman had disappeared. Sunlight and heat caused the vista beyond the trees to waver, as though out there was a flimsy dream, and here was what was truly real. She did not want the jar. She wanted nothing more than to walk away from the gift, from Mary's explanation, from the woman's obvious conviction. If only she had not been given this assignment from her mistress.

Leah had no idea how long she remained where she was, sheltered by the stunted trees and holding the alabaster urn. Mary's words about the risen man echoed through the silence. How was it possible for the woman to speak with such utter conviction about a dead man come to life and appearing to people within a locked room? Leah rose to her feet, set the urn and satchel on the stone where she had been seated, and began pacing among the trees. Her thoughts were as twisted as the roots lining the rocky soil beneath her sandals. Hope was a lie told to children. She would never hope again. She would never let herself be destroyed by expectations of a change in her circumstances, of a man who truly loved her, of the promise of security and safety and redemption. Never.

Then she heard footsteps.

CHAPTER TWENTY-THREE

The Burial Grounds

LEAH COULD SCARCELY TAKE IN what her eyes revealed. A moment before she had been alone, torn by her uncertainties and fears. And now Alban himself was walking down the trail, not far from her secluded place among the trees.

She froze as Alban turned in her direction. The intensity of the man's gaze reached across the sunlit expanse. Only when he scanned further around the perimeter did she breathe again.

The awareness that she, his betrothed, was a danger to him struck her heart with a dagger's force. Leah sought to push it away with silent insistence that it was not she who sought his life.

But though dressed in the garment of reason, the lie still rankled.

She heard Alban command, "Come here."

Her heart caught in her throat until a man replied, "Sire, I would rather—"

"I did not ask your preference, Crasius. I gave you an order!"

Leah carefully moved back another step, deeper into the trees, but kept the two men in sight. Alban wore a simple toga and sandals laced about his calves. He bore no weapon she could see save a knife sheathed at his belt. The satchel slung from his left shoulder was almost identical to the one Leah carried. The second man also wore simple Roman garb and bore what the maidservants called a soldier's mark. This was the callous stretching from beneath the ear around the top of the neck, where the helmet's leather strap chafed against desert sand. This man looked terrified.

"Sire, I came as you asked." He waved weakly toward the same trees where Leah stood. "Can we not step into the grove out of the sun?"

"The prophet's grave is here. Here we will remain."

The man wiped at his face with his arm and turned so his back was against the cliff's face. "Is it true what your message said?"

"I am a man of my word, Crasius. Tell me what I need to know, and I will offer you protection. You and your mate."

"How can anyone protect us from Pilate?"

"I carry a scroll bearing the prelate's own seal, granting me the authority to do whatever I deem necessary to carry out my orders." He patted his satchel. "Do you wish to study it?"

"I cannot read."

Clearly Alban had expected the response and waved it aside. "You are not a novice recruit. You know the punishment for deserting your post. There is no safety for you except through me. And all I need from you is the truth." When the soldier did not respond, Alban barked, "Speak, man! Your future depends upon it."

The soldier groaned, "I cannot."

Leah felt her entire body clench at what was likely to come next. She knew Roman legions ran on absolute authority. A centurion held the power of life and death. Justice was swift and brutal. Floggings, beatings, flaying the skin with iron combs—all were common practices among the legions. A soldier who disobeyed a direct command, as this soldier had just done, could only hope that his death would be swift.

Alban walked forward and gripped the man by his arm. "Come."

"Sire, mercy, I beg—"

"I said, come." But Alban's voice had gone mild, and he drew the trembling soldier to where a rocky overhang offered a narrow shadow. He pointed to an outcropping that jutted from the cliff like a shelf. The man now looked baffled as Alban guided him onto the natural seat. He pulled off his satchel and drew out a water flask. "Drink."

When the soldier tried to return the flask, Alban motioned for him to keep it. "You strike me as a good enough soldier. You do your duty and ask nothing more than a clean berth and a fair officer to whom you can report. Am I right?"

The man nodded as he, hand shaking, lifted the water bottle and drank again.

"The might of Rome is built upon the shoulders of men just like you. And when an officer gives you a command, you obey. But this time you have not. Why? The reason for the disobedience interests me as much as the reason you left your post."

"Sire, you wouldn't believe me." Leah could barely hear the man's answer.

"Were you drunk while guarding the prophet's tomb?"

"I had only watered wine with my meal, as I do every night. Nothing more. And nothing once I was sent from the garrison out here."

"What about your mate?"

"He was sober as I."

"I believe you. You see? Already I accept you as an honest man. So now I ask only that you tell me what happened. Everything."

The man shuddered and drank again. Leah could see his terror even from her hiding place thirty paces away.

Alban waited the man out.

Leah found his patience most disconcerting. Alban was nothing like she had expected, nothing like her own nightmares. All the strength and masculine force she had come to equate with brutal command were present, yet there he quietly stood, leaning calmly against the cliff wall, half in the shadow and half out, ignoring the blistering heat and the rising wind. Showing in a manner stronger than words that he was no threat to the terror-stricken soldier.

No threat. The concept was as strong as a conviction. She glanced back at the urn resting on the stone. Though the top was sealed with wax and bound with taut cord, a faint fragrance filtered through, of wild flowers and impossible hope.

Alban was not by nature a patient man. He found waiting one of his most onerous duties. Waiting for patrols to return, waiting for orders, waiting to be noticed, waiting for promotion, waiting for just that chance that would propel him upward. Even so, he restrained his impulse to press the man further.

Crasius had the look of a solid enough soldier. Strong, steady, experienced at battle. Yet he was clearly terrified. And Alban was sure it was not merely the threat of punishment that frightened him. In fact, the soldier obviously wished to flee *despite* the dire consequences.

Alban tested the man, searching beyond what he saw, probing, guessing. "You did not flee your post because of an attack. Something happened. Something beyond your abilities as a soldier."

The man's words emerged broken. "The entire world shook."

"There was an earthquake. Was that what frightened you away?"

"No. No, it was not that."

Alban already suspected as much. Earthquakes were common enough in this region, and no soldier would use such as an excuse to leave his post. Besides, there was no evidence around the site of violent tremors, no cracks in the earth, no pile of rocks shaken from the hillside.

Alban crouched to where he was eye level with the soldier. "Look at me, Crasius. Now listen well. I have been sent by Pilate to search out the truth about this prophet and his disappearance. Do you hear what I'm saying? All right. Good. Now I will make a confession of my own. Nothing I have heard so far makes sense. I too am a soldier. I receive an order, I obey. I see an enemy, I attack. But everything I have learned about this prophet, about his death and burial, only adds to the mystery."

The soldier nodded, took a ragged breath, then said, "There was an earthquake, as I told you. And then two . . . two beings . . ."

"Men?"

"Perhaps."

Alban slowly repeated, "Perhaps you saw men. Perhaps."

"They shone like lightning. Perhaps they caused the earthquake. I cannot say. But when they appeared, I froze." The words now tumbled from his mouth. "I have fought Rome's battles for nine and a half years. I have known a soldier's fear. My mate is a good man, a good Roman. And he fell over like he was dead."

"Because two men appeared bearing light."

"They did not *carry* light. They *were* light. And as I said, they might have been men. But I . . ." He wiped sweat from his face once more. "One of them—with no effort at all—rolled the stone set before the opening to the side. It had taken four of us to roll it into place. And then this . . . this man sat on that stone."

Alban gave that a pair of breaths. "Did the prophet walk out?"

"I stared at the opening. The other creature went into the cave, and his light was so strong I could see everything. The tomb was already empty."

"The prophet left during the earthquake?"

"The earthquake struck. The creatures appeared. The stone was rolled back. The cave was empty. It happened in that order."

"They rolled away the stone from a tomb that was already empty."

The man just stared numbly back at Alban.

"Could you have guarded the wrong tomb?"

"No, sire, we did not. We watched as the body was placed there. We put the stone in place and watched while the governor's own seal was placed on it. We stood our duty where we were ordered, before that same tomb."

Alban realized there was nothing to be gained by insisting that what the man reported was impossible. Crasius spoke as a good soldier would. The thoughts were set in marching order, although the man was gripped by tremors and his eyes searched even now for escape.

Alban said quietly, "Now tell me the rest."

The man looked away, took another breath. "It felt like these creatures were shining their light inside me. I saw everything I had done. Everything I had ever *thought*. That's why I could not move." He looked back at Alban. "I have followed orders all my life. I have done as I was told. But all of that meant nothing. These were my acts, my decisions and choices. This was *my life*. I was filled with a loathing and a dread. My time will come, and one day I will be seen as the person I really am." The man dragged his focus back to Alban. "The prospect has torn my nights to shreds."

Alban knew the man was waiting for him to scoff, to threaten, to rage. But he could not, because his instincts told him the man spoke truth. He steeled his emotions and held his tone even. "And your mate was knocked unconscious."

"He swears he remembers nothing." The man looked at Alban with eyes hollowed by fear and lack of sleep. "I wish it had been me there sprawled upon the earth."

"And then?"

"I finally got my mate up, and we fled. We went to the high priest's house. We were under his command. He was with some of the others—"

"The Sanhedrin."

"We tried to tell them what had happened. They would not believe us, but finally they gave us money and ordered us to say that the disciples had come and stolen away the body. They said they would protect us from Pilate and the tribune."

Alban straightened slowly. "They cannot, but I can. Report back to your garrison commandant."

The man looked up in disbelief. "I am free to go?"

"You and your mate both. If anyone asks where you have been, tell them the truth. You were under orders from Caiaphas until I ordered you back to garrison duty. If they want more details, tell them you are under Pilate's orders to say nothing more about the incident, and they should speak with me."

Alban waited until the man stumbled away. He then turned, took his own very hard breath, and moved toward the tomb.

To Alban, the tomb appeared to be the large sort of chamber a wealthy man might order carved out for himself and his family. The opening in the cliff face was reached by five steps. Stonemasons had fashioned a wheel of stone set into a narrow groove. Once the body was laid in place, the wheel would have been rolled along the groove, sealing the tomb.

Above him, other sealed tombs were joined to narrow trails cut from the cliffs. Most of the other tombs he could see had openings that would require crawling through them. This one, however, was tall enough that Alban would be able to enter simply by bending his head.

Alban rested his hand upon the stone wheel, observing the shattered wax seal. The diameter was that of a village millstone, rising to his chest. He believed the guard. It would have required several men to roll it into place.

Alban bent down and entered the tomb. It held to the common form, with an area three or four paces wide where family and friends could gather to mourn. The north wall was carved into a shelf large enough to hold two bodies, perhaps three. The air felt cool in spite of the day's heat. Alban reached over and touched the shelf. He ran his hand along the smooth surface, searching through his fingertips for answers his mind could not fathom.

He no longer questioned whether the prophet actually was laid here. He was also fairly certain that the prophet was indeed dead at that time. He knew crucifixions. He knew Roman soldiers. And he also trusted the word of Joseph of Arimathea. The man had carried a cold body and laid it in the tomb, wrapping the prophet in burial cloth. Joseph had handled a dead man. And he had help from another member of the Sanhedrin, another who was witness to the facts. Both men were acquainted with legalities and proper testimony.

So the prophet had been crucified, died, was taken down from his cross, brought here, and laid in this tomb. On this shelf. The tomb had then been officially sealed. Guards were stationed.

Then, according to every witness he had confronted, the impossible had happened.

Alban moved along the stone walls, probing with his fingers, tapping with the hilt of his sword, feeling his way over every surface. Was there another exit in the back or on one of the sides? Nothing. Not even a seam of any kind. The tomb was carved into solid rock.

He went over the floor of the tomb in the same manner, then turned his attention to the ceiling. Again, nothing. There was no way anyone could have exited the tomb in any other way than through the one opening. The one closed by the heavy stone and sealed.

He stood a while in thought, then ducked his head to emerge into the brightness of the sun. That along with his confusing whirl of questions caused him to squint and frown. Either a group of people, many of whom had never met one another, had developed an elaborate conspiracy to hide the truth from Pilate . . . or Alban had found it.

He lifted his head at a glimpse of movement across the clearing between the tomb and the trees. The figure of a woman struggled to move forward, her eyes glistening with tears.

He shook his head to clear his vision in the brilliant sun.

"Leah?"

CHAPTER TWENTY-FOUR

At the Tomb

THE FIRST WORDS Leah spoke betrayed emotions he could not comprehend. “I don’t know what to do.”

Alban stepped forward quickly. “Here, let’s move over into the shade.”

She allowed him to guide her back into the trees, as helpless as an invalid.

Alban bent his head. “May I ask what has brought you out here?”

She whispered again, “I don’t know what to do.”

He glanced around, saw nothing save a pair of crows stalking a mouse. “Are you alone?”

“I came with . . .” She shook her head a trifle. “It doesn’t matter.”

“You came with someone.” Alban spoke in hopes it would steady her. The expression in her eyes worried him. He had seen that shocked, confused gaze when riding into villages after bandits had left. Mothers staring at the ashes of their homes, but seeing only a life broken beyond repair. “A woman? A woman brought you to the tomb where Joseph and Nicodemus laid the prophet. Did you know where you would be going, Leah? Is that why the woman brought you here?"

When her only response was to begin weeping anew, he motioned her over to a rock. "Here, sit on this stone. Would you like water? No, I don't have any. The soldier . . . Never mind. Is that water you're carrying in your satchel?"

She made no protest as Alban lifted the satchel from her shoulder. She watched him pull out the jar. He asked, "What is this?"

Her voice was low and hoarse. "I suspect from the fragrance it is nard."

"Is it?" He sniffed the top. "Why are you carrying this perfumed oil?"

"She . . . Mary gave it to me."

He slipped the vessel back into the satchel and placed it on the rock beside her. She gripped it with both arms, hugging it to herself.

"Should I know this woman friend of yours?"

"She was . . . was the first to see him."

"First to see . . . ?" Somehow he knew the answer, "She saw Jesus?"

When she nodded, Alban knelt in the dust by her feet. There must have been a few eucalyptus trees among the grove, for the scent was suddenly very strong, as though it clung close to the earth and was more noticeable when he was on his knees. "Leah, please. This could be very important. Who is this Mary?"

"There are many Marys." She sniffed and pulled an end of her shawl up to wipe her eyes. Her hands were shaking along with the rest of her. "What have I done? I'm so confused. . . ."

Alban slowly reached for her hand, making certain he did not alarm her. The palm was wet with her tears. "You are safe now."

"I will never be safe."

"That is not true. I know how—"

"You do *not* know. You can't."

A rock dug into his left knee, but Alban stayed as he was. There was bound to be more at work than whatever this woman Mary told Leah. But he sensed that if he asked her directly, she would flee. He held to a patience he did not feel. "Can you tell me who all these Marys are?"

"They are with the prophet's disciples."

"Ah. I heard you were seen with them. Why did you go there?"

"Procula, my mistress, she sent me."

"So this Mary is among the disciples. But why did she bring you here, Leah? Can you tell me that?"

She stared at his hand holding her own. "To give me hope."

Alban had the impression that she wept that last word. "Did this Mary flee when she saw me arrive with the soldier?"

"She left before you came."

"You said she was the first to see Jesus. See him when?"

For some reason, his question caused Leah to go very still. Finally she said simply, "After."

"After the disciples stole his body."

"They did not steal him."

"Then . . . after he left the tomb on his own?"

"Yes."

Alban eased his legs so he now sat on the ground by her feet. "Do you believe that, Leah? Do you think this prophet Jesus actually lives again?"

"They do."

"Yes. I understand that." He saw that Leah no longer wept, and her breathing came more steadily. "What do *you* think?"

She looked around fearfully as though she suddenly realized

who she was, where she was. "We should not be here like this. Together."

"We are betrothed."

"But that gives us no right. It is not proper. Judaean custom forbids us to be alone."

"I am Roman. You are—"

"We did not take the vows under Roman law. You took the betrothal vows as a God-fearer and I as a Judaean. Either we are betrothed, with the Judaean customs in place—or we are not."

"We *are* betrothed."

Leah nodded, her eyes meeting his briefly. He could not tell if it was relief or fear he saw reflected there. He heard the deep sigh and saw the quiver of her shoulders beneath her shawl. "I am so afraid."

"Tell me how I can protect you, Leah."

She turned back toward him and raised fathomless eyes toward his. The tears still glistened in the corners. "I am so afraid of hope."

"Ah. I understand." And he was quite sure he did. "It is not merely hope, is it? It is also trust. In me."

A single tear trickled from her eye as she nodded.

Alban held back. There was much to tell her of his life. But not now. "Who has hurt you, Leah?"

Another tear disappeared beneath the shawl drawn across her face. She whispered, "Life. My father. Even my mother . . ."

"Tell me," he invited softly.

"We were a happy family. My father was a good man." The words gradually gained momentum as she began. "I was the youngest, and Father rather pampered me. Mother moved easily among the wealthiest and most prominent families of Verona." Her voice trailed off as though her thoughts were going back to a place she had not visited for a long time. Then, "Father was a good man. I loved him dearly. And then it all changed. He lost everything. Mother became ill with worry. Our friends vanished. Young men stopped calling upon my sisters. And Father . . . he changed utterly. He became angry and belligerent. He forgot about others and buried himself in solitude and self-pity. He married off my two sisters into dreadful situations. Eventually he would have arranged for my marriage as well, given enough time. I remember my sisters pleading, crying, but to no avail. I watched them both taken away. Still in tears, still begging. I couldn't understand how Father could have betrayed us so. Before, he had loved and protected, yet then . . ."

She stopped briefly to wipe new tears. "Word soon came that the brute who had married my dear older sister Portia had changed his mind. He had met a woman who promised a large dowry, so he divorced my sister and thrust her out of his home. She was left alone and penniless. He told her she could make her own way on the streets."

Alban reached for her hand once more. There was no other way for him to share her deep sorrow. No words with which to comfort her.

She stiffened, and he was afraid she would refuse to take his hand again. But she didn't seem to even notice. "They found her in a canal," she said simply, but the few words held more sorrow than he could imagine.

He remained still, willing her to accept his strength. She did not look at him. Did not even seem to be aware that he was yet beside her, holding her hand.

"I don't believe I will ever find peace."

"Someday you shall," Alban said softly. "If it is in my power to give it to you."

She stared at him a long moment, the expression in her eyes now dark with struggle. When she spoke it was in a low voice he had not heard before. "They are out to kill you."

"Who, the prophet's men?" He was astounded.

"No. From what I have seen, the followers of Jesus would never do that. No, it is Herod."

"This is about the Parthians?"

"Yes."

He leaned back as the realization struck home. "So the Parthians are in league with Herod Antipas, just as the fortress commandant predicted."

"Who?"

He waved her query aside. "Herod was feeding information about the caravans to the Parthians. They no doubt paid him well. So now they demand my head. Do you know when?"

"Soon. They will watch to find you outside the Jerusalem walls and isolated."

He rose and reached for where his sword should have hung, but his hand felt only air. "When did you learn of this?"

"Today. Antipas gave the orders before leaving for Herodion yesterday."

"It is unlikely the assassins could have already set up an ambush." Alban held Leah by her arm as she rose to her feet. "Even so, we should leave here."

They walked in silence back along the trail leading toward the city walls. Alban kept careful watch and did not speak again. They entered the main avenue behind a trio of shepherds, who shouted and whistled as they herded their sheep toward the holding pens just within the city gates. Alban waited until they were deep in the gates' shadows to ask, "Who gave you the information about this plot against me?"

"A member of Herod's household. He is only interested in himself and what he can get. He requires gold for everything, but in spite of all that, I believe the warning is real."

"You must not tell anyone what we have discussed. In fact, it would be best not to mention we have met. Can you find your way back to the palace on your own?"

With a quick nod she spoke again. "Was I . . . was I right to tell you?"

Her eyes were filled once again with doubt and fear. Alban longed to reach for her hand and bring it to his lips. Instead he said with all the feeling he could put into the words, "I am deeply in your debt, Leah. And I will repay you in the coin of trust."

The following morning, Procula again sent Leah off to the courtyard where the followers of the Galilean rabbi congregated. Leah felt torn. She longed for more of these visits. Yet she couldn't bear the thought that her reports back to Procula and the prelate might put these people in danger. She was confident that the prophet's followers meant no revolt against Rome's rule. But her mistress was far from convinced, and Leah once again entered the courtyard and took a position on a narrow bench near the outer wall.

As the sun and heat rose she moved farther into the shadows. Time passed slowly while she watched and listened. She was beginning to understand some of what she was seeing. It wasn't merely a crowded square, with individuals drifting in and out and small clusters gathered here and there in discussion. Guided both by her own observations and what the women had told her, she began to see beyond the surface. Jerusalem was filled with observant Judaeans who came for the first spring celebration, the Passover, and stayed until the second, Shavuot. Yet there was none of the frenetic tension that gripped other districts of this overcrowded city at this time of year. The longer Leah remained, the more she was certain that what Mary Magdalene had said was correct. These people gathered here and *waited*.

But waited for what? That was the question for which she must find an answer.

Two women entered at the far end of the square. Quite a few had been passing between dwellings that opened onto the plaza—airing blankets, shaking mats, bringing in firewood, or coming from the market with produce. But something about the two coming toward her drew Leah's attention.

As they neared the disciples' residence, one of them reached up and drew back her shawl. She turned to her companion to help free the shawl that had become caught in her hair. Both heads were now bare—one as dark as night, the other much lighter. Leah recognized the dark-haired woman from the market. They were almost through the portal when the girl abruptly stopped and looked at Leah. She walked over.

"Excuse me" came the lilting voice, "but aren't you the girl from the market? I think I remember your eyes."

Surprise warmed Leah's face. She rose to her feet as the young woman turned to her companion and said, "This is the one I told you about. Where we shopped for one another's hand." The two girls dissolved into merriment.

Leah managed a smile as the girl stepped closer and said, "I am Abigail. This is Hannah. And you are?"

"Leah."

The girl smiled. "Welcome, Leah. Are you waiting for someone?"

She was the most astonishingly beautiful young woman Leah had ever seen. Her eyes were dark, framed by thick lashes, her features delicate, and she had a complexion as rich and soft as the marble figure on Procula's corner shelf. Her hair glistened with deep auburn highlights in the sunlight. No wonder she used her shawl to hide her beauty. Any man on the street would be sure to find her desirable. And with all of the soldiers milling about the city . . .

Leah said, "I was in hopes of seeing Mary or—"

"Which Mary?" asked Hannah with a smile.

Abigail smiled too. "We have so many, we need give them another identification. Mary Magdalene, Mary of Bethany, Mary mother of James, Mary of Joppa, Mary mother of our Lord, and—"

"She wouldn't be waiting for Mary, mother of our Lord," Hannah interrupted.

"No, of course not," agreed Abigail, her teasing voice suddenly subdued.

"Mary Magdalene or Mary of Bethany," offered Leah. "Either one. Or Martha. I also would love to see Martha."

"I think the two Marys have gone out to the fields. But Martha may be in the kitchens. I will find out." Hannah stepped through the door and disappeared.

Abigail settled upon the stone bench where Leah had been seated. The girl blew playfully at a strand of dark hair that had managed to pull lose from its braid and lay against her cheek. The curl hung back for a moment, then fell forward again. She shrugged and laughed. Leah couldn't help but smile at her joy and obvious love of life.

"Do you come here often?" Abigail wondered.

"I . . . I've visited a few times."

"For a special task? Our vendor at the market that day told me you were from Pilate's household."

Leah's eyes must have shown her surprise.

"I did ask," the girl admitted with a slight flush. "I had not seen you in the market before. I'm sure I would have remembered you if I had."

"I go early," Leah explained, "to try to avoid the heat of the day and the rush. And find the best leeks." Now they both laughed.

"That's wise," Abigail noted, nodding her head so the curl moved up and down. "I am not the one who's usually sent to the market for the morning purchases. Actually, my duty is the laundry tubs." She shuddered in exaggerated fashion. "There is never an end to that work."

So much like Portia, thought Leah with a pang. Her sister would have chosen to be amused over continual tubs of dirty laundry. Not that she'd ever had that task. . . . Leah gave her head a brief shake and turned her attention back to Abigail.

"So you know Martha and her sister Mary," the girl was saying. "They are wonderful women. I don't know how we would manage here without Martha's capable hands and Mary's tender heart."

Leah nodded.

"Oh," announced Abigail, rising to her feet. "Here comes Hannah with Martha." Indeed, the two women were hurrying toward them from the doorway, Martha's hand raised in greeting.

Abigail looked back at Leah. "I'm so glad to see you again. I do hope you will come back often. I would love to talk some more. Just look for me at the washtubs." She smiled as she said it, adding another shudder.

Leah enjoyed the twinkle in her eyes. "I will," she promised as Abigail turned to follow Hannah toward the stairs leading to a second floor.

Leah watched her go, feeling her heart warm with the thought she had made a friend.

"I'm very glad to see you, Leah. When one finds good kitchen help, other hands are found wanting." Martha comfortably slipped her arm under Leah's and led her toward the kitchen.

Several more days passed while Leah continued to visit the courtyard and help with the meal preparations. She reported regularly to Procula, holding back nothing save her unexpected contact with Alban at the tomb earlier that week. From the centurion she did not hear a word. Had her warning come in time? She felt a pang in her heart.

Many of the palace servants, already jealous over her marriage and what they viewed as its promise of an enviable rise in status, were doubly resentful of her supposed freedom to come and go, sent out by the mistress herself. Only Dorit remained loyal among the household staff.

On the shelf above her pallet stood Mary Magdalene's jar of nard, almost as if Leah willed someone to steal it and free her from all the gift meant. Yet there it remained. These mornings, when Leah entered the kitchen, a place was set for her, and one of the young kitchen maids brought her meal. Leah protested, or tried to, but the senior cook pretended not to hear, which suggested that Procula had ordered it. When the men were banned from the baths and women of the household entered, Leah was informed that she was to accompany them. Leah knew the invitation was a polite command. She often found Procula there, always with a maidservant in attendance, occasionally with a female guest. Leah was introduced to these outsiders as a niece of Pilate, promised to one of his trusted centurions. As though Procula were forcing Leah to accept the marriage.

Leah masked her true feelings during the day, but her sleep remained broken. For hours on end, she relived the time in the grove. She had every logical reason to have remained silent about the threat. Yet she had gone ahead and warned Alban, and so sealed her own fate. Why? She did not have an answer.

Even so, when dawn would finally arrive and she rose wearily from her pallet, the sealed vessel given to her by Mary Magdalene was there upon the shelf. The faint fragrance gave her the impression of standing at the edge of a meadow. One lit by a sun far more gentle than that which illuminated the Judaean hills. Surrounded by the fragrance of wild flowers and by a peace that defied the shackles of her daily life—and her future.

Saturday morning, when Leah had finished a solitary bath, she discovered her servant's robe had been removed from the alcove, and in its place was one of Procula's older gowns. It was a custom among some Roman households to reward faithful servants in this way, granting them garments no longer wanted. Wisely, Procula had refrained from this practice, since it often created disharmony among the staff.

Leah knew instantly Procula had a purpose in mind, most likely some kind of audience. Leah shook her head in dismay. She had no choice but to hastily don the garment. In the kitchen she tried to assist one of the maidservants who was cutting meat for the day's stew, but the cook would have none of it, impatiently waving her over to the table and the waiting food. Leah could hardly swallow the fruit and flatbread, and she finally retreated to a bench by the side wall, one that granted her a view of the courtyard trees.

She did not wait long.

"Mistress?"

Leah wrenched herself around at the realization she was the one being addressed. "I'm . . . I'm sorry. Yes?"

"The prelate and his wife are waiting to see you now."

Leah followed the maidservant down a hall that connected the servants' quarters to the formal chambers. Together they passed through the main doors, upon which everything changed. On one side was a floor of untreated stone, the walls bare—like her life to this point. On this side, she walked across mosaic tile, down a hallway adorned with a sweeping mural.

They entered the smallest of the palace's three connected courtyards. Pilate's two personal servants, one of whom was always a seasoned warrior, stood in the shadows, where they remained silent but within immediate summons. The other, the governor's secretary, was a reedy middle-aged man with two blank slates, a writing instrument, and a rather tense manner. Both servants watched her pass. Leah knew the secretary recognized her gown as Procula's from the way his eyes narrowed.

Her mistress was seated on a backless chair next to her husband's throne. A faint cacophony of voices rose from the farthest courtyard. When the prelate was in residence, once each week the citizens of Judaea Province were allowed to request an audience. Pilate was dressed as an officer of Rome's legions. He intended to remind those who appeared before him that his word carried the weight of Rome's army. His expression matched his dress, stern and intimidating.

Leah bowed low as a woman might before the emperor himself, her forehead nearly touching her knees. She did not rise until she heard him say, "This woman remains a servant in my household, does she not?"

"Indeed, my lord," Procula answered.

"Then why does she come before me dressed as a free woman?"

Procula remained calm. "I sought to impress you, my lord, with her bearing and stature. She is indeed my husband's niece."

"The only thing that will impress me is an irrefutable report on these troublemakers," Pilate growled, but his demeanor eased somewhat. He called for his secretary. When the anxious little man stepped forward, Pilate ordered, "Bring in another chair."

Hastily the secretary tumbled his armload of petitions and

writing instruments on a table and complied. Pilate waved an impatient hand at Leah. "Sit."

Nervously Leah did as she was ordered. She had never before seated herself in the prelate's presence. But Pilate was in such a mood that to deny any whim would be testing fate.

"Your associations with the prophet's followers, they always take place in the same place?"

"Yes, my lord."

"Describe it to me."

Swiftly Leah described the courtyard and the interconnected rooms beyond the ancient doors, its large upstairs chamber.

"Are there strongrooms or weapons?"

"None that I have seen, sire. And none of the people go about armed."

"How did they come to occupy this place?"

When Leah hesitated, Procula prompted, "It is important that the prelate know exactly what you have learned."

Leah replied, "The day before the festival they call Passover, the prophet's disciples entered Jerusalem. They were told by him—by Jesus—that they would find a man, and they were to tell him that their master required his rooms. They did as they were told."

She waited.

Pilate's frown was fearsome. "These disciples enter the city the day before the largest Judaean festival. They find a house with a private courtyard and upper chambers where they are allowed to remain for the entire festival season?"

"That is what they said, my lord." She paused for breath and for courage. "And it seems they had never even met this man before."

"Are they feeding you myths to confuse me?"

"I do not think so, sire." Leah waited another moment, then

added, "To be perfectly frank, my lord, I do not believe they have lied to me about anything."

Pilate's chair creaked a warning as he abruptly sat forward. "Then tell me this: Do they plan a revolt against Rome?"

"I do not know. I think—"

He banged the chair arm with one fist, his gold armband cracking against the metal like a whip. "I don't want to hear what you *think*. I want to *know* what they are saying! Speak!"

"Sire, they talk of a kingdom." Leah concentrated on keeping her voice even in spite of the trembling in the rest of her body. "They discuss this continually. They speak of a free Judaea, but they call it by a different name." Leah saw his expression darken further and forced herself to remain at attention.

"Israel." Pilate ground out the name.

"Yes, sire. They speak of an Israel ruled by God himself."

"They say the Judaean God is to come down from on high and rule this dismal place?"

"Sire, they claim that their God has already arrived."

There. It was said. The lingering thought, the one that whispered over and over to her in the sleepless hours. She forced her gaze to remain steady on the man's face—this man who held the power of life and death over her.

To Leah's great surprise, Procula nodded with her entire upper body. Her slow rocking caused her husband to turn and stare at her. Pilate asked her, "You understand this?"

"What I know," Procula replied softly, "is my nights continue to be plagued by dreams of a man who has defied even death."

"Your headaches are gone, yet these dreams remain?"

"Almost nightly."

"I don't understand."

"No, nor I."

Leah had never witnessed such a discussion between them

before. Whatever conversations Pilate and Procula had, whatever counsel, whatever intimacy, was kept beyond sight or hearing of the entire household.

Pilate said, "I have noted you no longer offer daily gifts to the goddess."

Like most women of power, Procula had a small alcove in her private chambers dedicated to the goddess Diana. Leah had not noticed this change in her mistress's habits.

When his wife remained silent, Pilate asked, "Do you believe this man has come back from the dead?"

She met her husband's gaze. "I wish I knew."

"I could seal up the chambers where they are staying and expel these disciples from Jerusalem," Pilate mused. "Better still, I could order the entire group crucified. How many of them are there?"

Leah's lips trembled. "The rabbi's appointed apostles number eleven, sire."

"Hardly the makings of a revolutionary force," Procula remarked.

Pilate demanded, "Are there many beyond this group?"

"So numerous I cannot name or even count, sire. They come and go, so I am not sure of the number. But . . ."

"Yes? Go on."

"As I told you, I have seen no weapons, sire. Not one. In fact, all of them talk in words and a manner that are completely against the very concept of battles, of revolt. They speak of forgiveness. And hope. And love."

Pilate sneered. "You are in love with one of these disciples, perhaps?"

"I have never met one, sire."

"What, never? How then do you know what they are thinking?"

"Though the men keep themselves apart, some of the women

have accepted me. One of them, Mary Magdalene, has spoken quite openly with me. And Nedra, a servant in Herod's household. Occasionally two sisters named Mary and Martha. And a few younger women. All I know of the disciples, the leaders of the group, is hearsay. Though everything I have witnessed suggests the women have spoken the truth to me."

Pilate rubbed his chin, back and forth. "I am hearing rumors. Claims that this Jesus has been seen by others. Since the crucifixion, by Jupiter!" Pilate waved an impatient hand. "All the impossible nonsense you would expect of these Judaeans."

Procula asked, "Is there anything else you can tell us, Leah?"

There was, though it no doubt would cost her dearly to say it. She let out a slow breath. "These followers are certain Jesus has risen from the dead. What they argue over now is whether he is a prophet or . . . or something else."

Pilate watched her intently. "These Judaeans will argue over their religion endlessly."

Leah took a breath. "I am hearing a new word—at least to me—rather often. Some are calling him *Messiah*. But others disagree. According to their holy writings, if he is the Messiah he must deliver to them the kingdom."

Pilate's eyes seemed powerful enough to brand her skin. "So they *are* planning an attack?"

"As I said, sire, I have listened carefully, and I hear nothing like that. They seem to expect this Jesus to deliver the kingdom by himself. I sense that words are very important to them. They are precise when they speak of these spiritual terms. The word they use about Israel is *redeem*. The Messiah will redeem Israel."

Pilate snorted. "The prophet told me himself that his kingdom was not of this world. Your report is as bewildering as that of your betrothed."

Procula murmured, "Which suggests they might be speaking the truth."

"What? A man was scourged and then crucified. His side was pierced by a soldier's spear. He died and was entombed. And now he has risen from the dead and is threatening the might of Rome?" Pilate's laugh was savage. "A dozen new crucifixes will end this once and for all."

Procula sat straight in her backless chair. "I would counsel you to have nothing more to do with this group, my lord."

Even Pilate's most trusted advisors knew when to remain silent. Yet Pilate did not lash out at his wife, as Leah might have expected. He simply stared at her.

"You remember my first dream and our discussion that day—what I said to you then."

"I did what I could. I washed my hands of the entire affair."

"Just as you should now."

"But if they are threatening revolution . . ."

"You have heard two reports, that from the centurion and now from your niece. She has been in your household for three years. In all that time, have you once known her to speak an untruth?" Procula gave her husband a chance to counter, then turned to Leah and said, "What now?"

"Mistress, I was invited by the one known as Martha to accompany her to Bethany, a village a short walk from here."

"I know of it," Pilate said dismissively. "It is a place of poverty and ne'er-do-wells."

"She wishes for me to spend a Sabbath with her and friends. They want me to remain there for a few days longer, so that we can study together. She says another man will join us, someone named Cleopas, who met Jesus along a road—"

Pilate leaned forward, cutting off her remarks. "You are to go, and you are to return and report everything you hear and see to my wife. Perhaps we will finally learn something of importance, something that can be *proved.*"

Procula asked her husband, "You will not act against the disciples?"

"I will stay my hand for the moment. But I want this matter resolved." His eyes burned into Leah's. "Either you and the centurion find answers that make sense, or I will end this once and for all."

Thus it was that Leah found herself once again on her way to the compound of the prophet's followers. Today, however, Leah felt anticipation rather than her previous dread. Gradually she was sensing a genuine kinship with the women she met there. It was the closest thing to family that Leah had known for several years. Procula had insisted she take more gold, and the coins jingled softly. Clearly Procula thought she might bribe her way into the inner circle. Leah was certain this was utterly impossible. Perhaps she could stop at the market and purchase something for the day's cooking pot. She had shared many a meal and had so far contributed nothing. In light of her assignment, surely Procula's coins could be put to good use.

In spite of the storm clouds, the morning felt hot and smothering. Her step quickened as she thought ahead to time spent with these women. She learned so much from them. They all seemed to have a special sensitivity toward spiritual matters, even the younger ones such as Abigail and Hannah. Leah longed to understand their faith in the face of such immense uncertainties, their trust in God, despite those, like Pilate and Herod, who saw them as great a threat as their crucified leader.

Gradually Martha had become Leah's mentor. In some

unexplained way they were so alike. But it was Abigail, with her winsome ways and youthful enthusiasm, who drew Leah most of all. Though the lovely young woman spent her days bent over tubs of soiled clothing, Abigail remained joyous. Leah could no more understand her than she could ever hope to be like her. But it was so inspiring to be in her presence for at least part of the day.

After stopping at the market, Leah arrived at the compound and found Abigail at the washtubs, pouring water over garments strewn across stones. Leah quietly watched as her new friend pounded the clothing to cleanse away the ground-in dirt, then doused them in water before twisting and thumping each piece. It was backbreaking toil. Leah saw the sweat-covered brow, the long tapered fingers dipping again and again into the water. It was easy to imagine the beautiful girl residing in some luxurious palace. She did not belong here, surrounded by muddy ground and beating soil from roughly made garments.

Abigail must have sensed a presence and glanced up. When she saw Leah, she flashed a smile, then quickly adopted an exaggerated grimace. "I have only a few more thousand to do. I will be with you shortly."

She shook the water from her hands, pushed aside her long dark braid, and straightened, one hand on her back. She groaned and pretended to limp her way out of the mud that had formed around the rocks where she worked.

"Shall I bring you a drink from the well?" Leah offered, laughing in spite of herself.

"I will come with you. It is past time for a rest." Abigail's eyes shifted to the darkening skies. "I was hurrying to beat the storm. But I don't think I will make it."

Leah nodded at the laundered garments stretched out on the rocks to dry in the sun. "Can't you bring the wash into the courtyard and string it about on the walls? I can help you."

"The rain will rinse them further. They will dry when the sun shines again. It doesn't take very long in this heat."

They walked together to the well, and Leah drew the water to fill the drinking cup. When they both were refreshed, they moved to a bench in a shaded area and settled against the stone wall.

"I was hoping you'd be able to come today," said Abigail.

"I've had other duties."

"So what do you do at the palace?"

"I mostly was maid to Pilate's wife, Procula. The mistress is now served by a new maid, but I still assist wherever I am needed. I often take her the first meal of the day. I help in the kitchen. I used to go to the market every morning."

"It sounds as if you have had many duties."

"I'm not as busy as you with your washtubs. And I do not have nearly the responsibilities I had . . . until recently. Some days I feel quite useless. Especially seeing how hard you labor."

"Oh, I don't mind the work. Someone has to do it—and they have all been so good to me."

"Have . . . have you no family?"

Abigail's eyes held an unusual shadow. "Not any longer. Three years ago, I lost my entire family." Her eyes filled with tears.

"I am so sorry," Leah said, reaching out a hand.

"Thanks to the followers . . . the goodness of our Lord, I have a place to serve and to sleep." Abigail made a visible effort to push aside her sorrow. "And what about you? Have you always been with the prelate? We do not know much about his staff."

"No, I have been with his household for coming on three years." Leah had no desire to say more about her own background.

"I'm sure you serve well. That was one of the lessons our Lord taught us. 'Servants, serve well your masters. For this is right. And in so doing, you do it as to the Lord.' "

"You knew him? The prophet?"

Abigail's eyes still shone with unshed tears. "I was one of those he healed," she said simply. "A friend brought me to hear him speak. Afterward we got close enough that he saw me. . . . He had the kindest eyes I have ever seen. I never thought such joy or peace would have been mine to claim, especially after my loss. The healing of my heart is a miracle I live with every day."

Leah thought of the prelate's command to obtain helpful information, not just observations and guesses. It didn't seem right to pry, but her master was getting more and more impatient. "Will you tell me about what happened?"

Abigail nodded. "Our village is three valleys west of here. After my family died, I was taken in by a local shepherd and his family. They cared for me well enough, but I had lost the will to live. Months passed, but my sorrow remained a burden that never left me. I did not eat, I rarely left my bed. And then one day they heard the Lord was coming to Jerusalem. They put me on their own donkey and brought me here. He was healing people outside the Temple. I was one that he touched."

She hesitated. Leah wondered if that was the end of the story.

"I was taken in by believers here in the city. I worked in their household." Her voice lowered. "Then they crucified our Lord. Our world changed."

Another silence. Leah heard thunder rumble in the distance. The air smelled of rain.

Abigail seemed oblivious to the approaching storm. "I still see the shepherd family who took me in, but I'm happy here. It's the most content I have been since . . . since I lost my family."

She shared with Leah a most radiant smile and added, "And now we wait."

Leah's hidden motives caused her to flush. "And just what are you waiting for?"

"We aren't certain. But we are sure he will let us know at the right time."

"Do you mean his kingdom?" pressed Leah.

"His kingdom is not one like we have understood. But he will reign from a throne. And when he does, it will be with the power of love."

"Love? Not revolution?"

"No. Jesus never taught revolution, the kind with swords and battles and bloodshed. He talked about a revolution of love. Love your neighbor. Love your enemy."

Leah was stunned. "How can the man expect that?"

Abigail thought for a moment. "I think that's what his revolution is about—one that changes a person to be able to do something even that impossible."

"Do the others . . . do they believe as you do?"

"Oh yes. The new kingdom will be one of restoration. Of peace. We will no longer have need for instruments of war."

A sharp flash of lightning ripped at the clouds overhead and was followed by a crack of thunder that shook the ground beneath them. Abigail laughed as she lifted her face to the rain. "We'd better head for the kitchens if we don't want to be drenched," she said. "Although it would be fun to stay out and play in the rain. I loved to do that when I was a child. My mother was always dragging me in. . . ."

Leah noticed the shadow in Abigail's eyes again, but then the girl sprang to her feet. "Come!"

Leah felt a sudden urge to tell Abigail about her own mother and the burdens she carried. As though this younger woman might hold the answer to healing her own heavy spirit. But she remained silent as Abigail pulled Leah toward the door and shelter.

CHAPTER TWENTY-FIVE

In the Presence of Caiaphas
Two Days Later

As Alban crossed the Antonia Fortress central courtyard, he found himself filled with a feeling so subtle he could not even give it a name. Yet this new awareness was powerful enough that he felt as if he could observe diverse experiences being forged together toward something new. He could not identify a reason for this change in perspective. Progress toward answering Pilate's pressing demands remained slow. And he had heard nothing from Leah for eight days. Yet despite all this, gradually his search and his world seemed bound with something that defied his warrior's pursuit of cold, hard facts.

As he passed from the courtyard's sunlight into the shadows of the gates, a legionnaire on duty at the fortress entrance said, "A moment, centurion."

Alban took an instant to bring the day back into focus. "Yes?"

"One of the Temple guards brought this for you."

Alban made no move to accept the parchment. "You're certain this is for me?"

"He asked for you by name," the soldier replied.

With Leah's warning at the forefront of his awareness, he accepted the parchment and stepped back into the shadows.

The document was of woven linen, and held but one word. *Come*. Beneath it was the Temple seal, used by Caiaphas, the high priest of Jerusalem. Alban had seen the seal often enough, stamped upon documents nailed to the synagogue door in Capernaum.

Alban returned to the sunlight. As he expected, a young lad stepped from across the cobblestoned lane, making it instantly clear he had been posted there, waiting for Alban. "You are the centurion?"

"I am." Alban held up the parchment. "And I am ready."

The youngster led Alban through streets and winding lanes to the shop of a famed seller of perfumes, a man who brought expensive wares to the elite and wealthy of Judaea. Alban had not been in the place himself but had passed it several times and heard of its renown in the Roman baths. Customers came from as far away as Damascus for flasks of the celebrated aromas. Alban had never thought of perfume for Leah. Perhaps it was a worthy gift to consider the next time he found himself with gold coins—whenever that might be.

His guide looked like a Judaean slave and probably worked for the shop owner. The lad cast a glance at Alban, then turned into the dark passage beside the perfumery.

Alban wondered why he was not being shown to the front entrance. Was this surreptitious entry for his anonymity—or that of Caiaphas? The sweet fragrances followed them down the otherwise foul-smelling alley. The boy stopped and lifted a hand to indicate a low-curtained doorway. The stout wooden door was propped open to let in a bit of air, Alban assumed, and to accommodate those who knew of this hidden entrance.

A servant waited on the other side, clearly alerted to his approach. The servant shut and locked the heavy door behind him. The room's only light came from a trio of oil lamps hung by chains from the high ceiling. Alban's eyes took a moment to adjust to the chamber's dimness.

He then spotted Caiaphas standing by the back wall. The high priest wore formal robes and an air of stern dignity as he lifted his chin defiantly. Here was a man who would never bow to Caesar or any other Roman.

Alban acknowledged the high priest with a simple nod and waited. He would not be the first to speak. The priest had called this meeting. Let him declare its purpose.

There were no reclining couches or even benches in the dim, still room. The servant placed a single wooden stool on which the priest could seat himself and began fluttering a fan above him in the hot, overly scented air. Caiaphas lowered himself with a sigh. Alban knew the priest intended this all to be insulting, forcing the Roman to remain standing. Yet a curious emotional distance kept him calm.

Alban had long made it a habit to observe and learn from human nature. Clearly this religious ruler considered Alban to be beneath him in every way. Yet in the presence of this powerful and devious man, Alban found himself looking *beyond* the moment and their conflict to something else, something just out of reach. He was still searching for whatever that might be when Caiaphas demanded, "Has your mission proved to be successful?"

"Somewhat." Alban turned to the servant and asked, "May I please trouble you for another seat?"

The servant glanced at his master, who nodded. He swiftly left and returned with a matching stool. Alban eased himself down. "My thanks."

Caiaphas asked, "The young lady to whom you have been betrothed. What is her name?"

"Leah."

Caiaphas lifted his chin once more. "Unless you are indeed a God-fearer, the ceremony is worthless and more. It is a sacrilege."

Alban found himself searching past the man's belligerent tone. The high priest was so consumed by the maneuvering required to stay in power that he could not take a single easy breath. Caiaphas had eyes that burned with authority, yet his gaze was forever restless, constantly searching for hidden enemies, unknown threats. Here was a man Alban would normally have both feared and detested, for a suspicious man was liable to attack without warning. Yet now, in this strangest of moments, Alban felt what he could only describe as a twinge of sympathy.

He had come to trust his instincts enough to make a decision that he would not even have considered previously. Alban decided to treat this foe as a friend.

He replied, "It has never been my desire to cause any Judaean offense. Especially in matters related to religion."

"I am hearing reports of your investigation that disturb me. I demand to know precisely what you have learned."

"Sire?" Alban cocked his head. "Surely a man in your position would understand that a centurion takes his commands only from Rome."

Caiaphas made a process of adjusting his robes. He muttered, "It was a request, nothing more."

"In that case, I would gladly answer any question you might have, sire."

"There is continued talk about the dead prophet. You have heard it?"

"I have."

"They are saying he has been seen—again."

Alban nodded. "I have heard this as well."

The high priest's voice rose once more. "Who is behind these absurd claims?"

"Word comes from many directions. People speak of it in the markets. I have heard it in the streets."

"As have I. But they all trace back to the leaders of the dead man's group, yes?"

"I have never met one of the prophet's disciples, sire."

"I forbid you to refer to that man as a prophet!"

Even the man's sudden wrath did not touch Alban. He felt a calm that did not seem like his own. "I search for the same answers as you, sire."

"I need no answers!" The high priest bounded to his feet. "I need nothing except for this problem to be gone! I need nothing save for you Romans to stop meddling in business that is none of your concern!"

"My apologies, sire, but Pilate has a different assessment of the situation. And it *is* his concern."

"The prelate fears revolution? Have him retreat back to Caesarea and leave Jerusalem to the Sanhedrin! We of the Council know what is the best course of action." Caiaphas stalked the room's narrow confines. "All this poking and prodding only stokes the same fires your so-called 'prophet' fueled. He fed the masses *and* their discontent."

"What are you referring to when you say 'fed'?"

Caiaphas stopped and stared at Alban. "Eh?"

"You said the prophet fed them."

"I said no such thing!" The fact that Alban remained composed only heightened the priest's ire. "You want to know what happened? Fine! I will tell you! A rabble-rousing Galilean upstart bribed the poorest of the poor with food, gathered the hordes with a charlatan's promises of healing and revolution until they could no longer be ignored. He was finally tried and condemned in the court of Pilate himself."

"After a court of your Sanhedrin failed to do so," Alban inserted mildly, "when it was clear that the witnesses against the prophet had been bribed."

"Lies!" Caiaphas slammed a fist into his other hand as if to strike out the words. "He had a just trial. He was convicted. He was crucified. Your soldiers gambled for his garments. He died. He was taken down and laid in a tomb. And it was from this tomb that his disciples stole away his body!"

"And that is where the mystery begins."

"And I tell you there is only one mystery!" The man was shouting. "Why you Romans insist upon stirring up more trouble over a man who was never a prophet and who is now dead!"

"I find it all very strange," Alban said. "The man is crucified and laid in a tomb after one of the Sanhedrin wrapped him in proper burial fashion. He was cold in the bonds of death by the testimony of two witnesses who carried him to the tomb. Guards were set in place and the tomb was sealed."

Alban looked directly at Caiaphas. "Yet when those unsuspecting followers who thought they would find the dead man there arrived at the tomb, they found it empty and the linen cloth carefully folded and left in full view. I understand this would have been the prayer shawl used by all religious Judaeans, and it is your custom to use this as the face covering at burial. My question is this: Who, stealing a dead body, with Roman guards nearby, would stop to fold a cloth and leave it behind? Thieves are always in a hurry, even when not being pressed for time by guards of Rome. Yet someone did this. . . . Unusual, don't you think? It puzzles me."

Caiaphas revealed a glimmer of surprise, a flash of doubt that darkened to concern. Many of the Judaeans who lived in the larger cities of Judaea and the Galilee were men like Caiaphas, educated and sleek and powerful. The man's robes swinging behind him were a study in two rich cultures, Greek and Judaean. His internal state seemed to reflect this duality, this conflict. Clearly Caiaphas was a man who considered himself religious—after all, he served as the Temple's high priest, just like his father before him. Yet Caiaphas was also a sophisticated man, used to dealing with worldly power. The ruling council derived their power from the Romans, the same people they clearly detested and wished out of their homeland. Of course they were conflicted.

Caiaphas resumed his pacing. "We were right to insist upon the criminal's death. His crowd of followers grew every day. Soon Rome would have been blaming us for the troubles. There would have been a price to pay had Caesar smelled a rebellion."

"Did he preach rebellion, this Jesus?"

"The Galilean announced himself as 'the Promised One'! Absurd! How could this be when Israel is ruled by Rome? Dangerously absurd! Yet the riffraff was deceived by his silky speeches. They even started calling him *Messiah*." The word seemed to lodge in the high priest's throat like a bone. "So now the Galilean is dead. That much I know. I watched the imposter die, I received the report that he had been buried and the tomb sealed, and I and the priesthood went through the purification rites, though none of us had touched the body. But we all felt a need to separate ourselves from this pretender before starting our Passover. And I deeply resent the fact that you insist upon raising the issue again!"

Alban rose slowly to his feet. "I appreciate your concern, sire. But I regret that I cannot end my search. I am a soldier, and I must continue to obey the prelate's command. And the prelate is not yet satisfied with the information he has received thus far."

"There are no further answers required! The matter is settled!"

"Respectfully, sire, there are questions for which I must have answers. Two of which I had hoped you might assist me with." Alban waited until the high priest lifted his gaze. "First, why did you order the tomb's guards to insist the disciples had stolen the body, and give them a large sum of money for their silence? I request that you please do not deny it, sire. I have found the guards and retain their sworn statements."

The quiet was so complete Alban could hear the priest's breaths, sharp jabbing intakes. The servant stood as if carved from stone.

"And second, how would you describe a man who has risen from the dead? I know it sounds absurd—I can scarcely believe those words have come from my own mouth. But I am increasingly drawn to wonder if this might—just might—have happened. What would you call such a man? A prophet? Or something more?"

CHAPTER TWENTY-SIX

Pilate's Palace, Jerusalem

LATER THAT DAY, Alban presented himself at the entrance leading to Pilate's residence, saluted the guard, and said, "The centurion Alban. I have business with the governor's household."

The guard gave an informal wave for him to proceed inside. Alban was too anxious about what lay ahead to object to the man's casual air. No battlements, no cave full of Parthians, no menace in the night could cause a greater shiver in his gut than the encounter ahead of him.

At the entrance to the door to the palace itself, a guard he did not recognize demanded, "Your name and purpose?"

"The centurion Alban sends his respects and asks to see Leah, niece of Pilate and servant to the mistress Procula."

The guard smirked. "Wait here, centurion."

Alban settled onto the bench closest to the exit. A hummingbird flitted overhead, a feathered jewel that flashed through the sunlight like an arrow. He could not have guessed at the passage of time, but it seemed like hours he waited.

And then she was there before him.

He rose and gave a noble's bow. "I wish to offer my sincere greetings."

Leah was followed at a discreet distance by another woman, one with a crone's face and deeply seamed features. Leah motioned toward her and said, "This is Dorit, my closest friend in Pilate's household."

Alban bowed toward the servant as he would a lady of the realm. "An honor, madam."

Clearly Leah felt close to the woman, for her eyes softened and she said, "Dorit, will you sit please?" The woman took a place on another bench a dozen paces away, her eyes never leaving Alban's face.

Alban motioned toward the bench he had occupied, and Leah carefully sat at one end of it. He could not take in the fact that this woman was his betrothed. She was both tall and strong yet seemed also weak and broken. Her gaze was intelligent yet fractured with old pain. She was queenly but wore a servant's robe. He knew most in Roman society would find her too tall, too direct, too strong, too tainted by her family's tragedy to be interesting or appealing. Yet never had he imagined he might one day come to call someone such as this woman his own. "I thought perhaps I had dreamed you were so beautiful. I find my eyes did see correctly, and my memory has remained true."

Leah flushed and dropped her gaze to the stone tiles. "I don't know what you see. I am an ordinary—"

"No, please," Alban said, stopping her with an outstretched hand. "I cannot accept that word to describe you."

Leah was silent a long moment, then said quietly, "I had just been wondering how I might send word to you. I don't even know where you are staying."

He sat down on the other end of the bench. "Above the Antonia Fortress stables, across from the main portals."

"I have just learned that the disciples left yesterday for Galilee. They were told to meet Jesus upon a mountain there where he taught. The women among his followers tell me it is just north of Tiberias."

"I know it well." He inspected her closely, wishing he knew how to take away the veil of sorrow across her eyes, far more concealing than the end of her shawl. "Once more I find myself in your debt, my lady. I must thank you again for what you told me at the prophet's tomb. I understand what it took for you to warn me."

Leah whispered, "If you tell anyone, I will not last the night."

They were in plain view of the old woman and the guard, though both kept their distance. Alban kept his voice low. "I have not told a soul, and it will remain so." Alban leaned close enough to catch a trace of her fragrance, a mixture of soap and lavender and a long day's toil. "We have both been battered by life's unfairness. But this does not diminish us."

"How can you say such things of a woman you do not know?"

"Because I see in you what I am not yet able to describe in words."

Leah's chin quivered. She took a long breath and seemed to regain her composure. Alban watched the action and was so moved by her fortitude he wished he could disregard the watching eyes and take her in his arms. Instead he settled a bound bundle in her hands where they rested in her lap. "I would be very grateful if you would accept this token of my gratitude and my very warm regard for you."

Leah made no response, but her hands fumbled with the tie. She opened the packet and breathed out a long sigh.

The robe was made from a fabric as soft as any Alban had ever felt. It was simple enough, nothing that might attract any jealous attention of others within the prelate's household. Yet a freedwoman of station might wear such as this. Alban supposed a lady of stature would be at ease crossing the central plaza of Jupiter in this garment. "I saw this and knew it was made for you."

"I cannot accept such a gift."

"Please, Leah, I cannot now imagine it gracing any other woman but you."

Her gaze and her hands remained upon the robe. "It is the most beautiful gift anyone has ever given me."

"You will keep it, then."

She hesitated for enough time to stroke the robe again, then gave a simple nod.

"You make me very glad."

Then she did something that astonished him. This woman who was able to mask her interior world, this woman of such immense inner strength she humbled him, this woman wept a single tear.

Alban resisted the urge to ask her why she wept. To probe would only cause her further distress. There would be time for both of them to share their most sorrowful secrets. Time as well, hopefully, to find solace in each other. He said merely, "If Pilate is to be believed, he has offered me a position on his staff once I complete this quest."

She blinked fiercely and took a determined breath. "My mistress speaks of this as though it has already happened."

"The other officers on his staff are both Roman and wealthy. I am from Gaul. And I am hardly a man of means."

She tried to give him back the robe. "Oh, Alban, you must return this."

He settled the gift and her hands back in her lap, his heart warmed by hearing her speak his name. "I confess my poverty only because I can't give you the home you deserve."

"During the past three years, I have slept on a pallet in the servants' quarters. I share the chamber with slaves." She was silent a long moment, her hands stroking the robe. "You give me something I do not dare even name."

Alban felt his heart swell with an unfamiliar emotion. His connection to this remarkable woman was no longer about vindication of his name, nor career advancement, nor wealth and power. What he felt was beyond any desires he had ever held, beyond anything he had ever known for another human being.

Alban saw their chaperone shifting around on the bench and knew their time had come to an end. He rose to his feet and moved to where he blocked the woman's view of Leah.

"Leah, I sense something is happening with you," he said quietly.

She almost wept the words, "How do you know these things?"

"Because I believe I am going through something similar. Can you tell me?"

"I don't know if I can find the words to explain it. The people I have met who follow this Jesus. They . . ."

When she didn't finish Alban said, "Though you do not understand, still you are convicted. As am I."

She rose to her feet, clasping the robe to herself with both arms. "Who *is* this Jesus?"

Once more Alban gave her a courtier's bow, more for the benefit of the watchers than for Leah. "That is what I intend to find out."

With a trembling smile, Leah echoed, "And I as well."

On the day they were to travel to Bethany, Leah left the palace before daybreak to head to the now-familiar plaza. She found herself anticipating these visits more and more, though they troubled her long after she returned to the palace. She was surprised at how often the words and actions of her grandmother now became part of her whirl of thoughts. Things she had easily dismissed as a child returned unbidden to mind, and with them came an understanding of their meaning. To her dying day, the woman had cherished her Judaean roots, the faith of her fathers. Leah longed for the chance to have discussed her recent experiences with her. Now, though, it was her responsibility to ferret out the truth on her own.

When she reached the courtyard and entered the kitchens, she found Martha and Mary busy making preparations for the journey ahead. Mary came up beside her and put a hand on her shoulder. "I'm afraid we have some bad news," she said gently. "Abigail has had an accident with the washtubs. She spilled boiling water on herself."

Leah felt her throat constrict. "Oh no—where is she?"

"Resting in her room."

"Is she . . ." But Leah could not finish her question.

Martha said, "She is in pain. We are doing all we can."

Mary said, "One leg is badly burned. The other was only splashed a bit. It will heal quickly." She squeezed Leah's arm. "I will take you there."

Abigail lay on a cot in her simple upstairs room. The injured leg lay atop the cover, wrapped in a cloth that oozed some kind of dark liquid. She smiled wanly as Leah came through the door. The pain was clear in her face.

"Oh, Abigail. What have you done?"

Abigail watched as Leah pulled a stool over close to the bed. "I was lying here thinking of the Master."

Leah seated herself and reached to take the girl's hand. The bond between them was growing strong. Abigail murmured, "I remember his eyes when he passed, the way my heart was instantly healed. I know it sounds silly, talking about sorrows being lifted."

"It doesn't sound silly at all."

"It brings me comfort right now, remembering him in that moment. I feel as though my pain makes the memory clearer."

Leah stared at the girl's slender fingers, felt the callouses from her work, the strength even in pain. "You remind me so much of my sister. Her name was Portia."

"You say 'was.' . . . What happened to her?"

"She's . . . gone." It was strange to be speaking of this, especially now. But the words rose unbidden from her heart, as though seeing Abigail in pain had heightened her own loss. "Portia was born to sing, to laugh, to shower everyone around her with joy. Just like you."

"I felt that way as a child. My mother said I was born to make her smile. I thought I lost that ability forever." Abigail searched Leah's face. "You miss your sister."

She swallowed hard. "So much."

"There is pain in you. And much strength. You are stronger than I could ever be."

"I don't feel strong just now."

"You have handled your distress alone. I could never do that."

Leah stared into the beautiful face and for once saw beyond the shadows of pain. "I wish . . ."

"What?"

If only your Master were here now, thought Leah, surprising herself. Then she found herself asking Abigail the most astonishing question. "Is there any chance that . . . that Jesus might come . . ."

"We never know," Abigail responded. "He comes at unexpected times. Suddenly he is here. Then he leaves us again. We do not know."

The answer did not satisfy Leah. "Isn't there some way he can be—well, summoned?"

Abigail smiled in spite of her obvious pain. "He is not our servant, Leah. He is our Master. Even when he is not visible, we know he knows and cares about us. He is as close as a prayer."

Prayer! Of course. They all prayed. They believed. And their God had answered. Abigail's quiet faith in the face of scalding injuries was a mystery beyond Leah's understanding. "I was invited to visit Bethany. Perhaps I should stay with you instead."

"Oh, Leah, you must go. There is so much you will learn. Please. Please don't let this keep you here. I have many to help me."

Leah reached a hand to Abigail's shoulder. "If that is what you wish—I will go."

Abigail relaxed against her pillow. "And I will pray," she said simply.

The little group left for Bethany as soon as Leah came from her visit with Abigail, the four women taking turns riding a single donkey. It was a practice Leah had seen often enough upon the local roads. Families walking long distances would, one by one, take their turn resting their weary bodies. The road was jammed long before the sun strengthened into the full light of day. Travelers hastened in both directions, departing Jerusalem in hopes of celebrating the Sabbath with their families, or hurrying to arrive within the city walls before the Temple trumpet sounded the evening prayers.

Leah, Mary Magdalene, Mary, and Martha were accompanied by the sisters' brother Lazarus. He was a small man, standing scarcely as tall as his energetic older sister. He carried an expression that greeted every sight with quiet wonder.

Leah could see how Mary was very much like her brother, small-boned and quiet. They both had a gentle smile and demeanor that Leah found almost otherworldly. She was more at home around

Martha, who bustled as though the day moved at too slow a pace to suit her. Leah liked her no-nonsense manner and the direct way she met gazes and conversation alike. When Mary Magdalene settled upon the donkey for her turn to ride, Leah left Lazarus and Mary and moved forward to walk alongside Martha.

Their dusty road passed along the base of a high hill blanketed by olive trees. The leaves glinted silver in the sunlight. Martha must have noticed where Leah was looking and said, "That was the Master's favorite place to pray."

Leah liked how the women felt no need to either pry or waste breath on idle conversation. "Was?"

"Who knows what he does now. Or where." Martha shrugged, her answer like her walk, direct and swift and blunt. "Does he go to heaven and then come back to meet with his disciples? Does he dwell here in some secret place? My sister and brother love such questions. I have no time for them myself."

Leah hesitated, then confessed, "I find it easier to speak with you."

"That's because we're doers, you and I. I recognized it the first time we met. You came into the kitchen, and you picked up a knife and began paring vegetables. You knew what needed doing and you did it. My sister is so different from us both. Every time the Lord visited, Mary dropped whatever she was doing and clung to his every word. Her eyes never left him. Once I chided her for not helping with the meal I was preparing, and our Lord rebuked me for it."

"What did he say?"

"That Mary had chosen to do the best thing, and that it would not be taken from her." Martha spoke as matter-of-factly as she would about the weather. "I saw then that there are many ways to serve our Lord. Some like you and I do it through action. Others like Mary do it through reverence."

Leah pondered on that for a time, then confessed, "I find your brother to be rather unusual."

"Yes, he is different from the rest of us," Martha said briskly. "Especially since . . ."

It was not typical of Martha to hesitate. Leah prompted, "Yes?"

Martha glanced her way. "Since Jesus raised him from the dead." Leah stopped in the middle of the road. "Tell me, please," she implored.

The story of Lazarus and his emerging from the burial tomb, the death garments streaming about his body, took the rest of the journey. Midway through, Martha was joined in the telling by Mary. Leah's turn came upon the donkey's back, and the two sisters walked on either side while Mary Magdalene and Lazarus walked on ahead. He said nothing about the experience, though he did not appear uncomfortable with the retelling. In fact, whenever he met Leah's gaze, he smiled. When a turning in the road and the jostling travelers blocked the pair from view, Leah asked quietly, "What does he say of it?"

"He says he remembers little," Mary said. Her voice also resembled her brother's, a soft sibilance carrying a trace of otherworldliness. "It seems what he does recall is not meant for this earth."

Martha shot a look across the donkey's neck to her sister. "You've never told me that before."

"I have no way of knowing whether I am right or not. But I have spent much time thinking on it. Jesus also does not speak of his death, but he tells us what we are to do. He says that all is well. He gives us his love and his wisdom. But no explanations about what actually happened, or what will come next." She looked ahead toward where her brother walked with Mary Magdalene. "I think our dear Lazarus may have come very close to God. And what earthly words could describe such a moment?"

The village of Bethany had neither central plaza nor market nor even a tavern. They took a heavily rutted lane that meandered up and over a rocky terrace. Backyard corrals were built from whatever rubble was nearest—branches, mud, stones, bits of cloth and furniture and discarded bedding. It was the poorest village Leah had ever seen, midway down a rise and somewhat sheltered from the wind but facing into an empty valley of rock and desert shrub and lengthening shadows. Mary Magdalene saw her expression and said quietly that the name Bethany in the ancient Hebrew tongue meant "a house of affliction." She also said it was one of their Lord's favorite places, one he returned to time and again.

The house was of a common design. The lower floor was split into two chambers, a kitchen and a larger communal room. Up an outside stairway were two more rooms, sleeping chambers for the women and the men. Above that was a flat roof, high sided so that the people who slept there on hot summer nights were granted privacy. The simple home was neat and clean. Martha took charge of the meal preparation as Leah joined her in the kitchen. The others began preparing the table and setting a fire.

Leah was shaken to the core by the story of Lazarus. She had been hearing of miracles performed by Jesus for weeks. But this one struck her very hard indeed. She was grateful for Martha's willingness to leave her in silence, glad also for the normal tasks that occupied her hands and allowed her mind to roam. She finally came to settle upon precisely what had left her world tilted slightly upon its foundations.

Her hands paused in their chopping of vegetables to add to the broth simmering over the coals. She said to Martha, "I feel I can speak frankly with you."

"I was wondering when you were going to let out what you've been chewing on," the woman said with a little smile.

"I am betrothed . . ." Leah took a breath and started again. "I am betrothed to a Roman centurion."

Martha stepped over and took the knife from Leah's trembling hand. "Let's set this aside before you cut yourself. Here. Sip some water. Better?"

"Yes."

A voice in the doorway said, "It is almost sunset."

"We'll be ready on time. We always are." Martha turned back to Leah. "Tell me."

"My sisters were imprisoned in terrible marriages with men who saw them only as chattel. I fear the same thing happening to me." Leah's voice shook along with her hands. She looked up at Martha. "The betrothal was not of my choosing. Soon after, I was given information that the centurion was going to be assassinated. I thought this was my way out. I almost let him die. But I didn't."

Martha reached over and put a hand on her shoulder. The hand was thickly calloused, yet the gesture carried an uncommon gentleness and comfort.

"I've hardly ever cried," Leah said now, her voice low. "It is one of the few things I have taken pride in through this whole impossible experience. I did not weep even through all that happened to me and my family. But now I want to cry all the time."

"I don't think you've allowed yourself to hope either," Martha said. "What is the centurion's name?"

Leah lowered her head, tears forcing their way down her cheeks.

Martha gripped her hand and peered into her face. "Try."

Leah whispered, "Alban."

"So your Alban has come into your life. He is no longer merely a name upon a betrothal document. He is a man for whom you have feelings. You hope that there might be a tomorrow for you together."

Leah grasped the woman's strong hand with both of hers. "But men fail—even good ones. They break up families. They rage and they wound. And then they leave."

"Some do. My own father died. My mother too. And finally, Jesus himself did not come when we sent for him, and my brother Lazarus died as well." Martha spoke in the same calm tone Leah had come to recognize. "Then, when all hope was lost, Jesus did come. Do you know what I think now?"

Leah shook her head.

"Mary and I have spent quite a bit of time with the Master. I saw him teach, I saw him heal, I saw him dine with his disciples, I saw him leave, and I saw him return. And this is what I think: I believe every moment of his entire life has been spent setting an example. Every breath, every act, every word, carries message upon message upon message. His every instant was meant to bring eternity into the moment and hope to this fallen world. The death of my brother, our time of broken mourning, our loss of hope . . ."

It was Martha's turn to stop and struggle with her emotions. Then she said, "He did this not only for us, but for everyone who witnessed that day. And for those like you who hear of it. He did this to show that even in the darkest hour, when there is no reason to go forward, no possibility of a better tomorrow, he is there to comfort, to guide, to heal. He brings with him the gift of hope. Impossible, glorious, joyful hope."

CHAPTER TWENTY-SEVEN

North of Jerusalem a Day's Journey

ALBAN WALKED DOWN a squalid village lane and thought of the city he had left behind. Despite Jerusalem's overwhelming crowds, particularly at festival time, the city showed a remarkable tidiness. But this Bedouin village, a day's ride into the Samaritan desert, held perhaps a thousand souls and prospered because it was located at the point where the Damascus Road separated from the one leading north to Galilee. The village included an underground water system that fed an oasis planted with date palms and olive trees. Broad dirt plazas, every one surrounded by taverns and travelers' markets, each held a well. The remainder was a haphazard scramble of corrals and vegetable patches and mud-thatched houses. Refuse was piled in the unlikeliest of places, and animals bleating from neighboring pens added their own stench. Alban swatted at the ferocious flies and appreciated Jerusalem anew.

The late afternoon heat had driven everyone indoors. As he returned from the stable to the inn, Alban passed a pair of donkeys huddled beneath an awning, their eyes shut against the flies.

Otherwise the lane he walked was empty. He sensed more than saw the men who followed him.

He had spotted trackers twice as he crossed high hills and pretended to inspect his horse's hoof while discreetly scouting the route behind him.

Now he purposely walked with a distinct limp, as though working out cramps from an overlong day in the saddle. But his body and mind were alert and on guard, thanks to Leah's warning.

What held his thoughts fast at the moment was his conversation with a bearded Judaean whose gaze and words had rocked his world. Anyone could love their friends, Joseph of Arimathea had told him. Even the Romans could do that. Even a warrior. Jesus had taught his followers to *love one's enemy*.

Alban stepped into the plaza and surveyed the empty area. But what he was thinking was that no one who taught such lessons could foment an armed revolution. Alban went on to consider the challenge to forgive his own brother—even after he had cruelly sought Alban's death, banishing him from home. Even to contemplate such a thing left Alban astounded and shaken to the core.

Alban forced himself to concentrate upon the danger at hand. He limped awkwardly toward the pair of lanes opening ahead. He lowered his head and shielded his eyes as though the sunlight was almost too much to bear. He selected the narrower lane, the one most completely enshrouded in gloom. Every town had such places as this, dark even at high noon, with high walls protecting family compounds on both sides. Alban took his time down the narrow alley, wondering if he might have unwittingly lost them. Then he heard the soft pad of footsteps behind him.

He arrived at a corner and leaned hard upon the stone, squinting and searching the various turnings as though uncertain which way to proceed. Alban pretended at deep weariness and walked slower still. But the harsh breath that hissed through his teeth was real enough.

Then he heard a soft *twang*.

Instantly he dropped and rolled. The arrow thrummed the air over his head and shot into the wall opposite, its feathers trembling at the force.

Alban came up with sword in his hand. One of his earliest lessons had been how to combine a series of actions into one smooth motion, how to change a moment of perceived defeat into unexpected strength.

Clearly his assailants had not expected the feint. The man in front faltered slightly, for Alban was neither screaming from the arrow nor open to a final strike. The second man tumbled into the first, forcing them both off balance.

Alban quickly stepped forward and used his sword hilt to hammer the first attacker between his eyes. The man remained on his feet, but his eyes fluttered and his hand dropped his blade.

When Alban saw the bowman raise his bow and take aim again, he took a half step to his right, placing the stunned foe between himself and the next arrow. The second man thrust at Alban with a wickedly curved sword. But he risked hitting his mate and the force was halfhearted. Alban parried the thrust easily and slid his own blade down the attacker's sword, slipping around its guard and digging his point into the attacker's hand. The man shouted and released his own blade in a clatter on the stones.

A voice shouted, "Behind you!"

Alban flattened to the earth in an instant. The air over his head whistled, and a metal-tipped mallet aimed for his head struck the wounded assailant, who howled in further pain. This third attacker again spun the hammer over his head and struck downward. But Alban was already rolling away and felt the earth near his head tremble from the strike. He jabbed his sword at the attacker's leg, but the man scrambled out of reach. Alban spun and leapt back to his feet. He yelled, "Take out the bowman!"

The third assailant snarled and closed and took a vicious swipe.

Alban parried the blow, his sword catching the mallet's metal face and breaking clean off, leaving only its hilt in Alban's hand.

Then he saw the fourth assailant. He shouted, "Toss me your sword!"

The answer was the clash of steel upon steel. He realized Linux was occupied with his own struggle and unable to help him.

Alban did the only thing that came to mind. He ran—upward.

He dropped his sword hilt and used a hitching rail to make an impossible leap and land upon the top of a wall. The two remaining attackers roared their anger. Alban sprinted down the wall as the stone behind him rang with the sound of metal upon stone.

Two steps ahead, the narrow wall made a right-hand turn. Alban knew his speed would not allow him to make the angle, so he accelerated and raced out into the air. All limbs windmilled, seeking a hold that was not there.

He landed in the dust, rolling and coming up against a cart's wheel. Alban scrambled under the cart just as one of the assassins raced within range and swung his hammer once more. The blow was so savage it broke the wheel. The cart tumbled over, nearly crushing Alban in the process. The load of bricks poured out, forcing the assailant to retreat.

Alban knew now was his best chance. He scrambled out, grabbing two bricks along the way. Even before he was fully on his feet, he loosed the first brick. He missed, but the throw halted the attacker for a moment. Alban took more careful aim and threw the second brick with all his might, striking one foe directly above his heart. The man's breath rushed out and he sat down hard, a look of stunned disbelief upon his scarred and bearded features.

Alban ducked the hammer's next swing and reached for more bricks. His attacker was grunting with each breath, the hammer's weight slowing his actions. Alban stepped in and clapped the bricks to either side of the attacker's helmet. The steel rang like a gong. Alban extended his arms out as far as they would go and struck again.

The man dropped like a sack.

Alban plucked the sword from the man's fingers. He swirled and thrust the blade at the neck of the stunned assailant. The man froze in the process of rising from the dust.

"It's over," Alban said.

"Explain to me again why we must go through all this nonsense," Linux said.

They were seated in an open-fronted inn on the plaza's western side, deep inside the awning's shade. The five attackers were lashed to a hitching post by the well, kneeling in the dust with their wrists bound level with their heads. The square was filled with villagers now, talking in low voices.

"Have you noticed," Alban asked, "how the village has suddenly sprung to life? As though they might have been aware of the attack before it occurred?"

"Of course I have," Linux said, sounding peevish. "And that is no answer at all."

Alban and Linux had planned carefully, then made as much noise as possible to announce their departure from Jerusalem. Their hardest task had been dealing with Jacob's insistence on coming also. Alban had to become rather stern, finally convincing the boy that his presence would put Alban's life in greater danger.

Alban had left Jerusalem alone. Linux had left at the same time but on the road toward Caesarea, which departed from the city's opposite side. Once beyond the hippodrome, Linux had made his way overland, circling back around the camps beyond the walls.

"The village could well be a hiding place for the bandits," Alban now said patiently to his partner. "Or at least a point for information to be exchanged. Think of it: The bandits pay for a safe haven at the juncture of the two most important roads east of Jerusalem."

Linux waited as the nervous tavern keeper placed food and mugs of something hot before them, then scurried away. "I still don't understand why you won't let me lash these fellows behind my horse and drag them back to Pilate."

Alban rose to his feet without responding. He carried his empty mug out into the waning sunlight. The villagers backed away as he approached the five bandits. Alban ignored the surrounding peasants and reached for the rope attached to the well's overhang. He pulled up the leather bucket, set it on the well's ledge, and filled his mug. He walked to the closest attacker, who flinched at his approach. Alban held the mug to the man's cracked and dusty lips and said, "Drink."

"You're wasting perfectly good water," Linux called over to him.

"Be a friend and fetch my sack." Alban let the man drain the mug. He filled it again and gave it to the next bandit. He continued until all had drunk. He then exchanged the sack from Linux for the mug, opened its neck, and pulled out the scroll. He said to the bandits, "I am going to assume at least one of you speaks Aramaic. No band would dare enter this far into Judaea without at least one to speak for you." He held it so the golden eagle caught the sunlight. "This scroll bears the Imperial Eagle and the governor's seal. It grants me full powers within Judaea."

Alban motioned with the scroll to Linux. "My friend serves on the prelate's personal staff. He wants to take you back with him to Pilate. You know what will happen then. You will be questioned in the Roman fashion."

A moan could be heard from one of them.

"And then," Alban continued, "you will be crucified."

He settled the scroll back into the sack and cinched the top shut. Alban handed the sack back to Linux. And he waited.

Finally one of the men muttered, "What do you want?"

The attacker who had wielded the hammer barked out a guttural command. Linux's blade flashed in the sunlight and came to rest upon the attacker's neck. The man went silent.

Alban said, "I am going to give you a choice. I have fought the Parthians. I know they are men of valor and fierce warriors. So I offer you this: Tell me what I want to know, and my friend will transport you to Tyre. There you will serve upon the galleys for five years."

"It is the same death," one of them scoffed. But his voice trembled. "Only slower."

"Nothing is the same as an interrogation and crucifixion," another shot back.

"We don't know if we can trust him," put in a third.

"Five years," Alban repeated. "And then you will be freed. You have attacked a Roman officer upon a Roman road. You deserve far worse, as you are well aware."

The hammer wielder started to speak but was silenced as Linux pressed the sword more firmly.

The first attacker said, "What guarantee do you offer?"

"My word as you hear it now. Answer my questions, and I will put everything in writing."

"We do not read—"

"I do," Linux said. "I will confirm what is said, upon my oath as an officer. Though I say it would be far better to hang you on a Golgotha tree."

"Three questions," Alban said. "First, you are Parthians, yes?"

"We are."

This time Linux pressed the blade before the one with the mallet could even open his mouth.

"The Parthians are responsible for the attacks upon the Damascus Road?"

"Not all," another muttered. "But most."

"This village is your point of contact?" When he received a grudging nod from one attacker, he went on, "You have watchers in place who report when caravans are passing, and which route they take."

"We have spies everywhere," the hammer wielder reported, pride in his voice in spite of the knife in his neck. "Even in the palaces of Caesarea."

Alban said to Linux, "You will tell Pilate?"

"His questioners would have obtained this same information."

"Perhaps. But with me they did not have fear and pain staining their answers."

Linux lowered his blade and eyed Alban with new respect. "Pilate was right in what he said. You have the makings of a hero about you."

Alban obtained parchment and a writing implement from the innkeeper. He wrote carefully, invoking Pilate's name and his own authority. "You will ensure the admiral is aware of my agreement?" he asked Linux.

"My own document will travel with yours, and I will personally select trustworthy guards for the journey. Though I still feel—"

"We obtained all we needed."

Linux thumped his fists upon the table. "I ask again, why do you not want to hand these men over to Pilate?"

"It is not about Pilate." Alban continued writing. "I do not approve of crucifixions. Sending them back to Jerusalem would guarantee their fate on crosses."

"Crucifixions maintain order."

"I maintain order throughout all Galilee, and I have never required it."

"You are not most other men," Linux replied, admiration in his voice.

Alban finished the document, reread it, then left it to dry. "In truth, this quest of Pilate's has left me even more averse to such methods."

"Now I am truly astonished. How could searching Jerusalem for the body of a dead Judaean influence you at all?"

Alban stared out over the plaza. The sun was almost upon the horizon now, bathing the dusty village in hues of ochre and bronze. "Would you ever be able to forgive your brother?"

Linux rocked back in his seat. "Why would I even consider such a thing?"

"A worthy question." Alban nodded. "And my brother went one further than yours. He paid men to kill me."

"Over supper on the way to Caesarea, you told me you'd break your own oath of fealty to bring battle to him." Linux cocked his head. "Is this how you are after battle, morose and full of dark regrets?"

"It's not that."

"I have heard of such things, you know. Though you should

take care to whom you make such confessions. Some would count you as weak."

"I told you. This quest has filled me with questions for which I have no answers."

"Well, I can certainly help you with this one." Linux had features which adapted quickly to his swift-changing moods. They hardened now into the stone of old anger. "The answer is, you will never need worry about forgiving those who wrong you. Your brother and mine share one quality: They are both scum of the earth. But we are warriors and officers of Rome. We are not thinkers. We are wielders of Rome's might, and we bring chaos and fire and havoc to all who defy Rome's power. We keep such musings down deep and use them to fuel the soldier's thrust of weapons and his cry of war."

Alban nodded as though he agreed. Yet inwardly he continued to listen to a faint whisper, like a song just beyond the range of his hearing, but one so compelling it caused his soul to cry out in return.

CHAPTER TWENTY-EIGHT

The Village of Bethany

JUST AS THE SUN touched the western horizon, another guest joined the group for the traditional Friday-evening meal in the home of Lazarus and his sisters. Cleopas was greeted by the others with a familial embrace, the same informal warmth that marked so many of the contacts Leah had witnessed between followers of Jesus. Though poverty marked the household by what it did not hold, Leah noted that the home held a richness of spirit that money could not buy. She sat at the table's far corner, taking this opportunity to observe. The group clearly respected her distance. Happy conversation swirled around her after the Sabbath rituals, and she couldn't help but contrast it with her own family meals during her formative years.

Leah knew she tended to idolize her childhood, as though everything had been fine before disaster had struck. But in truth her family had always been focused upon wealth and power and status. They had judged happiness in earthly terms, and conversations at table had centered on how much they possessed and how well they lived in comparison to others.

But these people had almost nothing. The sisters and brother, orphaned while still very young, obviously struggled for their daily needs. Even the Sabbath candles they lit were of such poor quality they sputtered and constantly threatened to extinguish themselves.

And yet they were happy in a manner that did not so much defy their poverty as simply accept it and be content. Leah studied them and found herself wanting the same for herself.

Cleopas was a large man with a stonecutter's hands, yet he spoke with a voice as gentle as Lazarus's. When the newcomer looked her way, his eyes held the same glow, his voice the same warmth. "So you are in Pilate's household?"

"I am, yes."

"How did you come to be here with us in this grand place?" he asked with a smile.

"I was sent to spy on you."

Cleopas looked around the rest of the table. "She speaks the truth?"

Leah replied, "Would I make up such a thing?"

Mary, the sister of Lazarus, gave Leah a smile of her own. "She has spent too long in the kitchen with Martha."

"There is nothing wrong with frank speech," Martha stated.

"So, my honest lady." Cleopas turned back to Leah. "What does Pontius Pilate wish from us?"

"I was sent by his wife, Procula. She had suffered dreadful nightmares and terrible headaches since . . ."

"Since the night before the day," Martha supplied with a nod.

"She became better after Mary Magdalene prayed for her," Leah added.

"I pray for her still."

Cleopas showed no surprise at any of this. "Her dreams and her pain are gone, and she continues to send you anyway?"

"Pilate wishes to know where the body of Jesus of Nazareth is and whether the disciples are a threat to Rome. And Procula is also concerned about this."

"And you? What is it you want?"

Leah looked across the table and took strength from Martha's calm gaze. The words seemed to form themselves. "I wish for . . . for my heart to be healed."

Cleopas's hand came down on the table hard enough to clatter the dishes. "Well said, young woman!"

Lazarus, who had said the least during the previous exchanges, now prompted, "Tell her of your experience, Cleopas."

"She would be more interested in what happened to you, old friend."

"She heard about Lazarus on the road today," Martha said briskly. "Tell her, please."

Though his features went somber, his eyes gleamed stronger than the candles. Cleopas looked at the table for a moment, then began, "I hail from the village of Emmaus. You know it?"

"No, I have not heard of it."

"There is no reason you should. Emmaus is nothing more than dust and hovels and poverty. I earn my living shaping walls for wealthy homes in the Upper City. I once repaired the wall of Herod's palace."

"And now about the day," Martha said, gesturing with her hand.

"I'm getting to that. It was the first day of the week, the first week after Passover. You know what happened on Passover, yes?"

"She knows."

"Our Lord was crucified." Cleopas said it anyway. "He died on a cross, and he was buried. My friends and I, we could not leave the city. The sun had set and we were bound by our laws not to travel. The sun set and rose and set again. But for us, all was darkness.

Hope had died on the hill with Jesus that day. A storm swept in with the earthquake, and our souls remained caught in that same storm long after the winds had stilled and the earth stopped shaking. We in that upstairs room wept and we moaned and we were sick unto death. Our bodies still breathed, but our life was over.

"Finally the next morning my friend and I were preparing to set off. When suddenly the door bursts open and . . ."

Cleopas was strong in the manner of a man who had toiled his entire life. He wore simple garments that were patched and patched again. Leah was certain she was listening to a man who was able to face the worst life could dole out, shoulder his burdens, and push forward. This man covered his face and could not continue.

Lazarus reached over and touched his arm as Martha said softly, "Mary Magdalene came running in and cried out that she had seen our Lord."

The other Mary picked up the account. "Peter and some of the other disciples raced back to the tomb. Peter found the *tziddick*, the prayer shawl that at burial is wrapped around the head, set aside and folded upon the tomb's stone. Just as he had seen the Lord fold the prayer shawl every day they were together. Peter came back shouting that the Lord still lived."

Cleopas wiped at his face. "Forgive me, please." He looked around the table. "You finish for me," he said to Lazarus.

"It is your story. Take your time. Leah needs to hear this from you."

Cleopas stared at the table between his hands. "I had seen him die. I saw the soldiers approach to break his legs, and they found him already dead." Cleopas sighed hoarsely. "Peter was always the impulsive one. I feared he was grasping at straws. The Lord was gone. To hope again, and have the hope crushed, would have been unbearable."

Cleopas took another breath. "My friend and I left. We walked the road leading from Jerusalem, and we spoke of what the women might have seen, what Peter could have meant, and all the while we returned over and over to the simple fact that Jesus was gone from us, and the light of the world was snuffed out."

Leah glanced around the table. The group had gone completely still, as if they held their breath as one.

Cleopas went on, "Then another joined us on our journey. He asked of what we spoke. We could not believe someone leaving Jerusalem had not heard of our Lord's trial and death. We told him in snatches—it was hard to say more than a few words at a time."

Cleopas looked at the flickering candles for a long while. When he began speaking again, his voice was firm and calm. "Then he started talking with us. He spoke with a rabbi's knowledge. More than that. He made the Scriptures *live*. He explained how all that had happened, the trial and the rejection and the scourging and the death, had all been according to the Scriptures and the prophets. Even the fact that the leg bones had not been broken—everything. He . . ."

"He brought hope back into your hearts," Mary Magdalene supplied.

Cleopas nodded. "When we arrived at our home, the stranger made as though to continue further on the road—"

"Wait," Leah said quickly, leaning forward in disbelief. "You did not *recognize* him?"

Mary Magdalene said, "Over and over it has happened. At the tomb I thought he was a gardener."

Leah sat back at her place, her mind whirling with questions.

Mary continued, "The Lord was no longer a carpenter, a simple rabbi who taught profound truth. He had none of the dreadful wounds. . . ." She stopped and bowed her head.

"He was more than healed," Martha said. "He was transformed."

"I did not know him," Cleopas affirmed. "Neither of us did. Even so, we could not let this stranger continue upon the road. The sun was setting and bandits in that area are out in droves after dark. We urged him to come and stay the night. He agreed. We prepared a simple meal. He reached for the bread, lifted it in his hands and blessed it, then broke it into pieces." Cleopas turned to look at Leah. "It was as though a veil dropped from in front of our eyes. He offered the bread around the table, and in that moment we saw our Lord."

The glow on his face reached to Leah at the end of the table. Cleopas said, "And then he was gone. But we knew with certainty our Lord lived still. Our hearts burned with the truth. They burn within us still."

CHAPTER TWENTY-NINE

On the Road to Tiberias

ALBAN LEFT THE BEDOUIN VILLAGE soon after twilight and rode in solitude beneath the moon, the desert a vast silver sea. Hour after hour he rode until he arrived at an oasis fed by a bubbling spring. After a perfunctory search of the perimeter he determined he was the only wayfarer that night. He ate a solitary meal of flatbread and goat cheese, staring back over the route he had just taken. There was little chance he had been followed. The attack had been foiled, and any village messenger had at least a day's journey to reach Herod or the Parthians.

As he leaned his back against a date palm and listened to the soft evening wind rustle the dry branches overhead, he allowed himself to consider his recent proximity to death. A soldier was trained to put this kind of experience aside, to use it as simply more fuel for strength and determination to survive. Both a blessing and a curse, a warrior knew death better than anyone.

Alban struggled to his feet. He knew he could not sleep—not yet. His horse snorted and backed as far as its hobble permitted. Alban reached out to gentle the steed, then moved away. His thoughts chased him like hounds. He had made the best of a life he had not chosen. He had no reason to lament. Wasn't he a good man, as he had heard others affirm?

Palm fronds in his path became sentinels that barred his way forward. Alban pushed through, battering against the thoughts that also assaulted him. It was impossible that a dead Judaean prophet could trouble him so. Yet that was how he felt. As though the man had risen from the grave specifically to disturb his nights and his days.

Alban paused, holding his breath as he stared out over the empty desert beyond the oasis. He was certain he was no longer alone.

He quickly unsheathed his sword and circled. "Who goes there?" he called.

The branches waved and the wind hissed its warning.

"Show yourself!" Alban dragged sandaled feet across the uneven surface, never lifting them clear of the ground. It was a warrior's tactic he had learned as a child watching gladiators in the arena, so as not to lose touch or traction. Those who lived to fight again left circles in the sand, where each step created shallow furrows. Always keeping a double-stanced balance. Always ready for the attack.

"Come out and fight!" He had spent a lifetime on alert, just like now. The moonlight flickered upon the blade's cold steel, and then the light shifted so the blade seemed stained by old blood.

Alban stalked out across the desert, climbing the nearest hill. He made another circle, the blade now shining silver and black. The oasis was a dark shadow below him.

And the sense of another's presence followed him there as well. But there was no longer a premonition of danger. Alban had the sense of someone unseen ahead of him on the climb to the top of this dune. Now out in the open where the wind could fully encircle him, without branches blocking the stars, the night surrounded him with its sounds.

And someone whispered his name. Someone who *invited* him to . . . to what?

Was the only way forward to release his shields and his weapons, both those in his fists and those built around his heart?

He sat listening to the night for a long time.

Alban's journey continued northward and brought him to Tiberias late afternoon on Saturday. It was only upon his approach to the city, when he discovered it wrapped in weekly silence, that he realized his moonlit encounter had occurred at the beginning of the Sabbath.

He had awakened at the oasis just after dawn, certain of two things. First, his encounter the previous night had not merely been imagined. And second, he was through fighting the truth. All the answers he had learned forced him toward the same conclusion—one that required faith more than logic. The prophet did indeed die upon the cross. But Alban no longer questioned whether it was possible Jesus also lived. His experience on the hilltop allowed him to honestly say, *Yes, I am willing to believe*. If the prophet was who he had claimed to be, and Alban was feeling more and more like that was the case, he was ready to give him the allegiance due him. Whatever that might mean.

The urgency of the quest had shifted. Far more pressing than Pilate's command to discover the *facts* about Jeus was a growing hunger within Alban to know the *truth*.

He knew such a commitment would change his life. Where he had once sworn total allegiance to Rome, that would now be relegated to a subservient place in his life. Yet Rome was a demanding and jealous ruler. Strict and unwavering, her edicts were not to be questioned or refused. Alban had no doubt there would be a collision of wills. Rome's or God's? Yet he would not—could not—turn away.

Tired and stained from the road, Alban slowed his horse's gait as he came to the synagogue and heard voices lifted in fervent prayer. The Sabbath quiet meant the inns and market booths were all closed. But shuttered windows could not fully contain the Sabbath chants or the fragrance of the incense as he passed.

As in Capernaum, which lay still farther north, the synagogue fronted the town's central square. Empty market lanes opened to either side. Alban slipped from the saddle and led his horse to the central well to ply the rope until the leather bucket filled the trough. His horse snorted greedily as it drank. Alban filled the bucket once more to drink his fill. As he lowered himself onto the well's stone wall, the sun slipped behind the western rooflines.

The synagogue door behind him creaked open. Alban turned to see a bearded man step slowly into the early evening shadows. Alban rose to his feet.

Realizing he still wore his sword, Alban slid the belt from around his waist and slung it across the horse's pommel. He hesitated, then removed the leather sack containing Pilate's scroll from his shoulder and added it to the pommel. He wanted to meet this man as unencumbered as he could.

Alban recognized him as one of the senior elders of the town with whom he'd had contact in the past. But it was not yet the close of the Sabbath, and Alban was a Roman. The elder seemed hesitant.

Alban walked slowly toward the man. The elder said, "You are the centurion, yes? The God-fearer?"

Alban took a long breath. "I am." And this time he knew it was true.

"Forgive me, sire. Now I see you more clearly. Of course, of course. But may I ask why have you come here?"

"I seek . . ." Alban hesitated. He finally said, "I seek the truth about Jesus."

The elder smiled. "As do we all."

"I did not feel up to the journey to Jerusalem for the feasts," the elder told him as he led Alban along the street. "For the first time in sixty-eight years, I did not go. My son and grandson and great-grandson, they have gone for me. Was I wrong not to travel? At this most important of festivals?"

Alban was familiar and comfortable with the Judaean style of conversation, asking questions without expecting answers. But he said, "It is not only the journey. Life in Jerusalem during the festival seasons can be difficult."

"Just exactly as my grandson said."

The elder's name was Eli. They had first met when Alban had started the practice of visiting each of the towns under his jurisdiction at least once every three months, permitting anyone to bring whatever complaint they had. Eli had been one of the city fathers who sat with him and advised on matters of Judaean custom and religious laws.

"Well, here we are." The elder stopped before an unpainted door.

Alban could not help but gape. He had seen enough such structures to know he was before the village *mikveh*, the ritual bath. "Is it permitted?"

"You are a God-fearer. You are road weary. We are instructed by the holy texts to offer God-fearers our hospitality." He fitted his hands together in what Alban knew was a formal gesture of welcome. "When you are done here, please join my family in the meal to mark the Sabbath's end."

Alban fumbled over his thanks. After retrieving clean clothing from his saddlebag, he opened the door to the white-washed interior. He piled his sweat-stained garments onto the lone bench and pushed through the curtains. The contrast between this unadorned chamber and Roman baths could not have been greater. A simple wooden barrel stood in one corner, and he used the rainwater to rinse himself, then took the steps leading down into the bath. The pool was perhaps a dozen paces long and half as wide. The only illumination came from two oil lamps. Alban settled into the water and felt his overworked sinews begin to relax. The water was cool but not uncomfortably so. Beyond the whitewashed wall, a child laughed. He thought of Jacob—how he missed his impish grin and unstinting devotion.

Alban dressed in the fresh clothing. When he emerged, the elder rose from his position against the wall and led Alban down a narrow village lane.

"You spoke of Jesus of Nazareth," the man said as they walked. "His disciples were here. But they have already returned to Jerusalem. I spoke with them before they departed."

"Do you know why they returned so soon?"

The elder reached a point where both the lane and the village ended. He stared out over the Sea of Galilee's calm waters, like a burnished copper shield in the waning light. "Jesus told them to do so."

Alban knew the elder was waiting for a response. He thought of several, then finally said, "Last night I stopped at an empty oasis. Just after moonrise, someone I could not see came to me."

"How did you know he was there?"

"I cannot truly explain it to you," Alban replied slowly, turning to look at his host. "I thought he whispered my name. My heart burned like a torch within my chest."

The elder smiled through his beard. "Come. You must be hungry."

They dined in a covered courtyard underneath a steadily darkening sky. They were joined by at least a dozen family members. Alban respected the elder's silence and said nothing through the course of the meal. In truth, he was too full of conflicting thoughts to know precisely what to say.

The children also were subdued, shooting glances of awe and not a little fear at him. When everyone had finished eating, Alban watched the elder stand to light a candle made from three braided strands. Eli prayed over the flickering flame, his hands up to either side of his head, speaking in the ancient Hebrew tongue. His final amen was echoed by everyone at the table, even the youngest. His wife handed Eli a ceramic vial, from which he took a pinch of spices, sprinkling them over the candle. Instantly the patio was filled with the fragrance of incense.

At his place at the head of the table, Eli seated himself again and said, "We light the candle and ask the Lord Jehovah to illuminate the week ahead. We sprinkle spices into the flame and remind ourselves that the Sabbath should remain a sweet scent in our lives, flavoring the days to come."

"I wish I knew how to thank you for the honor of being included in this meal." Alban turned toward the women seated at the table's far end. "I am deeply indebted to you all."

"A Roman comes into the village as we invoke the final Sabbath prayers," Eli responded. "He waits at the well, silent and watchful. He comes alone. When I appear, he strips off his weapons and approaches with empty hands. What is this, I wonder? What has happened to change the course of our destiny? Could it be as the prophets have said, that the day will come when we will beat our swords into plowshares?"

"I do come in peace. But I am only one man."

"How else can we become reconciled, except one individual at a time? This Jesus you seek did not come to address nations. He washed the wounds of lepers. He dined with sinners. He healed all who came to him. One person at a time."

Alban realized he was occupying the only other chair. He suspected it normally went to Eli's wife, who now sat with the other women on one of the long benches. At some unseen signal, the women rose as one and began gathering dishes. The children scampered off. The young men sat in utter stillness, only their heads turning between the two as they talked.

Alban asked, "What happened here among the prophet's disciples?"

Eli stroked his beard for a time. When he spoke, Alban recognized the fashion of a Torah lesson, not answering directly. "While Jesus walked among us, we knew him as Rabboni, as Teacher and Master. Yet he came to serve. If he has indeed risen from the dead, then only one word truly applies. One title. Just one."

"Messiah," Alban said. "I have learned the word, but I do not know what it means."

"The Righteous One. The Redeemer of Israel. Comforter. Light to the Nations. Wonderful Counselor. Mighty God. Everlasting Father. Prince of Peace." The elder did not so much speak the words as chant them in a soft rhythm. "The One for whom we have prayed these two thousand years and more."

Alban settled further into his chair and waited.

"The disciples came to Galilee just days ago because they were told to do so, first by heaven's own messengers and then by Jesus himself. They arrived, but he was not here. So in the middle of the night watch, they went fishing. They caught nothing. As they rowed back toward shore with the dawn, a stranger called to them to cast their net once more. They did not want to, of course, for the water was shallow, there would not be any fish, and they were very tired. But they did so and could not lift the net, it was so full. At that instant, they recognized the man standing on the shoreline. Overjoyed and full of excitement, they waded ashore. Jesus sat with them, ate with them, and taught them the next lesson. That of tending his flock and reaching out to the world with his message of love and peace and redemption. And then he told them to return to Jerusalem—and wait."

Alban sat and listened to the crickets and other night sounds surrounding them. A bird of prey called to its mate. Fishermen passed below them in the nearby lake, the oars creaking softly. Finally he said, "You accept all this as truth."

"I do indeed. And how could this be?" The elder's chair creaked as he leaned forward. "Because I heard his teachings myself. I saw him heal sick people, feed them from baskets that never got empty. I knew then he was a prophet from God. Now, after seeing the disciples' faces, their features illuminated by something from within, and hearing their eyewitness testimonies, I believe he is something more. I believe he is the Messiah, the One whom the ancient prophets told us would come."

The town's only inn was full, as the main market was the first day of each week. Alban could have demanded a room from the innkeeper, but in truth he had no desire for company. Instead he camped by the sea in a sandy cove used by fishermen. The rocks rose up high behind him, forming a natural windbreak. The beach smelled strongly from the nets draped over upturned boats and the drying racks along the rock wall. Alban slept in snatches, waking to the sound of lapping water and the echo of the elder's words. The next morning he bathed in the lake's chilly waters, ate a breakfast of bread and dates, then walked his horse back into Tiberias.

The town was a very different place today, the central plaza turned into a noisy bazaar. The synagogue's front courtyard served as a classroom where young boys studied scrolls as somber greybeards marked their progress. Alban hitched his horse along a side lane and stood by the waist-high wall, waiting for Eli or another of the elders to finish expounding on a passage. Eli did not look over until one of the youngsters plucked at his sleeve and pointed.

He quickly came over. "Forgive me, centurion."

"I wanted to thank you once more for your hospitality."

"You honored my family and my home."

"I accept your words about Jesus as truth. How I will be able to express this to Pilate is beyond me."

"I would urge you to ask the Lord our God for guidance."

Alban pondered that. Such simple words, spoken so naturally. Yet holding such impossible challenge. He, a Roman officer, should ask the God of the Judaeans for help. "Pilate told me to determine one thing more: whether Jesus was a threat to Roman rule."

The elder must have been expecting this question. He folded his hands formally and began, "In the book of Isaiah, one of our holy texts written by a prophet of old, there are these words: 'Of the increase of his government and peace there will be no end. He will reign on David's throne over his kingdom, establishing and upholding it with justice and righteousness from that time on and forever. The zeal of the Lord almighty will accomplish this.' "

Alban leaned against the stone wall that separated him from the synagogue and the elder. "You are saying that Jesus will rule, but he will do so in a manner different from how Rome rules."

The elder smiled. "You would make an able student."

"Do you expect Rome to simply fold its tent and walk away?"

"I cannot say. It will be as God wills."

Alban pondered all that he had heard. Overlaid upon the elder's statement was his recollection of the previous night's conversation, and beyond that the healing of his servant lad, Jacob. He recalled the prophet describing Alban as a man of faith. The invitation in those words—ones he had not understood at the time—captured something deep within.

The elder added, "I think all will be revealed in the next week."

"What makes you say this?"

"You are not the only one who has spent the night in reflection. The final festival of the spring season is this coming Sabbath, fifty days after Passover. In Hebrew it is called Shavuot, though many now call it by its Greek name, Pentecost. It marks the end of the spring harvest, and the day carries a divine purpose. We are called to draw near to the throne of God, to receive an earthly foretaste of the splendor to come."

"What does this have to do with possible revolt against Roman rule?"

"I do not know, centurion. Perhaps nothing at all. But I think that in six days the risen Messiah will reveal his plan for mankind." The elder lifted his hands in the traditional Judaean blessing. "Go in peace, centurion, to love and serve the Lord."

CHAPTER THIRTY

The Village of Bethany

LEAH AWOKE IN TIME to watch the dawn star slowly fade with the rising sun. She was surprised at how refreshed she felt, for she was sleeping little in Bethany. The days had been spent in hours of toil and more hours of study. Martha and Mary read well and knew the Scriptures as thoroughly as Lazarus. Cleopas often studied with them too. When it came time to pray, the men moved into the common room while the women prayed in the kitchen. Yet their voices resounded throughout the small house, joining them in a quiet force that resonated through Leah's entire being.

Each night she had lain in the upstairs chamber she shared with the other three women, listening to their quiet breathing. So many thoughts kept her company, many of them impossible and frightening. And yet she was slowly coming to a remarkable sense of peace. Not even the tumult in her mind when she thought about the centurion or the prophet could disturb her calm.

Leah stood for a long moment, her head scarf in her hands. Her thoughts reached once again across the miles to her mother and her remaining sister. What would they think if they could see her now? She had seldom given a moment's consideration to the Judaean blood flowing through her veins. Yet she now donned the covering signifying that heritage. She also saw it as something connecting her to this community of believers. Could she live as they lived? Did she really want to be one of them? How would it change her life if she acknowledged her right to call herself a Judaean? Certainly there was nothing to be gained socially, politically, or economically. No, the reverse was more likely to be true. So why was she even contemplating it?

She did not have the answer to that. She only knew she was drawn to those deeply buried roots. A yearning drew her to these Judaeans, a sense that here lay the answer to her soul's emptiness. She knew that once she accepted the customs, the life, the faith that made her one with this people, there would be no turning back. She would not be a Judaean today and a Gentile tomorrow. It was all—or nothing at all.

Yet precisely what religion was drawing her? Leah already sensed that there was a growing divide between the traditional Judaean community and the followers of Jesus. This new group still observed the religious Laws, attended the Temple, and honored the Sabbaths and holy days. But hadn't their own Temple leaders conspired to make sure Jesus was killed? Where did she fit? And what of her betrothal to a Roman centurion? She still had no answers.

Leah descended an outside stairway so steep it seemed little more than a slanted ladder. As with the other mornings, she found Martha already at work in the kitchen. The woman paused long enough to nod once, then came over to greet her with a swift hug. "How did you sleep?"

"Enough," Leah replied. "I slept enough."

"I often find it remarkable how time for reflection can erase my need for more hours in bed."

"And I find it remarkable," Leah replied, "how well you understand me. Even when I don't understand myself."

Martha shrugged, looking rather embarrassed. "My sister is the one who sympathizes best. She listens with her entire being. I find it difficult to stop my work long enough even to let someone finish a thought."

"But I do not want to distract someone from what she is doing. You and I are so much alike I feel as though we are related."

Martha eyed her with the same piercing quality she had revealed their first night in Bethany. "Does this mean you have another question for me?"

"There, you see? You know before I speak."

"Make yourself useful while you talk. Seed those pomegranates and squeeze the juice. Lazarus enjoys nothing more than fresh pomegranate for breakfast." As Leah began working, Martha went on. "So what did you want to ask me?"

"I have never met Jesus. But I feel as if I know him." Leah shook her head. "How can that be?"

Martha poured milk into a churning bowl and began stirring. "The first time Jesus appeared to the disciples after he rose from the dead, one of them was not present. When Thomas returned and heard what had happened, he said that unless he was able to touch the Master's wounds, he would not believe. A few days later, when the disciples gathered for their evening meal, Jesus appeared again. He invited Thomas to do just that—inspect where the nails had pierced his hands and feet, and put his own hand into the wound made by the soldier's spear. Thomas exclaimed, 'My Lord and my God!' Do you know what Jesus said in return?"

Leah had stopped her work to listen, and she now shook her head.

"He said that Thomas had believed because he had seen. But blessed were those who believed who had *not* seen."

Leah put down the knife, wiped her hands, and crossed the kitchen to stand before Martha. "I want to believe."

Martha's smile was more beautiful because it was rather rare. "My dear one, you *already* believe. What you want to do now is *follow*."

By the time they began the climb to Jerusalem, the five were weary from the journey and the hot, dusty road. Leah was grateful for the others' silence, as it granted her time to reflect upon all she had heard. Over and over she silently repeated, "My Lord and my God." She savored the joy flooding her heart, replacing the turmoil she had known for so long. If she needed any further evidence that these impossible events were real, it came in the form of this undeniable peace and joy.

She knew she would not be willing to give it up for anything in the world. She was certain this newfound faith would cost her, but the price could never be too high. Even if it included losing the man she realized now she could learn to love. . . .

The newfound clarity in her heart and her vision left her certain that Alban was a good man, and that she was coming to care for him. At the same time, she suspected that belief in Jesus would not likely be compatible with the duties of a Roman officer, especially one who might be next assigned to crush this new and troubling sect—whether or not their leader was back from the dead. She could not help feeling fingers of fear around her heart.

She wiped dust from her eyes and straightened her shoulders. Her resolve remained intact. She would present her last report to Procula. When the woman told her husband, Pilate might well declare the betrothal invalid and prohibit Alban and Leah from going through with their marriage. There was a bitter irony in all this—possibly to be granted the freedom she had been sure she desired, only to have that freedom now cause such deep pain.

Or, worse, an angry Pilate could have one or both of them killed. For a moment, fear again engulfed her. Yet this was followed by a new experience, one so vivid she glanced behind her to see if someone followed. She heard a voice, though no one was near enough to account for it. "I am with you, Leah, always."

She faltered for a moment at something she had almost forgotten. Of another voice that had called to her, in the depths of her illness, reaching through her fevered state and bringing her back to health. It was the same voice that spoke to her now. She was sure of it.

Martha glanced her way, then looked at her more carefully. "You look happy, Leah. Are you?"

"Yes," Leah replied. "Oh yes."

Since Procula was not expecting Leah at any certain time after returning from the Bethany visit, she went straight to the believers' compound to see Abigail. The girl was in her bed when Leah entered her room. After warm greetings and hugs, Abigail assured Leah that the scalded leg had begun to heal, and the pain was not as severe.

Abigail told Leah, "In a day or two I shall stand again, I'm sure. I might even begin to walk with a stick. Hannah has already found one for me—a long one." Abigail laughed as she stretched her arm upward. "Nathanael had it cut down to proper size. I would have needed to be Goliath's size to use it."

The same strong-smelling black ointment was still smeared on the burn. Abigail wrinkled her nose. "I don't care much for the smell, though I am getting used to it. But it has worked its good."

Leah nodded her understanding. "I am so relieved that you are recovering." She paused, then said, "I have news of my own."

Abigail's eyes grew wide. "Your bridegroom has fulfilled his requirements?"

Leah turned sober. "Not yet. But it's even better than that." She took a deep breath, then said, "I believe Jesus is alive, that he loves me and has forgiven me."

"Oh, Leah, I've been praying. . . . Come here. Let me give you another hug." Tears were already starting in her eyes, and Leah found she could not keep her own dry.

"Oh, I'm so glad. So glad," said Abigail in Leah's ear as they embraced. "Does Martha know? Mary? Nedra? We had agreed we would not stop praying until you too believed."

CHAPTER THIRTY-ONE

Between Tiberias and Jerusalem

ON THE RIDE BACK into Jerusalem, Alban felt as though his entire world had been shaken and put back together in a manner he scarcely recognized. A soldier's task was to read the terrain, ferret out any enemy or risk, and conquer both. But he no longer knew who or where the enemy was. Only on one point was he certain: Jesus was alive and deserved unwavering allegiance.

When Alban arrived back in his chambers above the fortress stables, young Jacob was pathetically glad to see him. Linux had not yet returned from ferrying the Parthians north to their five-year punishment on a galley. Alban allowed the lad to prepare a meal because Jacob desperately wanted to do something for him. But he insisted Jacob sit with him as they ate. Alban described briefly what had happened to him, skipping over much of the ambush and spending more time on his mystifying encounter on the hill above the oasis. He was uncertain how much Jacob understood. Nor did it truly matter. Alban spoke as much for his own benefit as the lad's.

"And because I now have a new Master," Alban concluded,

"I don't know what will happen in the future. I do not even know what *your* future will hold."

Jacob quickly said, "I will do as you wish, master, whatever it is."

"What I wish," Alban replied, "is that you too learn about Jesus and discover what he has in mind for you."

"I want to serve you."

"And for that I thank you, Jacob. But there is more for you, my lad."

"You saved me from bandits who murdered my family," the boy exclaimed. "You have treated me as you would your own son. What else should I do but follow you?"

"Do you understand what I have just told you?"

"Not really, master." Though he spoke softly, the words were plain. "But you do. And that is enough."

Alban found it necessary to swallow hard. "I know you desire to be a Roman soldier. But God knows what he wants you to be. You will find his path and follow it. To be a man of war is not enough. I accept that now. You must also seek to be a man of peace."

"Are you saying I should not be a legionnaire?" Jacob asked quietly, a frown reflecting his disappointment.

"I am saying that God will show you what he wants you to be. Of that I am certain."

"But you will not send me away."

"I will never send you away. How could I ever get along without you?"

After their meal, Alban wrote a message for Linux, saying he needed to take care of a legal matter, then could be found at the disciples' meetinghouse. He then went to the formal baths, taking Jacob with him. After a few complaints from the boy, they scoured their bodies with a pungent mixture of soap and perfume and sand, rubbing and dousing and rubbing some more until their skin glowed.

This was followed by the hot bath, then the steam room, and finally the cold bath. Afterward they dressed in togas belted with woven fabric since Alban would not be carrying his weapon.

He stepped back a pace. "I *thought* I remembered what you looked like under all that dirt!" he quipped.

Jacob grinned, his teeth shining bright in his face.

The Antonia Fortress central courtyard rang with the boisterous voices of off-duty soldiers. A group of them gambled in the forecourt over a design carved into the flagstones. Alban was filled with conflicting emotions. He had known this kind of atmosphere all his life. It was his world. But how much longer? He walked into the main hall feeling like an outsider.

The tribune's aide was seated in the commandant's outer office. He nodded in response to Alban's salute. "Is this the lad?"

"Yes."

"So you're Jacob." The officer handed Alban a parchment, one corner weighted by a wax seal. "This is a fortunate day for you, boy."

Alban talked of other things on the way back to their rooms, waiting until they had entered and seated themselves to say, "This is for you."

"What is it, master?" Jacob made no move to accept the document.

"It is called manumission. It means you are no longer a slave but a free man."

"I didn't ask for it. I don't—"

"Jacob, listen to me."

"No, master. I won't accept it." He turned his face away.

"Look at me, lad. I've already told you. I'm not sending you away. But we're both moving into an unknown future. I need to be certain that if anything happens to me, you'll be free and you won't become someone else's slave." Alban thrust the document into Jacob's hands. "Stow it someplace safe. It holds your future."

Jacob did as he was told, but when he returned, his face was creased with very real sorrow.

Alban asked, "What is it, Jacob?"

"What *is* going to happen to you?" he sobbed.

Alban rose to enfold him in his arms. "Maybe nothing," he said as the boy wept against his chest. Alban did not want to unnecessarily alarm the boy, yet he refused to lie to him. Alban tousled Jacob's hair. "I'm asking you to trust me on this. Now, let's take a walk. There is something else I need to do."

They followed the main market avenue west. The easiest place to find in all Jerusalem was the Temple, dominating the city's highest hill. At the gates, Alban stood to one side, observing the throngs who came and went and watching for a break in the stream of people passing through into the Temple grounds.

Some carried animals that bleated and struggled against the arms that held them, no doubt alarmed at the cries of death and the smell of blood from their kind as they were given in the ritual sacrifices. Gradually Alban began to make out an odd sense of order within the chaos. Numerous families brought their newborn babies, probably for blessing. Many couples came surrounded by merry well-wishers, there to acknowledge publicly the exciting news of their recent marriages and the commencement of new families. Most that came and went were characterized by a common sense of fervor, of passion.

Jacob asked, "What are we waiting for, master?"

"Remember, you are free now. I am your master no longer."

"What should I call you, then?"

"My soldiers call me sire, my friends call me Alban. Which do you prefer?"

It was good to see the lad smile. "I don't know. I'll try them both."

"Take your time. Either is fine." He patted the lad's shoulder. "I'm waiting for an opening in the crowd."

"This is the Temple, and it is the festival season," Jacob observed. "As long as the gates are open, crowds will keep coming and going."

"Then let us do our best right now."

But as soon as Alban crossed the lane and started toward the gates, he noticed a change. Though he was not in uniform and bore no weapon, clearly these people knew him for the Roman he was. A space was made for him and Jacob, the expressions surrounding him suspicious and hostile. Alban clenched his jaw and moved forward, keeping his gaze straight ahead.

The guards to either side of the main portal watched him but made no move to stop his progress. He passed from the gate's shadow into the large Temple courtyard and stepped to one side. The crowd streamed past him, many continuing to cast surly looks his way.

Alban took stock of the vast area. The Temple, directly ahead, was an enormous structure with a triangular roof. Between him and the place of worship was a vibrant, noisy throng—everyone seemed to be in motion. At various points about the compound were corrals for lambs and cages for birds. Elsewhere tables had been set out, where money changers plied their trade. Alban had heard of this from the Capernaum elders, who spoke of the practice with disgust.

Jacob pointed to the left and asked, "What is that?"

Spaced around the outer wall were broad stone shields. "I have heard of these," Alban told him. "They were set in place by Herod the Great. The inscriptions of all the shields are the same, a warning written in Latin, Greek, Aramaic, and Hebrew, all the way around the plaza. They say, 'No unbeliever may pass beyond this point, upon pain of death.' "

"But why?"

"The Temple and the inner courtyard are only for Judaeans," Alban replied.

A colonnaded veranda ran down the far side of the courtyard. At several points along its length, men stood and expounded on religious themes. Alban had heard that Jesus had spoken here at the Temple, and he now regretted he was too late to hear him.

He turned and found a guard watching him. Alban walked over and bowed to the Temple officer. He received nothing in return but a defiant stare. "May I ask, where does one offer sacrifice?"

The man's ire was instantly transformed to astonishment. "You?"

"Yes."

"You wish to offer . . . You cannot."

"What do you mean?"

"You are Roman, yes?"

"I am from Gaul."

The guard waved that aside. "You are a Roman legionnaire. You are not welcome here."

The man's loud tones were attracting the attention of other guards. Alban bowed again and backed quickly away. Now all the guards were casting angry glances at him. But Alban had not come intending to offend anyone and had no wish to cause trouble. He thought swiftly, then dug into the purse at his waist. "Here." He spilled coins into Jacob's hands. "Do what is necessary. Buy what you can with that and make a sacrifice."

"But, sire—"

"Do it for both of us. I'll wait for you outside. Hurry."

Alban turned away, heading for the entrance. The guards scowled him back through the gates.

Only when he was outside and standing in the shadows across from the portal did he think about the significance of his experience. He was forbidden to make a sacrifice. He was excluded. Whatever the Judaeans experienced inside the Temple area, it was meant for them and them alone.

He had come simply seeking the God of the Judaeans. Back there in the Galilean night, he had come face-to-face with the certainty that Jesus was both human and divine. And now Alban sought to find him, to know him. Where better to begin than in the Temple where Jesus had often taught?

"Sire?" Jacob tugged on his sleeve. "It is done."

Alban managed a smile. "Good lad."

His mind and heart heavy, he followed Jacob through the winding streets, not really aware of their surroundings.

Then he remembered Jesus had already helped him once, bringing Jacob back to health when Alban had asked.

His task was simple: Find Jesus. Ask directly for his permission to join this teacher's group. After all, Alban was a Gaul who had become a Roman. Why not a Roman who had become a follower of Jesus?

Alban heard the tumult long before he saw it. He and Jacob climbed the cobblestoned lane to discover a crowd filling the square from side to side, with more in neighboring alleys. Alban slowly worked his way through, Jacob right behind him, acutely aware that something momentous must have happened.

The noise inside the plaza was so loud Jacob could scarcely be heard. "Sire, what is going on?"

"I can't make it out." Alban gripped the boy's arm to keep them from being separated. "Where do the disciples meet?"

"Inside the doorway on the plaza's other side."

"We will try to make our way there." The mass of people grew increasingly dense until Alban was forced to shoulder his way through.

Once through the portals, the crowd combined into a solid wall. He looked at Jacob, who motioned toward the stairs. "I have heard there is a room at the top!"

Jacob's words drew the attention of several men standing beside them. One asked, "What do you seek?"

"I wish to speak with one of the prophet's disciples," Alban answered.

"Most are at the Temple praying. Why do you seek them?" Then the man looked at him more closely. "Are you the centurion betrothed to the woman called Leah?"

They were jostled heavily from behind, and Jacob was thrown against Alban. "I am," he said, steadying the boy.

The man motioned to them. "Come."

He threaded his way through the crowd to the stairs. They climbed slowly behind him. The man led Alban and Jacob into a chamber that held a long table down one side. A few men were seated at benches, deep in conversation. In the far corner four men stood with their heads covered by prayer shawls, rocking gently.

"Now, then," he motioned them onto benches. "What is it you wish?"

"You are a disciple of Jesus?"

"He called me, and I came."

Alban felt the man's simple response resonate through his being. He nodded his understanding. "I am in awe of you, both for being so fortunate as to be called and for being wise enough to answer as you did."

The man clearly approved of Alban's response. "You may speak freely."

"May I ask your name?"

"My name is Bartholomew, but my friends call me Nathanael."

"I am Alban and this is Jacob."

"A Roman led into our fold by a young Judaean." Though probably not much older than Alban, Nathanael had the deeply creased features of a man born to hard labor, and his beard held a silver streak. He smiled down at Jacob. "I have seen you about, have I not?"

"Yes, sire."

"Did you come seeking answers for this man?" He gestured toward Alban.

The man was still looking at Jacob, but Alban knew the question was really directed at him, so he explained, "I sent him, first to find the disciples, then to learn where the prophet's body was. And finally to determine if your group was a threat to Rome."

Nathanael lifted his gaze to Alban. "And who was it who sent *you?*"

"Pontius Pilate."

"Did you find the answers you sought?"

"Those and more besides." Once again he was struck by eyes that held more than intelligence, more than intensity. "Nathanael, I come here wishing to speak with Jesus. I am not a complete stranger to your Teacher. We did not meet, but he knows of me. He healed the lad here."

"You are the centurion from the Capernaum garrison?"

"I am."

"I was with our Lord that day upon the road." Nathanael's gaze returned to Jacob. "So you are the young servant Jesus healed."

"Yes, sire."

The disciple looked back at Alban. "And you are the man whom the Teacher praised for being of such strong faith."

Out of the corner of his eye Alban saw that some nearby had ceased their discussion, and two of those praying had slipped the prayer shawls down about their shoulders to better observe. Alban pressed what he interpreted as his advantage. "Is that not enough reason to permit me a moment with him?"

"You misunderstand, centurion. It is not possible for you to meet with Jesus, because he has returned."

"Returned? Back to Galilee? I just came from there—"

"He has returned to heaven."

"Where . . . where is that?"

"A worthy question. At his instructions, we met our Lord outside Jerusalem on Mount Olivet, a favorite place of his. Before our very eyes he was lifted into the sky. We watched until he entered into a cloud and was lost to our sight. Then heavenly messengers appeared to us and said we were to watch and pray, for he would be coming back for his followers."

He had wanted to speak to Jesus. Now that he was coming to believe all he was discovering about the man, he was determined to know more of the Master's teaching. There was so much he needed to learn. To understand. How he envied those who had traveled with him, who had listened to his daily teaching and been able to ask questions and get answers. And now . . .

He turned to face Nathanael. "Do you think he will return soon?"

"All we know for certain is what he told us, which was to watch and wait. We are to stay in Jerusalem until we are given his command."

"Then he will be back? Here?" Alban's spirits lifted with hope.

"That is our understanding and our prayer. But before that

day, he has promised to send a gift to his believers, one called the Comforter."

Alban shook his head in bewilderment.

"The Comforter will teach us all things."

"How will I recognize him?"

Nathanael sobered, then quickly responded, "Jesus will make this clear. How, I do not know. But I have no doubt that it will be so. Until that time we will wait—and pray."

CHAPTER THIRTY-TWO

The Disciples' Courtyard

After reporting to Procula about her stay in Bethany, Leah returned to the disciples, ordered by her mistress to seek out anything of signficance. Leah no longer made any objections. Though the search for a threat to Rome from the followers seemed utterly futile, Leah was grateful now for any reason to return.

She climbed the cobblestone lane and worked her way through an enormous mass of people. Bewildered at the sudden increase in numbers, she managed to enter on the side closest to the disciples' dwelling. She had not moved far across the courtyard when she caught a quick glimpse of Alban, on the other side of the square. She was puzzled, but then all of Jerusalem seemed to be crowded into these streets. Was this the beginning of the riot Rome had feared? Had they called for the army? Fear gripped Leah as she strained to spot any other Roman guards in the crowd. She saw none.

The centurion seemed to be alone save for the young lad who had been present at their betrothal. They had managed to find a niche within the plaza's far wall, one where shadows protected them from the worst of the heat. Alban was surveying the gathering with a sober expression. But it was the lad standing beside him who was the first to notice Leah. The boy plucked at Alban's toga and pointed. Alban jolted upright and quickly began to scramble out from their position toward her.

Even when they were next to her, Leah had to nearly shout to make herself heard. "Do you know what is happening?"

Alban's response was lost to the crowd's tumult. But she could see now that something troubled him deeply. Leah motioned for them to follow. With great difficulty she led the pair toward the kitchen at the rear of the house. When they arrived, she discovered all work had been abandoned. But at least the place was relatively quiet. Leah heard her name being called by one of the women outside, but she did not respond. She asked once more, "Do you know what is happening?"

"I'm too late. Jesus is gone." Alban stared out toward the milling throng.

"What do you mean?"

He seemed not to hear her. Leah was close enough to see the lines of strain about his lips.

"Please, come and sit down," she invited. "There's no fire, so I can't make you tea. Wait, here's some bread. Have you eaten?"

The lad quickly said, "We've not had anything since early this morning, mistress."

Leah delved into the wooden vat at the back of the kitchen. After washing off the brine, she sliced the cucumber and then a wrinkled pepper.

Alban looked down at the plate she set between them. "If only I had come sooner."

His hopeless look disturbed her. She quickly ladled two cups full of water, found a bit of sheep's cheese under a cloth, a platter of flatbread under another. At least the boy showed an appetite. He wolfed down everything while Alban crumbled a bit of cheese.

"Eat something. Please." When he seemed about to protest, she hurried on. "I have something important to tell you. But I will not unless you eat."

The meal only seemed to heighten his sadness. Leah had so much she wanted to say. She finally could wait no longer. "I have found the answer I have sought."

He looked for a long time into her eyes.

She found herself shivering. But she feared if she did not continue, her resolve would weaken, and she must hold to this course. She must.

"The answer. It is here." She placed a hand upon her heart. "Within me. And though I cannot fully explain it, I know it is true. True and powerful."

Her eyes were so filled with tears now she could scarcely see him. Yet she could feel, if not see, the intensity of his gaze. She hurried on. "Jesus is the Messiah. Just as his disciples claimed."

She must say it all before he had the chance to respond. Otherwise she might never find the courage or the strength. "But, Alban, I do not see how I can be joined to a Roman centurion and to his government that threatens these people, my brothers and sisters, with destruction. They—we—plot no revolution. We only seek to live in peace, to worship God."

When Alban opened his mouth to answer, she pressed on, "Wait, please, I beg you to wait and let me finish. I know there is talk of the restoration of Israel. But I also know now that they expect this to be done by God himself, and in his timing. What earthly power, Roman or otherwise, would dare to stand against Jehovah?"

Alban seemed both bewildered and intent. "I am here," he said finally, "in search of Jesus. I came because I wished to give him my fealty." He hesitated. "I'm sorry. I speak as a soldier would. I do not know the proper way to speak of this. I want . . ."

"You want to follow him?"

"Yes. But Jesus is not here. So I must remain an outsider." Alban's features twisted in genuine pain. "Just as I am barred from offering a sacrifice at the Temple."

"I . . . I don't understand."

Alban related his conversation with the Temple guard. Jacob had finished his meal, and now, eyes wide, his head turned back and forth between the two as they talked. Alban finished, "When I arrived here, I asked for Jesus, only to learn he had been taken away—someplace called heaven. . . ."

Leah could not speak.

"You didn't know this is what has caused the furor here?" Alban asked her.

"No, I just arrived. . . . He is gone?"

"An angel told the disciples he would return. But this messenger did not say when." Alban looked despondent. "I don't know what to do. I don't know how to be accepted. I don't know how to approach this God."

"I do not know many things either," Leah said slowly. "But I know this. A way will be made. We will pray. And we must wait for Jesus."

Leah was greeted by a warm smile as she entered Abigail's room the next morning and found her standing by her pallet.

"Look at me," Abigail boasted. "I'm walking with my stick." Her dark eyes sparkled as she took three careful steps across the room.

"Oh, Abigail, this is wonderful." Leah clasped her hands together with joy.

"Martha said I might go outside if I continue to improve. Maybe even go to the market. I can hardly wait. Do you know how long I have been in this room? On that cot? But no more. I am going to practice with this stick. I am going to become so good with it that I can outrun Hannah." She lifted her stick and shook it, as if admonishing the quick-stepping Hannah.

"Where is Hannah now?"

Abigail lowered the stick. "She is still assigned to the washtubs in my place. That's the real reason I must recover quickly. She has been carrying my responsibility far too long."

"You're going back to the tubs?"

"Of course. That is my assignment."

"But—"

"I must learn to be more careful. I was trying to hurry when I slipped. It is not only Hannah who needs to slow down." She gave another quick smile. "Now—what shall we do today? I would love to get outside into the fresh air. Could you help me down the stairs?"

Once into the courtyard and open air, Abigail convinced Leah and Hannah, who had joined them, that she was feeling fine, enough so to venture to the market nearest the compound. The three heard strict warnings from every woman they passed, but Abigail assured them she would be careful. She still needed her walking stick, but in spite of that was in the best of spirits.

Before stepping out onto the busy street, the three young women folded one end of their shawls across the lower portions of their faces. Even so, Abigail was unable to hide her striking beauty. She walked with a grace even the stick in her hand could not disguise. The dark eyes danced and teased by turn. A few tendrils of hair escaped from their confinement to curl upon her brow, framing her face and adding soft femininity. Altogether, she made a picture so compelling that the gazes of many followed their progress.

Leah wondered as they walked if Hannah ever felt jealous

over her friend's astonishing beauty. If she did, she did not let it show. The two girls were the best of companions. As they chatted animatedly, Hannah carefully measured her steps to accommodate Abigail and her stick.

The crowds grew thicker around them. Leah allowed the two young girls to move ahead. Her thoughts swirled like the throngs moving to either side. She thought of Alban, and his confession of the previous day. How strange to find such joy and such concern in one moment! He sought to be a follower of Jesus, but could he? She had no idea whom to ask, or even if she should involve herself in this. She too felt such an outsider, she knew so very little about what was required of the followers. But to have Alban wish to join them and be barred from this group, and from her, was unthinkable.

Abigail caught sight of Leah's expression and demanded, "Whatever are you thinking?"

"She's thinking about the centurion, of course!" Hannah answered, and both girls laughed.

Leah was tempted to confess the worries that had kept her awake the previous night. But Abigail chose that moment to ask, "Have you planned a gown for your wedding celebration?"

"Gown? No, I haven't . . ." It had never crossed Leah's mind.

Abigail exclaimed, "You will want something festive for the wedding celebration. Mary and Martha and the others will plan one for the appropriate time. Let us help you find something to wear!"

"But . . . I don't—"

"Oh do. It will be so enjoyable."

"Please, Leah. I know the very place for beautiful garments," Hannah chimed in.

"But I don't even know when the wedding celebration will take place." *Or even if,* she added silently. The thought sent an arrow through her heart.

"One never knows exactly," said Hannah, shaking her head. "One is not supposed to know. That would take much of the fun and excitement from it. It's the not knowing that's so wonderful."

"That's why you must have your wedding garment all prepared in advance," Abigail explained. "You never know when your bridegroom might come. It would be unthinkable not to be ready to go at the sound of the wedding trumpet."

Leah found herself grateful for the chance to look ahead with anticipation. "I'm very grateful for anything you can teach me. Growing up in a Roman society has left me . . . what shall I say? Unschooled? I don't even know what the proper wedding garment is. When I went for the betrothal garments, Nedra came with me. I never could have done it without her."

"Now it is our turn," said Abigail, sounding delighted.

"But . . . but I don't have any way to pay for it," Leah confessed.

Abigail moved forward, her stick softly thumping across the cobblestones. "Then," she said with her customary brightness, "we will go look for the perfect wedding garments, and when you have the amount needed, you will know exactly what to buy."

It did not take long for Abigail and Hannah to encourage Leah's excitement. Their eagerness in examining the merchandise showed in their eyes and in the hands that gently fingered the fine linens and delicate cottons. The garments were white, some elaborately bordered. Leah even saw some with gold or silver threads gently interwoven among the red, blue, and purple adornments.

Then a more simple gown caught her eye, so white it shimmered in the sunlight coming through the open doorway. The cloth was light in weight and texture, with a dainty design that bespoke elegance. It slipped softly through her fingers as she caressed it.

"This is one you would like?" asked Abigail at her shoulder.

"Yes, yes, I would." Leah felt herself flush.

"I have found the perfect shawl to match it." Hannah moved up beside them, the white gossamer linen with its own decorations held out in both hands.

She was right, Leah admitted. They were beautiful together. But the price! Where would she ever find the money?

Then she remembered Procula's pouch, still securely fastened about her waist, under her shawl. The money that Procula had given her to spend on bribes, should bribes appear to be required, still lay at her disposal. It had been freely given her. Hadn't it?

But even as the thought came, she quickly dismissed it. It was not her money. It belonged to her mistress. It had been given for a certain purpose. But she had not paid any bribes for information. Now the money must go back to Procula. She would see to it as soon as she returned to the palace.

She thanked the shopkeeper and shepherded the two girls out of the store. "I think we must get on to the markets," she said briskly. "How is your leg, Abigail? Do you want to—"

But the girl wouldn't even let her finish the question. "I'm feeling very well, thank you, and let's go find some leeks!"

The sound of their laughter drew the attention of a Roman officer striding the lane ahead of them. Leah recognized Alban's associate, Linux, from the betrothal ceremony. Now she felt heat flood her cheeks. What would Alban think if he knew she had been looking at wedding finery, especially after she had been the one to raise the questions about whether she could actually give herself to a centurion? She felt sure Linux could detect her secret in her eyes. She looked quickly from side to side but saw no place to conceal herself.

Linux approached and bowed. "Leah, I thought I recognized you."

He straightened and glanced at her two companions. His gaze lingered upon Abigail, though much of her face was sheltered behind the shawl. Linux seemed to bring his attention back to Leah with some difficulty. "And am I to have the pleasure of an introduction?"

Leah looked imploringly at her friends. Was it proper to introduce two Judaean girls to a Roman officer? Then Abigail stepped back a pace and lowered her eyes in a respectful manner.

"Perhaps another time," Leah said softly. "We are anxious to complete our duties at the markets."

"Of course. Another time." Regret was clear in his voice as he inclined his head again. He gave Abigail one more look. "Another time," he said softly and strode away.

As soon as they were out of earshot, Hannah pulled on Leah's arm. "Was that your centurion?"

"No, that is Alban's friend. Linux is on the prelate's personal staff."

"He is *so* handsome," Hannah noted, awe in her voice. "And he certainly had eyes for Abigail."

"He was too bold," said Abigail with a shake of her head. "It was not proper. And he is Roman."

Leah let Abigail set the pace as they entered the bustling market. The conversation made her feel old and settled, hearing the women chatter about their impressions of the soldier. Yet she was hardly more than a year or two older. It made her realize how much her life experiences had shaped her.

Hannah turned to her and said, "And soon your own centurion will be coming for you."

Abigail brightened. "And you will meet him dressed in that beautiful gown you have chosen. Oh, you must be *so* excited!"

Leah hid her concerns by picking cucumbers and melons from the street vendors' carts. "We must hurry."

Leah was busy in the kitchen later that morning with preparations for the midday meal. She was stirring a large pot over the coals when Jacob appeared at her elbow.

"Mistress, could you please come with me?"

"Is Alban with you?"

"He awaits us in the courtyard."

She glanced at Martha, who nodded her understanding. "I am in need of a breath of air. I will come too."

Jacob led them into the courtyard, where Alban waited, his concern evident even before they spoke. Martha seated herself, motioning Jacob to join her a short distance away.

"What is it, Alban?" Leah asked softly as they stood by a short wall.

"Linux has heard from an ally in Herod's court. The tetrarch has been discussing us with a man called Enos."

"I know him. He is most dangerous."

"This guard has reported that Herod and Enos are conspiring to dissolve our betrothal and my claim for you as my bride."

Leah felt her heart squeezed until she could scarcely find the breath to ask, "Why would they do such a thing?"

"I think he intends to keep us permanently apart. Herod is angry because I survived the attack and fears I now know of his partnership with the Parthians. He wants me punished—and worse."

"He will do anything to save his own skin."

Alban took a very hard breath. "And further, I have been summoned to appear before Pilate."

Leah could read the alarm in his eyes. "What does that mean, summoned?"

"I have not brought him the news he wished to hear," Alban continued. "I have not been able to solve his problems concerning Jesus' followers. And now, when I tell him I seek to join their cause, I cannot predict what he will do. I know he will be terribly angry. I may escape with my head—but even that is in question."

Leah could only stare, her hand covering her mouth beneath the shawl.

"They all are afraid, Leah. The high priest, the Sanhedrin, Herod, along with Pilate—all are afraid of Jesus. Even if they will not admit even silently that he is alive, they are afraid of what he represents. Of what his followers believe about him. And most of all they are afraid of losing power."

"So that is to be their way—destroy any who embrace the truth of Jesus?"

"Perhaps. If they can."

When Leah was able to speak again, it was in no more than a whisper. "So what will happen to all of the followers? If the rulers would destroy even you—one of their own—what chance do the rest of us have?"

"I have no answer to that." His voice was husky with tension.

"What of us, Alban? The betrothal ceremony has already taken place. By law I belong to you now. I am your wife."

"That's true. By law." A grim smile turned up the corners of his mouth. "But the only way I can stake my claim now would be to steal you away."

Then and there the answer seemed perfectly clear. He had declared his allegiance with a far stronger conviction than she could ever have hoped. She replied, "So steal me."

She saw a flash in his eyes, then it faded just as quickly. "Don't jest, Leah."

"I am not one to jest. I have never been more serious."

"But the danger. When they discovered it, our lives wouldn't be worth a single farthing."

"I returned from Bethany fearing that my new faith would keep us apart. I arrive to find you have committed yourself as well."

"If they will have me," Alban finished grimly.

This would happen. She had no logic behind this certainty, nothing beyond the clear voice that had spoken to her heart in the middle of the night. Alban was one of them. "I am your betrothed. We are to wed." She heard the strength and certainty and desire in her own voice, and felt the breath catch in her throat. "I am yours, Alban."

He blinked fiercely, his face taut with emotions that turned his own voice hoarse. "Leah, I have no idea what tomorrow will bring. It might mean gallows. At the very least, my career is over. How could I ask—"

"You are *not* asking me. I am asking *you*. Our lives are in God's hands now. Perhaps he has plans, a mission for us to fulfill. Instead of a soldier of Rome, you might now be a messenger of God. But if not, then I still choose to be your wife, for whatever time he allows us to have."

His words sounded strangled. "But I have nothing."

"Then nothing will be enough. We will share it. And watch it grow into a happiness that will fill our hearts. God can do much with nothing. Have you heard the story of the little boy's loaves and fishes?"

"I am so tempted by this idea of yours." Slowly he shook his head. "But I cannot. I have given my oath. I must follow this through to its conclusion. We would be hounded to the ends of the earth. If only . . ."

She saw a change, a gradual dawning. "If only *what?*"

The silence between them seemed magnified by the square's tumult. Alban remained hunched over, staring intently at the stones by his feet.

Suddenly he straightened.

"What is it?" she begged.

Alban managed to smile. "I have an idea."

"Will you tell me?"

"Soon." He rose to his feet. "Please pray. For me, and for us. I will come back as quickly as I can."

CHAPTER THIRTY-THREE

Pilate's Palace, Jerusalem

THE MAN AND BOY walked quickly, taking the way that followed the ancient walls dividing the Upper from the Lower City. Jacob kept looking up into Alban's face, no doubt full of questions but deciding not to voice them. Then they saw Linux shouting and waving to them. "The prelate is waiting for you," he said quickly when he was close enough to be heard. "And I would advise sooner rather than later. Where have you been?"

"I went to warn Leah of the prelate's summons."

Linux shook his head dolefully, but said merely, "This way."

"Wait." Alban turned to Jacob and ordered, "Go to Simon bar Enoch and wait for me there."

"But, sire—"

"I do not like to order you about, but this time I must. Nor do I know how long this will take. But when I can, I will come for you."

Jacob must have realized Alban would not change his mind and started away, shoulders slumped and head bowed.

Alban watched the boy depart, then asked, "Linux, if anything happens to me, would you make sure Simon—"

"I will do what is necessary," Linux said. "If necessary."

As they approached the palace gates, Alban said, "Thank you for trying to help me, friend."

"We will know soon enough if it is of any use."

Inside the palace, Linux's expression became sterner still. Alban sensed that their time of traveling as cohorts would soon come to an end. After today, things would never be the same. If he had anything to say to Linux, it had to be said now. He slowed their pace.

Alban cleared his throat and began, "I asked you once before what would happen if you found yourself willing to forgive your brother."

Linux recoiled as if Alban had struck him. "You had best be working on your strategy to deal with Pilate rather than asking me such nonsense."

"But what if—"

"It could not happen, and you know it."

"It has happened to me."

Linux stared at Alban. "You've been spending too much time with that lot. They've damaged your thinking."

"I have never understood more clearly." Alban stopped Linux's response with a hand upon the officer's forearm. "I ask you again: If you found yourself willing to forgive your older brother for all his wrongs, would you accept that the impossible has happened?"

Linux's gaze tightened. "This is what your time with the Judaeans has taught you, how to ask the impossible of a Roman officer?"

Alban could have almost heard the bond between them snap. "I will ask God for this sign to be shown to you. And when it happens, remember my words today. Find me, and let us speak of the impossible made real." He held Linux fast with his gaze. "If not me, find another of the believers."

"You're one of the prophet's rabble now?"

Alban allowed himself a moment's hope. "If they'll have me."

Leah and Martha slowly walked back to the kitchen without speaking. But when Leah bent over the boiling vegetables, shoulders shaking, Martha came to stand beside her. Leah lifted tear-filled eyes to the older woman's face, and at the tender concern she saw there, she fell into Martha's arms, sobbing. When she found some control of her emotions, she recounted the dire news from Alban.

"I don't quite know how to ask this," Leah said, "but would you pray with me? For . . . for Alban? For me?"

Martha's face held both concern and confidence. "Of course we will pray. And would you like me to ask the other women to join us? We don't have to tell all the details, but I'm sure they would want to be part of this prayer time."

Soon a circle of women had joined hands with Leah to implore the Almighty to give Alban courage and wisdom. "And please protect his life and Leah's," Martha's sister prayed fervently.

When they were finished, Leah whispered to Martha that Alban had requested Nathanael be made award of the situation. Martha quickly sent a child to find him, and when he entered the kitchen, Leah briefly repeated the grim news, and Nathanael led them in another prayer. "I will ask the other disciples to pray as well," he assured Leah as he left.

Alban was kept waiting in the rear garden of Pilate's palace, watched by three very alert guards. Even so, Alban felt no distress as Linux slipped away. He knew he should be more worried. Yet he was filled just then with an image of people back in the believers' courtyard. People who knew how to pray . . . to a God who promised to listen.

He looked up at the sky and wondered if the God of these people—the God of Israel—would be willing to accept a prayer from a man who had walked his entire life as an outsider.

The garden grew intensely still, the silence as powerful as any voice Alban had ever heard.

He had no idea how long he stood there before a guard paraded down the path and came to attention with a salute. "Centurion, you are called."

Alban replied, "I am ready."

Alban was led into what he suspected was the most formal of Pilate's chambers, with a grand high ceiling, ornately carved walls, and a mosaic floor of onyx and semiprecious stones. Pilate sat upon a gilded chair, its high back shining ruddy in the light. Herod Antipas was seated to his right, Procula to his left. Alban glanced around the room, hoping his friend Linux had managed to implement the plan he had proposed. But the young officer was nowhere to be seen.

Alban knew a moment's regret, then pushed it away. He did not feel alone.

He marched forward, saluted Pilate, and said, "I come as ordered, sire."

The prelate scowled. "I expected your report long before now, centurion!"

Alban bowed to the prelate's wife and his guest. "I discovered the truth myself only days ago, my lord, and that was in Tiberias. I returned to Jerusalem the moment I had what you required."

"And yet you waited until I was forced to summon you! I should have you flogged!"

Alban stood quietly.

Procula offered, "My lord, perhaps you should hear what the centurion has to say."

But Pilate was not finished. "This is utterly unacceptable behavior, particularly from an officer I had thought to include on my staff!"

"My most sincere apologies, sire."

Pilate drummed his fingers on the armrest. Beside him, Herod's eyes gleamed fiercely. Pilate barked, "Are you ready with an answer? Do you come with a report to give?"

"Sire, the betrothal agreement stated that when I had fulfilled my obligations, those requiring answers about the Judaean sect, my rights would be acknowledged." He paused, drew a breath. "I have come to claim my bride."

Herod snapped, "Have you found the prophet's body?"

"No, sire. But I now have the answer. I know where he is."

Herod's swarthy face gleamed with malevolent anticipation. "I knew it! That ragged band of disciples stole the body away. Where did they take him?"

But Alban was not to be hurried. His eyes held Pilate's, not Herod's. "You promised me my bride when I brought the answer, sire. I do claim her now."

Herod narrowed his gaze and muttered to Pilate, "Grant the centurion his wife, and you will lose your hold over—"

"I am indeed sorry it took me so long, sire!" Herod's words were drowned out by a loud voice coming from the shadows of a doorway. Linux stamped forward, the bundle in his arms making a loud clatter. He marched to the table by the side wall, dumped his load, and offered an ostentatious bow to the three on the thrones. "Reporting as ordered, sire!"

"Yes, yes, all right." The governor sounded peevish. "What do you have there?"

"Items requested by Herod, sire." He tossed back one fold of the covering to reveal a small glimpse of the contents.

"I never . . ." Herod's voice slowly died.

Pilate rose slightly from his chair, peering at the items. "Are those Parthian weapons?"

Linux lifted a war hammer. The metal surface glinted dully in the light. "Indeed they are, sire."

"You've found some of the bandits who escaped?" Pilate inquired with some interest.

"Five of them, to be exact, sire. But I don't know if they were part of the original band defeated by the centurion here. We suspect these five to have been assassins."

"Parthian assassins operating here in Judaea?"

Linux merely stood and glared a warning at Herod.

Herod stammered, "I—that is, we—"

Linux finished, "We managed to capture all five of the men alive, sire. Thanks to the centurion and his cunning."

"Where are they now?"

"In Tyre, my lord. Awaiting transport to the galleys."

"On whose orders?"

"Mine, sire," Alban now put in. "We thought it best to offer them a hint of mercy."

"But they are bandits and assassins! They should already be hanging on Golgotha."

Linux answered, "At the time I thought the same, sire. But by offering them this leniency if they answered his questions, Alban gained information that was not tainted by fear. We learned a great deal, sire." The statement was followed by another glance at Herod.

Alban took up the telling. "We can confirm they were Parthians.

We identified their sources of information within Judaea and the Galilee, including certain villages upon the trading routes."

"Thanks to the centurion's wisdom, sire, we know where to station our garrisons." Linux's focus now remained hard and steady upon Herod. "We also know they had sources at the highest level of Judaean society."

Pilate looked from his officers to the ruler seated next to him, then back again. "I thought we were here to discuss the missing prophet."

"Indeed, sire." Linux bowed and flicked a glance toward Alban. "My sincere apologies. Might I take this opportunity to wish Alban every good wish for his marriage?"

The Judaean ruler hissed an angry defeat and subsided into his chair.

Pilate demanded, "What were you about to say, Herod?"

The ruler fingered his beard and muttered, "Of course the centurion should receive his bride. But such arrangements take time." He cast Alban a venomous glance. "Certainly someone of the centurion's rank and position would wish to make the celebration a proclamation to the world. I could order the preparations begun this very night, but—"

"We have no need of such, sire. My bride, Leah, and I will make appropriate arrangements."

Pilate studied Herod, then Alban, clearly at a loss at the tetrarch's sudden retreat into silence. "The request seems genuine enough, does it not?"

Herod fidgeted, finally thrusting himself forward in his chair to shout, "But where is the body? I demand to know! And if you don't fulfill your word, you will *never* claim that woman."

"I do keep my pledge," Alban declared. "Sire, every shred of evidence confirms what the disciples have said all along."

Pilate's face darkened in rage. But before he could speak, his wife cried out, "I knew it!"

All eyes swiveled to Procula.

"It is as my dreams have foretold!" Procula obviously found no triumph in her declaration, not even satisfaction. Her eyes glittered with a feverish intensity. "The prophet is alive!"

Pilate and Herod shared astonished confusion.

The governor demanded, "He did not die?"

"He was brought down dead from the cross, sire," Alban answered carefully. "He was buried, but on the third day the tomb was discovered empty. Not because he was stolen away. Roman soldiers would not have allowed that to happen, nor did they. No, sire, the tomb was empty because he no longer required it. He who was dead lives again."

Herod's voice rose even higher. "Then where is he now?"

"Jesus has now returned to his Father in heaven," Alban replied evenly. "But his presence remains here still."

"Get him out of here," spat out Pilate. "Remove him before I do so myself, piece by piece!"

A guard moved forward and Alban felt his arm in a firm grip. He did not resist. He felt thankful to be leaving the room.

"And he can have his bride," Pilate's angry voice shouted after them. "They deserve each other. But you will hear from me, centurion. You will hear from me!" The words echoed down the passageway behind Alban.

CHAPTER THIRTY-FOUR

Antonia Fortress

AS HE WALKED THE LANE leading to the Antonia Fortress, Alban knew the first lancings of fear. But it was not for himself. Not even with the prospect of the marriage hanging in the balance could the peace he carried be disturbed. What he feared was the fate of Leah—and of Jacob.

Alban now wound his way up the stairs to his lodgings above the stables. As he expected, he found the boy huddled in the corner. "Come out, lad."

There was no answer.

"Come here, Jacob. Please."

When the lad finally approached, head hanging low, Alban did what he had wanted to do a thousand times. He gripped Jacob and hugged him hard.

The boy wrapped his arms around Alban's neck and cried out, "I've never disobeyed you before. But I won't. I will not leave you."

Alban drew him over to a bench by the window. He pointed

out the guards pacing in front of the fortress gates. "You see them? For all I know they have orders to arrest me on sight."

"Then I'll wait for you here, sire."

Alban shook the lad but not hard. Just enough to get his attention. "What I'm trying to say is, my days of soldiering could well be over. Pilate is contemplating my fate."

"But you will always be a centurion," stated Jacob with childlike confidence.

"Perhaps not, lad. If so, I will serve to the best of my ability. If not—then God has other plans. And the same is true for you. I want you to promise me you will try to discover what plan God has for your life, and then follow it."

The boy dropped his head. "I have always done as you commanded, sire, except when you ordered me away."

"Listen to me." Alban lifted Jacob's chin. "There may come a time when the teachings of Jesus are violently opposed by the Roman guard. What then?"

Jacob gave no answer.

"I want you to be part of Simon's household. I want you to have someone to care for you, and his wife already does so. I have made a promise that you will be trained in the faith of your people. I want that to happen. I plan to . . ."

Jacob was shaking his head.

"Let me finish."

"No, sire—"

"You would be much safer there than with me."

"I want only to be with you!"

Alban rubbed a hand roughly over his brow.

"Let me stay. Please, sire. The lady Leah says I can. Even after you are joined."

"She told you that?"

"Yes. When you sent me to Simon's family, instead I went to

the courtyard before I came back here. Leah said if I wanted, she was happy to have me be a part of your house."

Alban leaned against the wall. "She has not told me this."

"She said you were already overburdened, sire. She told me to come back here and wait for you. She said if you agreed to this, she would send for me in time for the marriage celebration."

"You young rascal, you. You two have it all planned." Alban wiped his face a second time. "All right, then. Let's be off."

There was something else that needed doing. Alban approached the barracks through the main fortress courtyard. A group of perhaps thirty legionnaires were clustered about the dice pit. Alban found his friend Atticus standing apart. The older centurion leaned against the far wall and watched birds who pecked at bread tossed by two soldiers. Only when the senior of the pair glanced over did Alban recognize Crasius, the soldier he had last seen in front of the tomb. Alban showed the sergeant an empty palm. "All is well."

Alban moved toward Atticus. He searched for a way to ease into the conversation. "I owe you a great debt, old friend," he finally said.

Atticus blinked slowly. "You saved me from severe punishment, maybe death, over my abrogation of duties during the festival season. That is enough."

"It is not even the beginning. I will soon take my bride, Leah."

"The servant from Pilate's household? The prelate's niece?"

"The same. What is more, I love her. And none of this would have come about had you not approached Pilate on my behalf."

A glimmer of the old fire shifted in the Roman's gaze. "I should say congratulations, I suppose. Though how a woman such as she would ever be happy with a soldier's lot is beyond me."

"She assures me she will be just that. Whatever my future."

"Then I am glad for you." The fire in Atticus's eyes dimmed as quickly as it had appeared. "But you owe me nothing."

"I owe you a debt of life itself." Alban stepped in closer so his words would carry to the two men by the side wall. "I also bring news. The one I asked you about, Jesus of Nazareth. He did die upon the cross."

"Just as I have always said."

Alban saw the man's bone-deep pain. "How you must have suffered."

Atticus stared at the stones by his feet and did not respond.

"But that is not my only news." He beckoned to the other two, who cautiously moved closer. "The tomb was empty—just as the disciples declared. Empty. Because Jesus rose from the dead, just as it was reported."

This time, all three studied him. It was Crasius who whispered, "How can this be true?"

"It is true because he is the Messiah, come from God himself," Alban said. "It is not a fable. Not an illusion. It is real. Just as God has promised over the many years of Judaean history, his Anointed One has finally come."

CHAPTER THIRTY-FIVE

The Believers' Courtyard

ALBAN SPENT THE SABBATH NIGHT in his quarters above the stables. When he rose at dawn, he found Jacob soundly asleep on his pallet in the front room. Alban hated to wake the boy. Still, it was important they be on their way. He nudged Jacob, and the lad rolled over with a yawn.

They didn't stop for breakfast but took a piece of bread to eat as they walked. When they arrived, they found the courtyard to be already full.

They slipped to the alcove in the far corner, where they had spent much of the previous day. Jacob curled up in his cloak and went back to sleep. Alban must have dozed off too, for the next thing he knew, sunlight was tickling his face. He sat up and quickly looked around. It didn't look like they had missed anything.

Two men who sat nearby nodded an acknowledgment, and Alban dared to enter their conversation.

"Is this the day, then?"

"We do not know. But it seems an auspicious time to us," said the older of the men. "The day when Jesus was lifted into the sky, one disciple asked if he was now going to restore the kingdom of Israel. Jesus said it was not for them to know the day or the hour. Some wonder if this means the festival of Pentecost will come and go without his return. Others say we must watch and wait and hope."

They fell into a comfortable silence. After a time, Alban slipped through the doorway into the disciples' courtyard. He stepped into the kitchen area and found Leah helping to prepare a meal. Two other women he had seen before glanced over, nodded their greetings, and returned to work. When Leah walked over, he said, "I understand you and Jacob have been talking."

"Was I wrong to do so?"

He fought down a powerful urge to reach out and touch her. Though none of the women looked his way, he was certain all were watching. "It is a wonderful gift. To both of us." Her smile lit his heart.

"I can take a moment from my chores. Sit here on the bench. Would you care for anything?"

"Water, please."

She brought him a mug damp and chilled from the cistern. Leah settled on the bench a discreet distance from him and adjusted the shawl so it covered the lower portion of her face. Her eyes were like polished emeralds, brilliant and totally engaged. She said, "I have been thinking of what it might mean, to build a home with you."

"I can scarcely imagine such a thing," he confessed. "Since boyhood I have had no home except where I am."

"What do you miss about your homeland?"

Alban started to give his normal terse response to all such questions about his former life. But he found himself reveling in a newfound ability to look beyond old pain and anger.

"Winter," he said quietly. "I miss winter and the change of seasons."

Her eyes smiled, and in that simple act he felt as though they were joined together. Leah said, "Winter was rainy in the lowlands around Verona. But sometimes, when the air was very clear, I could see the mountains far to the north. Floating like clouds of stone and ice."

"I miss hunting stags through a frozen forest," Alban said softly. "I miss how a crow cuts shadows from a pale winter sky. I miss the company of a dear friend seated by a fire, surrounded by an empty glade. I miss the smell of horses in a warm corral."

Her eyes had gone soft. "You are very poetic. I could almost see it myself. You miss a life that was snatched from you."

Alban did not speak.

"You miss friends. You miss feeling as though you belonged to a place, and it to you." She took a long breath. "I have heard the women here speak of forgiveness. Do you think it would ever be possible to forgive those who stole your life away?"

He answered slowly, not because he needed to think things through, but because he was coming to terms with an answer he knew could not come from himself. "I think perhaps I am already beginning to do just that. But only because the strength is given to me from somewhere beyond myself."

Leah's eyes turned to focus on him. "How would it be, I wonder, to spend a lifetime searching out such answers—"

"Together." They whispered the final word as one voice.

Alban returned to find the plaza more crowded than when he had left. When Jacob came over, he asked, "What is happening?"

"No one knows. But more and more people keep coming."

Alban found them as secluded a corner as the overcrowded area had to offer, a shaded spot behind some empty water barrels. They watched as the last of the disciples returned from prayer.

Abruptly the entire plaza went silent.

Jacob whispered, "What is it?"

Alban pressed his hand onto the lad's back and whispered, "Wait."

A wind seemed to build from beyond where they sat. Alban felt it rushing from every corner, up and down and right and left, before him and behind. An *impossible* wind. He circled his arm around Jacob's shoulders and held tightly to him.

Across the mass of people, Alban saw Leah emerge through the portal. He lifted Jacob into his arms and started forward, but the crowd was so closely packed his progress was slow.

Then he saw lightning.

But there was no thunder. Nor did the power spark and vanish. Instead the light separated into individual blades, like pieces of flame hanging in the air. And each came to rest upon people throughout the courtyard.

Leah's head was bowed. Alban was filled with the conviction that she was immersed in prayer. He then witnessed a most amazing sight. One of the flames came to rest upon her.

Alban knew the sign for what it was: God accepted her, claimed her as his own.

Maybe she felt his gaze, because her head lifted and she looked straight at him. As he closed the remaining distance, he heard her say, "God loves you, and he has given to you the gift of his son, through whom you may have eternal life, eternal peace. His flame rests upon you."

With a shock, Alban realized Leah was speaking to him in Gallic. And not just any dialect of Gallic, but the language of his tiny province. For the first time in four years, he heard his native tongue. Spoken to him by the woman he loved.

His heart swelled with what was happening. He could not understand how she could know these words, but he didn't need to. He answered in Gallic, "Yes, yes, I believe this."

She looked upward, and he could see the flame above his head reflected in her eyes.

The wind stilled. The lights died away. He no longer saw the flames or felt the currents of air. But his heart burned with the truth he had seen, heard, experienced.

In the breathless silence, a voice called out from above, and the crowd turned to look up at a window in the upper room. A bearded man with the strength of a warrior stood in the opening and called to all below, "People of Israel, listen to this: Jesus of Nazareth was a man accredited by God to you by miracles, wonders, and signs, which God did among you through him, as you yourself know."

And Alban did know.

"That is Peter, the leader of the disciples," Leah whispered at his side.

"Therefore let all Israel be assured of this: God has made this Jesus, whom you crucified, both Lord and Messiah."

A man's voice carried over the vast audience, his anguish a piercing force, "Brothers, what shall we do?"

Peter replied, "Repent and be baptized, every one of you, in the name of Jesus Christ for the forgiveness of your sins. And you will receive the gift of the Holy Spirit. The promise is for you and your children and for all who are far off—for all whom the Lord our God will call."

Alban bowed his head in contrition, then in deep gratitude. He, a Roman, a Gaul, was accepted. The promise was for him also. "Thank you. Thank you, Jesus my Lord, for forgiving me, for including me, for giving to me also the gift of the Holy Spirit."

CHAPTER THIRTY-SIX

Pilate's Palace, Jerusalem

LEAH SAT UP ON HER PALLET just as the rising sun touched the window in the maidservants' chamber. A new thankfulness filled her being. No one had said so directly, but she was sure today was to be her *huppah*, the day her bridegroom claimed his bride.

She lay back and gazed at the ceiling, now bejeweled with slivers of sunlight. In her mind's eye she was seeing her bridal garments. The ones she and Abigail and Hannah had selected. Procula had insisted on buying them for her as her farewell gift. Her mistress had seemed reluctant to speak with Leah since her declaration that she was a follower of Jesus. But Leah found herself praying once more that Procula's nights would become calm and her spirit healed.

Then her thoughts turned to Alban.

He had been regretful he could not prepare the kind of wedding celebration he wanted her to have. She had tried to convince him that it did not matter. That a simple celebration would be exactly right.

It was true she would not have the traditional parade with

Judaean music and a flower-strewn pathway. She would not be carried on a litter with friends dancing before her. There would be no decorated bridal chamber in the center of the courtyard. Nor would there be a bountiful feast for friends to enjoy. But what did it matter? They were blessed to have this day at all.

The only thing that brought a fleeting sorrow to her heart was the absence of her family. If only her mother, her sister . . . But she resolved to not let that spoil her joy. The community of worshipers was her family now. And she would soon have Alban. Alban and Jacob.

She rose and dressed and prepared for the day, reflecting that this probably would be the last time she would waken in this room. Would lift herself from this pallet and roll it up and place it against the wall. She was not a slave, not even a servant. She would very soon be the wife of a centurion.

A little shiver went through her body. Alban was indeed a centurion, at least for this moment. What the future held, who could say? Pilate still had not given his mandate. Alban had been summoned to appear before the tribunal two days hence. They would not know the prelate's verdict until then.

Leah pushed the fears aside. She would not allow such uncertainties to intrude upon her happiness. She had much to do if this indeed was the day she would meet Alban at the courtyard of the followers. Theirs would be a simple celebration. Thanks to her newfound friends, however, they would have a festive meal, with singing and perhaps dancing to follow in the square. Abigail's small room had been cleared for their private use. The girl had removed her personal items and placed them in Hannah's quarters. It was enough.

No, Leah decided. It was much more than enough. It was wonderful.

She left to serve Procula's breakfast one more time. Tucked

under her arm was her urn of nard. She would present it to her dear friend, with the prayer that it would bring the woman hope.

Leah arrived at the believers' gathering place with a small bundle containing all her possessions. She had carefully folded the robe Alban had given her, once more caressing its soft folds. Nedra had come to the palace that morning and asked for her. With a little smile, the woman had told her she was needed at the courtyard, that she "should be prepared."

The two women were met at the entrance by two overjoyed friends.

"You are here. You are here!" Abigail and Hannah called as one. "Come, come. We will help you prepare."

With one on each side, Leah was led into Hannah's crowded quarters. The girls had pushed the cot tight against the wall and placed Abigail's rolled pallet on top of it. Everything they owned was stacked upon the bed to make room for the preparations.

"We told everyone they must stay away until the shofar is sounded. Enoch will blow it. He is posted at the doorway. When he sees the centurion, he will sound the horn."

"Martha is making some of Alban's favorite dishes," Abigail told her. "She has the kitchen workers fairly running with her instructions." Abigail ushered Leah into the small room, leaning upon her stick. "Your gown and shawl are right here. And your veil."

"It is so beautiful, Leah, it suits you!" Hannah exclaimed. "How do you wish to do your hair? I will lend you my silver comb. My father gave it to me."

Abigail eased herself down to the floor. "Here. Let me wipe the dust from your sandals."

And the fussing continued. Leah had never felt so cared for and loved. Like family.

She could have dressed herself much more quickly on her own, but both girls were intent on helping her. They stumbled over one another in the room's narrow confines, but no one minded. Finally the soft cotton robe was settled into place, the sash firmly tied, and the freshened sandals back on her feet.

Her hair was arranged and rearranged. Leah felt no need for the comb, but she did not want to disappoint Hannah, so she accepted it and exclaimed over its delicacy. They were just positioning her veil when the sound of the trumpet pealed through the air.

"He's here. He's here. Your bridegroom has come!"

The young women, already excited before, were now nearly feverish. Hannah's hands trembled with her voice. "Oh . . . the flowers in your hair are slipping. Let me fix them."

Abigail warned, "Don't tangle them in the veil."

"The comb is caught!"

Leah wondered if the two would undo all the work that they had done. "May I?" she asked. But when she reached up, she discovered her fingers were trembling as well.

Another long blast from the trumpet, then Leah heard excited shouts and loud cheers. She took a deep breath and fastened the veil as securely as her shaking fingers would allow.

When Leah entered the courtyard, she was astonished to see the transformation. A bench was pulled forward and centered in the space. Wild flowers and branches were arranged as a latticework shelter over the bench. Leah was ushered immediately to a seat there beside Alban. He looked at her for a long time, finally reaching for her hand as a cheer went up from the crowd.

The bearded man with strikingly intense eyes who had spoken to them from the upstairs window on the day of Pentecost now stepped forward. Peter was dressed in a dark robe, with a camel's hair outer garment tied upon one shoulder and hanging down both front and back. He lifted both hands toward the heavens, and every voice went silent.

"Our God, the almighty Lord of heaven and earth," he began in a clear, authoritative voice, "bless these two here before you with your grace. Grace to keep one another in sickness and in health. Grace to learn together to serve as you would have them serve. Grace to give them strength for daily toil and duty. Grace to keep them in the hour of temptation or weakness. Grace that will enable them to give and love and labor. Make them fruitful. Bless them with your presence. Wrap them in your peace. And multiply their love—for you, for others, for one another. In the name of our blessed Lord and Savior, Jesus of Nazareth. Amen."

The echoing amens resounded around Leah and Alban, and they looked at one another, Alban's deep emotion evident in his face.

Leah had never heard any blessing so touching or majestic. Soon, one after another, the community of believers stepped forward with greetings and Scripture recitations and advice for a long and prosperous marriage. There was singing and dancing and the sharing of goblets of wine. Children threw flowers and women placed kisses while men slapped Alban good-naturedly on the back or greeted him with the customary kiss or a formal bow. It was hard for Leah to take it all in.

She noticed Linux had arrived, but hung back silently against the coolness of the far wall. His eyes rested upon Abigail as she stood at the edge of the communal dancers, laughing and singing as the others whirled their way around the courtyard. Leah was concerned for her friend, but she pushed those thoughts aside and turned once more to look at Alban. His ready smile and strong yet gentle hand assured her that it was not all a dream.

Jacob had already found new friends and entered into their

noisy gaiety. The sun climbed overhead, and the crowded courtyard became nearly stifling. But the noise and activity swelled further. Everyone was having a wonderful time. Leah began to feel faint with the excitement and headiness of it all. And the wedding feast was still to come.

A loud clanging of metal pots and thumping of sticks and clattering of simple music makers drew the crowd toward the bench where the bridal couple sat. The dancers and shouters and noisemakers attempted to outdo each other with their laughing and cheering.

Jacob danced across Leah's vision in the middle of some whirling activity. Then he wheeled back and pressed close to Alban, shouting his joy and contentment as he wove his way in and out.

Suddenly there was a shout of another kind, piercing through the merrymaking. Leah knew Abigail's voice. She was crying out, "Jacob! Jacob!"

All eyes turned toward the sound.

Abigail. What had Jacob done? Had her friend been hurt again? Leah half rose from her seat. She felt Alban's hand on her arm. Then he too was standing to see what was happening.

Jacob had spun around at the sound of his name and was standing as still as a stone, staring at Abigail, who was maybe thirty paces away. Like him, she now had fallen absolutely still.

"Abigail?" His voice sounded small in the quiet that had fallen over the group.

And then the two were moving toward each other, arms outstretched, calling each other's name over and over again.

Leah could see the tears running down Abigail's face, but she could not understand their cause. What had happened?

"Jacob," Abigail was now saying, running a hand over his face, patting his shoulder, holding him close. "I thought you were dead."

Jacob gasped through his own tears. "They told me all the family was dead!"

She grabbed him close and wept some more. "I am the only one. Our parents are gone."

Alban held Leah's hands tightly in his own and let her weep. And soon Abigail and Jacob had joined them, and they all wept, then laughed, together.

The shouting and celebration resumed as the story of the wonderful reunion spread through the crowd. "I can't believe it. I simply can't believe it," Leah said over and over as she wiped her tears.

When the commotion had died down, Leah found herself closer to Alban on the bench. Although careful not to seem improper on this day, she did not move away. She felt elated and drained all at once. How could so much be happening on the very same day as their wedding celebration? *Alban's Jacob, a young brother of Abigail.* It seemed like another miracle. *We will need to make new family arrangements*, Leah was thinking quickly. *Will we gain one more—or will we now lose them both?*

And just as those thoughts flitted through her mind, the loud banging and chanting started again. She questioningly turned to Alban with the crowd weaving their joyful dance around them. He leaned over to whisper in her ear, "I think they are trying to tell us we are to enter the bridal chamber now."

Leah's heart began to pound, and her cheeks felt even warmer.

"Will you show me the way?" he asked.

She took Alban's hand and drew him through the cheering crowd, up the steps and through the flower-decorated doorway into Abigail's small room. Her cot had been removed. A petal-strewn pallet lay on the floor, covered with a soft sheepskin. Palm branches crisscrossed the single window to block some of the light and the noise of the celebration that continued on in the square.

Alban pulled her close and looked deeply into her eyes.

"I love you, Leah," he whispered. "I wish with all my heart I could give you the world. But I do not know what the future holds. What *our* future holds. I—"

"Shaa," Leah whispered back as she reached up to place a finger on his lips. "We will not talk about it now. We will not even think of it. We will think instead on Peter's prayer. Our lives belong to God now. He will give his grace. He does answer Peter's prayers, you know."

He released her to free his hands, one lifting her shawl and the other going to the loop that held her veil.

"Now?" he asked.

Leah nodded.

With a deftness that defied the strength and size of his fingers, her husband slipped the loop and let the veil fall.

He seemed transfixed. Studying her face. Running a hand along her cheek, then tracing the curve of her lips with one fingertip.

"You are beautiful," he whispered hoarsely. "Beautiful. And you are mine."

Leah closed her eyes and leaned against his chest. She could feel his heart beating against hers. She savored his words. Let the tomorrows bring what they would. She had today. She had her centurion.

A Note from the Publisher

The authors discovered a great deal of fascinating historical information as they began their research for this novel. Davis Bunn spent nearly two weeks in Israel, touring the country with a rabbi friend who provided invaluable insight and understanding of the setting, politics, and culture of the first century.

For additional background materials, please visit *www.thecenturionswife.com*. Some topics covered on this site include possible reasons for the two gospel accounts of the healing of the centurion's servant, the significance of the cup and the bread in communion, the connections between Passover and Pentecost, and an explanation of the complex Jerusalem power structure.

Questions for group discussion or individual study also can be found at this site.

Books by Janette Oke and Davis Bunn

Acts of Faith

The Centurion's Wife

Song of Acadia

The Meeting Place
The Sacred Shore
The Birthright
The Distant Beacon
The Beloved Land

Books by Davis Bunn

The Book of Hours
The Great Divide
Winner Take All
The Lazarus Trap
Elixir
Imposter

All Through the Night
My Soul to Keep

Heirs of Acadia*

The Solitary Envoy
The Innocent Libertine
The Noble Fugitive
The Night Angel
Falconer's Quest

* with Isabella Bunn

Books by Janette Oke

Canadian West

When Calls the Heart • *When Comes the Spring*
When Breaks the Dawn • *When Hope Springs New*
Beyond the Gathering Storm
When Tomorrow Comes

Love Comes Softly

Love Comes Softy • *Love's Enduring Promise*
Love's Long Journey • *Love's Abiding Joy*
Love's Unending Legacy • *Love's Unfolding Dream*
Love Takes Wing • *Love Finds a Home*

A Prairie Legacy

The Tender Years • *A Searching Heart*
A Quiet Strength • *Like Gold Refined*

Seasons of the Heart

Once Upon a Summer • *The Winds of Autumn*
Winter Is Not Forever • *Spring's Gentle Promise*

Seasons of the Heart (4 in 1)

Women of the West

The Calling of Emily Evans • *Julia's Last Hope*
Roses for Mama • *A Woman Named Damaris*
They Called Her Mrs. Doc • *The Measure of a Heart*
A Bride for Donnigan • *Heart of the Wilderness*
Too Long a Stranger • *The Bluebird and the Sparrow*
A Gown of Spanish Lace • *Drums of Change*

www.janetteoke.com

DAVIS BUNN has been a professional novelist for twenty years. His books have sold in excess of six million copies in sixteen languages, appearing on numerous national bestseller lists.

Davis is known for the diversity of his writing talent, from gentle gift books like *The Quilt* to high-powered thrillers like *The Great Divide*. He has also enjoyed great success in his collaborations with Janette Oke, with whom he has co-authored a series of ground-breaking historical novels.

In developing his work, Davis draws on a rich background of international experience. Raised in North Carolina, he completed his undergraduate studies at Wake Forest University. He then traveled to London to earn a master's degree in international economics and finance before embarking on a distinguished business career that took him to more than thirty countries in Europe, Africa, and the Middle East.

Davis has received numerous literary accolades, including three Christy Awards for excellence in fiction. He currently serves as Writer-in-Residence at Regent's Park College, Oxford University, and is a sought-after lecturer on the craft of writing.

JANETTE OKE was born in Champion, Alberta, to a Canadian prairie farmer and his wife, and she grew up in a large family full of laughter and love. She is a graduate of Mountain View Bible College in Alberta, where she met her husband, Edward, and they were married in May of 1957. After pastoring churches in Indiana and Canada, the Okes spent some years in Calgary, where Edward served in several positions on college faculties while Janette continued her writing. She has written forty-eight novels for adults and another sixteen for children, and her book sales total nearly thirty million copies.

The Okes have three sons and one daughter, all married, and are enjoying their fifteen grandchildren. Edward and Janette are active in their local church and make their home near Didsbury, Alberta.